ARIZONA
MOON

ARIZONA MOON

A Novel of Vietnam

J. M. GRAHAM

This book was brought to publication with the generous assistance of Marguerite and Gerry Lenfest.

Naval Institute Press
291 Wood Road
Annapolis, MD 21402

Library of Congress Cataloging-in-Publication Data
Names: Graham, J. M. (James M.), author.
Title: Arizona moon : a novel of Vietnam / J. M. Graham.
Description: Annapolis, MD : Naval Institute Press, 2016.
Identifiers: LCCN 2016026692 | ISBN 9781682470718 (hardback) | ISBN 9781682470725 (epub) | ISBN 9781682470725 (mobi)
Subjects: LCSH: Vietnam War, 1961–1975—Fiction. | Soldiers—Vietnam—Fiction. | United States. Marine Corps—Fiction. | BISAC: FICTION / War & Military. | GSAFD: War stories.
Classification: LCC PS3607.R3375 A75 2016 | DDC 813/.6—dc23 LC record available at https://lccn.loc.gov/2016026692

24 23 22 21 20 19 18 17 16   9 8 7 6 5 4 3 2 1
First printing

*This book is dedicated to all those
who left boot prints in the Arizona and remember the costs.
And to Linda, who rescues me daily.*

Acknowledgments

I'd like to thank the staff of the Naval Institute Press for their invaluable help in bringing *Arizona Moon* to print. They include Gary Thompson, who saw potential in the manuscript; Mindy Conner, whose editorial eye identified the right words (and the wrong ones); Nick Lyle; Robin Noonan; Claire Noble; Judy Heise; and Brian Walker. I'd also like to thank Walt Lyon, the first to read *Arizona Moon*, and especially Linda, my better half, my personal IT department, and my constant reminder that I'm not as smart as I think I am.

QUANG NAM PROVINCE, VIETNAM

October 1967, the Year of the Goat

The Arizona was scarred with trails that went in every direction, but to use them meant death. This was the most heavily mined landscape in Vietnam, where the booby-trappers and mine-layers had free rein to ply their deadly craft, and some had raised it to a high art. Every bit of unexploded U.S. ordnance in the An Hoa Basin found its way into the Arizona, creatively transformed into some horrific surprise for the unwary, the careless, or the unlucky. From Go Noi Island all the way south to where the Song Thu Bon twisted around the Que Son Mountains, every step was a gamble unless the boot print of the man ahead proved the spot reliable. You trusted only the ground you stood on. And even then you weren't completely sure.

The three-man fire team waded the shallow stream and climbed the embankment on the far side. They were the point element of Golf Company's 1st Platoon from the 2nd Battalion, 5th Marines, out of An Hoa combat base on the fifth day of a weeklong, no-name operation beyond the Song Thu Bon. The October monsoon season alternated blistering heat with blinding downpours that kept the river running brown and fast, and everyone in the platoon miserable. The trailing man carried a PRC-25 field radio, known affectionately as the "prick." An olive-drab towel hung around his neck, and he mopped his face with one end as he reached level ground. The morning heat that had transformed last night's rain into steam under the jungle canopy suddenly evaporated into a wide clearing. The three Marines stood a few yards apart catching their breath, water draining from the air vents in their jungle boots.

The point man squatted at the clearing's edge, his M16 tucked under an arm. He looked back at the other two. "This looks like the spot," he said. "Get Lieutenant Diehl on the horn."

Twisted wire from a C ration box made a makeshift hook that hung the black plastic handset from the pocket of the radioman's flak jacket.

He lifted it from the hook, held it to his ear, and squeezed. "Gimme One Actual," he said.

The radio hissed and a small, faint voice answered, "Roger, wait one."

Within seconds another voice cut through the static. "One Actual."

The radioman looked back into the trees as though looking in the lieutenant's direction might be helpful. "Be advised, we have the LZ, sir."

The radio squelched and the lieutenant's voice jumped the two hundred yards to the radioman's ear with all the force and power of two tin cans on a string. "How big a landing zone is it?"

The radioman turned back to the clearing, estimating the distance to the far side. "It's big enough. We got some trees in the middle to deal with, but the rest is low brush and grass."

The other two Marines moved off to the side, being careful to stay inside the concealment of the shade. The point man took deep gulps from his canteen.

The radioman held his M16 at his side by the sight mount as he listened. Finally he said, "Roger that," and hung the handset back on his flak jacket. "Diehl says to get around the clearing and set up security."

The point man seemed disappointed at missing an opportunity to sit until the rest of the platoon caught up. "Does he want us to go across or around?"

The middle man started along the edge of the clearing, staying just inside the tree line. "You can go across the open ground," he said to the point man. "We'll go around and meet you on the other side." The radioman followed him.

The point man calculated the shortest distance between two points of seclusion and the lack of cover in between. "Screw it," he said and fell in behind the others.

≈

Far back under the jungle canopy, 1st Platoon was stopped. Nearly every man was squatting or down on one knee, taking advantage of the delay to grab whatever rest was offered. The column stretched well over three hundred feet, with each man able to see only the man ahead and the one behind; heavy undergrowth obscured all else. In the center of the column Lieutenant Diehl stood beside his radioman and watched the shorter man try to hop the heavy radio into a more comfortable position on his back, the blade antenna whipping wildly.

"Stand still, Bronsky," the lieutenant said. He checked the notations written on the edge of his plastic-covered map. "We need to change freqs."

Bronsky dropped to one knee and leaned forward so the lieutenant could see the top of the radio. Two large knobs controlled the tactical frequencies, and Lieutenant Diehl turned them until the numbers matched those written on his map. He squeezed the handset. "Pounder One to Highball, over." He released the lever and listened to the static: nothing. He squeezed again. "Pounder One to Highball. Come in, over." The radio hissed and gurgled, and hissed again.

"Maybe we need the whip, sir," Bronsky said, pointing to the auxiliary antenna collapsed inside the narrow canvas case on the side of the radio.

"Maybe, maybe not," the lieutenant said, squeezing the handset again. "Pounder One to Highball." He turned the volume knob, making the static louder.

"Are you on the right freq, sir?"

"What do you think?" the lieutenant said. "Have you changed the battery lately?"

"Fresh this morning. Anyway, Clyde just came in loud and clear."

Birds flitted through the jungle canopy, feeding and squawking and ignoring the men below.

The lieutenant sighed. "Pounder One to Highball."

The instant he released the handset lever, a voice jumped back at him. "This is Highball, over."

Diehl extended a hand, pulling Bronsky back to his feet. "Highball, this is Pounder One. You busy?"

"Negative, Pounder. We're in the air. Your wish is our command."

"Be advised, our ETA at WL 477336 is zero five minutes. Copy?"

"Roger, Pounder One. Contact you this net, over."

"Roger, Highball. Pounder One out." Lieutenant Diehl held the handset out to Bronsky and pushed the folded map back into the bag slung around his neck. "I need Four," he said.

Bronsky turned to the man squatting ten feet behind him. "Papa Sierra up," he said just above a whisper.

The Marine spoke into the shadows behind him. "The lieutenant wants the platoon sergeant."

Receding voices called, "Blackwell up."

In less than a minute a tall, black Marine pushed through the brush, mopping his face with an issue towel. The elastic band around his helmet held a bottle of insect repellant and a waterproof cigarette case with a pack of Marlboros inside. Perspiration darkened the waistband of his jungle pants, even soaking his web belt. "Sir?"

"Who has the demo bags, Sergeant?"

Staff Sergeant Blackwell squinted as though the answer had to be forced out into the heat. "The Chief has one back in 3rd Squad, and Franklin has the other one up ahead."

"Okay," Diehl said, putting a hand on Blackwell's shoulder and walking him toward a kneeling man further ahead in the column, whispering instructions like a football coach sending a man in from the bench. "Tell Franklin to put charges on every obstruction in the LZ. I don't want anything standing higher than his ass." He stopped and looked back. "Make that Bronsky's ass. He's shorter."

Bronsky toyed absently with the cord on the radio handset. "That hurt, sir. I'm sensitive about my height."

Sergeant Blackwell had learned his tact and diplomacy as a drill instructor at Parris Island. "Both your feet reach the ground. You're fuckin' tall enough." He pushed through the foliage and disappeared.

The lieutenant got the attention of the man resting at the spot where his sergeant had just disappeared. "Move out," he said. The word spread up the column. After a few groans, the Marines rose and began moving again.

By the time the lieutenant's spot in the column reached the clearing, the embankment across the stream was slick with the mud of dozens of boots, and knee and hand prints decorated the slope where lost footing had been saved. Sergeant Blackwell already had the first half of the platoon setting up defensive positions around the LZ, and Franklin was busy placing a C-4 charge at the base of one of the tall trees.

When the lieutenant got to the top of the embankment, he turned and gave Bronsky a hand up. "Find Sergeant Blackwell," he said.

Before Bronsky could move, the sergeant came from the shadowed edge of the clearing. "Sir?"

"Sergeant, I want a couple of fire teams and one of the guns where they can cover this stream and the path we cut through the bush."

"Will do. I put the other 60 on the rise to the right of the clearing just beyond the tree line."

Bronsky extended a hand to the next man struggling up the embankment. Besides his pack the man carried two bags with straps that crisscrossed his flak jacket under a bandolier holding one hundred rounds of M60 ammunition. He had no rifle, but his web belt held a .45-caliber automatic pistol and four magazines. To the untrained eye he looked like all the other Marines, but he was one of two Navy hospital corpsmen assigned to 1st Platoon. As prime targets for snipers the corpsmen made a special effort to blend in, carrying their medical supplies in old demolition bags and occasionally trading their .45s for M16s, but the trip through any village, no matter how remote, would usually burst their bubble of invisibility when children would point and yell "*bac-si*," the Vietnamese word for doctor. If a five-year-old could pick you out, how difficult could it be for a trained eye behind a rifle?

Doc Garver, just under six feet tall, had always been thin, but the diet of C rations combined with long hours and little sleep had pared his weight to less than 150. His fair skin seemed incapable of tanning, and ruptured sun blisters on his forearms gave him the appearance of a pox sufferer.

"Doc, the lieutenant says the command post is here. Doc Brede can stay with 1st Squad."

Bronsky moved over near the lieutenant, and Doc Garver went to the shadows by the edge of the clearing. CPs tended to get crowded, and crowds tended to draw fire. Doc Garver's survival strategy was to be where the bullets weren't. He might have to go there after their arrival, but it was always wise to avoid the initial salvo.

Every few seconds a Marine came out of the jungle and crossed the stream. Each carried a bandolier of ammunition for the M60s, and some carried two hundred rounds, the linked cartridges strapping their chests like those on Mexican banditos in old westerns. One Marine hacked a branch from a tree with his machete and used it to haul new arrivals up the mucky incline. Lieutenant Diehl signaled one to wait, directing the others to break off to the left side of the clearing. The waiting man was a stocky lance corporal with a barrel chest. His face and arms were deep bronze, and his high cheekbones and broad nose framed piercingly clear eyes that could fix a man with a stare the way a mountain lion looked at its next meal. His strong chin supported a mouth often bordering on the edge of an intolerant sneer that seemed to warn people to choose their words wisely. His voice belied his forbidding countenance. The prepossessing lilt came out soft as velvet, but like his Apache forebears he was thrifty with words, and no one in the platoon could ever remember hearing him laugh.

Born into a warrior clan in the remote Cibecue community on the White Mountain Reservation in Arizona, his warrior ethic had led him to another warrior clan—the U.S. Marines. He had no interest in saving the Vietnamese from themselves or defeating communism or propping up the domino theory. His enlistment was the fulfillment of an ancient mandate. It was simply a matter of metallurgy: he was forging an Apache manhood, and the crucible was Vietnam.

"Chief. Go help Franklin set charges on those trees, and go easy on the C-4. I just want them down, not vaporized."

The Chief looked out into the clearing.

"You hear me, Chief?"

"Yes, General," the Chief said, lifting the demo bag and pulling the strap over his helmet.

"I'm not a damned general, Chief."

The Chief started into the clearing. "And I'm not a chief, sir."

Bronsky stifled a laugh but couldn't suppress a smile. "I guess he's the sensitive type, too, sir."

The lieutenant checked his watch, a black-faced chronograph he'd picked up at the PX in Da Nang. "Tell him that burning the company shitters for a week could put a nice crust on that sensitivity."

"Sir, pfcs don't tell anybody anything; it's our only perk. And Marines who want to stay healthy don't tell the Chief anything he don't wanna hear. I think the only reason he joined the Crotch and came to Vietnam is because he didn't get the chance to kill cowboys in the Old West." Bronsky watched the Chief kneel next to Franklin with a coil of det cord in one hand and a long, wide-bladed knife in the other that he used to cleave low branches. "Once when he was feeling talkative, he told me that if I ever saw him with paint on his face, I should run."

It was the lieutenant's turn to smile.

"He was serious, sir. That Indian is fuckin' crazy."

Sergeant Blackwell sent the last Marine who emerged from the jungle to a position on the left and returned to the lieutenant. "We expect to be here long, sir?"

Diehl glanced at his watch again. "We'll be gone in less than ten minutes. Better get the 3rd Squad leader up here quick."

The sergeant checked his own watch, mentally marking the spot where the minute hand would be when they were moving again. "Strader won't like this."

"That's the great thing about the system we have in the Corps. He doesn't have to like what I say, but he damned well has to do it."

Along the left side of the LZ, 3rd Squad were shedding their heavy equipment. Bulky flak jackets with their layered fiberglass plates lay open so the air could dry sweat-soaked linings. Marines stripped to the waist moved in and out of the heavy brush. Cpl. Raymond Strader, the squad leader, moved among them. His pack was off, but he wore his flak jacket and helmet. A thirty-day countdown calendar drawn on one side of his camouflage helmet cover had most of the days scratched out. On the other side was a likeness of a miniature helmet dangling a pair of jungle boots that trod on the words "short timer."

"Reach, how long you think we'll be here?" one of 3rd Squad asked as he passed. Some of the platoon were given monikers that suited their jobs, personalities, skills, or even physical characteristics. Corporal Strader was "Reach" because, as the designated platoon sniper, he could reach out and touch the enemy wherever he could see them. Instead of the M16 that had been newly issued to the Marines in March, Strader still carried the old M14, chambered for the larger 7.62-mm NATO round. It was heavier, but he preferred the feel of a warm wooden stock to the hollow plastic of the M16, and unlike the 16, the 14 was reliable.

"Don't get comfortable," he answered. "Knowing the LT, we'll be saddled up and moving before the supply chopper lifts off."

One of the Marines had his pants down around his ankles while he pissed into the tangled root system of a huge strangler fig that completely obscured its host tree. "Hey, Reach. How short are you now?"

"Shorter than what you have in your hand, Tanner, and nothing's shorter than that."

"You *wish* you packed my gear."

Strader pointed to the ground where the fig and the tree were locked in a struggle. "I'll be back in the world before the piss on your boots dries."

Strader was universally envied in the platoon. Not because of his experience or the responsibility he shouldered as a squad leader, but because he was coming to the end of his tour of duty. He was what everyone longed to be; he was short.

A Marine holding his M16 over his shoulder by the barrel like a baseball bat pushed through the brush. "Reach. Blackwell is looking for you."

"I'm not hard to find, Burke. I'm right here in Vietnam."

Burke turned back the way he came. "I think the lieutenant wants you most ricky-tick."

Sergeant Blackwell shoved through the foliage from the clearing side, letting midmorning sunlight in to wash over the men of 3rd Squad. "Strader, Lieutenant Diehl wants you at the CP back where we crossed the creek."

"I'm just getting my squad set up. Give me five—"

"I ain't givin' you squat, Corporal. The lieutenant wants you now, not five minutes from now. And take your gear. If Victor Charley decides we ain't welcome on his side of the river, we may have to *didi mau*, and I ain't comin' back for your shit."

Strader walked a few paces past a rotting stump blanketed with moss, snatched up his pack by one strap, and slung it over his shoulder. "Did he say what he wanted?"

Sergeant Blackwell gave Strader a look that said patience was being tested. "As a matter of fact, he did. He said he wanted *you*."

"Eat the apple but fuck the Corps," Strader said, heading back toward the lieutenant's position.

Strader stood just under six feet tall, and the heat and mountainous terrain of Vietnam had whittled his weight down to a respectable 165. His blonde hair was cropped close, not in the high-and-tight Marine Corps style that might get him mistaken for a lifer, but close enough that what hair was left didn't create a heat issue. Any career Marine could see that Strader was just passing through. He had no plans to climb the NCO ranks or maverick himself into an officer. Like most of the men in 1st Platoon, his dreams were of life after the Corps, if there was to be any.

In fact, Strader had never planned to join the Marines at all. After high school, he spent a year working part-time jobs, raising hell with his friends, and playing Russian roulette with the Selective Service Board. One day the morning mail included greetings from his benevolent country and an invitation to become a member of the U.S. Army. It wasn't a suggestion. He had fourteen days to get his affairs in order and deliver himself to the Federal Building in Pittsburgh. The problem had a limited number of solutions: there was no chance of a college deferment, his job wasn't considered necessary to the national defense, and he hated the winters in western Pennsylvania, so the ones in Canada were out of the question. The only thing open to him was a verified prior commitment. The Army couldn't claim you if you were already a member of another branch of the armed services. So a week before his report date, Strader, Raymond C., entered that same Federal Building and walked into the recruiting offices off the main lobby. His goal was to sign up with someone other than the Army, and for as little time as possible.

Small, cramped cubicles surrounded a large room, each partition stenciled with the name of a designated branch of the military and papered with brightly colored posters that made being a member of that particular service seem fun, exciting, and above all, patriotic. Strader's first thought was to find a spot in one of the reserve units, but as the petty officer in the Navy cubicle said, after choking back a laugh, "Unless people call your daddy Senator or Governor, you can forget that." He also said that he could provide valuable schooling that guaranteed lucrative employment when the enlistment was over . . . and four years wouldn't seem that long. The Air Force recruiter parroted the same sentiments and felt sure he could get Strader a first duty station somewhere warm and tropical, like Florida. The Army recruiter didn't even look up. His quota was secure. He wasn't about to perform and pass the hat when he already had a captive audience ready to be delivered.

And then a gunnery sergeant welcomed Strader into the USMC cubicle. His shoes shone like they were coated with glass, and the creases in his dress blue trousers and khaki shirt looked like they could slice bread. Rows of colorful ribbons were stacked so high above one breast pocket that they threatened his collarbone. Two marksmanship medals dangling over a pocket flap proclaimed him an expert with both rifle and pistol. The sides of his head were shorn close with a crew top. And he exuded confidence. Behind him on the wall was a portrait of Lyndon Johnson and, next to it, a large photo of the sergeant shaking hands with a Marine officer with enough stars on his shoulders to qualify as a constellation. Strader noticed that none of the men on the wall looked worried. In fact, judging for self-assurance, competence, and strength, the president came in a distant third.

"Don't pay any attention to anything those numb nuts next door told you," the sergeant said. "They couldn't say shit if they had a mouthful."

Strader was impressed. Here was a no-nonsense man who would give him some experienced advice—direct, straightforward, and ready to be carved into granite as soon as Raymond C. scribbled his name on a promise of two years of servitude.

Fifteen minutes later Strader left the building a future Marine private and feeling the master of his life again. It would be weeks before he realized that his life was actually like a car careening out of control, and he wasn't even the one driving.

〜

Waves of heat shimmered above the clearing, and Franklin and the Chief shed their packs and flak jackets as they worked at the bases of the condemned trees. Soon, in a pyrotechnical blink of an eye, the jungle's efforts to reclaim the clearing would be erased. The Chief's helmet was upended at his knees, and the remains of a block of C-4 sat on the webbing inside the helmet liner, the plastic wrapping partially torn away. Franklin watched as the Chief kneaded the pliable explosive into a pancake and folded it around a knotted loop of det cord. Rivulets of sweat ran through the bristles of the Chief's close-cropped hair and down his neck until his dog tag chain and a leather cord suspending a small pouch interrupted the flow. The pouch looked old. Bright beads sewn to the leather depicted the abstract figure of a small man running below a silver circle. Franklin watched the bag swing back and forth as the Chief leaned into his work.

"What you got in that bag, man?"

The Chief molded the C-4 pancake to the trunk of one of the trees, but it wouldn't stick to the slick bark.

Franklin pointed. "That thing around your neck. What you got in there?"

The Chief grabbed the stag-horn handle of his knife and in one quick move brought the heavy blade down on the trunk at an angle, opening a flap like a bird's mouth. The tree seemed to shudder, and clear juices flowed.

Franklin shifted a few inches back from the Chief's reach. "Then again, it ain't none of my business what you got in there." He busied himself with his own equipment. "You could have a million dollars in there. It ain't my business."

"How'd you know there's money in there?"

Franklin took on the look of the unjustly accused. "Just a lucky guess." He stowed unused chunks of his own C-4 in his bag. "You're shittin' me, right? You really got money in there?"

The Chief looked up with a wry smile. "Honest injun."

It was difficult to tell where the Chief's mood was going, so Franklin weighed treading lightly against his natural curiosity. "How much you got in that bag?"

"One penny."

Franklin wanted to ask if it was an Indian head penny but decided not to press his luck. "Like I said, it ain't my business."

"A shaman gave it to me."

Franklin gave the Chief a look like he knew he was being had. "A shaman. You mean like a witch doctor? So it's a magic penny?"

The Chief's look said the time for sharing was over.

It was the first time Franklin had spoken to the Chief at any length. "Yes" and "no" answers generally ended their conversations. He decided to press a little. "A lot of bag for one penny," he said, stealing glances so he would know to duck if he had to.

"There's more," the Chief said, not looking up from his work.

"Like what?"

The Chief attached the pull-ring igniter to the C-4 stuffed into the tree gash. Both Marines stood and hauled their gear back toward the CP.

"My honor," the Chief said, slipping an arm through one side of his dangling flak jacket.

"What?" Franklin struggled with his hands full.

The Chief touched the leather bag and his eyes seemed to soften. "The spirit bag. It carries my honor."

"That a fact?" Franklin said, looking at the pouch suspiciously.

"That's right. It's a fact." The softness was gone.

"Whatever you say, man." The Chief was always unpredictable, and Franklin knew it was best to walk softly and live to fight another day, preferably against another enemy.

Private First Class Franklin came from the streets of Detroit, where every other building in his neighborhood was slated for demolition. Like most black families in the area, his found frequent moves necessary. He had mocha-colored skin and, at six-three, towered over most of the members of his squad. His tall, lithe body gave him a stride that kept the platoon scrambling when he was on point; at rest he looked like an unfolded chaise longue, full of angles and joints. With his three-year enlistment, he would be a civilian back in Michigan before he was old enough to vote.

As Strader worked his way back through his squad, a young Marine with a tattoo of a helmeted bulldog on his arm held out a worn photo for him to see.

"Hey, Reach. Take a look at Deacon's wife."

Strader slung his rifle over his shoulder and took the picture. "Damn," was all he could say.

"Damn straight," the tattooed Marine said. "I'd lay comm wire across the DMZ bare-ass naked just to hear her fart over a field phone. I shit you not."

Another Marine stepped up and grabbed the photo. The left leg of his jungle trousers was torn from the front pocket down past the thigh, and his knee popped out as he walked. With only seven weeks in-country, Private Deacon was working hard to overcome the FNG label attached to fresh replacements, but most of the old-timers in the platoon still referred to him as a fuckin' new guy and hadn't bothered to learn his name.

"Did Bronsky put in a requisition for me? I'm droppin' shit everywhere. If I don't get new drawers I'll be walkin' around in my skivvies."

"I put in the order yesterday," Strader said. "And I thought I told you to shit-can the skivvies. The doc ain't gonna send you back to the rear for a case of crotch rot, no matter how bad it gets."

The tattooed Marine made a grab for the photo and missed. "Come on, man. Let me have another look. You think you're special because you're the only one in the platoon dumb enough to have on underwear?"

Deacon tucked the photo into the bulging cargo pocket on the untorn pant leg. "Maybe I need extra support," he said, cupping his scrotum in one hand.

The Marine with the bulldog tattoo picked up his M16 and held it out with one hand. "This is my rifle," he said, then grabbed his own crotch with his free hand. "This is my gun." He shook the M16. "This one's for fighting." Then he pulled up on his crotch. "And this one really wants to see that photo again."

"Screw you, Karns," Deacon said, turning away.

Strader shook his head and moved on. When he passed a Marine sitting against a tree and opening a small cigarette pack from his C rations, he stopped long enough to say, "The smoking lamp is not lit, Laney. And get your fire team squared away. We're deep in the Arizona. Charley owns this place, and he don't like visitors. We got less than two days left on this op, and if we can get back across the river with our asses intact, I'll consider it a victory."

Laney snapped the cigarette pack under the band around his helmet.

Strader waited. "You think you can do that?" he said.

Laney shrugged and said, "*Kohng biet.*" Like most Marines he had no practical knowledge of the Vietnamese language, but he had heard those words a thousand times in dozens of villages in the Quang Nams. Whenever a Marine asked for the location of any VC, the nervous villagers would nod their heads and repeat the phrase over and over. Marines new to the boonies thought they were saying, "Cong bad," affirming that these villagers were friendly—or at least sympathetic—instead of the words' actual meaning, which was simply, "I don't know."

"Well, you better find out before Chuck rains *beaucoup* shit on our heads."

"Don't sweat it, Reach. We got it together."

Strader knew there was no time now to put Laney's head right, so he went on, wondering what the young Marine's parents were going to buy with his military life insurance.

Beyond his squad Strader passed into Corporal Middleton's 2nd Squad. Middleton stood at the top of the embankment and watched as two of his men filled canteens in the creek. "Put halizone in those canteens," Middleton was saying. "If you don't have enough, ask one of the docs for more."

The innocuous-looking little pills changed the local water into a medicinal-tasting fluid, palatable only if extreme thirst forced your hand. Given enough time, halizone pills could kill the microorganisms that racked your bowels and played havoc with your internal thermostat, but they also killed any desire to put the liquid into your mouth. Strader once asked Doc Garver if the pills made the water sterile. The corpsman laughed and said that the only thing sterile to drink in the bush was your own urine. Strader thought that was a disgusting concept, but from then on he couldn't help looking at his own stream as though he were pissing lemonade.

Middleton caught Strader as he passed. "Reach, can you smell that?" Middleton had a little over nine months in-country and considered himself short. Over six months gave you delusions of shortness, but over nine made it official for purposes of bragging. You were on the home stretch, short for sure.

"What?" Strader said.

Middleton tipped his head back and sniffed the air. Strader did the same.

"I don't smell anything," Strader said.

Middleton sniffed again. "Yep, I can smell your woman's panties."

"You're not that short, and keep you nose out of my love life."

Middleton had once been a member of Strader's squad, and he credited his old squad leader for teaching him the ropes and keeping him alive when he was too new to do it himself. He was closer to Strader than to anyone else in the platoon.

"You know what I'm going to do first when I get home, Reach?" Middleton said.

"No, what?"

"I'm going to fuck for six solid hours," Middleton said.

"Sounds like a plan. What will you do second?"

Middleton seemed lost in thought. "Probably put down my seabag." He slapped Strader on the shoulder as he left.

Strader reached the CP as Bronsky pushed the radio handset up under the rim of his helmet and clapped a hand over the other ear to block out the ten million invertebrate voices that made the jungle seem to vibrate. The radioman stepped a little closer to the clearing so the short antenna would grab as much reception as it could from the sea of vegetation all around them. "Sir," he said to Lieutenant Diehl. "High-ball says they're about a minute out. They want to be advised on the smoke."

"Reach. What color smoke grenades do you have?" the lieutenant said.

Strader swung his pack to the ground. "One red and one yellow."

Lieutenant Diehl held out his hand. "Bronsky, tell Highball the smoke will be yellow." He stood waiting, arm extended, until Strader handed over the canister. "I'm glad we're using one of yours, Reach," he said. "It's kind of poetic."

"Why is that, sir?"

"Because a Marine should hail his own cab."

The lieutenant handed the smoke grenade to Franklin, who was standing off to the side with the Chief, and urged him toward the clearing. "When I signal, pop the smoke and start the fuses. And don't take your time getting back here. We won't be waiting for Doc to pull splinters out of your ass."

Franklin headed into the clearing, pulling on his flak jacket as he went. The Chief squatted where he was, always conscious of the size of the target he made.

"I don't know what you mean, sir," Strader said. "What cab?"

The lieutenant looked up at the cloudless blue sky above the clearing, appreciating the view generally denied him in the Arizona. "What is your DEROS, Reach?"

Strader looked at Bronsky, but the radioman turned away, busying himself with an imaginary problem with the handset.

Strader didn't need to calculate his date of expected return from overseas. "I've got three days and a wake-up," Strader answered.

"Hear that, Doc?" the lieutenant said. "Three days and a wake-up."

The corpsman was sitting on the ground, using his pack for a backrest. "Don't look for sympathy here. I've got five months and a wake-up."

The lieutenant stopped looking at the sky and turned to Strader. "This is your ride coming. When we get the supplies off the chopper, you get on."

Strader let his pack fall to the ground. His eyes darted about like an animal's looking for a way out of a trap. "I can't leave, sir. My squad's short two rifles now. The ones I have are a headache when we're in the rear. Out here in the boonies . . ." His mind raced to find some piece of logic that would dissuade the lieutenant, even though experience told him that two stripes never overruled one bar in the Corps. In the hierarchy of Marine Corps firepower, he was a mere peashooter.

Lieutenant Diehl put a hand on his shoulder. "We'll be back in a couple of days. You'll have plenty of time to buy everybody in An Hoa a beer before you go. You can even buy me one. So grab your gear. That's an order."

"Sir, I can't go."

"You can, and you will." The lieutenant tried to soften his authoritarian voice; he'd grown to like Strader. "Look," he said, "you should never have come on this operation. The Arizona has always been a nightmare, and the captain was sure we were going to step in it, like always, and you would be needed. But for some reason Charley is doing his best to avoid us—too busy doing something else, I guess—so you're just here for the exercise. There's no point."

"I can stay and still have a day left to get squared away after we get back."

Argument from subordinates wasn't tolerated in the Corps, but the lieutenant's fondness for Strader tempered his frustration. "You may not be familiar with military law concerning disobeying orders in the field. Chief! Get over here."

The Chief stood and jogged the few steps to where they stood, feeling oddly self-conscious. "Sir," he said.

"You ever shoot a white man, Chief?"

The Chief seemed stunned by the question. He wasn't at all sure what the lieutenant expected him to answer. "No, sir," he said, slowly and with caution.

Bronsky moved over beside Doc Garver. "Not that we know of," he whispered.

"Would you like to?" Lieutenant Diehl asked.

A broad smile spread over the Chief's face. He was trailing his M16 by the front stock and slowly raised it up with both hands. That Strader was his squad leader made the prospect even sweeter. "It would make my ancestors very happy," he said.

"Your choice, Reach. You go out on the supply chopper or on a medevac."

Strader could see that further resistance was not only futile but, judging from the twisted grin on the Chief's face, probably dangerous. He was sure the lieutenant was being facetious, but the look in the Chief's eyes left little doubt that if the order was given, he might enjoy pulling the trigger.

"Chief, please don't shoot Reach," Doc said. "I just got comfortable."

A distant pounding interrupted the farce. Every Marine in 1st Platoon sensed it; the sound seemed to emanate from their core, subtle thuds that punched the chest in rapid succession like little concussion grenades. At the lieutenant's command, Franklin pulled the pin on the smoke and tossed it into the tall grass a few yards away. It pinged, sending the spoon spinning into the air, and the canister spewed clouds of yellow smoke that billowed up from the clearing on columns of hot air like a drawing chimney. In seconds an H-34 helicopter streaked over the clearing at ninety miles per hour, just above treetop level. Anyone who wanted to take a shot at it would have to be quick on the draw. The huge radial piston engine staggered the trees and made the ground quiver as the helicopter banked to starboard and climbed.

The H-34, officially designated the UH-34 D, was the workhorse of the Marines in the northern provinces of I Corps. While the Army flooded the southern provinces with the UH-IE, which looked like a scorpion and became universally known as the "Huey," in the north, the Marines' mainstay was a flying truck that looked like a grasshopper. The H-34 was forgiving, it could outcarry the Huey, and it could absorb enough punishment to sink a battleship and still stay in the air.

Bronsky held the radio handset out to the lieutenant. He had to shout to be heard. "Highball wants a sit rep, sir."

Lieutenant Diehl grabbed the handset. "Highball, this is Pounder One. The LZ is secure, over. Do you read? The LZ is secure."

"That's good, Pounder. I'll just set down on top of one of those trees and you can climb up and get your supplies, over."

As Lieutenant Diehl watched, Franklin pulled the rings on the igniters and started running back to the CP screaming "Fire in the hole" at the top of his lungs.

Lieutenant Diehl grabbed Bronsky by the shoulder strap and pulled him toward the embankment. "Bring it in now, Highball. We're throwing out the welcome mat. Over and out."

Marines scrambled over the edge of the embankment, ducked behind high ground, and crouched behind any tree with enough girth to provide cover.

As the escort 34 swept away and banked steeply to port, the door gunner looked straight down on the jungle's canopy, a roiling green sea. The supply 34 started a straight descent toward the clearing.

The copilot signaled the crew chief that they were going in, and the chief and the door gunner tucked the butts of their M60 machine guns into their shoulders. In the jump seats by the door, two Marines in newly issued gear and jungle utilities, their new jungle boots without a scuff, looked at each other with thinly veiled apprehension as the chopper shook and vibrated. Clumps of dirt danced around the riveted floor like the little plastic players on an electric football game. As the crew chief had demanded before takeoff, their M16s held no magazines and the chambers were cleared.

The door gunner leaned over with a toothy grin not meant to be comforting and shouted over the noise, "Stay away from the rear of the chopper. You can't see the tail rotor spinning, and it will cut you in half. I don't give a shit about you, but after it cuts you in half, we won't be able to take off. So stay the hell away from the tail."

Three rapid explosions jolted the ground, and shards of tree trunks shredded the surrounding foliage. Three trees hopped spasmodically in unison and collapsed with a crash into the grass. Before the branches stopped twitching Sergeant Blackwell was into the clearing with a detail involving half the platoon. They snatched up the trees and dragged them into the jungle, pulling and twisting until even the uppermost branches were manhandled clear of the LZ.

Even before the trees were completely concealed in the jungle, the 34's tires were bouncing on their struts beside three splintered stumps. The huge rotors whipped the grass into a brown frenzy and tossed bits of tree trunk around like shrapnel. The crew chief was already pushing cases of C rations to the door. "Last stop, everybody out," he yelled, pushing a carton into the arms of one of the passengers. "And don't go empty-handed."

The pilot lowered the collective and adjusted the engine's rpms as a small group of Marines rushed the starboard side, stooping at the waist to avoid the deadly rotors. The two new guys hit the ground disoriented, each holding a case of C-rats under one arm. One of the approaching Marines pointed back to the edge of the clearing, and the replacements ducked down and headed to where the lieutenant and Bronsky stood watching.

The escort flew a wide arc above the clearing as cases of food and equipment were dragged through the cargo door of the supply helicopter and hauled away.

Standing next to Diehl, Strader watched the two new Marines approach. Their pants were bloused at the boot tops, and they wore their jungle utility shirts under their flak jackets, the sleeves rolled to the elbow. One set the C ration case at his feet and started to raise his right hand to the rim of his helmet.

"Don't paint a target on me, Marine," the lieutenant said. The new guy dropped his arm to his side. The other stood there, clutching his C rations.

Strader looked at the lieutenant with disbelief. "Two more FNGs, sir? I should stay to make sure—"

The lieutenant cut him short. He nodded at the grenade pouches on Strader's belt. "Reach, give these two hard chargers your frags and smoke. You won't need them."

Strader dug the grenades out and handed them to the new guy without the C ration case.

All the gear was offloaded from the helicopter now, and the pilot was increasing the engine's power. Lieutenant Diehl grabbed the radio handset. "Hold on, Highball. I've got one to go." The pilot's voice hissed through the speaker, and Diehl turned away and covered his other ear.

"Let's move, Pounder. I don't like your neighborhood."

Strader wanted one last appeal. "But, sir," he said.

"Chief, make sure the corporal gets on that chopper."

The Chief took a menacing step forward.

"Okay, okay. I'm going. I don't like it, but I'm going."

The two Marines started across the clearing toward the helicopter as the rotors whipped the air impatiently.

Corporal Middleton ran in from the side and caught up. "Blackwell says you're skying up, Reach. Is that true?"

"True enough, Carl. The lieutenant says I go or the Chief here will be wearing my hair on his belt. Right, Chief?"

"I'm not a chief, shitbird."

Middleton slapped Strader on the shoulder. "I'll see you in a couple days. Save me a beer." He turned and jogged back toward his squad.

Strader tossed his pack through the helicopter door and started to climb on, then looked back. "You wouldn't really shoot me would you, Chief?"

The Chief slung his rifle over his shoulder. "My name is Gonshayee, asshole."

The door gunner extended a hand and dragged Strader in.

The pilot worked the collective, and the huge open exhaust roared, the rotors spinning until they were a translucent blur. He adjusted the pitch of the main rotor, simultaneously increasing the engine speed, and the Chief ran for cover, disappearing in a swirling hail of debris. The machine rattled and shook until it seemed to test all the rivets that held its form together. With one more throttle increase, the pounding rotor beat the law of gravity into submission and the big green grasshopper lifted into the air, raised its tail, and climbed out of the clearing.

Corporal Strader stood in the door and watched his Marine family fall away. Unexpected sadness and overwhelming guilt swept over him as the helicopter moved above the jungle canopy and the arboreal wilderness swallowed up Golf's 1st Platoon.

The H-34 swung north with the escort close behind. The gunner sat by the door, casually holding the pistol grip on his M60 as it hung down in its mount. He whistled loudly to get Strader's attention and pointed to one of the jump seats. Strader didn't want to break his mental connection with his platoon. The crew chief cupped his hands to his mouth and shouted, "Sit down." Finally, Strader dropped into the seat. The air seemed cooler in the chopper. The rotor wash and speed whipped air currents about the interior, drying the sweat on his face. He noticed the crew chief pointing at him. He raised a defiant chin as if to say, "What the hell do you want now?" The Marine pointed at Strader's rifle. "Clear that weapon," he yelled.

Strader lay the M14 across his knees, released the magazine, and ejected the chambered cartridge. The jacketed 7.62-mm round gleamed in the shadowy interior of the helicopter, and he pushed it into the pocket of his flak jacket. The crew chief gave him a thumbs-up and turned back to his window.

In the last year Strader had been ferried about the northern provinces of I Corps many times in choppers like this one. He had flown from the top of the mountain outpost at Nong Son. His squad had dropped into the Phu Loc compound at Liberty Bridge to stop VC sappers from destroying the engineers' newly completed work. And he went with Sparrow Hawk to Tam Ky when a North Vietnamese Army push overwhelmed Marine defenses there. He might even have flown in this very 34 before, though he didn't recognize the crew.

The crew chief was sitting in shadow against the bulkhead, but the door gunner sat in a square of bright morning light. The green paint on his flight helmet was so scratched and worn that his name, stenciled in black letters, was illegible. His face seemed marked with acne, but on closer inspection Strader could see that the problem was caused by enthusiasm, not hormones or hygiene. The black spots were specks of cartridge powder burned into the skin, blowback from an overheated M60 barrel known as a cook off. Strader was sure the spots would have faded to mere shadows by the time the gunner was old enough to drink.

Strader leaned back, closed his eyes, and tried to enjoy the ride.

N guyen Xian Tho and Pham Long moved ahead of their unit to an outcropping that afforded a view of the valley. The distant explosion and sounds of American helicopters had drawn their attention and sent the other men with them to ground. Pham climbed to a higher vantage point, Nguyen's binoculars swinging precariously from his neck. Nguyen had threatened to make Pham's life very difficult if he allowed any harm to come to them. Pham concentrated on his hand- and footholds, blocking out his leader's voice. From the ledge he could see over the jungle canopy in the valley, and he trained the binoculars on the smoke rising in the distance. "*May bay truc thang, hai,*" he said, indicating that there were helicopters in the valley, two of them.

"*Boa xa?*" Nguyen asked. How far?

Pham watched one of the helicopters make lazy circles in the dis-tance. "*Hai kilometers,*" he said, rocking his hand back and forth to indicate the distance was only a rough estimate. He watched until the second helicopter rose from the jungle and continued watching as the two flew east until their sound faded to nothing. "*Thuy quan luc chien my,*" he said, looking down into Nguyen's upturned face. Nguyen shrugged and waved him down. So the American Marines were in the valley. It was no concern of his. He had his orders. He was to avoid contact with enemy units and deliver his cargo to cadres in the Quang Nams before the Lunar New Year for the Tet celebration.

Pham climbed down and returned the binoculars to Nguyen, who inspected them thoroughly before replacing them in the canvas case hanging around his neck. Hanoi had made it sound like his new assign-ment was a promotion to unit commander, but Nguyen felt like he'd been demoted to laborer. He was being sent down Uncle Ho's trail again, but this time as a coolie.

Before starting south, Nguyen's men exchanged their North Viet-namese Army uniforms for the *oa baba* that U.S. troops described as black pajamas. Some wore sandals made from old tire treads, and soft, wide-brimmed hats took the place of their usual pith helmets.

Nguyen and Pham backtracked to where they had dropped their equipment. Pack boards strapped with RPGs and mortar rounds lay next to a recoilless rifle and a Chinese 24 machine gun. Stretched out along the mountainside, the members of the NVA unit were already getting to their feet and hauling the heavy weapons up onto their backs. Co Chien and Sau Thao lifted the bulky machine gun strapped to two long bamboo poles that flexed under its weight. Truong Nghi, another student volunteer like Pham, followed with the gun's tripod balanced on his shoulders.

Pham helped Nguyen with his pack board of mortar rounds before swinging a mortar tube onto his own shoulder. "Couldn't we move faster if we went down to level ground?" he asked.

Nguyen ran a belt through his shoulder straps and cinched it tight across his chest. "The valley is heavily mined. We could move faster, but at what cost? I will not take the chance without a local guide. Even this high we are not safe, so step with care. And as you saw, the Americans are inside the trees, and we must move away from them." Nguyen leaned into his load and started off.

They had come more than forty kilometers from the Laotian border in the last five days, and their burdens were wearing them down. Their backs felt broken and their shoulders were rubbed raw. Each day they appreciated the time spent resting more than the day before. They originally pushed on through the rain, but their progress was so slow and the falls so frequent that it was decided that waiting out the downpours was wiser than losing a man to injury. Anyway, they had time.

"It's good to know our leader is concerned for our safety," Truong said, coming alongside Pham.

"Don't be a fool, Truong. His concern is for the cargo."

Truong moved close to Sau so he could speak unheard. "Is it true that the Americans call this area Arizona?"

Sau turned his head, trying to keep pace with Co so he wouldn't push or be pulled. "I've heard Nguyen say so."

"Why would they do that? I've read about their Arizona. How could this place remind them of it?"

Sau tried to shrug. "I don't know, Truong. The Americans think they are cowboys, so maybe they also think there are Indians here."

Truong dropped back a few paces, giving the concept some consideration. "I think they're right about that," he said. "There are Indians here. And we are the Indians." As an avid reader of western novels published in America, he felt happy somehow to be saying that. He suddenly experienced a surge of pride. In all his readings, he had never identified with the cowboys in the stories he loved so much, even though they were the main characters and obviously the intended heroes. He always thought of himself as one of the Indians.

The H-34 lowered gently onto the interlocking metal panels that Seabees had sledge-hammered together to make the runway at An Hoa combat base. On a rise overlooking the runway, a Marine air controller in a tower watched from behind a ring of sandbags as Strader jumped from the cargo door, the panels banging under his boots. The door gunner sat in the door with his legs dangling. He handed Strader his backpack. "Where are you headed now?" he said.

Strader swung the pack over one shoulder. "Pennsylvania."

The door gunner laughed. "That's a little outside our range. I think you'll have to find another means of transportation."

"That sounds like good advice." Strader waved and headed for the main road leading up to the 2nd Battalion command area.

The road continued on through the base and out the gate and in twenty-six hard-fought miles reached Da Nang. Heavy vehicles had ground the dirt into fine talc that rose in clouds with every footfall and turned into a muddy soup after a few minutes of rain. In the administration area the road was lined with plywood buildings raised up on blocks and topped with corrugated steel roofs. Each was screened all the way around and had a door at each end. A sidewalk of shipping pallets made a feeble attempt to keep boots out of the muck in the monsoon season, but during the rains the whole base was mud, the road was slop, and the bunkers on the perimeter filled with brown water. If you had the rank to travel by vehicle, you could step onto the sidewalk without tarnishing your shine. But if you walked, you waded through mud, and when you reached the sidewalk, every step you took left a lumpy boot print. Unfortunately, officers did not like a dirty sidewalk. In wet weather, Echo, Foxtrot, Golf, and Hotel commanders kept the office personnel busy scraping the muddy footprints back into the road.

The office pogues hated it when grunts were summoned to the company hooches; it always meant dirty work for them. The two groups seldom mixed on the base. The grunts resented the pogues because of the relative safety and comfort of their jobs, and the pogues resented the grunts because being in the land of elephants and seeing the elephants were not the same thing.

Strader dropped his pack and helmet by the steps in front of one of the buildings and went in. Panels on the side of the building blocked the sun and kept the interior in shade while an oscillating fan on top of a file cabinet bathed the room in a sweeping breeze. The room was populated with desks and files and a large table next to a wall that divided the length of the building in half. A large map detailed 2/5's tactical area of responsibility. From where he stood Strader could see the green spot in the Arizona marking the TAOR where 1st Platoon was now sweating. Since there was no one else in the room, he went up close to the fan and let the rush of air wash over him.

Before long a door in the partitioning wall opened and Cpl. Donald Pusic stepped into the office. His clean, starched jungle utilities had been tailored to fit, and his canvas-sided jungle boots were coated with Kiwi black. He smelled of soap and aftershave. In one hand he carried a file folder; the other held a cold Coca-Cola. He stopped when he noticed the Marine enjoying the fan. "Strader," he said, "is 1st Platoon back already?"

Strader held his flak jacket open on one side to let in the breeze. "No, just me."

Pusic moved behind one of the desks and shuffled some papers. "I don't remember the captain giving me any orders about you."

Strader tore himself away from the fan. He hadn't washed or shaved in five days, and his jungle pants showed every inch of his travels. They were rolled up above worn-out boots with holes abraded in the ankles and nearly every bit of black on the leather scuffed away. His forehead was divided by a tan line showing where his soft cover fit, and his arms were marked to the elbows with scabs from elephant grass cuts. He leaned his M14 against the desk next to a carved wooden placard warning against asking for favors that said: DUTY MARINES HAVE NO FRIENDS AND GIVE NO HUSSES. "Lieutenant Diehl sent me back. If you have any arguments, they're with him."

Corporal Pusic was a political realist when it came to the Marine Corps hierarchy. He never questioned officers. If a question was going to a lieutenant, it would come from a captain. The trick was to get the captain to ask the question. "I never argue with Lieutenant Diehl," Pusic said.

Strader leaned both hands on the edge of the desk. His arms were covered with tracks where sweat had eroded the dirt. "That's probably best, because it seems Diehl has decided to let the Chief resolve all his problems."

Pusic's eyes widened. "The Chief?" he said.

"Yeah. He was going to shoot me this morning if I didn't get on the chopper. And he likes me. Can you imagine what he would do to someone he didn't like?"

Pusic briefly imagined what horrors that might involve, then decided to regain some command over his domain. "What is it you want from me, Strader?"

"I want a hot meal and a shower, but what I need is some sleep. I need a rack."

Pusic leaned back in his chair. "Third Platoon is manning the lines. They're in the hootches along the runway on the mess hall side. There should be some empty cots."

Strader snatched up his rifle and headed for the door. "I'll be back in the morning for a checkout list. I've got three and a wake-up and I wanna get the paperwork done as soon as I can."

"So, you're going to leave your happy little family here?"

Strader stood in the doorway and looked down the road, across the runway, all the way to the distant Ong Thu shrouded in the Arizona haze. "I already did that," he said. "Now I'm going back to the world."

≈

After the supply chopper lifted off, 1st Platoon moved northwest of the clearing, the lead fire team hacking a path as quickly as they could. The point man swung his machete until his arm was spent, then the second man took over. The three Marines rotated point until the platoon had traveled more than a click from the LZ and Lieutenant Diehl called a halt so the supplies could be distributed. Replacement equipment, ammunition, and twelve cases of C rations had come off the chopper and had to be dispersed through the platoon. The men carrying the heavy cases were glad to hand them off to squad leaders. Bandoliers of M60 and M16 ammunition were passed out. The two M79 men split thirty rounds between them, and Deacon got his new pants.

Corporal Middleton dropped two cases of meals on the ground and snapped the wire banding with the slots in the flash suppressor on his

M16. Each meal had the contents printed on the box top, and some meals were more prized that others. Wieners and baked beans were a favorite, while ham and lima beans were universally despised; the combination of the ham and the beans just didn't work, and the Marines made it known which ingredient was the culprit by naming the meal "ham and motherfuckers."

Middleton flipped the cases over so only the unprinted bottoms of the individual meals showed. In theory, each squad member would choose an anonymous box in turn until the case was empty. Unfortunately, every case was packed exactly the same way, so the configuration was easily memorized; if you were too new to know or too late to pick, you either learned to love ham and limas or starved.

Middleton tossed a green bundle to Deacon. "Here, don't rip these," he said. "And I don't want to have to tell you again, lose the skivvies."

Deacon dropped his gear and started stripping off his torn trousers as fast as he could. He didn't want to be caught half naked if the platoon moved out.

Up ahead, Lance Corporal Burke was handing out C-rats to 3rd Squad in the same manner and with much the same results. Burke had eight months in-country and, though only an E-3, with Strader's departure now found himself in charge of a squad in the most dreaded area in I Corps. Sergeant Blackwell had promised to stay close, but since the sergeant had been with the platoon only a little over four months, he didn't find the promise comforting.

"Blackwell says I'm to honcho 3rd Squad," Burke said to the others as they stowed their new meals in their packs.

"Where the hell is Reach?" one of the Marines said, flipping his meals over to confirm what he would be eating.

"The lieutenant sent him back on the chopper."

It took a second for that to take hold. Reach was gone. They were glad to know that one of their own was going home, but his departure left a hole in the squad, an important hole that made them more vulnerable.

Sergeant Blackwell moved down the line, pushing the Marines to gather their gear and get ready to move. He found Deacon wearing only a helmet, flak jacket, and boots. "Do you think this is a nudist colony, Marine?" he said, watching as Deacon tried to dance into his new pants.

"Get those lily-white legs back into green before some VC takes a shine to your ass."

Whistles came from around 2nd Squad. Middleton laughed.

"It ain't funny, Middleton. You got a man doin' a striptease in the Arizona," the sergeant said.

Middleton laughed again. "He's just practicing for a section eight discharge."

"I am not," Deacon said, struggling to button his fly.

The sergeant looked around at the debris. "Get those empty cartons torn up and buried, and don't leave any of the wire here."

Middleton pulled his KA-BAR from his belt and tossed it to Deacon. "Here you go, Gypsy Rose. Cut up those boxes."

Deacon sliced away at the empty C ration boxes, worrying all the while that the "Gypsy Rose" label was going to stick and haunt him the rest of his tour. Being given the name of a stripper old enough to be his mother would be hard to live down.

Farther along, Sergeant Blackwell reached the CP. Two Marines in clean uniforms stood behind Lieutenant Diehl gulping water from their canteens.

"Sergeant, meet Privates Haber and DeLong," the lieutenant said. "See if you can find a place for them."

Sergeant Blackwell looked the replacements up and down. "Out-fucking-standing," he said.

The Chief stood directly behind the two, his M16 cradled in his arms.

"Chief, get back up to 3rd Squad and take these two with you," the sergeant said. "But tell Burke to keep them away from point."

The Chief pushed past the replacements and started up the column.

"Go on, you two," Blackwell said. "Stay with the Chief and watch where you step. This country tends to jump up and bite you in the ass."

Haber and DeLong hurried by, trying to watch the ground and keep an eye on the Chief at the same time.

Lieutenant Diehl unfolded his map and traced a line with his finger so the sergeant could see. "We're moving along here. I want to stay close to the mountains so we can get into the foothills tonight. You stay with the 3rd and try to keep the new blood out of trouble."

Dark clouds swept over the valley, visible from below as a change in the translucent quality of the light in the treetops. The air filled with the smell of the rain to come.

"Do you think we're gonna get soggy?" the sergeant asked.

The lieutenant looked up at the darkening shadows in the trees. "Count on it."

~

Two rows of barracks hooches faced each other across a wide, dusty space, interspersed with sandbag bunkers and twelve-man tents that held the rifle companies' personal gear. Beyond the hooches, past the barrel latrines and piss tubes made from rocket pods, was the southern end of more than three thousand feet of runway. Just past the runway, perimeter bunkers overlooked strands of concertina wire meant to keep whoever was beyond it from getting in, or at least to slow them down. Strader walked between the two rows, looking into each building as he went. The sounds of Armed Forces Radio emanating from one of the barracks told everyone within earshot the sad story of Billy Joe McAllister and a bridge on the Tallahatchie. It was one of the few current popular recordings to get AFR approval. Many of the lifers acted as though the sand in their boots was from Tarawa and Iwo Jima, and they saw rock-and-roll as a subversive noise that rotted the brain and loosened the morals. Most of the music AFR played for the troops had either a 1950s country twang or the innocuous big orchestra drone popular on elevators. If the clueless brass couldn't rock your world with Mantovani, they would try stirring your blood with John Phillip Sousa. Eventually the lower echelons learned to either do without or hum along with Pat Boone and Jim Nabors.

Strader pulled the screened door open. Two steps took him out of the sun and onto a plywood floor. No one was home except one of 3rd Platoon's corpsmen, sitting on a corner cot reading. He looked over his glasses as Strader entered. "Hey, Reach," he said.

Strader swung his pack to the floor. "Hi, Doc, any empty racks in here?"

The corpsman indicated the other end of the building with the paperback book in his hand. "There's some down on the end. You finally decide to join a good platoon?"

Strader pulled his pack up by one shoulder strap. "Well, Doc. Did you ever hear a gook say that something good was number three? I don't think so. First Platoon is number one. It's a numerical fact, and numbers don't lie."

The corpsman laughed. "I thought you guys were out poking the Arizona with a stick. What are you doing here?"

The floor vibrated with Strader's steps, booming as though he were walking on a drumhead. "I'm too short to be anywhere else," he said.

Most of the cots were piled with helmets and flak jackets. Packs and web gear filled the spaces in between. Military-issue shower shoes mixed with Ho Chi Minh sandals purchased from the enterprising locals who set up stands on the road just outside the wire. The three end cots on the right were empty. Strader dropped his gear on the one closest to the door and leaned his rifle in the corner.

"Are Brede and Garver okay?" the doc said over the music.

"They were this morning when I left." Strader sat on the cot and stripped away his jungle boots. His mottled green socks gave off a putrid odor like stagnant water. He peeled them off and tossed them under the cot. His own rank aroma mixed with the musty stink of the canvas cots and the essence of creosote and fuel oil that wafted through the screens on the hot breeze. He lay back on the bare cot and stared up at the rafters and the corrugated steel roof that was giving off heat like a convection oven. "Hey, Doc. I'm gonna catch some Zs. Don't let me miss chow, okay?"

The corpsman waved and turned down the volume on the radio.

Before Bobbie Gentry could sing Billy Joe under the muddy water below the Tallahatchie Bridge, Strader was asleep.

$$\approx$$

In an attempt to raise morale, the Seabees had put together some sheets of painted plywood that served An Hoa as a movie screen. Occasionally the bulletin board would announce a movie—meaning that the projectionist was going to light up the night with that screen and try to get through a film without taking fire from the wild country west of the base. Attending was a calculated risk. The prospect of a blazing screen surrounded by an audience of Marines sitting on empty ammo cases was often too much for the VC to resist, and the distant thump and swish of incoming mortar rounds would send the movie into a prolonged intermission. The VC might just as well have saved their precious ammunition, because the same powers that filled radio broadcasts with Andy Williams and Percy Faith also chose movies they felt were appropriate for troops in a combat zone. This wasn't a plus for attendance.

Strader was always on the lookout for little indicators that showed him how much the brass was in tune with the troops they commanded. He wanted to know that those making life-and-death decisions at least knew who their troops were. He was usually disappointed, and never more so than on his first trip to the base movie when the plywood came alive with the 1933 version of *Little Women*, adapted from the Louisa May Alcott novel. There, in glorious black and white, was indisputable proof that the brass at Special Services didn't have a clue. Or maybe they had an ulterior motive. Maybe they thought that the sight of Katherine Hepburn and Spring Byington waltzing sedately through Civil War America would curb masturbation. If that was the case, they sorely underestimated the libido and imagination of the average Marine. Strader generously chose to think that command just saw a movie title with the word "women" in it and, lacking a background in literature, decided that it might be something young men would enjoy seeing. None of those scenarios, real or imagined, filled him with confidence. But of one thing he was certain; it was insane to sit in the dark in front of a beacon of light that attracted bullets the way a streetlight attracts insects just to watch a cinematic version of saltpeter.

≈

The bank of threatening clouds covered the entire Ong Thu mountain range from south of the Song Vu Gia all the way north to the razorback below the Liberty Bridge. The rain started slowly, and the jungle's triple canopy held it back like an umbrella until it strengthened and forced its way through to soak the jungle floor. From below, the water seemed to be originating from the branches themselves. And the trees would hold the water, dispensing it over hours, keeping the jungle alive with drips long after the storm passed.

The North Vietnamese kept moving until the relentless rain made the footing sloppy and the energy spent for distance traveled seemed a poor investment. They finally sought cover in the underbrush. Sentries slipped away from the group to prevent surprises while the rest covered their equipment with oilcloths and rubber-coated tarps. They huddled together, holding the covers over their heads as makeshift tents.

Nguyen squatted shoulder-to-shoulder with Pham watching their tarp shed water in sheets. Raindrops beat at the thick fabric like little pummeling fists.

"You don't have to be here," Nguyen said, feeling oddly uncomfortable being this close to Pham.

Pham seemed confused. "I could sit with the others."

"I mean here in the South. It's not your place. You should have stayed in the capital where you belonged."

Pham's knuckles whitened as he twisted his hat into a wet clump. His hair, plastered to his face, was feeding drips onto the bridge of his nose. "I spent the last six months digging bomb shelters by the Bao tang My Thuat. My only part in the war was to make it safer for citizens to visit the art museum. I wanted to do more. I was ashamed when I heard the guns around the railyards at Duc Noi and Yeh Vien and near the harbor. I didn't want the war to be something that fell on me. I wanted it to be something I carried to the enemy."

Nguyen smiled. "Well, you got your wish. You are now 'carrying it' to the enemy."

"And when we reach our destination?"

"Then you will do what you are ordered to do."

Pham hung his head.

"Don't worry," Nguyen said. "I've spent over three years in the southern provinces, and I can assure you that just being below the Seventeenth Parallel will provide you with many opportunities to ease your conscience."

Nguyen was sitting with his arms draped over his knees, and Pham noticed a puckered scar on his hand where a bullet had passed through, leaving the little finger on his left hand permanently curled and a wrinkled mass of burn tissue below his sleeve that passed in mystery under the shirt to peek over the edge of his collar. "You must think me foolish," Pham said, searching Nguyen's eyes for some sign of understanding.

Nguyen smiled. "No. I think that you are a young man who didn't want to tell his grandchildren that his weapon in the war was a shovel."

Pham seemed to find some comfort in those words.

"Don't misunderstand me," Nguyen continued. "If you or Truong endanger this mission in any way, you will not return to your studies. You will obey my orders without question. If I say run, you will run. If I say hide, you will hide. If I say fight, you will fight. If you do not do what I say, you will die."

After that the two men sat without speaking, listening to the cacophony of crashing rain on the leaves surrounding them.

A few meters away, Truong crouched with Co and Sau under a tarp stretched over one of the bamboo poles from the heavy machine gun. The corners were pulled taut like a tent and provided excellent cover for the three men and the gun. They were dry and comfortable and hoped the rain would last hours.

Sau was working a wad of betel nut under his upper lip, and his wide grin showed an expanse of blood-red teeth. Probing his mouth with a calloused finger, he tried to find a comfortable position to lean against the gun.

Truong dug into a canvas bag with a wide strap that hung across his neck and removed a square package wrapped in heavy plastic over white linen tied with a cord. He looked nothing like the hard-edged veterans he sat with. Like Pham, he had interrupted his studies at Hanoi University to move equipment south. When the urgent call for help before the Lunar New Year swept the city, he, like many others, was caught up in the fervor.

Co watched Truong untie the cord and carefully unwrap the plastic and the white linen folded around the treasures. "You might get them wet," he warned.

Truong turned the small stack of books over in his hands, examining each in turn. "I wanted to check," he said. The top book had a scuffed green binding with the printed lettering on the spine worn away. It was the classic *Tale of Kieu* by Nguyen Du, a precolonial tale of love and lust for power. The book was a gift from his mother, and Truong had committed many of the verses to memory. He loved the Vietnamese authors, but the present political climate in the North repressed the publication of anything that did not align with communist doctrine. The *Lament of the Warrior's Wife* and *Complaint of the Royal Concubine* went from a prominent place on his parents' bookshelf to a bottom drawer in a back room. When he'd studied in Paris, though, all expression was open and Truong read all the censored authors with abandon. These writers may have been caged at home, but their books flew freely in the West. And as his *professeur de littérature* had pointed out, his tastes went much further west than the curriculum had intended.

The two remaining books had garish dustcovers illustrated for the pulp trade in America. They were French translations, driven into that language by popular demand. The first showed a Sioux Indian on horseback with a feathered shield racing alongside a locomotive belching a trail of black smoke. Truong turned the book in his hands. The dust-cover was worn, and small rips curled the paper at the edges. He held the book so Co could see the title. "*The U.P. Trail*, by Zane Grey," Truong said with a certain reverence.

"U.P."? Co asked.

"The Union Pacific. A railroad. They were a powerful force that drove the true Americans from their homeland for the sake of progress. The Sioux Indians, though proud and defiant, could not stand against a superior technology."

Co gave a nod of commiseration.

The other book's dustcover blazed orange and showed a cowboy astride a rearing horse on a rocky mesa. The title peeked below the cover's curling edges: *Frère de les Cheyennes.* Thuong held the book up. "Brother of the Cheyenne," he said, and pointed at the author's name. "By George Owen Baxter. A name used by the famous Max Brand."

"This Max Brand did not use his own name?" Co said.

Truong carefully stacked the books and began rewrapping them. "Even Max Brand was not his name. He was Frederick Faust."

Co shook his head as though expelling unwelcome information by centrifugal force. "So, this American was afraid to use his real name?"

Truong seem offended. "He had no fear, but German family names were not held in high regard during the Great War in Europe and he wanted to sell his writing. But in World War II he used his fame to get assigned as a frontline correspondent, even though he was well beyond a suitable age. He didn't have to go, but he went—and he was killed in Italy in 1944."

"The Italians killed him?"

"No. The Germans did." Truong seemed embarrassed.

Co covered his mouth with a hand, but a muffled laugh squeezed through his fingers. "Maybe he should just have used his real name."

Truong pushed the books into the bag and closed the flap. "I see you are familiar with irony."

Co's shoulders heaved against his stifled amusement.

At the other end of the heavy gun, the steady breathing and sagging head showed Sau was asleep.

"The point is, the native people of America fought against the Europeans. They defended their homeland against overwhelming odds. They fought with bows and arrows against rifles. They matched horses against locomotives and spears against artillery. I admire these people. They were brave and noble before the dragon."

Co scratched his chin in thought. "And you think we have a common bond with these people because we now face this dragon?"

Truong placed the bag as a pillow and lay back. "We share a common interest, a common enemy."

"Since we are not presently fighting red men on horses, I can only assume that these brave warriors did not slay the dragon."

"No. But like all the dragons that have come to Vietnam, they are blind."

"Blind?" Co asked.

"Yes. They underestimate us. They disregard our tenacity, and they ignore the simple fact that we will not lose because we will not quit. You remember, the French dragon lured the Viet Minh into Dien Bien Phu where they were sure they could destroy them with impunity because we could not put heavy guns into the mountains above them; but we did what they refused to expect."

Co leaned back against the machine gun. "So, you think that is what we are now doing to the American dragon—something unexpected?"

Truong tried to banish the worried expression from his face. "I do," he said.

They sat in silence for a while, then let the rhythmic beat of the rain on the tarp lull them into restless sleep.

First Platoon moved across the jungle floor, following the serpentine path cut by the point fire team. Shifts in terrain forced them to cross the stream many times. The rain seemed to grow heavier by the second, but the platoon pushed on to the northwest, working their way deeper into the Ong Thu range. Earlier, just before the rain, when their circuitous path took them to the edge of the trees, they could see smoke from village cooking fires in An Bang 3. Now they were back under the triple canopy again, fighting the rain and mud and heat. The Marines took comfort in the rain's ability to drive flying insects to cover, but they knew that when the rain stopped, the mosquitoes would be back with a vengeance, looking for a warm meal.

The rain fell straight and hard, drenching everything from the crown of the canopy to the root systems deep below the jungle floor. It gushed down the foothills, collecting in ever-larger channels, to the stream that would carry it to the Song Thu Bon. And it soaked the Marines of 1st Platoon. Water poured from the rims of their helmets, ran down their arms, and dripped from their hands and weapons. Every plant they pushed aside dumped more water on their clothing. It soaked their jungle pants and followed the contours of their legs into their muddy boots. Everything they wore became heavier and more uncomfortable. Wet clothing clung to bodies, making movement a strain against the unforgiving fabric. The wet straps and heavy web gear rubbed wet skin raw. Flesh absorbed the water, wrinkling fingers and toes, making every minor abrasion a reason for the epidermis to peel away. Every step pushed the platoon further into the painful adventures of immersion foot. Those with experience hoped the rain would end soon so they would have time to dry out a little before nightfall, because nothing was more miserable than spending the long night soaked to the skin, wide awake with teeth chattering from the cold.

The FNGs, Haber and DeLong, were finding the going especially difficult. Each step drained their energy and every muscle protested even the slightest rise in the terrain. Although they weren't yet aware of it, the rain was a godsend because it temporarily masked the heat. All too soon the rain would end, the heat would rise, and the jungle would become a steam bath, jacking their body temperatures up until they would feel like their helmets were the only things stopping their heads from exploding.

The lead fire team rotated the point frequently as the calluses on their hands turned spongy and peeled away against the dripping handles of their machetes, leaving pink patches of raw nerve endings. Haber followed DeLong in the column, and DeLong struggled to keep sight of the Chief's back as he pushed through the brush. Visibility was poor, and the crashing rain smothered the sounds of the Marines' movement, giving rise to spurts of panic when the path veered or the Chief increased his speed and DeLong thought he had lost the column. Within a few steps he would find a sign or catch sight of the Chief disappearing through the foliage ahead and a wave of relief would sweep over him. He had wanted to call out when the panic tightened his chest, but the others in 3rd Squad moved through the bush without speaking, and he didn't want to be the one to break the silence. It was one thing to be a rookie; it was another to embarrass yourself making a rookie mistake. He wondered how the terror of thinking he was lost would compare to the humiliation of having the platoon blame him for actually losing the way. He made a silent prayer as he went, not to keep himself safe, but that he wouldn't make a mistake that would shame him in the eyes of the other Marines.

Lieutenant Diehl radioed forward for the platoon sergeant and Blackwell stepped aside, letting the men file past him until the lieutenant reached his position. They leaned into each other as they walked so they could hear above the rain. "Meal break in fifteen, Sergeant," the lieutenant said, tapping the crystal on his watch. "Let's hope this rain stops by then."

Sergeant Blackwell nodded. "We're moving into some steep ground."

"It'll get a lot steeper," the lieutenant said, resting a reassuring hand on the sergeant's shoulder.

"I was hoping this was gonna be a cakewalk."

The lieutenant gave the sergeant his best all-American grin. "So far, it has been."

≈

Five minutes after 3rd Platoon's corpsman woke Strader from a sound sleep, he had his boots laced over his crusty socks and had pulled a wrinkled olive drab T-shirt from his pack, grabbed his soft cover, and was out the door into the pouring rain with his M14 slung over his shoulder. Leaping puddles, he moved away from the runway and toward the mess hall. The rain pounded the corrugated roofs, as though the drops were pebbles, and flew off the eaves in streaming arcs that made each building look like a fountain. The bunker sandbags had a polished sheen. A few other stragglers in ponchos were headed for a meal, and Strader wished he had taken the time to dig his rain gear out of the storage tent. But he was already drenched, and he was sure that soaking his rancid clothing in rainwater could only be a good thing.

By the time he reached the mess hall the line had moved inside, and he grabbed a partitioned metal tray with a wire hook on one corner and ducked through the door. Inside, wet ponchos hung through rifle straps or rolled into tight bundles dripped a wet pattern on the floor that followed the steam tables down the right side of the building. Big stainless steel coffee urns stood along the back wall. Strader followed the queue, collecting a strip steak, corn, mashed potatoes with a ladle of gravy, and a section of fruit cocktail. At the end, he dipped his canteen cup into a bin of ice and then filled it with water.

The personnel gathered for mess sat in groups segregated by assignment, MOS, or rank. The tanks and amtracs sat together. The 155 battery crews kept to themselves, their ears attuned to voices calling for a fire mission. The corpsmen from the battalion aid station made a small group at one table, sometimes joined by other docs assigned to the companies. Marines from line duty came and went in rotation, and the office personnel sat at the end of the sergeants' table by the urns where staff sergeants and gunnery sergeants voiced their gripes to first sergeants over coffee and cigarettes. The lower ranks secretly called it the lifers' table because they knew that these were the Marines who ran everything. The officers might give the orders, but the sergeants made the orders happen. They knew how things worked and how to get things done. When something was wrong with the green machine, the sergeants were the wrenches the officers used to fix it. The sergeants themselves identified more with the hammer than the wrench. You could tighten up a problem, or you could hit the problem so damned hard that it would fix itself.

First Sergeant Gantz looked up when Strader passed. He pinched his nose with one hand and covered his coffee cup with the other. "Damn, Marine," he said, "do you have to stink like that?"

Strader stopped and let the miasma that surrounded him spread. "I blame it all on Charley," he said.

A gunnery sergeant on the other side of the table wrinkled his nose and waved Strader on. "Victor Charley doesn't have to smell you," he said.

Strader lingered longer than any of them appreciated. "I guess I *could* use a hot shower."

The first sergeant jerked his head toward the other end of the mess hall as though Strader's odor was giving him spasms. "Keep moving, and make sure that shower happens real soon."

Strader finally started to move again. At the end of the sergeants' table, Corporal Pusic looked up from his tray with a disdainful glance at Strader's condition, as though he hadn't seen it earlier. There was plenty of empty space on either side of him, but Strader just nodded and moved on.

Halfway through the mess hall, a squad from Golf's 3rd Platoon was in from the lines and wolfing down their meals like starving dogs. Strader slipped in next to a lance corporal with the ace of spades drawn on the back of his flak jacket and a mouth bulging with half-chewed strip steak.

"Reach," he mumbled, spraying little bits of meat across the table.

Strader already had his face buried in his upturned canteen cup of ice water, and rivulets of cool heaven were running down his neck to join the rainwater in his T-shirt. He gulped and gulped until the cold made it too painful to swallow. His cup hit the table with a clunk that sent a splash of ice over the rim. "How's it goin' Ace?" he said. "The Crotch treatin' you right?"

"The Corps couldn't love me more if I was Chesty Puller."

Strader sliced off a piece of meat and forked it into his mouth. Ace finished chewing his wad of steak and started to shovel in another load. "Doc tells me you're too short to talk to."

"No, but you'll have to talk fast," Strader said, gulping more water. "Things cool here?"

Ace had to chew awhile before the chunk of steak in his mouth was small enough to talk around. "Chuck's been probing the line on and off, especially on the north end of the runway. Nothing serious, though. They just fire off a few rounds every once in a while to make sure we aren't getting any sleep. They did light up the CAP unit in the vill a couple of nights ago. They had a mad minute going until 2nd Platoon went to the rescue. Other than that it's been samey same."

Ace watched with amusement as Strader drained the rest of his water then crunched a shard of ice between his teeth. "You must be really short to be worried about being on this side of the wire. How much time you got?"

Strader added a spoonful of corn to the fragments of ice he was chewing. "Three and a wake-up."

Ace washed down his steak with a gulp of coffee and showed Strader his best grin, studded with bits of strip steak. "I guess you'll be sleeping in your flak gear tonight."

"I ain't gonna get twitchy, Ace. I got nothing to worry about with you on line, right?"

The squad from 3rd Platoon had to get back to the perimeter so other Marines could get a shot at a hot meal. They gathered their gear and pulled away from the table. Ace had to finish his beans and coffee on the fly. "You know I'll kick ass, Reach. But if they get past me, you're on your own." He caught up to the squad dunking their trays in the rinse barrels outside, and they disappeared in a splash of puddles.

Strader went back to his food, taking his time cutting his steak into bite-sized pieces and chewing slowly. He was in no hurry. He could take all the time he wanted. He could go through the line again and sit until the mess sergeant threw him out. And he would have done that, but he wanted to use the showers while it was still daylight. He just hated being caught in the dark in nothing but a towel and flip-flops.

First Sergeant Gantz leaned down the table toward Corporal Pusic and cocked his head in Strader's direction. "You know that Marine, Pusic?" he said.

Corporal Pusic turned in his seat to look at Strader as though he had no idea who the sergeant was referring to. "Oh, yeah, that's Corporal Strader."

"Is he one of yours?"

Corporal Pusic hesitated before answering, his mind racing to search every possible scenario his answer could create that would cause Sergeant Gantz to bring a world of hurt into his life. He was stymied.

"Yeah. He's Golf, 1st Platoon." He couldn't imagine that anything Strader did would reflect badly on him. But he also knew the vagaries and unpredictability of sergeants. He waited for the other shoe to drop, but the sergeant just rapped on the table with his knuckles and went back to his coffee, leaving Pusic to feign an inordinate level of interest in his meal. He didn't want to do anything to provoke the wrath of the sergeants. He had cultivated a very beneficial relationship with them. They were especially useful when the officers of Golf Company came to him with a problem or an assignment. And when problems were solved and assignments were successfully completed, the officers saw Pusic as an indispensable cog in the company wheel. Although the credo of the Corps was that every Marine was a rifleman first, Pusic wanted to be needed right where he was, and he didn't want anything to tip the delicate balance away from that. If he had anything to do with it, no one would ever even consider that he might be useful elsewhere.

The drumming of the rain on the roof slowed to a few scattered taps, and the runoff trickled to a stop. Marines who had been in no hurry to finish while it poured took the opportunity to clear their tables and head back to their areas. Pusic watched them through the screens as they went, picking their way around the larger puddles, leisurely skirting the surrounding buildings. He could walk back to the company office now without getting soaked, so he rose to go. He turned to look for Strader, but the table was empty. Things were looking up.

≈

As the storm rolled away across the An Hoa Valley, the NVA troops bundled their waterproof covers and lashed them to the bamboo poles and the barrel of the recoilless—anyplace where they could provide a cushion for weary shoulders. The jungle canopy continued to leak the dregs of the storm, but not enough to convince Nguyen to delay departure. The Americans were somewhere in the valley, and he was anxious to move out of their reach. His orders demanded that he stay away from them.

Nguyen spread a map across his knees as the others crouched around him. "We are here," he said. His finger followed the contours of the mountains north and stopped west of Huu Chanh 1. "We will rest here tonight, and tomorrow we will push all the way to Minh Tan and boat across the Song Vu Gia." His finger stopped on the village near the river. It looked like a great distance. "Tomorrow will be a difficult day. I suggest we cover as much ground as we can before nightfall to ease our pains tomorrow."

Truong pointed to the large circle drawn on the map that encompassed the entire Ong Thu mountain range and covered most of the valley from the Que Son Mountains to well beyond the confluence of the Song Vu Gia and the Song Thu Bon. "Is that circle the place the Americans call the Arizona?" he asked.

"This circled area is the home of our R-20th Doc Lap Battalion," Nguyen corrected him. "Thanks to them, we will have a safer passage here." Nguyen folded the map and waved it in front of him like an emperor indicating the expanse of his domain. "This is Doc Lap's hunting ground. Here intruders pay a bloody penalty for trespassing."

Truong and Pham exchanged glances. "I hope they know we aren't the intruders," Pham said.

Nguyen rose and began strapping on his heavy gear. "This place has no secrets from the 20th," he said. "Every footprint here is at their pleasure. The Americans would do well to remember that."

As Nguyen adjusted his load, Pham and Truong helped the others lift the heavy machine gun and situate the poles on their shoulders. "And yet the Americans are here," Truong whispered.

The weapon bearers shifted their loads until they settled into a reasonably comfortable position and the NVA column moved north.

5

The Marines wove a jagged line just east of the Ong Thu foothills. When the rain stopped, 1st Platoon stopped as well. Clustered in small groups, they worked their C rations into palatable meals. Lance Corporal Burke spent some time with Haber and DeLong showing them how to make a stove out of a cracker tin using the little P-38 can opener that came with the meals. He showed them how the trioxin heat tab would suffocate unless they cut little triangular holes around the top and bottom rims on the stove, and told them that if they hung over the stove and breathed the fumes, they would suffocate too. He made sure they left the lid partially attached to the meal tin, or B-unit tin, so it could be used as a handle to lift it away from the heat. "And make sure your stove is on level ground," he added. "It'll dump your meal on the deck if the balance is wrong." He wasn't surprised to see that Haber was opening a tin of ham and lima beans. "And don't touch the heat tab. Just because you don't see any flame doesn't mean it isn't burning. If you time it right, you should be able to cook a meal and a coffee before one tab burns down."

Both Haber and DeLong were still working on the obstinate tinfoil packages containing the little heat tablets. Burke pointed to their canteens. "That base water in those canteens?"

They looked confused at the question.

"Did you fill those canteens at An Hoa or from the stream we've been wading through all day?"

"An Hoa," they said in unison.

"Okay, that water is safe. Don't drink the water you get out here unless you treat it with halizone for a half hour. Do you need some?" DeLong dug into a pocket and came up with a little brown bottle with a screw top. "Good," Burke said. "If you're smart, the next time you write home you'll ask your folks to send you packages of Kool-Aid. It won't kill the halizone taste, but it covers up some of the ugly."

Doc Brede moved along the line of resting Marines, stopping at each position for a few seconds. He was still chewing on a flaky white roll wrapped around a slice of ham when he reached Burke and the replacements. "I hear the lieutenant gave you a promotion," he said with a wry smile.

Burke kept stirring the tin of turkey loaf bits on his makeshift stove. "Of all the things I can remember wanting lately, being squad leader wasn't one of them."

The doc kept smiling and chewing. "You've got no problems. Just ask yourself 'what would Reach do?'"

Burke tested the temperature of his turkey with a tentative spoonful. "All I want is to do what he's doing right now."

"You and every other swinging dick, me included. Hey, tell your squad to change their socks before we move out."

Burke swallowed a bigger bite of turkey and washed it down with a swig from his canteen, his sour expression an outraged gourmet's review of the taste. It was the first time anyone had referred to the squad as his, and he was surprised at the weight the words carried. "What makes you think anyone has dry socks?" he said.

"Well, tell them to wring out what they have and switch." He looked down at the new guys working on their meals and raised his voice. "You two, hang your wet socks on your pack straps until they dry," he said. "Change them as often as you can. Whoever said that an army travels on its stomach was full of shit." He noticed Haber's tin of ham and limas and handed him some processed cheese spread. "Stir this in. Maybe you can kill those motherfuckers before they kill you." The doc took another bite of his ham roll and moved on.

Lieutenant Diehl squatted over his own boiling tin of beans and wieners while chewing on a cheese-coated cracker. The sergeant stood nearby, shoveling spoonfuls of chopped ham and eggs into his mouth as quickly as he could, because the stink of hot ham and eggs could change your mind about eating them if you lingered. Bronsky was sitting on the ground leaning against his radio, slurping juice from a tin of peaches. He tipped the tin up, draining the last drops. "I've got two pound cakes I'll trade for a fruit cocktail," he said to anyone within earshot. Fruit cocktail was the most coveted tin in the combat meals, so there were no takers. He made a show of stuffing a little pack of C-rat Winstons into an accessory bag stuffed with Kents and Chesterfields. Everyone knew that he didn't smoke, and also that as long as they were far from the PX, time was on his side.

The lieutenant had his grid map laid out at his feet, its OD canvas case holding it flat. The plastic-coated map showed all the grids with the coded thrust points marked. He waved Sergeant Blackwell over. His finger wandered vaguely over the map above their present position. "You ever hear of any units working the Arizona across the river for five days and not butting heads with the 20th VC Battalion?"

The sergeant squatted next to the lieutenant. "No. From what I understand, they always make it a point to show how jealous they can be when it comes to this mosquito-infested shit hole."

The lieutenant nodded and absently tapped the map. "Right. And yet here we are, alone."

"I don't think we're alone," the sergeant said. "I guess we just ain't wandered close enough to anything they care about protecting."

The lieutenant stared at the map. "Maybe. It just seems crazy to me. Something is going on."

Sergeant Blackwell ran a hand over his close-cropped hair. "What seems crazy to me is one platoon of Marines hoping to piss off a battalion of VC. I'm not so sure I feel comfortable grabbing that tiger's tail."

Lieutenant Diehl glanced around, making sure the Marines within earshot were occupied with their meals. "We're an example of firepower on tap, Sergeant. We pull the tiger into the open, and superior technology rains a shitstorm down on its head."

The sergeant seemed skeptical. "We just have to hope that shit can rain faster than the tiger eats."

Diehl pointed to a spot in the foothills west of one thrust point marked with an automobile designation. "I want to be here by nightfall, about four points off Cadillac."

The sergeant looked at the spot, calculated the distance in his mind, and nodded. "Not a problem, sir." He watched as the lieutenant slowly dragged his finger east. It jumped foothills effortlessly, flew across marshes, skimmed rice paddies, and dragged through villages on its way to the blue line that would be the Song Thu Bon, and beyond the river, the relative safety of An Hoa. He noticed that the first village the finger passed through out on the valley floor was just north of a small body of water and was peppered with the locations of a number of dwellings. It was clearly marked Huu Chanh 1.

≈

After digging his seabag out of the 1st Platoon pile in the storage tent, Strader soaked in the shower until every stain from the Arizona was washed away. He lathered and scrubbed, and scrubbed again, until his skin felt abraded and new. He changed into a laundered set of jungle utilities and switched his decrepit boots for a pair of Corcoran jump boots that he'd kept wrapped in a set of stateside utilities in the bottom of the seabag. The all-leather boots felt stiff and unforgiving compared with the supple old jungle boots that had long ago conformed to the contours of his feet. He remembered a year ago when the Corcorans felt comfortable. But like the rest of him, his feet had undergone a change. Not that anyone would notice by looking. It took the Corcorans to remind him that a change was there.

Third Platoon's hooch was empty now with everyone manning the bunkers west of the runway. Strader went out the back door to a piss tube buried in the ground about twenty-five yards from the building. He always felt self-conscious urinating in the open. He looked across the runway to the line of bunkers, and beyond the wire to the wild country surrounding the village of Duc Duc. All of the brush and trees outside the concertina seemed to promise that someone was there looking back. He hoped they weren't looking over the barrel of a rifle. It would be a long shot to his position at the tube, but when you're standing there with your fly open, you can't shrug away the feeling of being exposed. And he knew something about long shots.

The fading light was turning the countryside into an ominous gray mass of shadows and made the runway look like a long, black scar. The danger you could see coming at you in the daytime you now had to hear or sense. As he watched the Ong Thu Mountains vanish into the distant darkness, Strader felt guilty that he was feeling vulnerable here inside the wire while his platoon faced another night out there. He slung his M14 over a shoulder and followed the runway past the sandbagged air control tower, skirted the fuel revetments, climbed the embankment, and headed for the EM Club. Lights were coming on all over the base.

Inside the club, Marines were jockeying for position along the bar and crowding the tables packed into the narrow room. A ceiling fan turned slow circles with just enough speed to swirl the clouds of cigarette and cigar smoke. Behind the bar, two Marines were serving cans of Budweiser from large stainless steel coolers, keeping to the daily allotment of two beers per Marine. The first sergeant who ran the club oversaw the distribution and called anyone out who tried to come back for seconds, although it was common knowledge he didn't subscribe to those restrictions with his own consumption. Above the door, a bare lightbulb illuminated a hand-lettered sign: THROUGH THESE POR-TALS PASS THE MEANEST SONS OF BITCHES TO EVER SHIT BEHIND A PAIR OF BOONDOCKERS.

Strader pushed his way in and, when a spot opened up, made his way to the bar. The harried bartender plunked down two Buds and levered them open with a hook-nosed church key that sent a spray of foam into the air. There was no saving one to open later. Strader took his beers and made a hole for other Marines to shoulder their way in. Three of the four men at the table closest to the door got up to leave, and the group at the next table immediately requisitioned two of their chairs. Strader moved in quickly to the one open chair remaining. "Okay if I sit here?" he said to the lone Marine left at the table.

The Marine waved a welcoming hand. "Take a load off," he said.

Strader leaned his rifle against the wall and drained half of the first beer. He sat with a beer in each hand, looking at the Marine across from him. "First Platoon, Golf Company," Strader said.

The Marine had three chevrons on each collar and a crushed empty on the table in front of him. "Fox Company, 3rd," he said, taking a gulp from his uncrushed can. Strader noticed that his eyes were bloodshot and that getting the opening in the beer can aligned with the opening in his face took a concentrated effort.

"Is Fox here?" Strader asked, wiping his chin with the back of his hand.

"No. We're at Nong Son. I've been in three days for dental work." He stuck a finger in his mouth and pulled his cheek aside, revealing nothing but a slack tongue. "Abscess," he slurred around a wet finger.

Strader nodded in sympathy.

The Marine drained his beer, then lowered it into the shadows beside him. When he set it back on the table it was full again. He noticed that Strader noticed. "I bought enough Tiger Piss from the mama-sans to keep my canteen full for a week. Let me know if you need to be topped off."

Strader shook his head. "No, thanks. I plan to be asleep in about an hour."

"I plan to be unconscious soon myself," the sergeant said, taking a long pull on his refill. He followed Strader's gaze to a mimeographed sheet tacked to the wall by the table. The ink in the machine was low, and the sergeant had to lean closer to make out the faint letters. The sweet perfume of mimeograph ink still clung to the paper, which offered such useful information as the times of reveille and retreat, the hours for mess and sick call, the uniform of the day, and chaplain's hours. At the bottom it announced the movie scheduled for tonight: *A Thousand Clowns*, starring Jason Robards. He tapped his finger on the sheet. "There's irony for you," he said.

Strader emptied his first can and started on the second. "What do you mean?"

The sergeant pressed his finger hard into the sheet. "It's a perfect example of what's wrong with this damn war."

Strader had to take a closer look at the posting to see what he might have missed. "A thousand clowns?" he said with a confused look.

"No. Here," the sergeant said, and stabbed the paper with a dirty fingernail. "Jason Robards."

Strader was lost but tried hard not to show it. He'd had many senseless conversations with fellow Marines when they were drunk, and he suspected this was going to be another one.

The sergeant gave Strader a conspiratorial glance and lowered his voice. "I heard Jason Robards got torpedoed twice in the Pacific during World War II."

"Okay, so?" Strader said.

The sergeant reached into his pocket and slapped a little P-38 can opener on the table. "Well, can you explain this?" he said.

"It's a C-rat opener," Strader said, sure now that drunken blathering was about to be raised to a new level.

"Not just an opener, a John Wayne can opener."

"So it's a John Wayne, so what?" Strader said.

"John Wayne never served in the military. Lots of movie stars served in World War II. Some were in combat, too, but not John Wayne."

Strader finished most of his remaining beer in anticipation of a quick departure.

"For Christ's sake, Captain Kangaroo was a Marine during the war." The sergeant held the can opener up and shook it so the blade flapped back and forth. "This shouldn't be called a John Wayne. It should be a Jason Robards."

Strader finished the rest of his beer. "Or a Captain Kangaroo," he said.

"Right," the sergeant said, looking at the opener with a new appreciation.

Strader stood and hefted his rifle from its spot against the wall. "I get your point," he said. "For a minute I thought you were just talking bullshit."

The sergeant tossed the opener onto the table. "I was," he said. "That was the point. If we can't recognize a little piece of obvious bull-shit, what chance do we have with the big sneaky ones?"

Strader gave the sergeant his best impersonation of John Wayne's casual, one-fingered salute and pushed through the door into the night before he could be subjected to slurred theories about life preservers and Mae West never being in the Navy.

Just beyond the EM Club, light flickered on the makeshift movie screen as the opening credits of *A Thousand Clowns* scrolled up. Strader followed some Marine-shaped shadows past the projection hut to the rows of upended crates and ammo boxes. The glowing tips of cigarettes pinpointed the positions of the small group of viewers, further accentuated by sharp smacks directed at attacking insects. He stood in the back and watched Jason Robards cross a rubble-strewn lot to a New York tenement and climb the stoop to the front door.

"Who the hell is that?" came from the shadow standing next to him. Strader turned away from the screen. "John Wayne," he said and moved off into the night.

≈

When the sun dropped below the ridge, the eastern slope of the Ong Thu slipped into a tableau of opaque shadows. Under the jungle canopy, sundown was a short and merciless process. While the open fields and paddies were still bathed in gray twilight, under the trees, patches of blackness swam together like spilled ink, and the comfort of the visible world vanished.

The NVA cadre shed their burdens and settled in for a night of rest. They could not risk cooking fires, so they peeled the banana-leaf wrapping from their *tam thom* rice balls and ate them cold. All down the line tired, dirty fingers picked out clumps of the sticky rice, compacted them into balls, and slipped them into mouths, savoring each bite as though it were the rarest of delicacies.

Truong and Pham shared a spot against the sprawling roots of a dipterocarp tree with foliage finally reaching the sky more than forty meters above their heads. They sat in silence, hungrily devouring their portions of rice. Pham paused to drink from his canteen. "I've been having dreams," he said, watching Truong lick the rice from his fingers.

"About home?"

"No," Pham said, holding up a large pinch of rice. "About food."

Truong smiled. "You dream of dry *banh chung* without the mung paste or meat?"

"That's not funny. I dream of *ban cuon*."

"*Ban cuon*?" Truong said with a disappointed expression.

"Yes. I feel the dumplings in my fingers. I see the steam rising. I taste the onions and pork and mushrooms. The sauce stings my tongue. My eyes water."

"When I think of all the food you could be dreaming of, food that isn't sold by any street vendor in the city, I want to cry also. Why not dream of lobster or a juicy filet?"

Pham seemed embarrassed. "Well, *ban cuon* isn't the only food in my dreams."

The tone of the conversation was piquing Truong's interest, or at least his taste buds. "What other culinary delights invade your sleep?" he asked, as though he were a blind man asking a poet to describe a sunset.

Pham dropped another bit of rice into his mouth. "It doesn't matter," he said.

Truong stopped in mid chew. "My salivary glands say it does matter. And make it good. I need a tasty story to go with this rice."

"You won't be satisfied," Pham said.

Truong held up the remains of his rice ball. "Do I look satisfied now? You have my permission to torture my appetite."

Pham wiped his mouth with the back of his hand. "*Pho*," he said, not daring to look at Truong.

"*Pho*," Truong said in disbelief. And after a long pause, "What broth on the noodles?"

Pham sniffed as though the aroma of his dreams were hanging in the air. "I think, beef," he said.

Truong nodded slowly. His mind was debating with his appetite, and it appeared *pho* was something they could both work with. "One thing is certain. No one will ever accuse you of having extravagant tastes."

"I wasn't describing my tastes, only my unconscious dreams."

"Well, your unconscious mind is certainly plebeian."

Pham bit into a hard biscuit and pointed the jagged edge at Truong. "Maybe so, but every cold meal I eat tastes like ambrosia dipped in *nuoc mam* when I close my eyes."

Nguyen stopped at the base of their tree and knelt down, placing the butt of his AK-47 in the dirt. Pham and Truong were the unknown quantities in his unit, and he wasn't comfortable with them pairing up. It had the potential to double the impact of their inexperience. He pointed a finger at Truong. "You stay close to Sau and his group tomorrow. This is a dangerous place and we have a long way to go before we reach the river. We won't sleep again until we're north of the Vu Gia."

"What about me?" Pham asked.

Nguyen fixed Pham with a hard stare. "You'll be with me."

Sau and another man came out of the shadows, their faces hovering in the dark above their cartridge vests like ancient masks carved from granite. Nguyen spoke to them in hushed tones. He pointed down the slope, and the two disappeared into the darkness, moving silently through the foliage with practiced efficiency; the wind made more sound in passing. Little communication was needed. They knew what had to be done and how to do it.

Pham and Truong couldn't help comparing themselves with the other men in the unit, and the comparison made them feel like children. These were men who ate on the run. They didn't appear to tire, and if the situation demanded it they didn't stop for sleep or food or water. They could be absolutely motionless for hours or march without rest. It seemed that only death would stop them, and Pham and Truong weren't sure even that would do it.

Nguyen stood and lifted his rifle. "The sentries are posted, so get some sleep. We'll be moving before daylight." With that, Nguyen turned and faded into the night.

Once he was gone, Pham and Truong felt the night close in. Although they knew that the other men were all around them, they heard and saw no one, making the two neophytes feel alone in the jungle. Fear and worry might have kept them awake, but since they came south exhaustion ruled their nights, and they let the darkness flow over them like a warm cloak. Before long, they slipped into a fitful sleep.

First Platoon continued to cut a meandering line through the foothills as the setting sun lengthened the shadows. The point fire team chose their course more by the path of least resistance than to avoid the likelihood of danger. When the light faded to a wisp of existence the lieutenant called a halt, sending Sergeant Blackwell to spread the word up the column to hold position and wait. The Marines immediately knelt or squatted, thankful for the respite. Their clothing and gear were still wet, and they knew to expect an uncomfortable night when they finally went to ground and their body temperatures began to fall.

In the center of the column, the lieutenant glanced at the luminous dial on his watch. He wasn't interested in the time—there was no schedule to be maintained—the visibility of the dial against his wrist was setting the timetable. When the wrist disappeared and only the dial was visible it would be time to move again. One of the hard lessons learned in jungle combat was never to be caught in your last daylight position when night fell. If it was possible for you to be seen, you assumed you were being watched, and when the night made you invisible, you moved. In a while, the lieutenant reached out and touched Bronsky's arm, and word went down to Sergeant Blackwell to get the column up and moving again.

If Private DeLong found following the Chief in daylight stressful, following him in total darkness pushed him to the edge of panic. He cursed himself for every slight noise he made, not because he feared he might give away his position but because it masked any sounds coming from the Chief, and he was using his ears to keep track of the Marine ahead of him. Though the air was cooling, sweat poured from his face. He was startled by the hushed voice of Lance Corporal Burke close behind him. "Tighten up the intervals." Stumbling, DeLong pushed ahead until his outstretched hand met the E-tool hanging from the Chief's pack. The Chief turned sharply and slapped his hand away. For once DeLong was happy about the darkness because he couldn't see the expression on the Chief's face. If the looks he had received during the day were any indication, the one he was getting right now would be downright terrifying.

The going was slow and difficult, with each Marine feeling his way through the jungle as though he were blindfolded. Stumbles and falls were followed by a flurry of curses that covered everything from the stinking country to the Corps to the God responsible for jungles and darkness and all discomfort in general.

The lieutenant knew that moving through the Arizona in the dark was a potentially lethal game of blind-man's buff, so when he felt their last position was far enough behind them, he called another halt and told the sergeant to set up a night perimeter with the CP in the center. The Marines stripped off their packs, and those who had them dug out jungle utility shirts and put them on. The squads quickly worked out a two-hour watch schedule. Sergeant Blackwell went whispering squad to squad, selecting men for the listening posts that would be set up below and above the platoon. He leaned in close, almost finding his victims by Braille. The LPs were an early warning device designed to save the rest of the unit from deadly surprises. They were the canaries in the coal mine. And though the concept was sound, it it seldom worked out for the canaries.

Third Squad was at the head of the column when they stopped, and in the highest position when the sergeant felt his way into their area. "Burke," he whispered with as much authority as a whisper could command.

"Over here," Burke answered.

The sergeant poked blindly into the spot the voice came from until he reached an obstruction wearing a flak jacket. "I need an LP up the mountain about a hundred feet," he said into the darkness.

"Anyone in particular?"

"It's your squad," the sergeant said. "But make it a three-man LP. Send one of the new guys along. He can use the experience, and with three, maybe somebody can get some decent sleep."

"Send three and make one a new guy. Are you sure it's my squad, Sergeant?" Burke asked, feeling safely anonymous in the dark.

"Maybe you want me to radio the base and get Strader to make the decision for you."

It was difficult to have a conversation with someone when you couldn't see faces. You couldn't get a read on someone's intent. What seemed to be anger might be sarcasm. Then again, it might not. "It's my squad," Burke relented, turning to the invisible men around him. "Tanner, Chief, take one of the FNGs and set up an LP about one hundred paces upgrade."

A steady stream of bitching in a Southern drawl issued from Tanner's position. "Shit, Burke. Why me? I thought we was close."

"We'll still be close, Buck. At least as close as a hundred paces can be. But do me a favor, make the paces long ones."

Tanner made a show of temper gathering his gear, but it was completely wasted because no one could see it. Even Tanner couldn't see it himself. "Shit, man. I hope you ain't gonna let a little power go to your head."

"I don't have any power. I just have headaches." Burke tried to sense the spot in the blackness in front of him where the Chief might be. "Chief. Where the hell are you?" He was startled when a voice as smooth as whipped butter sounded in his ear. "Here," was all it said.

Burke reached out but felt nothing. It was like talking to a ghost. "Collect one of the new guys and head up the mountain. And stay sharp." He had often seen the Chief dragging the blade of that big staghorn knife across a whetstone, honing it to a razor's edge, and he immediately regretted using the word "sharp." Now that he was squad leader, he would have to choose his words more carefully.

The Chief took a few steps and reached down into the dark, catching hold of the collar of a flak jacket. "Which one are you?" he asked.

A voice feigning enthusiasm drifted up. "DeLong," it said.

The Chief tugged, pulling the Marine to his feet. "Let's go."

Haber pushed DeLong's rifle into his hands as he was hauled away. The two privates weren't on the buddy program, but they had been traveling the same path together since Okinawa and took some comfort in a shared misery. Being the new guy in an established unit was difficult, which made a companion going through the same experience invaluable. Now, as the three Marines moved off into the night, he was the single odd man out for the first time, and his relief that the Chief's hand had found DeLong's collar and not his was a reason for considerable guilt.

The LP detail left the perimeter, crossed a shallow ravine, and started up a lower slope of the Ong Thu. The Chief led the trio, followed by DeLong and then Tanner, who was keeping an audible count of his steps.

"Thirty-one, thirty-two, thirty-three."

Each number made DeLong flinch, and his apprehension grew with the count. The idea that the growing numbers emphasized how far they were from the platoon was somehow a secondary concern to the actual sound of the counting that seemed to say over and over to anyone listening in the darkness, "Here we are." He wished Tanner would be quiet but didn't feel he was in a position to say so. Suddenly, the Chief stopped and came down a few paces. He reached through the open front of Tanner's flak jacket and grabbed a fistful of T-shirt. "Shut the fuck up, Anglo," he hissed, the kind of hiss that could make a snake change its mind about biting. Then he was climbing again with DeLong and Tanner playing catch-up. After a few yards Tanner muttered, "He made me lose count."

≈

Sau squatted in front of a large tree hosting a cluster of tetrastigma vines on their climb to daylight. And just as the vines used the tree, a parasitic rafflesia plant clung to the vine. Though Sau knew little of plants, he knew death, and the enormous rafflesia flower gave off an odor many likened to a rotting corpse. When the breeze shifted with the vagaries of the forest, Sau had to cover his nose with his hand.

He used the stock of his rifle planted between his feet for balance, unwilling to sit or lean against the tree. To stay awake on sentry when you needed sleep, you took an uncomfortable position and stayed in it. His comrade sat a few feet away with his arms folded across his knees and his head balanced on his arms. He would be allowed to sleep until it was his turn to assume an uncomfortable position.

The wind changed direction and swept up from the valley, and Sau closed his eyes and let the coolness wash the plant stench away. But something rode in on the wind, something different. He gripped his rifle barrel with both hands and slowed his breathing so the sound of it wouldn't interfere with anything he needed to hear: mosquitoes buzzed through the thermal waves rising from his skin; something with small teeth chewed to his left; and the breeze from the valley twisted leaves on their branches until they snapped. Sau held his breath and cupped a hand behind one ear. Something snapped again. Then something crunched.

Sau turned his head slowly and gave a slight whistling chirp, no more than the sound of a distant bird or a small rodent. The other sentry's head snapped up, and he reached immediately for the grip on the AK at his side.

"*Nghe ma*," Sau whispered, alerting his companion to listen to the movement.

Both men raised their weapons and slowly and soundlessly pushed the safety levers into the middle position. Each man gripped the front stock with some force. In full automatic the heavy AK would climb, and this would be a problem firing downhill.

The newly awakened sentry aimed blindly into the dark and waited until sounds in the trees below drew his barrel to its target. Sau was right. There was movement.

They waited motionlessly, letting the sounds pull their rifle sights like divining rods are pulled to water. Their fingers hovered over triggers and the butt plates pressed tightly into their shoulders. Their heads moved as if on gimbals, ears jockeying for better reception. The sounds were close, but they didn't seem to be coming any closer. And then, suddenly, the movement was gone, leaving only the squealing conversations of wildlife and the pounding hearts of the two NVA, who now had to determine their aim by memory alone.

"*Luu-dan*," the sentry said, the word barely audible on his breath, and Sau felt the wooden post of a hand grenade touch his knee.

Sau pushed it away. "Nguyen," he said, "now," and the sentry evaporated into the night, soundless as a wraith.

The rising moon found random openings in the cloud cover and shot beams of gray light through the canopy, projecting a faint and flickering show on the jungle floor. Sau watched down the barrel of his rifle as the interplay of moon and cloud repeatedly gave the gift of vision and then swept it away.

The sentry was back within minutes with Nguyen close on his heels. He resumed the vigil while Nguyen and Sau moved behind the malodorous tree.

"Do we have trouble, Sau?" Nguyen asked, trying to hide the apprehension in his voice.

"There was definite movement that stopped on the mountain just below us," Sau said, watching the play of moonlight across Nguyen's face.

"How close?"

Sau moved his head in closer for emphasis. "Twenty meters, maybe less."

Nguyen halved the volume of his whisper. "Just twenty meters?"

"They could be closer," Sau said.

Nguyen stood silently, letting the impact of the information penetrate his sleep-fogged mind. Recriminations flooded in. They should have moved during the storm. They should have moved in the dark. They wouldn't be here now if they had only kept moving.

"How many are there?" he asked.

"Not many," Sau said, wiping sweat from his eyes. "Probably two. I think it is a watch post for their unit. We work in pairs. They work in pairs."

"And you say they are as close as twenty meters?"

"Or closer."

"Then their main unit is not far," Nguyen said, more a voiced thought than a communication.

A prolonged break in the clouds bathed the undergrowth in dancing shards of light, and Sau peeked around the tree. "I think we will find out how far in the morning."

"We cannot be here in the morning," Nguyen said firmly.

"If we move now they will hear," Sau said.

Nguyen turned the options over in his mind. "So we can fight them now in the dark or wait and fight them in the light of morning. Either way, we will have carried these weapons all this way for nothing."

Sau glanced around the tree again. "There may be another way," he said.

Nguyen grasped Sau's shoulder and pulled him around. "If you have an idea, you won't ever find me more willing to listen."

"If their sentries weren't so close we could move on, and there is a chance the main unit would not hear us."

"But they are close," Nguyen said.

Sau drew his thumb across his own neck under his chin. "Then we change that."

Nguyen seized on the idea like a drowning man to a lifeline. "It will have to be done silently, without alerting the other Americans."

"It will be difficult," Sau said.

"But it can be done?"

Sau shrugged resignedly. "Do we have a choice?"

7

The three Marines settled on the flattest piece of real estate they could find—six feet of level ground with a couple of small trees that didn't eat up the space. "Who wants the first watch?" Tanner asked, making himself comfortable with his back to one of the trees. "Nobody? Okay, I'll take it." The first watch was the easiest because everybody was still alert and the dark and the boredom hadn't had time to work on the need for sleep. In three or four hours it would be a different story. "Hey, new guy. Do you have a wristwatch?"

DeLong moved in close. "Yeah, I have a watch. And the name's DeLong."

"Okay, Deeeee Long. Give it here."

DeLong hesitated. Someone he didn't know or trust was asking him for his watch, and it made him leery. It wasn't a family heirloom or even a very expensive watch—his father had bought it for him at the Sears in Milwaukee—but it was something from home, something the Marines had not issued. It was a connection, one he did not want to lose.

"Come on," Tanner said impatiently. "You'll get it back when the Chief wakes you."

DeLong reluctantly unbuckled the band and handed over the watch.

The watch face was black with white numerals and hands, and Tanner held it out and rocked the crystal in a shaft of moonlight. "This'll work. I'll wake the Chief in two hours. He'll wake you in four. I would give you the second shift, but then you would have to wake the Chief, and that can be tricky. Who knows what he would do in the night to someone he didn't recognize. Right, Chief?"

A few feet away, the Chief cleared a spot so he could stretch out. The ground was wet, and he lay back on his flak jacket and balanced his head on his upturned helmet. It wasn't comfortable, but it would do. He didn't answer.

DeLong spread out his flak jacket and lay down on his side. He wrapped his arms around his body, tucking his hands into his armpits, trying to stay warm. His body heat had baked some of the wet out of his clothes, but they were still damp enough to make him shiver when a breeze invaded, or when he thought of where he was. He couldn't imagine being more miserable.

Tanner sat cross-legged against a tree with his rifle on his lap. He tilted his head back and sniffed. "Damn. It smells like something died around here," he said.

≈

The lieutenant reported his position to the com shack in An Hoa, calculating the distance and direction from his last thrust point and making sure the 155 batteries had 1st Platoon's grid coordinates marked on their maps. It paid to be able to get quick fire support in case things went wrong, and in the Arizona, they tended to go wrong in a hurry.

The two M60 machine guns were in position, the watches were assigned, and claymore mines had been placed in likely approaches. More than half the platoon was now asleep. The extra radio went with the listening post on the lower slope, and Bronsky checked with them every half hour for situation reports. The radios were turned down to their lowest squelch settings, and only Bronsky spoke. "Pounder to backfield. Pounder to backfield," Bronsky whispered. "Sit rep. If your position is secure, key your handset twice."

A short silence was followed by two distinct bursts of static.

"Roger, backfield. Back in thirty. Out." There would be no contact with the other LP until morning.

Though it wasn't raining, moisture was thick in the air, a physical entity the Marines could reach out and touch. It made breathing more difficult. It clung to their skin and seeped into the fabric of their clothing. It made the air itself visible. It accumulated on the leaves and wept down from their drooping tips. It also impeded sound. Faint noises would spend all their energy fighting their way through the heavy, wet air, giving the slightest of whispers very little hang time. It made everything seem close and claustrophobic. It made the jungle feel alive and the Marines feel even more isolated than they were.

≈

Strader sat on the side of his cot looking through the screening into the blackness west of the wire. A few Marines from 3rd Platoon were asleep at the other end of the hooch, their breathing steady and deep as though regulated by a metronome. The rest were manning the lines. The base was completely dark. Some Marines were at their watches, monitoring radio frequencies, tracking units in the bush. Some were in bunkers, watching and waiting. The rest were in their racks and grateful to be there. Strader felt he was the one Marine out of place. He slipped out the door and walked to the embankment above the runway. Cloud shadows sweeping along the dark aluminum plates gave the runway a sense of movement like a channel of running water. The illusion was only slightly spoiled by a breeze coming across one of the two-hole latrines that carried the smell of fuel oil, fried maggots, and the menu from the evening mess processed through a few dozen Marines. Strader scratched at the ground with the tread on his Ho Chi Minh sandals. In a few days he would be on his way back to the world and Vietnam would be nothing more than a year of bad memories. But as he stood looking into the endless night of the distant Arizona, he had never felt so far from home.

~

Nguyen and Sau crept through their unit, carefully rousing each man in turn as they went. Before long, all were up and alert, listening as Nguyen laid out their situation in detail. They would get their equipment ready to travel without making a sound, then wait in absolute silence for the order to move while Sau and a group of his choosing dealt with the problem. Whether noise would matter when the order to move came would depend on the success of the night's work, and that could be hours away. Pham and Truong listened intently.

"I volunteer to go with Sau," Pham said.

Nguyen pretended not to hear. He nodded to Sau, who went through the group making his selections. It was evident from the speed of his choices that Sau already knew which men he wanted.

Pham didn't like being ignored. "I said I'll go."

Nguyen moved close to Pham. "This is by invitation only, and you aren't invited."

"I don't care if it's dangerous," Pham said.

"And I don't care that you don't care."

Sau whispered to Co and two others, Binh and Duong, and sent them to prepare. Another man stepped out of the shadows. His leathery skin was the color of bronze, and his unusually high cheekbones gave his face a perpetual squint.

Nguyen put a hand on his shoulder. "Vo, you make five."

Vo nodded and followed the others into the darkness.

Nguyen turned to the remaining men. "We will have to carry their loads as well as our own." He looked into the darkness where the five were gathering what they needed and spoke softly, almost to himself. "And we may have to carry it far because I'm afraid there is little chance that they will be returning."

Truong seemed shocked. "There is little chance?"

"Do not feel bad for them. If they fail, we will likely share their fate." Nguyen seemed to stare at Pham rather than Truong. "If I were a betting man, I wouldn't wager five dong that any of us will be smiling by this time tomorrow." He started to leave, then turned back. "Now get ready. If there is any shooting, we will have to get away from here as quickly as we can. But if our comrades are successful, we will leave slowly and quietly. Unless you are like Pham and don't mind the danger, you should pray they are successful." He slipped into the darkness.

Truong followed Pham back toward their sleeping area. "For a minute there I thought our noble leader didn't like our odds," Truong said. "But I think it's just you he doesn't like." Pham didn't answer.

The heavy weapons were still being readied for travel when Nguyen returned. The five soldiers committed to the detail filed past like condemned men en route to their execution. They had stripped to black shorts and dark headbands, and each carried at least one edged weapon. Most of these were short, deadly looking knives with the blades darkened. There were a couple of long blades, machete-like, more tool than weapon, and Co complemented his own short knife with a hammer with a heavy, square head. They padded along behind Nguyen on bare feet and dissolved into the blackness of jungle clinging to the slope of the Ong Thu.

When it was anticipated that additional firepower might be needed, Nguyen had sent another man to join the sentry at the tree. He carried a Russian PRD light machine gun, an elongated AK with a drum magazine hanging from the receiver. Another drum was slung in a canvas bag over his shoulder. A bipod hung from the end of the barrel. Nguyen knelt beside them. "If things go wrong, empty your weapons into the valley," he said. "Rake the mountain. We'll need time to get clear, and you must give us that time." The two nodded and Nguyen turned his attention to the others. "I've given them their orders should the worst happen. If you have to come back quickly, come low." He rested a hand on Sau's shoulder. "How long?" he asked.

A small gust of wind cooled the sweat on Sau's body, and he shivered involuntarily. He hoped Nguyen didn't mistake the shudder for a sign of fear. "Five hours, maybe more."

"*Chuc may man*," Nguyen said, patting Sau's shoulder.

Sau looked at the men waiting in the shadows. They looked like a gang of cutthroat pirates from the South China Sea. "We won't need luck," he said.

Tanner was sitting in the bowl of his upturned helmet, his back against one of the trees. The helmet rim dug into his cheeks, but at least his ass was off the wet ground, and the irritation was enough to keep him from nodding off. The jungle throbbed with the squeaks and squeals of countless insects, broken occasionally by the distant screech of a predator finding prey. Tanner let the noise feed his mind. The primeval tune played over and over until he was sure that any sound that didn't fit the natural track would draw his attention. He kept a hand on the grip of his M16 waiting for that sound.

The Chief lay a few feet away with his legs crossed and his arms folded across his chest like he was asleep at a picnic. His breathing was so shallow as to be imperceptible, and his face was a mask of serene composure. Tanner knew he wouldn't snore or twitch or even change position until his watch.

Just beyond Tanner's feet, DeLong lay on his side with his knees hiked up and his arms pulled inside his flak jacket in an attempt to preserve body heat. He lay still and tried to keep his eyes closed, but he couldn't sleep. It was his first night in the bush. The end of his first day, his first long, miserable day, and it was so new and alien that he couldn't imagine a year of days like it. His occasional glances at Tanner and the Chief weren't meant to reassure himself that he wasn't alone, but to have visual proof that becoming accustomed to the life of a grunt was possible. He tried not to move, so the others wouldn't know he was awake. Spending the night on a lonely LP in a Vietnam jungle shouldn't be something that would make a Marine lose sleep, even if it was a first night, on his first LP, in his first jungle.

～

The five men spaced themselves in an irregular line and, on Sau's command, faded slowly into the undergrowth. They would feel their way with their fingers and toes, slipping through the leafy stalks and branches with no more disturbance than a slight breeze would make.

Since plants were less forgiving at their bases, they would remain on their feet for as long as possible. When they were close to the enemy they would be forced to crawl, slicing the plant stalks close to the ground with their knives. It was a game of inches. The closer they got to the target, the slower they would move; in the end, their progress would barely be measurable.

Though Sau was certain how this night would unfold, he had no doubt that he had selected men who knew what to do and how to do it.

After two hours Sau's men had covered half the estimated distance to their target, but they suddenly stopped and squatted in unison when a distant exchange of small arms fire erupted to the north. To the educated ear, the pops and cracks of the battle told the story. The gunfire echoed across the valley from some dark spot beyond the terminus of the Ong Thu. That nothing larger was introduced told Sau that the clash was taking place some distance from any American compound. He suspected that elements of the R-20th Doc Lap were plying their trade against Marines from one of the outposts at the bridge. The moisture-laden air and the thick foliage made it difficult to determine a precise distance. What sounded far away might be deceptively close. All the five could do was sit on their heels and wait for a reaction from below.

＝

After giving the Chief a furtive nudge with the barrel of his rifle, Tanner weathered a contemptuous glare and then handed over DeLong's watch. The two sat together listening to the gunfire.

"Sounds like Hotel Company out at Phu Loc," Tanner whispered.

The Chief looked at the watch then stuffed it into the breast pocket on his flak jacket. "Maybe."

Tanner leaned back against the tree and tilted his helmet down over his eyes. "Get some, Hotel," he said to no one in particular.

DeLong thought that pretending to sleep through a firefight, even a distant one, might be a bit transparent, so he raised his head a little and looked at the Chief.

The Chief turned his head slowly. "It don't mean nothin' to us," he said and turned back to the mountain.

DeLong wanted to remind the Chief to take care of his watch, but instead he lowered his head and went back to his make-believe sleep.

~

Bronsky sat with the radio handset to his ear monitoring the frequencies bouncing around north of their position. The sporadic chatter of gunfire interrupted the quiet slumber of the valley. The lieutenant knelt at his side.

"What's going on?" Diehl said.

Bronsky listened intently to the handset then turned to the lieutenant. "A night ambush out of Phu Loc made contact. Sounds like a squad of Hotel's 3rd Platoon."

"How serious?"

"I think it's all one-sided now. They're on the horn to An Hoa, but they ain't requesting any medevac."

The distant firing petered out and was followed almost immediately by the boom of man-made thunder. A hushed swish and a loud pop left an illumination flare dangling from its parachute over the valley. The empty canister spun in whooping somersaults on its fall to earth as the harsh glare like an arc welder's torch stabbed through the trees, pushing in piercing shafts of artificial light at oblique angles. The upper valley was a stark, gray tableau with the only movement the flare rocking peacefully under its silk canopy. Anything in the open that moved would be picked out by the eerie light and become a target for Hotel's squad. But there was no firing. As the flare's light began to fade, a second round sailed north from An Hoa, bathing the valley in a fresh glare, and a new parachute began its tranquil descent.

"I think the VC broke contact, sir," Bronsky said.

The lieutenant moved back to his sleeping position and stretched out. "Switch back to our freq, and stay sharp. Our LP below may get some movement later."

"Yes, sir," Bronsky said, and clipped the handset to the strap ring on his helmet to keep it close to his ear.

~

The artillery compound at An Hoa was far enough from the barracks area that the voice alert for a fire mission wasn't audible, but the report of the big 155-mm guns jolted the earth and the concussion shook the screening on the huts. Strader was asleep under a poncho liner on his corner cot when the first round slapped him awake. He was on his feet looking across the runway before the shot was halfway to its target. Being awakened by the muzzle blast of a 155 was akin to being struck by lightning, and Strader stood vibrating from his scalp to his toenails. When the flare burst open he could see from the distant glow that it had been called in far north of his 1st Platoon and he relaxed. There were other sleepers in the building, and a voice came out of the darkness. "Reach, you think your guys stepped in some shit?" The first flare dimmed and the second round's shockwave swept over the building.

"No. It's just illumes headed out toward the bridge." He waited to see if the illumination rounds were followed by a flurry of high explosive rounds, but the base was quiet, and after a while he knew that the gun crews were standing down. Strader flopped back on the cot and pulled the poncho liner up under his chin. "I think they're okay," he said.

$$\approx$$

After the last flare extinguished, the five NVA waited until they were sure there would be no response from the Americans on the hill below them. Finally, they raised themselves up as one and began inching downward again. Their progress was now being determined by the density of the clouds that drifted across the face of the moon. When their surroundings were plunged into total darkness, they chanced movement. When the nimbus clouds thinned to a wispy translucency, the five stayed frozen in their spots, reluctant to even blink their eyes. They were close now, and their progress was agonizingly slow. Each man fought against the adrenaline trying to gain control of his system and the searing pain from back muscles crying out for relief.

With no way to pinpoint the enemy position, their fear was that they would stumble into it without warning, so each time they stopped, they strained their ears in hope of picking up any sound that could provide direction. But each time they heard only the voices of the jungle. After a particularly long period of obstructed moonlight allowed a few tentative paces in succession, the cloud cover ended abruptly and the five turned to stone.

$$\approx$$

Perched on his upturned pack, the Chief held out the watch and waited for a break in the clouds. Finally, the moon cleared and a shaft of light touched the crystal face. Leaning over, he gave a tug on DeLong's bloused trouser leg. When the new guy sat up, he pushed the watch into his hand. "It's your watch," the Chief said.

DeLong dragged a hand over his face as though he were wiping away four hours of sound sleep. He wasn't sure if the Chief would be fooled or would even care, but he felt the subterfuge was worth the effort. "Yeah, that's mine," he said.

The Chief leaned in close so his face was nearly touching DeLong's. Even in the diminished light DeLong could see the intimidating spark of intolerance in the Chief's eyes. "It's your turn to stand watch," the Chief said, with emphasis.

"Oh, yeah. Okay. I'm awake, I'm awake," DeLong said, getting onto his knees and immediately regretting the move as the soggy jungle floor soaked his legs.

The Chief turned away and stretched out in his earlier spot.

DeLong glanced at Tanner asleep against the tree. He imagined having to awaken the Chief because of some noise or movement he couldn't identify, and he solemnly swore to himself that in that event, he would rouse Tanner first, no matter what.

DeLong followed the Chief's example and sat on his pack. The plants around him moved in and out of filtered gray light, and he felt the responsibility of being the only one watching them. Before, through the other watches, when he lay on the ground awake, he knew that someone else was awake with him. Now the sound of steady breathing told him he was on his own.

After the flares died during Tanner's watch, the jungle had returned to its natural hum and drone and still remained unchanged. DeLong knew he would listen to the same sustained litany of the countless species that serenaded Tanner and the Chief, only now the concert seemed to be a command performance for him only. He hoped he would be able to notice if someone was singing out of tune.

≈

Sau's attention was drawn to slight noises just ahead. Not as close as he had feared, but close enough that hushed whispers were discernible. He was fairly sure there were two voices, and he signaled as much to the men closest to him. All of the five were near enough to detect the sound and movement for themselves, even Co, who was on the extreme left flank and now knew that he alone would be entering the position from that side. With a little luck, within the hour they would be in a position to strike. They would be close enough to choose their targets. Less than an hour would seal their fate, and not only theirs but the fate of their comrades up above them on the side of the Ong Thu.

≈

DeLong sat with his M16 across his knees, his right hand clamped on the handgrip, his index finger resting on the side of the trigger. His thumb played with the end of the select fire switch. If he had to, he could flip the switch to full automatic and empty his magazine into the bush in a split second. He could shred the trees with 5.56-mm rounds in the blink of an eye, and his only concern then would be a fresh magazine. He felt along the web belt at his waist for his extras. The M16 had been recently issued to the Marines and came with very few accessories, so everyone carried his magazines in old M14 pouches. They didn't hold the smaller magazines tightly, but the Corps was famous for making do with what it had. He snapped one of the flaps open and felt inside, touching the top of the magazine so he would know which was the front in case he had to load it in a hurry.

In training on the ranges at Lejeune and working field problems at Pendleton, you always had a sense of power when you held your weapon. Having it in your hands made you feel prepared and capable, even invincible. And when you added the combined firepower of a squad or a platoon, you had the feeling that nothing could stand against you. But now, sitting in a dark, wet jungle on the other side of the world with his M16 and nearly one hundred rounds of ammunition hanging from his belt, he felt inadequate. He knew he had the potential to do a lot of damage to an enemy, but he still felt exposed and naked. There was a nagging suspicion that what he had might not be enough. If the rifle in his lap was all the protection that stood between him and a ride home in a flag-draped coffin, he wished that it at least felt like more.

DeLong looked at his watch, safe at home again on his wrist, and tried to calculate the time difference between Vietnam and Milwaukee. He thought it would be late afternoon, a cold afternoon. It was probably snowing there this very minute. It occurred to him that time zones were a silly construct of the human imagination. There was no difference in time. This very second existed all over the planet. At this second his father was probably at work, and whatever he was doing, he was doing it now, not yesterday or tomorrow. His mother was probably picking his sister up at school and laughing and bickering with her over the channel on the car radio. And they were doing it this very second. It seemed somehow comforting that this second existed both here and back in the world and that his family was living it, sharing this individual second with him.

A remote rumble echoed in the east and grew as a group of Hueys crossed high over the valley, leaping the Ong Thu on their way west. They might be from the base at Marble Mountain or from the Army squadron that bivouacked on empty ground beyond the runway at An Hoa, but whatever their origins, rhythmic thuds from the big turboshaft engines floated down to earth like snow on a Milwaukee lawn and melted into the jungle noises, and DeLong looked up into the trees in a hopeless and futile attempt to see them.

When he looked down again, the jungle on the mountainside had taken on a new configuration. There seemed to be wet faces in the foliage. He tried to blink the apparitions away, but instead of vanishing, they came on in a rush. In a single deft move, DeLong raised his rifle, flicking the safety lever to full auto. He squeezed the trigger. In that very second, he saw the fullness of his error: the clearing of weapons with Haber on the helicopter; hurriedly slapping in a magazine as the platoon moved away from the LZ; the distraction of the moving column and the rain. He'd never pulled the charging handle, never jacked a round into the chamber. And no matter how hard he squeezed the trigger now, he couldn't change that.

The jungle was alive and leaping on him and past him. Strong hands clawed at his face, forcing their way into his mouth, and he bit down hard as a searing pain paralyzed his throat. The gritty sensation of sharp metal ground against his vertebrae and something warm spilled into his lap. His breath rushed out with no chance of returning. In that second, that world-encompassing second that existed here as it did in Milwaukee, Pfc. William DeLong knew he would not see Wisconsin snow again. A surge of anger that would have been voiced with a snarling scream made a wet, airless whisper, and his life's blood flowed over his hands and wrists and coated his Sears wristwatch, smothering all the seconds that would define the here and now as well as all his seconds to come.

In that second, that final second for DeLong, two other NVA fell on the sleeping Tanner, smashing the wind from his lungs, and before his gasps could regain the slightest bit of it, they severed everything that made the recovery possible.

≈

Co waited on the side until Sau and his men sprang forward, then broke cover in long strides. He expected to be giving whatever help might be needed to silence the two enemy sentries, but at the first sounds of struggle a third figure stirred on the ground in front of him. Co instinctively stomped down on the butt stock of a rifle as the American grabbed for it. Instead of aiding the others, he was forced to deal with a sentry on his own, losing precious surprise. Panic seized his chest as the promise of success quickly decayed into failure before his eyes.

The Marine pulled up hard on the rifle, breaking the stock. He immediately released the weapon and rolled away, came up on one knee, and drove a large knife deep into Binh's side as he knelt over the sentry against the tree. As Binh's body curled around the blade, the Marine jerked it free. Binh sank to the ground with a moan. Co, standing over the American, listened to him fill his lungs with air for delivering a scream designed to awaken the entire valley, and he swung the hammer with all his might. The peen met the Marine's head with a sickening thunk, pitching him onto his side before a single utterance escaped. He lay still.

Sau grabbed Vo's arm and fought his own charged nervous system to construct a whisper.

"Tell Nguyen to go, now," he hissed, and Vo scrambled up the side of the mountain.

The unmistakable smell of fresh blood permeated the quiet space that now seemed overly crowded.

Binh groaned, clutching at his side, and Sau grabbed one of the Marines' towels and pushed it into the wound. "Can you walk?" he asked.

Binh nodded, but when he tried to speak, thick red blood gushed through his teeth.

"Duong. Help me here," Sau said, and the two reached under Binh's arms and lifted him to his feet, causing Binh to groan anew. Bloody air bubbles exploded from his nostrils, and Sau knew that the blade had pierced a lung.

Co picked up one of the Marines' rifles and started looking for others.

"Leave them," Sau said.

"These weapons are a danger to us," Co said, holding the rifle out.

"Not that one."

Co looked down at the rifle in his hand. The butt stock was cocked at a strange angle.

"We must go quickly," Sau said. "Leave everything and help with Binh."

Reluctantly, Co laid the broken rifle across the legs of the Marine sprawled against the tree and turned to the still form in the weeds. He shoved a shoulder with his foot, rolling the body onto its back and leaned down, knife in hand. A focused beam of moonlight framed the head. Gravity had directed streams of blood from the head wound to illustrate the face, and Co looked down on a savage countenance, half red, the rest streaked with random lines. The blood and the man's facial structure gave Co the odd impression he was looking at war paint. Then he noticed the leather pouch with its dangling fringe and bright beads. He stood up and pointed down with the tip of his blade.

"An Indian," he said.

Sau and Duong were moving away, supporting Binh while he pressed the soggy towel to his side and wheezed and gurgled with each step. They weren't listening.

Co watched them leave then turned back to the body at his feet. "A real Indian," he said. "Truong will never believe me." He leaned down again and brought his knife to the Indian's throat. In one quick move he sliced through the rawhide cord and lifted the beaded pouch free. "A damned Indian," he said to himself. He hurried to catch up with the others. In less than half an hour the rising sun would push the night from the face of the Ong Thu. The fruition of the long night's work took less than a minute. A minute full of short, harsh seconds.

Birds in the highest branches of the canopy began to announce the sunrise to come. Those few tentative voices beckoned to others, and in little time the trees were alive with a celebration of the morning. The Marines of 1st Platoon saw it more as avian braggadocio at having survived yet another night. The birds weren't saying that a new day was coming, but that a new day was here and they were still alive. It was a point the Marines occasionally felt compelled to make themselves.

Private First Class Deacon wiped at the mist that clouded the lenses of his glasses. He stood the last watch in his squad, and the cloying moisture at ground level seemed determined to obscure his vision. He reached over and shook the shoulder of the man next to him. Private First Class Franklin blinked awake and leaned up on one elbow.

"What you want, Deek?" he said.

Deacon leaned in close and pointed up the mountain with his glasses. "I think I heard some noise up there."

Franklin looked up through the moisture-laden air. "What kind of noise?"

"I don't know. Like someone fell or something. But more."

"Shit. It's probably just the LP coming in," Franklin said, rolling onto his back.

Deacon replaced his glasses, which were already starting to fog up again. "I don't think so. They wouldn't come back yet. It's too dark. Some nervous FNG might light 'em up. And Strader would be warnin' us his people were comin' in."

Franklin rolled onto his side, facing away. "Strader is gone, Deek."

"Well somebody would say something. Blackwell, Middleton, even Burke. Somebody."

Franklin rolled back and gave Deacon a stare. "You know what your problem is?" he said, and then continued before Deacon could answer. "You ain't got no idea how the chain of command works. You and me is both pfcs. When you got something to report, you tell someone that got more rank than you. That way the info goes uphill. When you tell another pfc, the info just goes sideways, and that means it ain't goin' nowhere. Plus, you're telling someone that don't give a shit and couldn't do anything if he did." Franklin rolled away again. "Especially if he just wants to sleep."

"You think I should tell Middleton?" Deacon said.

Franklin raised his head slightly. "That would be my professional advice," he said and lowered his head again.

Deacon got to his feet and carefully felt his way to the dark spot where his squad leader slept.

Middleton, instantly awake, took Deacon in tow and went up the line, going man to man until he found Sergeant Blackwell.

The sergeant sat up and wiped jungle dew from his face with the towel he used as a pillow.

"I don't remember leavin' a wake-up call with you, Middleton," he said.

"Deacon here says he thinks he heard something up the mountain."

Deacon chimed in. "It sounded like somebody fell—hard and a lot."

"Maybe the LP is coming in and someone slipped."

"Too early," Middleton said, with Deacon nodding in agreement.

The sergeant looked at his watch. "You tell Burke?" he said. "They're his people up there."

"Not yet," Middleton said.

"Well, get up to 3rd Squad and interrupt Burke's beauty sleep. I'll be there in a minute.

Middleton turned to go and Deacon started after him.

"Where the hell are you goin'?" the sergeant said. "You're on watch, aren't you?"

Deacon stopped. "Yeah," was all he said.

"Then get back to it. Middleton can find his way without your help."

Deacon seemed disappointed, as though something important that he'd discovered was being taken away. Middleton had already vanished into the darkness, so Deacon just turned and headed back to his squad.

Middleton made his way to 3rd Squad's position and shook Burke awake.

"Don't tell me," Burke said. "Diehl left and now I'm the platoon honcho."

"No, but that's a scary thought. My man on watch says he thinks there's movement up above us on the mountain where your LP is."

Burke sat up and set his helmet on his head. "He thinks?"

"He said it sounded like someone fell down."

Burke stood and stepped over to the new guy standing his first watch. "New guy," he said. "You hear anything up there?"

Haber sat with his knees drawn up and his rifle gripped tightly in both hands as though an attack was imminent. "I don't think so," he said.

Burke looked to Middleton at his shoulder. "You got one who thinks and I got one who doesn't."

Lieutenant Diehl and Sergeant Blackwell came out of the shadows with Bronsky and his radio close behind. "Burke," the lieutenant said. "When is your LP due to start back?"

Burke checked the luminous dial on his watch. "About fifteen minutes," he said.

The lieutenant consulted his own watch. "They wouldn't have started back early, would they?"

"No, sir. They aren't suicidal."

"Then they wouldn't be falling down," the sergeant chimed in.

"Well . . . ," Burke said.

"Well what?" the lieutenant said, looking up into the mist clinging to the side of the mountain.

"They wouldn't be falling, but they might get knocked down."

Sergeant Blackwell wasn't known for his patience. "You're not making any sense, Marine. Spit it out."

Burke never liked presenting problems to officers, and it wasn't any better doing it as a freshly minted squad leader. "The Chief is on that LP, and if he caught one of the others asleep on watch, he might just administer a little Marine Corps justice."

The lieutenant reached out and pulled Bronsky close. "Call the other LP in. Tell them not to wait, to get back now."

Bronsky took his radio off squelch and reached out to the LP below, covering the mouthpiece with his hand to mask the noise.

The lieutenant tried to identify the shadows standing around him. "Who is this?" he asked of a dark form.

"Middleton, sir."

"Go back down the line and warn everybody that the LP below is coming in early. And don't just tell the watches. Make sure everyone knows it."

The silhouette that was Middleton dissolved into the night, and the lieutenant turned to Sergeant Blackwell. "I'd like to know what's going on up there," he said.

"Could be nothing. Maybe it's like Burke said. The Chief was just administering an attitude adjustment."

"Maybe," the lieutenant said.

The sergeant mopped his face with the towel hanging around his neck. "They won't be expecting anyone climbing up to check on them. It makes for the kind of surprise that ends in a friendly fire incident. The Chief may be a scary son of a bitch, but he's squared away. If he hears movement coming toward him, he'll chew it a new asshole. Maybe we should wait until they're due back."

"That's what's bothering me. Whatever else the Chief is, he's sharp and on the ball. I don't think I've ever heard him make any noise, anywhere. He wouldn't make noise on an LP for any reason." The lieutenant sensed nervous movement near him. "Burke," he said.

"Sir?" Burke answered, a lilt of question in his voice.

"Take your squad up there and get your people."

Burke checked his watch dial again. "You mean now, sir?" he said.

"Now, Marine," the lieutenant said.

Burke swallowed so loudly he was sure it was audible across the valley. "Yes, sir," he said and turned on his heels. "Mount up, 3rd Squad."

There was a flurry of activity as the remaining five members of 3rd Squad gathered their equipment.

"Am I still on watch?" Haber asked as Burke passed.

"Not anymore. Get your gear and move out."

After Burke gave their marching orders to the rest of 3rd Squad, the lieutenant found him and pulled him aside. "Make sure you all stay sharp. If Charley took the LP, they had a reason, and that would be to hit us on a blind side. I don't know what you're walking into, so keep your shit tight." He watched Burke's outline waver. "I'll bet you wish Reach was here."

Burke seemed to stiffen. "No, sir. Strader's a friend of mine. I wouldn't wish that on him." A silent pause stretched out to the breaking point. "I just wish I wasn't."

A commiserating chuckle escaped from the lieutenant's lips as he spoke over his shoulder. "Bronsky. I'll get the LP's radio. You go with Burke. And let me know what the hell is going on."

The earliest gray tint of morning began drawing faint shapes from the jungle shadows, and the birds filled the trees with their raucous symphony as 3rd Squad started up the mountain.

≈

Vo stood beside the two sentries at the rafflesia vine and watched as the small group emerged, struggling under the weight of Binh's limp body. He brushed past the expectant gun barrels aimed down the hill and took hold of Binh's arm. The three bearers' breathing was hoarse and labored from the climb, in marked contrast to Binh's shallow, wet wheezes. Sau's own gasps left little room for words. "Is Nguyen gone?"

Vo draped Binh's arm over his shoulder and lifted, causing a weak groan. Whether it was weak because Binh knew his sounds could endanger the group or because he no longer had the ability to project sound was anyone's guess. "Yes, and we will need to hurry to catch them," Vo said. He looked at Binh's face, eyes rolled back to white crescents. "Should he be moved?" The two sentries handed their weapons to Sau and Co and lent fresh energies to the effort while Duong pressed the sodden towel to Binh's wound.

Sau cradled the RPD machine gun in his arms in relief; compared with Binh, its weight seemed insignificant. "He shouldn't be moved, but he must be; he will be."

With that, the men lifted Binh and swept him along, his head lolling lifelessly. They followed the path of their comrades along the slope of the Ong Thu and left the beautiful flower of the rafflesia and its stink of death behind them.

The eerie predawn grayness gave the mountain landscape the feel of a faded black-and-white photograph. Burke's squad moved through it carefully, expecting the worst and sweeping the trees with their eyes over the sights of their rifles. Flanks were out and pushing through the underbrush muzzles first. The platoon below them was prepared for an enemy assault, and the climbing squad was more than concerned that they could be caught in no-man's-land in the middle of a firefight. Even if the LP became spooked by their approach and cut loose, the platoon might take it for an attack and pour everything into the mountainside.

Bronsky moved up the middle behind Burke and Haber. He kept the radio handset to his ear, making sure the lieutenant was on the other radio. The squad spread out over enough ground so there was a good chance one of them would stumble into the LP. Burke suddenly called a halt. They were a good distance from the platoon now, and everyone stood still, listening to the jungle taking its first morning breaths.

Bronsky moved close to Burke. "Maybe we should call out and let them know we're coming. I don't like the idea of surprising the Chief. He scares me when he's calm. I hate to think what he's like when he's startled."

"We'd be letting anybody else know, too. Don't you think there's someone out there more hostile than the Chief?" Bronsky wiped his face, and Burke noticed for the first time that the radioman had his .45 automatic in his hand. The handgun was Bronsky's only weapon, and Burke couldn't remember the last time he saw it out of its holster.

"I don't know," Bronsky said. "But I'll tell you one thing. If we have to fight someone when we get up there, I hope it's just the VC."

Burke waved a hand and the squad crept upward. Bronsky looked back down the mountain, but they had traveled out of sight of the platoon and nothing seemed to be there but a lethal potential.

It felt like they had been climbing for an hour, but they were less than five minutes from the platoon when one of the flanks waved Burke over. The flank man had his helmet off and was wiping his forehead with the back of his arm when Burke got close enough to see the expression on his face.

"What?" Burke said. The Marine's clenched jaw muscles rippled and he just pointed with his rifle and shook his head. Broad leaves hid a small level spot with trees, but before Burke could push them aside, a sickly sweet odor filled his nostrils. The smell was not unknown to him. He looked to the flank man, but the Marine wouldn't meet his gaze. Bending the leaf stalks slowly, Burke caught sight of a pair of legs in jungle boots stretched out on the ground in a casual pose; beyond them a body lay face-up, eyes staring blankly at the trees. "What the hell," he said, pushing through the leaves, snapping the butt of his rifle to his shoulder, and sweeping the space with his aim.

Tanner lay against the tree in the weak gray light with his legs spread and the front of his flak jacket caked with congealing blood. His head hung awkwardly to the side; an ugly red gash at the throat showed white rings at the parted windpipe. DeLong lay on his back by Tanner's feet, skin as white as parchment and his eyes flat and blank. Beside the tree, the mound that was the Chief lay, his face a streaked mass of red drying to brown flakes at the edges. Insects drawn to an easy meal were already beginning to land on the bodies.

Burke tore his eyes away from the sight. "Get security on this spot," he said, loudly enough for everyone to hear, then, "Bronsky."

The rest of the squad moved around the LP and formed a loose semicircle above with their weapons trained uphill. Bronsky and Haber stepped in and froze. Haber seemed transfixed, unable to look away from DeLong. He took short, deep breaths and gulped like something was working its way up that needed holding down, something that had to be controlled because if it got loose he could never get it back again.

Burke noticed. He had seen that look on fresh faces before. Vietnam was something you had to work into gradually. In a month or six weeks, a new guy's mind would have built up a tolerance to the sights of combat, but when circumstances dumped a full measure of horror in front of you without warning on your second day in the field, it could fill your mind beyond its carrying capacity. This Marine was getting too much, too fast. "Hey . . . ," he said, unable to think of a name to match the face. He stepped up and touched Haber's shoulder, trying to break the trance. "Which one are you?"

Haber didn't hear him. His senses were entirely devoted to vision. His mind was recording the pale nightmare that could only inhabit this transitory space between night and day. The image of DeLong was searing itself into his brain so it could be projected onto the inside of his eyelids for the rest of his life every time he closed them, and the promise of dawn would never be the same.

Burke shook his shoulder. "Whichever one you are, go over on the right and stay alert."

Haber looked at Burke like he was speaking in a foreign language.

Burke spoke slowly and gestured this time. "Go over there and cover the right flank."

Haber turned and moved away like a somnambulist.

Bronsky still stood with his .45 in one hand and the radio handset in the other. "His name is Haber, and he's the one that's still alive." He looked down at the Chief's right hand, still gripping the stag-horn knife with its long, bloody blade. "Son of a bitch," he said.

Burke lifted the M16 from Tanner's legs and held it up. "Look at this. The buffer assembly is completely broken."

The radio hissed a whisper and Bronsky held the handset to his ear. "Yes, sir, it's bad." He stooped to see the matted blood adhering to the hair on the side of the Chief's head and noticed an almost imperceptible rise and fall to the chest inside the flak jacket. "We need the docs up here, quick!"

The corpsmen made short work of the distance between the platoon and the LP by giving no consideration to stealth or noise. Speed was their only concern. Sergeant Blackwell was close on their heels, pleading with them between breaths to slow down and at least pretend to demonstrate a little caution. Within a few seconds of their arrival both corpsmen were working at the Chief's side, having quickly determined that there was nothing to be done for Tanner and DeLong. Doc Brede removed the Chief's web belt and slid the stag-horn knife back into its sheath while Burke helped Doc Garver peel away the flak jacket. There were no other apparent body wounds, so they concentrated on the bloody patch above his right ear, dabbing and peeling and probing until they could get a clear idea of the damage.

Burke and Sergeant Blackwell hovered over them. Not that they were so interested in seeing the corpsmen ply their trade. That was a spectacle Marines generally avoided; it was difficult to function if you considered the realities of combat, but it gave them an acceptable target for their attention and provided an excuse for not looking at the other bodies.

"This isn't a stab wound," Brede said, looking up into the sergeant's face. "The others were cut, but not the Chief. Something slammed into the side of his head."

Bronsky picked up the broken M16 and held it out. "Something like this?"

Blackwell took the weapon, examining the butt stock. "What do you mean? Are you saying Charley didn't do this?"

Bronsky leaned toward the sergeant and lowered his voice to a con-spiratorial level, as though the Chief might be listening. "I can only see what I see. No dead dinks and a scary-ass Indian with a bloody knife in his hand."

Blackwell looked at the M16 again.

"And there's that," Bronsky said. "The Chief has a dent in his head and Tanner with a busted rifle in his lap."

Blackwell quickly squatted beside Brede. "I need to talk to him, Doc," he said.

The corpsman pushed back the Chief's eyelids and flicked a flash-light across his eyes. "Not a chance. He's out cold." He lifted the cor-ner of the battle dressing tied over the wound and looked into an ear. "There's no spinal fluid leaking from his ears, but that doesn't mean the skull isn't fractured. I really don't like his pupil response."

"You mean he isn't going to wake up?"

Brede stashed the flashlight in his bag. "He has serious damage. I can't say when he'll be conscious again."

Bronsky leaned over the sergeant's back. "So you don't know if he'll be out for a minute or a month?"

The corpsman was unrolling a bundle on the ground next to the Chief, a portable nylon litter with six loop handles. "That's about right," he said.

"Then fill him with morphine," Bronsky said. "He's a ticking time bomb."

"Can't give him morphine with a head wound."

The sergeant moved back so the two corpsmen could lift the Chief onto the litter.

"What if he wakes up in a bad mood?" Bronsky said.

Doc Brede gripped the Chief's wrist, timing his pulse while his partner began filling out casualty tags for Tanner and DeLong.

Sergeant Blackwell took the radio handset from Bronsky and squeezed. "Give me One Actual," he said. The lieutenant came on immediately. "I've got two routine and one priority to go," the sergeant said. "And it ain't pretty. No, sir. If they were here, they're long gone." Blackwell moved away from Bronsky, stretching the handset cord out to its limits. "By 'if' I mean maybe this isn't enemy related. There's no sign of Victor Charley, but the Chief had a knife in his hand and the others were split open. That's right, he's the priority, but he's unconscious and Doc Brede doesn't know when that will change." Blackwell moved back toward Bronsky as though the tension on the cord were reeling him in. "Right, sir. I'll make sure he's secure. Roger, out."

The sergeant returned the handset and caught Burke's attention. "We're taking them down. Get the web gear from Tanner and the new guy and strip the belts clean."

With Doc Brede's help, Burke got the belts free of the bodies and removed the ammo pouches, canteens, and personal battle dressing packs. It was an unpleasant task, and Burke and the corpsman didn't look at each other as they worked. Each felt like he was committing a violation, and it was best accomplished without thought and without considering whose body they were manhandling or the life that had inhabited it only hours earlier. They felt they should apologize for taking their things, or say how sorry they were that they were dead, but they said nothing. They worked as unobtrusively and efficiently as they could and hoped that would be enough.

The web belts were adjusted and fitted around the Chief's torso at chest and stomach level, pinning his arms to his sides. While Doc Brede made sure the belts wouldn't interfere with breathing, the sergeant untied the Chief's bootlaces then knotted them together. Glancing up, he saw disapproval on the corpsman's face. "This is bullshit," the doc said.

The sergeant tugged on the laces, making sure the knots would hold the Chief's ankles together. "It's only a precaution," he said. "As much for his safety as ours."

Brede pointed over to Tanner lying on the portable litter Doc Garver had provided and DeLong cocooned in a poncho liner. "The Chief wouldn't do that," he said. "He might kick the shit out of them when they got back to the platoon, but he wouldn't screw up an LP, no matter what."

"Come on, Doc," Bronsky said. "You ever look into his eyes when he's pissed? I'll bet it was just like the last thing General Custer ever saw."

"Knock it off," the sergeant said. "I didn't ask for any opinions." He pointed at the packs and equipment on the ground. "Burke, get your squad to police up their gear and follow us down with the bodies." Before he heard an answer, the sergeant swung the Chief's pack and web gear over his shoulder and grabbed the stretcher loops at the foot end. The docs each took a side and lifted, then started down the slope on unsteady feet.

Burke distributed the gear and sent Tanner's body down with his escort. "Sling your weapon," he told Haber as he stood with Bronsky by the bundled poncho liner. "Bunch the liner up so you have something thick to grab." Bronsky took the feet, and the three lifted DeLong into the air, stretching the poncho liner tight. "If you start to lose your grip, say so, and we'll set him down. Okay?" Everybody nodded and they left the little flat space with the two trees.

The sun cleared the Que Son Mountains in the east and dumped warm light into the An Hoa Valley, filling the rice paddies with morning reflections and flooding the treetops of the Ong Thu. Golden shafts pierced the canopy, spearing the rich mountain soil at random spots, not by the sun's design but simply as the day's first targets of opportunity.

The portable litters provided reliable grips for the bearers, but the three carrying the poncho liner fought a constant battle to maintain handholds. They bunched and twisted the edges of the liner, trying to find enough material to give their straining hands a good grip. Bronsky, at the feet, had the lightest burden, leaving the bulk of the load to Burke and Haber, who immediately discovered a newfound respect for the concept of dead weight. They had to set the body down frequently to establish better handholds, and Haber concentrated an inordinate amount of attention on the liner to avoid looking at the stiffening cargo it carried.

Haber felt ashamed that he couldn't look, although he knew nothing good would be gained from it. But there was a deeper shame that came from last night's relief that DeLong was the one chosen for the

LP. Plain luck had decided who was being carried and who was doing the carrying, and the idea that serendipitous events were likely to be the controlling factor in his relationship with life and death here left him rattled. When he shipped out, Haber's father, in a clumsy attempt to be comforting, said that life was a crapshoot and that he could die crossing the street. Haber knew that was true, no matter how remote the possibility, but this was the first time he had witnessed the mortal dice being tossed, and the guilt at coming up a winner was eating his insides. In the midst of his self-recriminations he was barely aware that he had received his first wound in Vietnam. It was deep, extremely slow healing, and didn't even leave a mark.

≈

The group carrying Binh moved along as close to a run as they could manage. Initially Binh would flinch with each jolt, but eventually his body went slack, leaving his head to swing wildly on loose sinews. Sau called a halt to check on him. Binh's rheumy eyes were only partially open and unseeing. Sau pulled one of the sentries aside. "Go on ahead and tell Nguyen to prepare a place for Binh."

The sentry looked over at Binh and back to Sau in confusion.

Sau placed a hand on his shoulder and moved him away from the group. "Binh's final place," he said. "Go, quickly."

11

The procession of Marines stumbled and slid down the mountainside under their heavy loads, arriving at 1st Platoon's level breathless and back-weary. They placed the two bodies apart from the Chief, and Lieutenant Diehl gave them a cursory inspection. His jaw tightened, setting his facial muscles rippling. This wasn't the first time he had lost men under his command, but it always hit him as a personal failure. The prospect of dying in combat was an accepted risk among the troops, but being responsible for men who died in combat took some time and practice to reconcile. The idea that these deaths were caused by one of his own seemed to question the quality of his leadership and his ability to judge the character of the men he led, and as he looked down on the Chief's blood-streaked face, he couldn't see how he had made such an error. He couldn't believe he had been that wrong. "What can you tell me, Doc?" the lieutenant asked Brede, who was wiping the Chief's bloodstained face with a damp wad of gauze.

"Not much, sir. Blunt force to the head above the right ear." The corpsman slipped a hand under the battle dressing. "There's damage—a depression and a sharp ridge of bone. He definitely has a skull fracture. If he was conscious I might have some idea—slurred speech, confusion, even vomiting—but all I'm seeing is shallow breathing and weak pupil response." The corpsman took the point of a safety pin and pushed it into the Chief's arm above the wrist, getting no reaction. "It ain't good, and he's been unconscious for a long time. I can't find cerebrospinal fluid leaking from his ears, nose, or mouth and there's no blood in his eyes, but that doesn't mean there's no intracranial hemorrhage."

The lieutenant looked up to the web of branches supporting the jungle canopy. "Can he be cable-lifted out of here on a jungle penetrator?"

Doc Brede looked at Doc Garver, who scrunched up his nose as though he'd just caught a whiff of something foul. "I wouldn't do that, sir," he said. "That's a rough ride, and I'm guessing the inside of his skull isn't smooth anymore. He gets jarred around enough and sharp bone could cut into his brain causing a hemorrhage. He could have a stroke. It could kill him."

"So we need to get him to an LZ, ASAP," the lieutenant said as Sergeant Blackwell handed him the damaged M16. He turned the weapon over in his hands, then squatted down beside Brede. "Do you think a smack on the head with this Mattie Mattel piece of plastic could cause all that damage?" he said with his voice lowered so the suspicion wouldn't spread into the platoon.

"I don't know. I suppose so," Brede said. "I never saw anybody get hit with one. But like I told Blackwell, I don't think the Chief did Tanner and the new guy. He's a hard case, but he's not a mental case."

Bronsky stood just behind the lieutenant, waiting for the inevitable order to make the call for a medevac. He made a sweeping gesture with his arm. "Look where we are, Doc. We're all mental cases," he said.

"Speak for yourself, Bronsky," the sergeant said.

The doc gave Bronsky a sour look. "I don't think geography can be held responsible for your unfortunate mental status," he said.

Bronsky stifled the urge to defend himself. He knew the corpsmen were sometimes all that stood between a Marine and a trip to graves registration, and he liked to think that if the situation presented itself and he needed their help, they would be motivated to do their best work.

The lieutenant unfolded his map and searched the terrain east of their position. "Sergeant, get out your map," he said.

Sergeant Blackwell pulled out his plastic-coated map and held it next to the lieutenant's. Grease pencil notations spotted the face, and small crosses were marked in strategic spots in a seemingly random pattern.

The lieutenant jabbed his own map with a finger. "This is the closest spot with enough open ground for a chopper," he said. "Take 2nd Squad and get the Chief and . . . the other two . . . down there."

The sergeant compared the maps and made a quick mark in the area indicated. "That could take some time. It's well over a mile."

"Don't worry about it," the lieutenant said. "It's mostly downhill. I'll get the chopper in the air, and I have to let Five know what the situation is here."

Blackwell scratched at the back of his neck. "Do we have to involve the exec? You know how he is. He just might fly out here."

"I doubt it. But there's got to be security for the Chief, and he'll want to know why."

A solid policy of covering your own ass was familiar to all sergeants, and Blackwell knew that the lieutenant could do no less. But once Diehl got the executive officer on the horn, the Chief would be plunged into the bureaucratic maze of the military justice system, and the full weight of command would land on him like a B-52 payload. His future looked grim. On the bright side, though, the Chief might get lucky and die in transit.

"Bronsky," the lieutenant said, "go with the sergeant and keep me apprised of the Chief's condition."

"Shit," Bronsky said, seeing the chance to rest his aching back fade away.

"What was that, Marine?"

"Yes, sir, Lieutenant. I said, 'Yes, sir.'" Bronsky turned and followed Sergeant Blackwell in search of Middleton and 2nd Squad.

～

The team swept Binh's limp body along at a jogger's pace, easily following the path blazed by the main unit. Binh's limbs dangled loosely, and the wound in his side, a dry, ugly gash, seemed to have discharged all the blood it was capable of losing. Sau sent the remaining sentry, the only one with a firearm, ahead of the group as security.

After a while the sentry stopped suddenly and raised his long-barreled machine gun to his shoulder. The men carrying Binh stopped and let him slump to the ground without ceremony. Ahead, one of the main unit's weapon bearers stood with a short-handled shovel and waved them on. He had a white cloth draped over one shoulder and pointed with the shovel to a spot just off of the trail.

The sentry lowered his weapon and looked at Sau. "Binh is home," he said, indicating the man ahead on the trail. The others raised their heads tentatively, their breaths coming in hoarse gasps.

Sau nodded without speaking, and they got Binh aloft again and followed the digger to a spot a few meters downgrade where a mound of fresh soil was piled beside a shallow grave. The grave walls were studded with roots that had been cleaved away to make room for the new resident. As they lay Binh beside the hole, Sau's deep breaths took in the rich aroma of the newly turned soil. It was pungent and dank and filled with the fertile promise of growth. Sau looked around as though committing the spot to memory, but he knew that it would be anonymous in a few days and impossible to find in a week.

The digger could see that the group was nearly spent, so he knelt and pressed a hand to the side of Binh's neck and lowered his ear to the center of his chest. He looked at Sau and the others, then just looked away. It was not news. It was simply a confirmation of what they all had known since their last stop. It was clear that they were no longer hurrying to save Binh's life, only to save his body.

The white cloth was spread on the ground, and Co and Duong lifted Binh into the center of it while the digger handed a small bag and a coin to Sau. Sau took the offerings, wiping the sweat from his face with the back of a forearm. As the others wrapped the cloth around Binh's body, Sau knelt by his head. The digger handed Sau a saucer of water from his canteen, and Sau poured it over Binh's face and wiped away some of the dirt-encrusted blood. The rest of the group stood silently while Sau opened Binh's mouth. Death was beginning to claim the muscles, and Sau had to use some force. He took as much rice from the little bag as a pinch of his fingers could hold and let the bits fall through Binh's teeth, then he dropped in the coin. He could leave this world now with proof that he wanted for nothing and had no hunger. Sau stood as Duong draped the folds of the cloth over Binh's face.

"His old name will not do in his new place. He will now be known as Trung, the faithful and true, and a more fitting name could not be imagined," Sau said.

The digger looked to the path, and Sau knew that their mourning period was over. They lowered Binh into the trench and with shovel and hands covered the shroud-wrapped body until only a slight bulge marked the grave. In time, joss would be burned and prayers offered, but for now, the need was to rejoin their unit. Sau placed a hand on the mound. He was sure Trung would understand.

S trader hit the chow line early and took a corner seat where he wouldn't be jostled by traffic while he worked his way through a mound of scrambled eggs with sausage links and grits, refilling his coffee cup when it emptied. Marines moved through the morning mess at a steady clip, and Strader could easily tell those coming off night watches in desperate need of some rack time from those who were fresh from their barracks with hours of uninterrupted sleep behind them. A couple of sergeants were at their table nursing coffee in personalized mugs and savoring the first cigarettes of the day.

The space behind the steam tables was alive with activity, and the clang of empty stainless steel bins being shuttled away and generously filled replacements being dropped into their spots filled the room with a sound of industry that battled the din of voices for dominance. This was Strader's favorite time of day. Everything had a new beginning. The sun hadn't had time to bake the life out of the air, and the aroma of sausage and bacon and freshly ground coffee beans created an atmosphere he found relaxing, almost peaceful. And the morning brought another day to be scratched off his short-timer's calendar.

The mimeographed checklist in his pocket set the itinerary for his remaining time at An Hoa. He planned to tick through the column of mandatory destinations, getting the appropriate signatures in the pre-scribed spaces, going from department to department until the page was exhausted, every line a signed testimony to his qualifications to go home. Supply would want back all the equipment he was issued, and in a condition that met the supply sergeant's satisfaction. The armory ser-geant would go over his weapon with the scrutiny of a diamond cutter. His pay records would be examined. His service record would be rifled in search of legal infractions. His seabag would be searched. He would be quizzed, questioned, warned, threatened, and ignored. But he would endure. And the day after tomorrow he would fly away, finally awaken-ing from a bad dream.

At the bottom of the page was a space reserved for the captain's signature. It was just a formality. He liked to speak with each of his Golf Company Marines who managed to complete a tour unscathed, as though he was curious about the secret of their success. At the end of the meeting, he would always shake hands and give the Marine's shoulder a fatherly pat. It was vaguely odd and uncomfortable for most of the men, but they could see from the emotion in the captain's eyes that he was genuinely pleased to be sending home a survivor.

Strader slung his rifle over his shoulder and carried his utensils and tray outside. While dunking his tray in the first rinse barrel, filled with steaming brownish water that floated clumps of uneaten food, he decided his first stop would be the battalion aid station. All Marines feared the possibility of a medical hold stopping them from catching the freedom bird, so he meant to get the poking and prodding out of the way first. If he had a communicable disease that couldn't be shared with the rest of the world, he would rather know it now before he wasted his time slogging through the rest of the list. An intentional and strategic rumor circulated about a strain of venereal disease called the "black clap" that would get you a permanent hold. The rumor even went so far as to create an island where you would be sent. You could never go home. The rumor was designed to curb the sexual appetites of lonely troops with nuclear hormones approaching critical mass, but had about as much effect as the neutered movies and comically graphic VD lectures.

By the time Strader reached the main road through the company area, morning traffic had begun to grind the earth into reddish talc. Each step raised little explosions of dust that coated his Corcorans. Heat waves rose from the corrugated steel roofs as the rising sun turned them into sizzling hotplates. Just beyond the company hooches the battalion laundry had the canvas drapes pulled down and the cardboard sign on the door that marked it closed for business. He knew that the Vietnamese women who ran the laundry would be waiting at the wire for entry, anxious to begin the day of washing and folding and starching and earning their fat little bundles of military payment certificates that they tucked quietly away in their pockets.

Supply and the armory were quiet, too, and before he turned off the road toward the amtrac area and the battalion aid station he could see the local entrepreneurs beyond the wire readying their stands for the day's commerce. Out there, the mama-sans sold anything you might want or need. You could get boonie hats and Ho Chi Minh sandals, cigarettes and Tiger Piss beer, and with the right amount of MPCs, or even greenbacks, you could buy a Coke, a cold and frosty Coke chilled with ice donated by the German medical clinic out by the road.

The battalion aid station was in an actual brick-and-mortar building with real walls and doors and a floor that didn't flex under your weight. The base side showed a face of stucco with high windows. Around back, a helicopter pad led directly to a triage unit with lines of hard-topped gurneys that had to be hosed down regularly. If Strader timed it right, he would be in before the crush of sick call monopolized the docs' attention, but not so early that the morning workload wouldn't be an incentive to get him out of their hair as quickly as possible. He let the spring slap the screen door closed behind him.

The room had a concrete floor with benches against the walls; on the far side an enlisted man sat behind a counter, one hand around a mug of coffee, the other thumbing a copy of *Stars and Stripes*. He glanced up casually then returned to the paper. The collar pin on his utilities identified him as a Navy chief petty officer. The Navy chiefs ran the Navy the way the higher-ranking sergeants ran the Marines, and like the sergeants, they had little tolerance for the lower ranks.

"You're too early for sick call," he said without looking up again.

Strader crossed the room, leaving faint dusty footprints to mark his passage. He slid the mimeographed checklist onto the counter beside the newspaper. "I'm not sick," he said, pointing to a line on the list. "I just need a doctor's John Hancock so I can check out of this resort."

The CPO pushed the checklist away with the side of his hand, never taking his eyes away from his newspaper. The one thing a chief liked less than a lower rank was a lower rank with attitude interrupting his morning quiet time.

"You'll have to be examined," he said. "Have a seat."

Strader grabbed his checklist and went to one of the benches. On the way he looked through a door marked DENTAL. The walls were lined with metal cabinets with glass doors. A portable dentist's chair was pushed back, and a pair of scuffed jungle boots stuck out awkwardly from the footrest, toes pointed tensely to the ceiling. Strader hung his soft cover over the barrel of his rifle and leaned back against the wall.

Behind the counter a bank of file cabinets flanked a metal cupboard, the kind that made sounds like a tympani when the doors were slammed. On top sat a helmet with the camo cover removed. Puckered bullet holes decorated the metal surface on one side and jagged edges marked the exits on the other. "What's with the helmet?" Strader said.

The CPO glanced over his shoulder at the helmet as though he needed a visual refresher, then back to his *Stars and Stripes*. "It's just to remind our field corpsmen not to be heroes."

"That ought'a do it," Strader said.

The screen door swung open and a young Navy officer entered at a pace that said time was money. The tails of his long white coat flapped in his wake like a luffing sail, and the black stencil on his breast pocket was a caduceus with a big D over the serpents. Strader got to his feet quickly, but the CPO barely took his attention away from his reading.

"That emergency here yet?" the officer asked.

"Yes, sir," said the CPO, turning a page. "He's waiting for you in the chair."

The officer disappeared through the door marked DENTAL in a flurry of white linen.

Strader sank back onto the bench. In a few minutes he could hear the officer asking questions and getting muffled and garbled responses, as though the speaker had a mouth full of fingers. The mumbles were soon followed by groans.

Strader looked at the CPO. "My teeth are fine," he said.

Another page was flipped. "Good for you."

≈

The duty officer from the com shack made his way across the road and scaled the pallet walkway and steps into the company office in three strides.

Corporal Pusic had just finished drawing a fresh coffee from the stainless steel urn the mess hall provided every morning. He looked up as the young officer barged in. "Good morning, sir," Pusic said, holding his cup in the air. "Can I get you a coffee?"

The lieutenant shook his head and waved the notepad he carried. "First Platoon needs an evac."

"That's Lieutenant Diehl," Pusic said, slipping behind the safety of his desk. He always felt more comfortable behind the desk. It was a symbol of the authority delegated to him by the captain and served as a little DMZ, three feet of gray metal insulation from the angry, the needy, and the demanding. "Shouldn't we radio the squadron at Marble Mountain?"

"A chopper came in this morning with a sick crew member. It's sitting idle by the air control tower now. It could be at 1st Platoon's coordinates before one of the Evil Eyes from the 163rd would be half-way here."

Pusic started to sink into his chair, then thought better of sitting in the presence of a standing officer. "I could call the tower and tell them to get the chopper in the air," he said.

"I can do that, Corporal," the lieutenant said testily. "But Lieutenant Diehl requested security. What I want from you is a body to go along."

"They're sending back a VC prisoner?" Pusic asked, hoping the officer wasn't considering him for the job of chaperone.

"Not VC. The security is for one of ours."

<hr>

As Strader climbed the grade from the BAS, an M-274 mechanical mule bounced by in a shower of dust, a pair of jerry cans staggering across the flat bed behind the driver and passenger. Strader stepped aside so he wouldn't be enveloped in the red cloud that chased the mule up the road. A first sergeant clung to the low rails that surrounded the bed and cursed the inventor of the little machine that seemed dedicated to putting a permanent dent in his ass. The lance corporal at the wheel, his legs angled at the pedals hanging over the front of the machine, noticed the sergeant's discomfort and downshifted, leaping the mule forward, spinning the tires, and lifting the front wheels off the ground. Before the sergeant could unleash a stream of invective, the driver swung over to the walkway and stopped in front of the company office.

The first sergeant hopped out, rubbing the crease the bed rail had pressed into the seat of his starched trousers. "You should get the suspension checked on that thing," he growled, trying to get some circulation back into his feet by stomping on the walkway planks.

The driver revved the little engine like it was a hot rod lawnmower. "It ain't got no suspension, Sergeant. They built this little beauty to haul ass and rattle bones."

"Well, it better haul your ass out of here before I think of some creative way to rattle your bones."

With that, the driver popped the clutch and the little mobile platform lurched forward and disappeared over the rise leading to the runway.

Farther back on the road, Strader trudged along, his rifle slung on one shoulder and his cartridge belt draped over the other. He had timed his visit to the BAS with perfect precision. By the time the Navy MDs had dragged themselves away from the officers' mess a line had begun to form at the counter and the CPO had retreated into a back office with his paper, leaving a third-class corpsman to deal with the medical complaints.

Strader eavesdropped on the litany of maladies. After announcing to the room to clear all weapons, the corpsman listened with a thinly disguised lack of interest as each Marine described the problem that brought him to sick call. He would scratch his chin, then fill in the space on the sick call form for the medical complaint while saying it out loud as though he were dictating to a stenographer. It seemed that most everyone was falling into one of three categories: if they shivered with the chills, he diagnosed "ague"; if they felt dizzy, he proclaimed it to be "vertigo"; and if they just didn't feel good, the problem was "general malaise." A few wandered outside the scope of his diagnostic purview. One Marine kept dancing from one foot to the other while pulling on the seat of his pants. Strader guessed dysentery and was happy to hear that the corpsman concurred. One pulled the neck of his T-shirt down to reveal a red boil on the back of his neck that seemed to have an eye in the center of it. The next man in line stepped back a pace. The corpsman wrote "carbuncle" and sent him to the bench. One of the crew from the 155 battery swore he couldn't hear anything out of his left ear, and to prove it he said "huh?" to every question the corpsman asked.

A Navy lieutenant pushed his way into the room and everyone on the benches snapped to their feet. The officer waved them down saying, "At ease, at ease," as though the Marines' stubborn adherence to military protocol was a nuisance and the newness of having it directed at him was more than a little embarrassing. The Marine Corps officers accepted the required courtesy as a necessity, a demonstration that reinforced military discipline. It was an exercise clearly intended to define the difference between enlisted and officer. However, the young Navy physicians were a different breed. They were generally conscripts who had discovered, much to their chagrin, that upon achieving the MD they had pursued through years of postgraduate work they were suddenly and eminently eligible for the draft, even if they had served before and used the G.I. Bill to get the coveted medical education that now turned to bite them in the gluteus maximus.

The corpsman pointed at Strader. "Sir. That one needs a medical clearance so he can DEROS out of here."

The officer hooked a finger in Strader's direction. "Come with me," he said. He held his hand out and wiggled his fingers until Strader realized that he wanted the checklist. He handed it over as they walked.

The doctor was tall and lanky, and his frame swayed when he walked as though the physics of his structure was in a state of flux. His hair was cropped close enough to make his ears appear oversized, and his gray military eyeglasses emphasized the whiteness of his skin. He perused the information at the top of the sheet. "Strader, Corporal," he read.

"Yes, sir," Strader answered.

"Going home, huh?"

"That's the plan, sir."

They passed a couple of examination rooms and stopped in front of the third. "Where did you go for R&R, Corporal?"

"Sir?"

"You did go on R&R, didn't you?"

"Yes, sir. About six months ago."

"Well?"

Strader looked down and noticed that the doctor's boots weren't terribly scuffed, but the bottom half of the canvas sides was stained dark, like something red and sticky had infused the material again and again until taking permanent root. "Bangkok, sir," he said.

The doctor's eyebrows rose almost imperceptibly. "And have you experienced any burning during urination since then?"

"No, sir," Strader answered indignantly.

"Does that mean you were lucky or that you took the communicable disease classes to heart?"

"Well, the condom lecture stuck in my mind."

"I didn't think applying prophylactics was something that required instruction. What do the Marines have to say on the subject?"

"The sergeant just said to put the rubber over the tip and roll it on until you ran out of one or the other."

An awkward smile spread over the doctor's face as though it was visiting a place where it used to live but no longer felt at home. "Okay, okay. I just wanted to see if you had fun on R&R. Mine comes up next month and I'm doing a little comparison shopping. So, you recommend Bangkok, then?"

"I guess so, sir. You would probably want to stay at the R&R Center at the Windsor Hotel. Beer is expensive, though, about twenty baht, which is about a dollar, especially on Patpong Road, where the clubs are."

The doctor set the checklist on the exam table and pulled the black government pen from his shirt pocket. "Are you saying you couldn't afford to get drunk?"

"No, sir. I was shit-faced every night, and most days, too. But I have to admit that most of my money went to some very lovely escorts. Twenty-four hours for five hundred baht. After seven days, I needed to come back here for a rest."

The doctor leaned over the checklist, glancing at Strader all the time. "Five hundred baht, twenty-five dollars," he said.

Strader seemed embarrassed and shrugged his shoulders. "Right, sir. It's kind of like trying to buy your way back into the human race."

The doctor nodded and turned his attention to the illegible signature he was affixing with a flourish. "Didn't bring back any souvenirs?"

"Like I said, sir, the condom lecture had a real impact."

The doctor smiled again. "Go home, Marine," he said, and within minutes Strader was headed back to the company area with the checklist folded around one less hurdle to the finish line.

~

First Sergeant Gantz entered the company office as the duty officer from the com shack was applying a level of pressure on Corporal Pusic that might pry one of Golf Company's personnel loose.

"Good morning, sir," Gantz said. "Can I do anything for you?"

The officer turned away from Pusic's desk, flipping open his notepad. "Your 1st Platoon had some trouble in the Arizona last night, Sergeant, and needs a chopper. I've got one short-handed sitting on the runway, but Lieutenant Diehl requested a security escort."

"They're sending a VC back to intel?" Gantz asked, heading for the coffee.

"More likely the adjutant. The security is for one of ours."

The sergeant turned, empty cup in hand. "One of ours? Sounds like we should notify the aid station that a psych case is coming in."

The officer glanced at his watch. "We've got plenty of time to organize a reception. What I need now is one of your people on that chopper ASAP." He made a point of looking at his watch again, and then waved his notebook. "First Platoon's workhorse will be at the LZ in fifteen minutes."

Pusic grabbed his starched soft cover from its perch on top of a file cabinet. "Should I double-time over to the officers' mess?" He wanted to get clear of the office while decisions were being made that might affect him personally if he were within sight.

Before the lieutenant could respond, Sergeant Gantz cut in. "Don't bother the captain at breakfast, Pusic. Get over to the platoon area and find somebody."

Pusic's relationship with the platoons was already less than cordial. The Corps was divided into the haves and the have-nots, and Pusic was definitely aligned with the haves. They always viewed his arrival in the hooches with suspicion, as though he were intelligence gathering for the staff or delivering bad news in the form of an order from above. If he showed up now just to pluck someone from the safety of his rack and send him into the Arizona, the grunts would not look on it favorably. Though they knew the order was coming from command, they would hold it against him anyway, and the animosity would just feed his alienation. His mind raced for an out.

"Third Platoon was manning lines all night and the 2nd is the Sparrow Hawk reaction platoon," Pusic said. "With units in the Arizona, they'll pitch a bitch about reducing strength."

Sergeant Gantz turned back to the coffee urn and filled his personal cup illustrated with first sergeant's stripes on one side and a bulldog in a World War I doughboy helmet on the other. "I don't give a shit who you get, but get someone."

From where he stood behind his desk, Pusic could see through the screening to the dusty road in front of the office. On the far side of it, Strader trudged along with his M14 slung upside-down on one shoulder and his belt of magazines dangling over the other.

Pusic's out was being delivered as though by divine providence. If he was going to piss off one of the troops, who better than one who was leaving in a couple of days? He pointed a finger in Strader's direction.

The sergeant, sipping his coffee as steam vapors rose above his razor-cut hair, let his attention follow Pusic's finger. "Who's that?" he said.

"That's Corporal Strader. You saw him last night in the chow hall."

The sergeant took another sip, squinting over the cup. He wasn't making the connection.

Pusic stepped around the buffer zone of his desk feeling a rush of relief wash over him like a blast from the fan. The focus of bad tidings was swinging away from him to another target, and all he had to do was play the spotter and direct fire. "He's the one from the chow hall you told to get away from our table and take a shower."

A flash of recognition ignited the sergeant's eyes. "He's one of ours, right?"

"Yes, he is. First Platoon."

The sergeant shoved the screen door open until the spring vibrated in protest. "Strader, get your ass over here," he said.

Strader hesitated when he saw the door of the company office swing open and the first sergeant's bulk fill the doorway. He hoped he hadn't drawn the sergeant's ire just by walking by. He didn't want to spend one of his last days in An Hoa burning latrine barrels or filling sandbags, and he knew how creative the sergeants could be when they took it upon themselves to cause someone a ration of discomfort. There was always a chance that the sergeant's interest lay elsewhere. But then he heard the hard-edged summons. His shoulders sank as the balloon of promise he had just begun to inflate with the first signature on his checklist sprang a leak. He jogged across the road, small dust clouds rising above his ankles.

Pusic retreated behind the safety of his desk and returned his crisply starched and sculpted utility cover to its spot on the cabinet. It seemed prudent to divorce himself from the proceedings as much as possible. Whatever hard feelings Strader might develop in the next few minutes, it was best they were directed at the sergeant or the lieutenant. He dropped onto the wooden office chair and leaned back, making the abused joints creak.

The sergeant leaned out of the door as Strader reached the walkway. "You got an hour free," the sergeant said.

Strader let the belt slide from his shoulder to hang over his forearm. "Well, I'm pretty busy, Sergeant," he said, noticing the officer peering over the sergeant's shoulder.

"That wasn't a question, Corporal. You *do* have a free hour, and I'm gonna use it."

Strader had hoped that what little time he had left on the base would be free of petty griefs, but if it wasn't to be, he resigned himself to a lost hour and would consider it well spent if it got the sergeant off his case. He should have skirted the command area and passed anonymously behind the storage tents, and he could only blame the intoxication of his impending freedom for making him careless.

"There's a 34 sitting by the control tower. Go get on it," the sergeant said, fighting the function of the door spring and steadying his coffee cup so a spill wouldn't mark the steps.

"Where am I going?"

"First you're going down to the runway. After that, just go where the chopper goes."

The lieutenant pushed his head into the sunlight. "I'll be radioing the chopper to take off in three minutes."

The sergeant looked through the screen door and down the road as though he could see the chopper waiting. "When it lifts off, be on it." He freed the door to close with a slap.

Strader stood frozen on the walkway staring at the closed door, which hummed with the spring's tense vibration. His mind raced to formulate a response that would dissuade the sergeant from inflicting the one-hour headache he was facing, but he knew from experience that trying to reason with top NCOs usually led to more problems and bigger headaches. From inside the office he could hear an oscillating fan set to high sweeping the room with a lighthouse beam of rushing air and a voice repeating coordinate numbers to the air control tower. An hour's busy-work was one thing—it generally cost little more than sweat and frustration—but flying over the countryside in a chopper involved a certain amount of risk, and he was becoming comfortable with the idea that his danger days were at an end. He cursed himself for letting his mind relax.

The sergeant's face appeared behind the screen door. "What is your malfunction, Marine? Did you not hear my order? If you are not on that chopper in three minutes I will bring a shitstorm of hurt down on you that will make your grandchildren cry. Do you hear me, Marine?"

Strader simply looked at the sergeant, then nodded. His shoulders sagged and his lungs expelled a long flush of air in resignation. He hopped down into the road and headed for the runway.

At the edge of the plateau that held the offices the road sloped downward, and he could see the big green helicopter sitting by the tower, the giant grasshopper nose pointed at him like an entomologist's hallucination. The huge main rotors hung lifeless in an arch, but as he watched they started a slow movement, turning lazily at first but growing in speed until the centrifugal force began to affect the rotor sag and the curvilinear motion stretched them out onto a flat plane where the aerodynamics of their design could do their work. He could hear the big-throated exhaust in the distance. If the chopper lifted off without him, the sergeant could make enough trouble to delay his departure, and he didn't want to spend any additional time in-country answering a charge of disobeying a direct order. He slipped his rifle from his shoulder and started to run.

His feet struck the roadway like little explosions, and the web belt beat the heavy M14 magazines against his leg. As he reached the spot where the pathway to the platoon area met the road, the hot rod mechanical mule driver slid to a stop in front of him. The bed of the machine was empty of jerry cans now, and Strader waved for him to wait. "Hold up," he said. The driver sat calmly, gripping the wheel that pushed at him from the oddly angled steering column. Strader pulled up against the mule. He caught his breath and pointed down at the runway. "Can you run me down to that chopper, fast?" he asked, fresh beads of sweat speckling his forehead and upper lip.

The driver turned his head casually as if to verify the existence of the helicopter. "Why not. Hop on, man."

Strader tossed his belt onto the bed and hopped backward over the side rail, letting his legs dangle. Before he could settle, the driver popped the clutch and the mule swung wildly onto the road, spewing a roostertail of dust like a powerboat's wake. Strader had to scramble for a handhold on the rail to prevent being tossed off. The driver worked his way through the gears as smoothly as a Grand Prix racer, and Strader could see that the Marine clearly enjoyed his work. There was little enough enjoyment to be had in Vietnam and you found what pleasure you could, and it was obvious to Strader that this Marine loved driving the crazy little machine. The engine whined as the driver slapped it deftly into high gear, and Strader could barely hold onto his rifle and the mule both as the uneven road slammed the springless wheels and drove the flatbed to the edge of control.

The driver looked over his shoulder at Strader, stretched out on the bed and bouncing about like so much loose cargo. "Hang on, man," he said, laughing and wrestling the wheel. Strader felt the body blows as he went airborne and the bed bounced up to meet him on his way down. Each impact was like being hit by a pro lineman.

In less than a minute the mule left the road and rolled onto the interlocking metal plates of the runway, leaving a red cloud hanging behind. The driver steered under the chopper's bulbous nose and slid to a stop next to the wheeled strut by the starboard door. Strader crawled off the bed feeling as though his joints had aged forty years. He walked gingerly to the rear of the mule to retrieve his cartridge belt, compacted into a bundle against the tail rail. "Thanks, I think," he said, rubbing his abused hips.

"No sweat, man." The driver spun the wheel and drove straight up the embankment, past the control tower, and down along the rear of the platoon hooches that bordered the runway. He was having a good time, and for that Strader's envy went with him.

The helicopter's rotor wash met the attacking dust cloud that followed in the mule's draft and flattened it to the runway. The wash whipped at Strader, and he had to clamp his utility cover to his head with a free hand.

Masked in shadow just inside the door, a Marine bent over the swivel-mounted door gun. He had the M60's long feed cover standing tall and was carefully setting the linked belt of 7.62 ammunition on the feed plate. When he looked up from his work, Strader recognized the pinpoints of black powder stain on the teen surfer face, which filled out in a wide grin. "Hey, man. How was Pennsylvania?" the door gunner said.

"Don't be a smart-ass," Strader said, tossing his cartridge belt through the door to land with a clunk on the metal floor.

"You our security?" the lance corporal asked, extending a hand.

Strader grasped the offered hand, locking thumbs, and with a heave the gunner hauled him into the chopper. "Security for what?" Strader yelled inside the noisy compartment.

"Prisoner escort," the young Marine said, used to economizing on words in deference to the noise. He stepped to the gun mount at the port window and repeated the same loading procedure as with the door gun.

"I'm here to babysit a *chieu hoi*?" Strader said incredulously.

The door gunner was concentrating on positioning the rounds on the 60's feed plate. "I don't think its VC. It's one of the grunts."

Strader's eyes narrowed as they always did when another MOS used "grunt," often meant as a slur. He retrieved his belt from the floor and swung it around his waist, locking the post link in front, and clearing his weapon before he was told to. "There's just the two of us? Where's the crew chief?" he asked.

The young door gunner opened his mouth and pointed into it with a dirty finger. "Bad tooth," he said. "Infected. Swelled his jaw like a wad of chew."

Strader nodded, remembering the nervous boots in the dentist's chair.

The copilot stomped his foot on the deck between the cockpit seats to get attention in the rear. He slapped his hand against his helmet, and the gunner went to the door and pulled on his own helmet. The rotor speed increased and the helicopter shook. The young Marine whistled at Strader and pointed to the gun in the port window. Strader set his M14 on the floor against the bulkhead and pinned it there with his foot, grabbed the butt of the M60, and pressed it into his shoulder, grateful for the sturdy gun mount that would steady his stance when the deck pitched. Chopper crews developed sea legs to compensate for the undulating surface beneath their feet, but Strader would stagger around the deck like a drunken sailor without something solid to hold on to. Having a position at the M60 was a blessing.

The windsock on the pole by the tower scooped what little breeze there was, and with a change in the collective, the big machine's tail drifted around to face the wind head on. An aureole of dust billowed out beneath the chopper, and with a gradual adjustment of the cyclic pitch it moved forward and climbed away from its little corner of the runway.

Strader watched the base drop away over the barrel of the M60 and pulled himself closer to the opening to see the full expanse of the west side of the perimeter. The chopper increased speed and banked in a wide arc above the base, climbing as it went. It was best to gain as much altitude as possible before crossing over the wire, not so much to discourage VC snipers from taking a shot as to make the inevitable shot as difficult as possible. After making a wide loop over the base, the 34 leveled out and headed its grasshopper nose toward the muddy brown gash the Song Thu Bon made in the landscape, and the Arizona beyond.

From his spot at the gun port Strader could see the straggling wisps of morning mist and dissipating clouds rising in the heat. Had he not been a thousand feet in the air in a shuddering machine with nothing between him and a smoking hole in the ground but the fabled Jesus nut on the main rotor, he would have enjoyed the scenery like a tourist. He peeked through the gun port at the paddies and villages and rivers far below that consolidated into a patchwork quilt of greens and browns, but the height stirred a flutter in his stomach and he dropped down into a jump seat and leaned back against the bulkhead, content to watch the door gunner pop C ration Chiclets into his mouth until his cheeks bulged.

13

The slope of the Ong Thu eased as Corporal Middleton's reinforced squad got downgrade from the bulk of 1st Platoon. The heat of the morning sun striking the top of the jungle canopy pushed the temperature on the ground to a greenhouse level, and the squad members were drenched in sweat from the strain of their loads. Where the grade was steepest, they slid and stumbled, barely maintaining control of their charges. The Marines carrying the bodies took the lead and moved at a quicker pace, fully aware that the ones they carried could no longer be harmed. The six carrying the Chief worked under different constraints. They chose their footholds carefully, and when gravity overpowered their efforts, they froze or adjusted their path, or simply set the nylon litter down so Doc Brede could check the Chief's vital signs and peer under his eyelids. When they were on the move, the corpsman stayed at the top end of the litter and tried to stabilize the Chief's head when the terrain had the bearers fighting to stay upright. Once they crossed the stream—the same one that had repeatedly blocked their path the previous day—the landscape leveled out some and the Marines could focus on dealing with the weight alone, without the distraction of dangerous footing.

With the stream behind them, Sergeant Blackwell called a halt. He checked his watch. "Take five," he said, "but don't get comfortable."

The litters immediately went to the ground and canteens were hoisted while the corpsman bent over the Chief. Bronsky found the sergeant and handed him the radio handset. "It's Lieutenant Diehl," he said.

The sergeant took the handset and squatted down, spreading his map at his feet. His heart was still beating rapidly from the descent and his breath was labored. "Sir," he said.

"Yes, sir. We're at valley level now." He looked at the map then consulted his watch. "I estimate LZ Mike in ten." He gathered the map awkwardly with one hand and stood, listening intently. "Wait one," he said. From where he stood he could see the corpsman pressing his fingertips to one of the Chief's brachial arteries. "Doc?" he said with trepidation in his voice.

The corpsman looked back over his shoulder and nodded.

"That's affirmative, sir," Blackwell said, clearly relieved. Though the Chief still showed no signs of consciousness, it was good to know they hadn't killed him on the trip down. He listened again. "Roger, sir. Out." He returned the handset to Bronsky and checked his watch again. "Saddle up in two minutes," he announced to a squad just beginning to appreciate the illusion of weightlessness they were experiencing.

The pulse in the Chief's wrist seemed stronger than it had up on the mountain, and Doc Brede laid his hand on the Chief's chest and timed his respirations. The heat on the valley floor seemed to have increased, probably from their proximity to the jungle's edge, the corpsman guessed. The beads of perspiration dotting his face formed into rivulets, and as he bent over the Chief, a drip that had blazed a path to the end of his nose fell free and struck the Chief's face at the inner fold of his right eye . . . and the Chief flinched. It was nothing more than an involuntary tic, a reflex spasm, but it was enough. It was a positive sign, an unexpected sign that allowed the doc to dare to be optimistic. He grabbed the Chief's hand again and pushed his thumbnail down hard on one of the Chief's cuticles. The arm jerked under the belt restraints and the hand pulled free of the doc's grasp. He quickly looked back over his shoulder. "Sergeant," he said, unable to hide his enthusiasm.

Sergeant Blackwell moved in his direction. "We have to get goin', Doc. How's he doin'?"

"I'm starting to get a response from the Chief. I think he may be coming to."

The sergeant looked down at the body banded in web belts and motionless as a corpse. "Are you sure?" he said.

"As sure as I can be under the circumstances."

As long as the Chief was unconscious, the sergeant was content to see him as a medical problem, an inert package that presented no more difficulty than the logistics of transport. But if the Chief came out of it, there was a good chance the situation would change. "Can't you keep him out?"

The corpsman shook his head. "I can't keep him out just like I'm not waking him up. I'm only an interested party watching things happen I can't control."

"That's my concern, Doc. I don't want anything to happen I can't control, and if he wakes up pissed off, I'm going to have a problem." The sergeant looked around. "Middleton," he said. "Move your people out."

The corporal got his squad going; the men raised the litters with a chorus of groans and followed the point man away from the mountain.

The sergeant walked alongside the corpsman. "The sooner we get the Chief to the LZ the better," he said.

The corpsman watched as the Chief bounced along between the struggling Marines. "Maybe we *should* try to wake him up, Sergeant, for his own sake."

"Negative, Doc. They can deal with that at battalion aid. Let's just worry about getting him on that chopper." Rather than enter into an argument with the corpsman, the sergeant moved ahead until all three litters were behind him.

The docs had the upper hand in the platoon's medical matters. They were responsible for the physical well-being of the men, and their medical opinions were seldom questioned. Technically, they could even evacuate men over the objections of officers, though Blackwell had never actually seen it happen. He knew waking the Chief up for his own good could surely be problematic, and if there was going to be a battle on the way to the LZ, he was going to do all he could to make sure it wouldn't go into the records as an Indian war.

≈

Arc lights burst behind the Chief's eyelids like a mad minute of misfiring synapses. He was vaguely aware of movement, and the pain in his head was sharp and hot, piercing his thoughts with fire. Sounds were far away and came in drones and unintelligible growls. He was at the bottom of a black lake with refracted daylight faint and far away. He wanted to kick and claw his way to the surface, but he felt constricted and helpless. The same murderous clamp that squeezed his skull wrapped his body in a claustrophobic cocoon that smelled of burning wood and tasted like copper pennies in his mouth.

The burning odor stimulated a memory, and he found himself looking across the glow of a campfire on the high desert of New Mexico. His father and grandfather looked back, their familiar stoic faces bathed in golden light, and spoke to him of the expanse of stars that splashed the heavens from horizon to horizon and the need for the trek to the great tree. Sparks rose on erratic thermals above the fire, and the round, youthful face of Noche Gonshayee watched them spiral skyward in streaming coils that stayed alive as negative strips of ghost light when he closed his eyes.

When he was born, everyone at White Mountain remarked on the shape of his face, and his grandfather took to calling him Kle-ga-na-ai, Moon. Before long everyone on the reservation used the nickname. But the name was a personal thing, a construct of his people, and when he left White Mountain he found little use for it. Whites' propensity to call him Chief seemed to resolve the name issue, though not to his satisfaction.

Every crack and crease in his grandfather's weathered face seemed like an old map of home that soothed his mind, and the warm light of the remembered fire was relaxing as it held the night at bay. Moon knew the place and time as a journey from his youth. His father had made this trip when he was young, as his grandfather had in his time. Now it was Kle-ga-na-ai's turn to make the family pilgrimage to the tree. Usually the trek was made by father and son, but Benito's pickup truck was available, so his grandfather rode in the cab while Kle-ga-na-ai and his father sat in the bed and watched Arizona turn into New Mexico. He could feel the jolts and jars as the old Dodge hauled them past Coyote Canyon to Tohatchi, then on to Naschitti.

Kle-ga-na-ai's great-grandfather, recounting the history of his people to the younger generations, told of his band of Chiricahua raiders who led a detachment of cavalry and an angry mob of ranchers on a merry chase. But the Apache knew the desert—they *were* the desert— and the Army broke off the pursuit, effectively deflating the resolve of the ranchers to carry on.

After crossing a wide, scorching mesa, the Apache finally made camp at the foot of a lone butte that bore a great tree at its head. When Kle-ga-na-ai's great-grandfather climbed the butte to survey the land for their pursuers he was struck by the power of the lone tree. Wind and heat had bent and twisted the trunk, forming knobby branches and deformed tendrils that pointed at the heavens in green defiance. The gnarled roots clung to the butte with steely tenacity. He ran his hands over the bark, blasted smooth by sand, and knew that among all trees, this one was truly Apache. It fought the world with an Apache heart. It was a brother.

When Benito dropped off his passengers, a good twenty-five dry, hot miles on foot lay ahead, an unforgiving distance in the high desert. They carried bedrolls, water, and dried, salted meat—enough for five days. They expected to feel privations and to suffer as a necessary component of the trip. Their tenacity would be an offering to the tree, a tribute to its own tenacious heart. And they wanted the feeling of accomplishment, a feeling the world often denied the Apache.

They wrapped their heads in traditional style. Kle-ga-na-ai's head wrap felt wet; and the sun must have been especially fierce because his head could barely contain the drumbeat that was trying to pound its way out. They slept among the sagebrush under the infinite expanse of distant worlds and rested at midday, thwarting the sun's plan to exhaust their water, and in two days' travel stood at the foot of the great butte, looking up at the proud, misshapen tree. The arduous trip sapped the grandfather's reserves of vitality, but the sight of the lonely mound, so familiar in his youth, brought back energies of that distant time and made him anxious to climb, as though his greatest need was to erase the distance between himself and a long-estranged friend.

Kle-ga-na-ai's father led, skirting patches of cliffrose and fernbush, circumnavigating the grade so they arrived at the plateau by a kinder slope and came at the tree across a bald surface swept clean by the same winds that had sculpted the tree. As the older men walked across the top of the butte at a casual pace, Kle-ga-na-ai couldn't contain his anticipation and ran ahead to claim the honor of arriving first, an accomplishment that would give him great cachet among his friends at White Mountain. But being first left him confused. Up close, the tree was gray and dry with long, twisting cracks where the relentless sun had sucked all the moisture away. The ground was littered with brittle branches and twigs. Once flagged with legions of obstinate leaves, they now lay scattered among the roots like so much kindling. He looked back to where the others had stopped and marked the disappointment on their faces.

What was expected was not always what had to be endured.

Kle-ga-na-ai's grandfather sat on the ground and crossed his legs stiffly. The shadow cast by the tree fractured the sunlight and coated his image in a mosaic of shapes created in concert by both the victor and the vanquished. "The tree is dead," he said, announcing the fact to the world.

Kle-ga-na-ai's father stood silently as sunlight and shadows played across his face. But the boy's round face held eyes with the acuity of a hawk's. He pointed into the twist of branches above his head. "No, it's not," he said. His position at the trunk shaded his eyes from the sun, and he could see one branch where small pennants of green fluttered in the wind. The men came close and followed the youngster's direction. The tough old tree had marshaled its resources, concentrating what sustenance it still possessed on the living tissue it had left.

The weathered lines in the grandfather's face formed into a broad smile, and he apologized to the tree for having doubted. The tree was alive and Apache to the core, as it always had been.

They camped on the plateau and made their fire from the tree's castoffs, and in the middle of the night, when the thirst of the sun was blocked, they poured their canteens into the roots at the base of the trunk.

The trip back across the arid mesa was more difficult than anything Kle-ga-na-ai had ever experienced or even imagined. Their thirst could not be quenched and came in spasms. The sun cracked their lips, and they traveled as much as possible after sundown, erecting shade tents made from their bedrolls during the day. They hoped to come upon an errant barrel cactus that would give up its juices, but they tripped only through endless sage interspersed with four-wing saltbush and desert spoon. The occasional Apache plume brought smiles that tested the lost elasticity of their lips. Kle-ga-na-ai's grandfather had made a walking stick from one of the old tree's fallen branches, and he waved it in the air when Benito's pickup appeared along the distant road, looking like a rust-colored boulder in the Painted Desert.

They had provoked the Usun and the sun he created and won a gamble, but each felt the wager was worth it. They had reached their destination and given sustenance to an old friend, and now the three Apache walked the last steps side-by-side, equal in their effort and their discomfort and bonded by the experience. But every step under the sun's dispassionate assault snapped glaring spots in Kle-ga-na-ai's vision, and he hoped that Benito had thought to bring plenty of water. Maybe a drink would ease the pain in his head.

He could still feel the old truck wobble over the uneven ground as he lay on the bed listening to his name being called again and again. He looked up into his father's face, but the pain clouded his vision and he tried to blink away the apparition he was finding it difficult to recognize. His father seemed to have forgotten his name.

"Chief, Chief."

The upside down face that hovered over him was lined with fatigue, had stubble on its chin, and wore glasses that reflected light into his eyes. "Chief," it said again.

His mind scrambled through the pain, trying to find some cohesion, some connection with the blur wavering over him while other voices pressed in, hollow and faint, echoing with an annoying reverberation. "He hates being called that, Doc," one of the voices echoed.

The visage above him fractured into a grotesque, shimmering mask. "I know that," it said. "Chief," the voice said with intentional emphasis.

Doc Brede had noticed that the Chief's eyelids were fluttering as though they were fighting to open. Either that or the head trauma was causing a seizure. He had the Marines lower the litter to the ground.

Kle-ga-na-ai felt the truck stop rocking. Hands gripped his face, and he felt they had a magic that froze his entire body. He tried to focus his thoughts. His consciousness floated between two worlds and he tried to speak, but the desert world had dried the words on his tongue. He felt he could find his place with a drink of water. "*Tu*," he said in a whisper so dry it barely crossed his lips. "*Tu*."

The face leaned in, framed by a covered helmet with a frayed edge along the rim. The Kle-ga-na-ai of childhood began to dissolve like a morning memory of a dream, and the Chief squeezed his eyes closed and willed his mind to find a reality he could hold on to. "Water," the Chief said in a dry croak, choosing a place, or letting the place choose him.

The corpsman tipped his canteen and soaked an end of his towel, then squeezed drips into the Chief's mouth. He couldn't risk having him choke on too much water. A fit of coughing with a brain injury could be catastrophic. The Chief opened his mouth like a hungry bird, and Brede squeezed in more.

With the litter on the ground, the bearers faded apart, each finding his own inconspicuous spot in the brush. They didn't need the sergeant's admonition of "one round will get you all." Seeking anonymous ground in the Arizona was second nature.

Another face hovered over him, and the Chief felt his mind climbing out of a deep well toward recognition, but he couldn't justify his place in time, and his memory was lost. As hard as he tried, his mind couldn't find the information that would put him here, in this place, at this time. And the feeling that he was paralyzed planted a seed of panic that was taking root. "What happened?" he said weakly, feeling the refreshing sensation of wet terrycloth being dragged over his face. Cool trickles ran over his cheeks, down past his ears, and dripped from the back of his neck.

A black man looked down from what seemed a great height. "That's a good question, Chief," he said. There was a stern quality to his voice, a familiar quality, but the Chief couldn't conjure the name.

The closer face, the one inverted over his, stared into his eyes. "You have a head injury, Chief. You've been unconscious."

His mind couldn't verify that information, but it did explain the searing pain. It also explained why he was unable to move. "Am I paralyzed?" he asked, a flicker of fear invading his voice. He looked up at the face and willed it back into his memory by sheer force. "Doc," he said, almost a question.

The face broke into a smile. "Good man," it said. "I don't think you're paralyzed at all. Wiggle your fingers for me."

The web belts constricted his arms, but his hands were free and he tapped his fingers against his legs.

"Now move your feet."

He couldn't pull his legs apart, but he rocked his feet back and forth with no trouble.

"You're good, Chief."

"But I can't move." He raised his head gingerly and winced at the pain. When he opened his eyes he could see the web belts wrapping his body. "What the hell is this?"

Doc Brede looked up at Sergeant Blackwell. "Yeah, Sergeant. Tell the Chief what this is."

Blackwell checked his watch. He didn't have time for explanations, even if he wanted to provide one. "Let's go. Move it out," he said.

Marines came at the litter from all sides and raised it from the ground. They followed the sergeant, each keeping to an irregular cadence in his own mind, rocking the Chief as though he rode in a mobile hammock.

"Let me up. I can walk." The Chief looked down at his chest and the emptiness there, then tilted his head back so he could see the corpsman traveling at the head of the litter. "What's going on, Doc? Where's my spirit pouch?"

The corpsman poured more water into the towel from his canteen. "What pouch?"

"The one I wear around my neck. Where is it?"

"I don't know, Chief. You didn't have it on you at the LP."

The Chief looked around with a growing panic. "What the hell is going on, Doc?"

"Something happened last night on your LP, Chief. Tanner and the new guy are dead and there's some confusion about how they died. Don't you remember anything?"

The Chief's mind raced through the previous hours, searching for anything that could anchor him to the present one, but they were blank. He feared the void would offer up something that would drop him into a world of hurt far beyond what his head was now providing, but there was nothing. It was a vast and empty expanse of possibilities. He squeezed his hands into fists and strained against the belts. "Turn me loose," he said. He struggled with the restraints, raising his knees and kicking with his bound feet. He spit and cursed. He questioned the parentage of the surrounding Marines and threatened their physical well-being, and he did it in a voice loud enough to frighten birds in an area where remaining inconspicuous was the key to survival, for birds and men.

The Marines carrying him staggered with the violent movement. "Cool it, Chief," one of them said.

He rocked back and forth, ignoring the pain the movement was causing in his head. The Marines were finding it hard to walk and hold onto the litter. The Chief's contortions twisted their wrists and threatened to pull arms out of sockets.

"Hold up," the sergeant said. He tapped Bronsky on the shoulder, holding out his hand. "Give me your weapon," he said.

The radioman looked confused. "Huh?"

"Give me your .45, Marine. Now."

Bronsky removed his pistol and dropped it into the sergeant's hand.

As he took the few steps to where the Marines struggled with the rocking litter, the sergeant examined the weapon and checked the chamber. "Chief," he said. His voice had a hard edge to it that was all business with a promise of finality.

The Chief looked up at the sergeant and the muzzle end of the Colt .45 that was pointed at his face. The barrel opening seemed as huge and black as a tunnel. He could see the sergeant's eyes staring down the sights. They weren't blinking and they weren't friendly. "You can stop what you're doing, or I'll stop you."

Everyone froze, including the Chief. There was an awkward silence while the sergeant's steady hand kept the weapon pointed at a spot between the Chief's eyes.

"People with head injuries get agitated," Doc Brede said. "It doesn't mean anything."

"I'm a little agitated myself, Doc," the sergeant said. He moved the pistol in closer and thumbed the hammer back. "Chief. We're ass deep in the Arizona and I'm not going to let you endanger any more of my people, so you can go easy, or you can go in a bag like Tanner and the new guy. You decide."

The Chief blinked at the .45 barrel's opening, imagining his life disappearing into it, and stopped struggling.

The sergeant lowered the pistol to his side, nodded his head, then fixed the Chief with an icy stare. "You won't get a choice next time," he said and turned away, slowly lowering the hammer on the weapon.

The Chief watched him walk away. "I am one of your people," he said. The words seemed odd coming out of his mouth. It was the first time he had ever said them to someone who wasn't Apache. He realized he had acknowledged the Corps as a tribe. A tribe he belonged to. Since joining the Marines he had always had a difficult time finding a home for his loyalties. Could he have two?

The line moved out again and the corpsman stayed close to the head of the litter. "Be cool, Chief," he said.

"What did I do, Doc?"

"I don't know that you did anything, Chief, and neither does anyone else. But it looks bad." The corpsman nodded toward the bodies being carried ahead. "They were both killed with a knife."

"My knife?"

The corpsman shrugged.

The Chief looked up at the Marines straining to keep the heavy litter moving forward. Sweat poured from their faces. The nylon loops bit into their hands and stretched their arms into twisted cords. But they worked as a team, carrying one of their own. And he knew they would not stop.

"I wouldn't hurt my own people, Doc," the Chief said.

"I know, Chief. Be cool."

Up on the face of the Ong Thu, Lieutenant Diehl moved the rest of the platoon to the LP site and established a perimeter. He stood in the small clearing with Burke and Doc Garver at his side. Pools of blood soaked the ground, and swarms of gnats spiraled over the puddles, swooping in to land on the darker spots, taking what they could of the free meal. The air buzzed with the little opportunists, which stuck to sweaty faces and threatened the dark, inviting openings of noses and ears.

Burke pointed down. "Tanner was lying against the tree, here, and the Chief was next to him."

The lieutenant looked at notes made yesterday and stuffed into the pocket of his map case. "Where was . . . DeLong?" he asked, uncomfortable that he didn't immediately know the name of a Marine under his command, especially one already dead.

Doc Garver indicated the spot. "He was on his back over here." A fresh swarm of insects swirled in a congested flight pattern over the slick ground.

The lieutenant surveyed the clearing, committing it to memory. He might have to provide a detailed account and answer the kind of questions that could satisfy a military court. He wondered what questions the families would ask if they had the chance. The least of all might be: Why did two decades of hope and effort end as a puddle in a nameless patch of jungle on the other side of the world? He was glad he would only be facing court inquiries.

The platoon encircled the LP site and a private first class entered the clearing from the high side. "Laney says it looks like someone came through the bush up there," he said.

The lieutenant looked uphill into the tangle of foliage. The frenetic chatter of birds that had filled the canopy since sunrise was beginning to diminish as the unlimited supply of insects sated their night's fast. "Show me," the lieutenant said, starting upgrade. He was glad to get away from the clearing with its growing population of buzzing feeders and gruesome reminders of Marine lives lost.

They followed the man upward single file and soon came upon Laney crouched in the bush. He pointed to some stalks cleaved off near ground level. "These are fresh," he said, rubbing his thumb over an exposed stump. "Someone came this way recently." A shrill tweet sounded behind a bank of broad leaves, and Laney left the others standing there and went in that direction like a lovesick bird responding to a mate's summons. He returned quickly. "We have a blood trail, sir. Someone made a wide path going up the mountain, and they were bleeding out."

Without waiting for the others the lieutenant dashed off in the direction of the birdcall, driven by the promise of redemption for his platoon. Maybe the weight he had carried around all morning, dragging him down like a five-G force, would be lifted and the shadow of murder that darkened his platoon would vanish in the light of day. He found another Marine standing beside a large, variegated leaf marked with a blood splatter. A wide swath of plants was trampled, and the Marine pointed up the path. "They went that way," he said.

Laney and Burke went where the trampled plants led them, following the trail of dark drips and splotches. The lieutenant was close behind. "Hold up, you two," he said. "We have wounded VC in the bush, and we don't know where. Get your squad up here. Laney, your team is on point." He looked around. "Where the hell is my radio?" From behind Doc Garver came a hesitant voice. "Here, sir." The radioman pushed past the doc.

The lieutenant grabbed the radioman's shoulder strap and pulled him close. "Clyde, as long as you carry that box we're joined at the hip. If I even think about using the radio, you better be close enough to slap the handset into my hand. It that understood?"

"Yes, sir."

"Now get me Blackwell on the horn. I think we should let him know the Chief is in the clear."

"Yes, sir."

≈

The rotors pushing the H-34 westward strobed the morning sun into slices so thin they were indistinguishable to the human eye. The big green machine split the air at a speed far beyond what the grasshopper aerodynamics of the fuselage seemed to suggest possible, and the airspeed scooped turbulence through the open door that whipped the folds of Strader's uniform against his arms and legs. The corporal's rank pins on his collar slapped at his jaw line. He watched the young door gunner leaning back against the front bulkhead, oblivious to the aerial scenery that flashed by the door just inches away. While Strader was aware of being thousands of feet in the air in an awkward machine that from all appearances had no right to be flying, the gunner seemed at home in his office doing his job, the same as he did every day, and the view from the door that twisted Strader's stomach into a knot seemed only more of the same to the younger Marine. He appeared as inured to the sight as any bureaucratic pencil pusher in a high-rise building would be to the view from his office window.

Strader knew when they crossed the Thu Bon that they were headed into the wilds of the Arizona. Just yesterday he was sure that the only way he would see the place again was in his nightmares, but here he was, being dragged back into it as though it were a big, malicious green magnet. He leaned forward, elbows on knees, and stared at the worn surface of the chopper deck. Why was it you were never finished in the Corps? No matter how much you did, there was always one more thing to do. It was like trying to reach a destination by going half the distance to it with every move. If you could cover only half the journey each trip, theoretically you could never arrive. If you couldn't leave until you were done but there was always one more thing to do, you could never leave. It was the kind of conundrum that played with the brain and made for sleepless nights.

The gunner leaned forward and tilted his head like the RCA Victor dog listening to his master's voice. He waved at Strader and pointed at the M60. "We're getting close," he yelled, swinging the door gun to his shoulder. Strader gripped the 60 at the window. He could see the northeastern curve of the Ong Thu range in the distance, pointing its threatening finger in the direction of the Marine base at Phu Loc. He glanced at the door gunner over his shoulder. The Marine caressed his M60 with the casual familiarity of someone who knows his tool intimately, the way a carpenter knows his hammer and a mechanic knows his wrench. He could push the capabilities of his weapon to its limits and, as his marked face showed, beyond.

Strader had never been overly confident in his own skill with the M60. He appreciated the kind of firepower it added to a squad, but it was heavy and hungry for ammunition and took some practice to master. You had to learn to lead your targets and guide the tracers in like they were at the end of a long, flexible rod. Strader had only fired the gun from ground positions, and he was sure the difficulty was compounded when it was mounted on a moving helicopter. He imagined it would be like shooting skeet while riding on the back of another clay pigeon. He hoped it wouldn't be necessary to pull the trigger.

The villages of Dai Khuong and Phu Loi 3 passed below, and glints of sunlight ricocheted from the lake beyond Nam An. Just beyond Phu Loi 3, a stream of tracers rose up in front of the helicopter, reaching blindly for the heavens, waiting patiently for the machine to fly into them. But the flyers had seen that tactic many times before. The pilot banked sharply to port, increased speed, and then leveled out. The maneuver evaded the streaming bullet trap, and before the shooter had time to correct his aim, the helicopter covered enough distance to make it no longer a viable target. The sudden pitch of the deck froze Strader's blood, and he was sure that his grip on the bulkhead was damaging either his hands or the fuselage. He had to force his eyes open to see if the gunner was still in the compartment. The door gunner leaned casually against the front bulkhead looking at Strader with a toothy grin. He held his hands out like wings and mimicked the radical path the helicopter had just taken. He laughed, but the sound was lost in the engine noise and the ringing in Strader's ears.

The squad of Marines at the foot of the mountain, using the pilots' radio frequency, directed them to the edge of the trees where green smoke marked the LZ. While the copilot kept up a running dialogue with the squad, the pilot banked the helicopter toward the green clouds coming from the open ground just beyond the tree line.

The big grasshopper swooped in, and with the deft manipulations the pilot swung the tail around and set the machine down with the wide starboard door facing the mountain. Before the struts took the full weight of the helicopter, Marines were moving out of the trees, bent over their loads. The gunner watched them emerge, struggling with the bodies wrapped in green, and his hand tightened on the grip of his M60 until the knuckles were white. The post sight at the end of the 60's barrel moved slowly across the face of the mountain, sweeping the thousand invisible places where malevolent eyes could be watching. His finger hovered over the trigger, waiting for the first sight of a muzzle flash.

The first group of Marines reached the helicopter and slid a body in a poncho liner through the door. Strader abandoned his gun and pulled the body away from the opening, making room for the ones coming. He knew from the way the Marines handled the body that there was no reason to be especially gentle. He recognized the faces that turned and ran with stooped bodies. He wondered what familiar face was hidden inside the poncho. Immediately, the second group moved in and Corporal Middleton helped Franklin lift Tanner's body onto the chopper deck. Strader could see there was no undue care taken with this body either, and he helped the gunner pull it unceremoniously into the shadows. Corporal Middleton stayed at the opening. "Hey! Our corpsman needs that litter," he yelled above the noise. The gunner rolled Tanner's body onto its side, and Strader jerked the litter free. He crushed it into a bundle and handed it to the waiting corporal. "Here. Don't say I never gave you anything," Strader said.

Middleton stood dumbfounded, his mouth hanging open. "Reach. What the hell are you doing here? Are you out of your damn mind?"

Strader watched the third group moving in with their litter. He could see from the attention they paid that this one held live cargo. He shrugged his shoulders. "It wasn't my idea, Carl," he said. "What's happened here?"

Now it was Middleton's turn to shrug.

The third litter arrived feet first, and Middleton stepped aside so it could be turned. Doc Brede strained to set the Chief's shoulders onto the deck while others threw bundles of equipment in after him. Three packs and the Chief's cartridge belt with the stag-horn knife hit the deck along with three M16s. "Look who's here," Middleton yelled, slapping Doc's shoulder and pointing into the compartment.

Doc Brede looked up as Strader reached for one of the litter straps. "Reach. Are you insane? Lieutenant Diehl is going to tear you a new asshole."

"Where is he?" Strader said, looking expectantly toward the tree line.

"He's not here, but I am," Sergeant Blackwell said, stepping up to the helicopter with Bronsky in tow. "The only one who has no business being here is you."

"I couldn't agree more. But the first sergeant didn't give me a choice."

"Gantz sent someone with three days left in-country on a joyride into the Arizona?" Sergeant Blackwell said, shaking his head. "He must be crazy."

"You won't get any argument from me," Strader said.

He knelt down so he could talk to Blackwell without so much volume. "Why is the Chief restrained?"

Before the sergeant could respond, Bronsky pushed his face into the opening. "Don't let him loose, Reach," he said, and pointed at the bodies in the shadows. "He did that."

The Chief raised his knees and kicked his bound feet at Bronsky's head but fell short.

"See?" Bronsky said.

The Chief lay back and closed his eyes as though the kick had taken more out of him than he had to give.

The copilot stuck his head out and whistled down at the Marines like a bird from a high perch. They all looked up. He tapped the face of his wristwatch with an anxious finger indicating it was too long to be on the ground in the Arizona. Sergeant Blackwell gave him a thumbs-up sign and pulled his people away from the chopper. They ducked from the rotor wash as the engine speed increased, and the bulky machine pulled up from the valley as though it was sucked into the air by a giant vacuum. It banked to port showing its underbelly and headed away from the Ong Thu.

～

Sau's little band of NVA moved across the face of the mountain at a runner's clip, following the new vanguard carrying his AK in one hand and the shovel in the other. His brown legs churned up the ground; the others, already worn out from transporting Binh's body, felt they were in a footrace and losing badly, but they pushed until their lungs burned. They knew the only thing that was important was rejoining Nguyen, and they would run until their chests exploded to make that happen.

Far ahead, Nguyen knew that Sau would drive his little group to follow his path like wolves on the scent and could overtake his group within the hour—if they weren't intercepted by the Americans. This prospect caused Nguyen some concern. Most of Sau's group were unarmed, and clashing with even a small enemy unit would be fatal—and the Americans could be anywhere. They could leapfrog ahead or come from above; they could drop a blocking force in Nguyen's path while a larger unit came up from behind; they could decimate the NVA with artillery or strafe them from the air. And the only thing that prevented any of this from happening was that the location of Nguyen's unit was unknown and would remain that way as long as they kept moving.

If he could just get through this day and night and cross the Vu Gia before daylight, things would be better. They would be out of the Marine base's region, and while the obligation to catch them would transfer to other units, Nguyen was confident he could fade into the countryside.

Yesterday he had warned his people that today would be long and difficult, but he saw now that his threats did not begin to approach the problems this day could bring. The topography of the Ong Thu was becoming so steep that it slowed their progress to a crawl, and Nguyen decided to angle their path in a gradual descent toward the valley floor where the terrain was more cooperative. His map indicated that the Ong Thu swung to the east well beyond the marshy lake, and his exhausted and overloaded unit would have difficulty climbing over the razorback that blocked their way. If they were to reach Minh Tan 1 by midnight, they would have to cross open ground north of the lake and skirt the geological roadblocks that gradually spent themselves at the village of Phu Phong 3. From there they could follow a tributary straight into Minh Tan.

Nguyen was stooped under the load of two RPGs with rockets, two rounds for the recoilless rifle, and an extra pack and roll. He looked like a vagabond merchant in dire need of a cart. Pham and Truong staggered up with the heavy machine gun crushing their shoulders. They were bareheaded, and streams of perspiration plastered their hair to their skulls. Nguyen stepped aside and let them pass. "Do you feel you are making an adequate contribution yet, Pham?"

Pham tilted his head in Nguyen's direction. Words bubbled up to his lips and he imagined unloading them on their arrogant *dai uy,* but that would take breath, and the heavy gun had a prior claim on all of his air, now and in the foreseeable future. The two young men stumbled on, exchanging glances filled with both the pain they felt and the pain they wished.

Nguyen watched them go, feeling a sense of satisfaction in their discomfort. He enjoyed seeing the privileged bourgeoisie get a taste of the labors of war. But he also felt a nagging spark of pride in their efforts, and he couldn't begrudge them the honor of having asked for the taste. He looked up as tiger shrikes flitted through the canopy trading chattering screeches with trogons vying for a swarm of beetles just in from the valley floor. The treetops were alive with the aerial jousting.

The NVA maneuvered their heavy weapons away from the steep slopes and across the undulating foothills until vertical shafts of light from open ground penetrated the tree line, illuminating the jungle floor. The marsh that led to the western rim of the lake was just visible from there. Clumps of razor grass sprouted from the soft, black soil, and barricades of bamboo shafts marked the contours of the shoreline.

Nguyen wobbled on unsteady legs to the head of the column and stayed there until the northern edge of the lake was past. He signaled a halt, and the men behind him sank as though their loads had driven them into the earth like tent stakes. They let the weapons roll off their shoulders, and each man lay gasping for air while his heart pounded against the inside of his ribcage. Nguyen slipped out of his shoulder harness and eased his pack board to the ground. While the others seemed to be drifting into a vegetative state, he scooped up his AK and moved to the edge of the tree line. He stuck his head out and looked north.

The huge expanse of the Ong Thu that defined the western boundary of the An Hoa Valley might have gone on indefinitely, but the Song Vu Gia forced it into an eastern dogleg, where it dissolved into the misty distance. From where he stood, Nguyen could see the direct line across the clear valley floor to where the razorback melted back into the earth. The terrain looked solid. They could wade through the low grass meeting little more obstruction than the occasional dry paddy dyke. But it was open ground—a lot of unprotected open ground. After nightfall, he would not have given it a second thought. Even in the fuller phases of the moon he would have set off across the valley with the full column, but in daylight they would have to move in groups. It was a calculated risk, but he didn't like the other options. He could wait for nightfall and hope the pursuers didn't track them down; a bet he knew he couldn't win. Or he could continue fighting the foothills all the way around the Ong Thu's dogleg with no chance of reaching the river crossing by midnight, forcing them to wait through the day tomorrow near Minh Tan 1 for night to fall again without being detected. Or he could run the diagonal in daylight. These were the calculations forcing him to choose the lesser of three evils, but the term "lesser" was problematic because the differences between the three were negligible in terms of risk. Each held a possibility, if not a likelihood, of disaster. He couldn't wait, but it was dangerous to go on.

Nguyen carefully removed his binoculars from their case and scanned the open ground, being sure to stay far enough back in the tree line so no glare would reflect from the lenses. Everything looked quiet and inviting, but the Americans had the resources to change that with blinding speed; and if they did, he would have to provide assistance for anyone caught in the open. While he turned the possibilities over in his mind, Pham came up behind him and looked over his shoulder. Nguyen lowered the binoculars. "We're going to cross here," he said without turning to look at Pham. "We'll go in four shifts and move quickly."

"I volunteer to go first," Pham said, rubbing his shoulders in a futile attempt to massage away the pain.

Nguyen turned slowly. "Why, because you are not afraid?"

Pham's shoulders were stooped and his face was drawn and haggard. He'd had little sleep last night, and there would be no rest today and none expected tonight, at least not until they crossed the river. He stared at the open ground that seemed to go on forever, a sea of brown grasses undulating in the morning breeze like the surface of an ocean. "It's a long way across. I think I am afraid."

"Good," Nguyen said, a little more harshly than he intended. "Anyone spotted out there could become target practice for the Americans. He would be helpless."

Pham nodded and tried not to lick his lips so Nguyen wouldn't know that fear had drawn the moisture from his mouth.

"Since I need someone to provide help for the helpless, you will not be going first. In fact, since I have use for the heavy machine gun you have been carrying, you will in all likelihood be one of the last to cross." Nguyen waited for an objection, but none was forthcoming. "This is no favor, going last. The first to cross will have the advantage of surprise. All those after that will be following a known path. Being predictable here is not a good thing." Nguyen could see that Pham felt he was being rebuked but was too tired to put up an argument. "Your group will use the Chinese gun to provide security for those in the open." He wrapped the binoculars in a cloth and slipped them into the padded case. "At least by going last you will have more time to rest."

"But the gun . . . I have no experience—" Pham started to say.

"You will not be firing the machine gun," Nguyen interrupted. "You will do what the gunner tells you to do, then help carry the weapon across. With any luck you will not be asked to make a heroic gesture."

While they spoke, two of their men leapt up from their positions at the tail of the column and aimed their weapons back along the trail. Something was moving fast back there, and the whole exhausted unit scrambled from where they lay to find cover they could defend. Nguyen and Pham ran toward them as far as a fallen tree, then dropped behind the trunk, using it as a bench rest for their AKs. They pressed their cheeks against the rough wood of the butt stocks and followed their sights back into the foothills. Pham's shoulders felt raw and bruised, and he knew the AK's recoil was going to be painful. He hoped he would not wince and spoil his aim.

When the first visible target waved his shovel over his head, the tension rushed from everyone. Pham turned his face away and rested his head on his forearm. Nguyen was over the tree and running back to his unit as Sau and Co and the rest flooded out of the undergrowth. They were met with wide grins and much slapping of backs. Canteens were offered. Arms were thrown around shoulders. Cleared sitting spots were contributed. Nguyen felt his spirits rise as he watched his most trusted men mix back into the column, but he was startled at their appearance. Streaks of dried blood stained their arms and legs and sloughed from their bodies in grotesque slabs. Blood-drenched clothing had dried stiff and hard.

Sau smiled when he saw Nguyen coming.

"It went well?" Nguyen said, both wanting and not wanting to reach out and touch Sau.

Sau tilted his head and looked away. "Not for Binh," he said.

"He honored his country and his family," Nguyen said, knowing it sounded hollow.

An awkward silence followed while each man seemed to search for something meaningful to say, but found nothing.

Finally, Nguyen looked back along the broken path. "How much time do we have?" he asked.

"There was no sign of anyone pursuing us, but we moved very fast. Just because we didn't see them doesn't mean they aren't coming. I expected helicopters over us by now."

Nguyen looked up. "That is a puzzle. It seems you have confused them somehow. I don't know how or why, but I'm thankful anyway."

Truong stood beside the Chinese machine gun adjusting the leafy branches lashed to the barrel. Co took another swallow from a canteen then passed it on. He held his hand out to Truong. "I have something for you," he said, dropping the beaded leather bag into Truong's hand.

The figure stitched into the face of the bag looked like a dancing kachina doll. Truong looked up at Co then back at the bag. "Indian?" he asked.

Co shrugged his crusty shoulders without answering.

Truong held the bag by the cord, letting it swing freely. "One of them was an Indian," he said. Sadness clouded his face, and he looked at Co with genuine pain in his eyes.

"He was just another American in a uniform." Co paused, clenching his jaws. "And he killed Binh."

Co could see the battle of competing emotions on Truong's face. Binh had been a comrade. They had shared hardships and meals and slept under each other's protection, but in all of the western novels he loved, Truong's sympathies were always with the Indians. Co began to turn away, and Truong grabbed his blood-streaked arm. He held the bag up and squeezed it tight. "Thank you," he said.

Nguyen stepped past and pointed along the tree line. "Co, take the heavy gun north about one hundred meters and find some high ground where you can cover the valley. We'll be crossing here in groups."

Pham and Truong hoisted the heavy gun back onto their bruised shoulders as Co began gathering his personal equipment from the pile laid at his feet, strapping his pack on over the dried streaks of Binh's blood.

The second Bronsky switched the Prick 25 to the platoon's frequency, the handset came alive. "Yes, sir. I was on the air tac with Highball. No, sir. They just lifted off. Yes, sir. Here he is." He turned the handset over to Sergeant Blackwell.

"This is Four," Blackwell said. "Yes, sir. Yes, sir." He gave Bronsky a puzzled look then turned away. "Most ricky-tick, sir. Roger, out." He returned the handset to Bronsky without looking at him. "Franklin, get your team on point. We gotta get back fast. The platoon is on the scent of something and they don't wanna wait." He grabbed Bronsky by the radio's shoulder strap and pulled him close. "You get on the horn to Highball and tell them to cut the Chief loose. The gooks hit the LP and the lieutenant thinks the Chief got a piece of one of them."

Shock and confusion worked in tandem to create a dumbfounded look on Bronsky's face. "You're shittin' me," he said.

"I wouldn't shit a first-class turd like you, Bronsky. Now get your ass in gear and do it on the run."

The evac detail moved off at a fast pace, retracing their path from the Ong Thu.

The helicopter gained some altitude heading east when the pilot banked steeply to port, running north along the face of the mountain. It was wise to avoid the anxious trigger fingers around Phu Loi 3 and give the village a wide berth by sticking to the contours of the mountain. The pitch sent Strader staggering over the bodies to his gun position, and he leaned forward against the bulkhead and looked through the gun port directly down onto the valley floor. He glanced back. The gunner was sitting with one hand on the M60 and gazing casually at the expanse of sky that filled the opening in front of him. Strader knew that he could never respond to these radical aerial maneuvers with that kind of nonchalance, and if he was ever lucky enough to set his feet back on the ground in the world, he would never go any higher than a stepladder.

When the deck leveled out, Strader could see the copilot looking down on them, adjusting the mouthpiece on his radio. He was nodding when he drew his head back, and when his face returned, the gunner raised his right arm and stuck his thumb in the air for the copilot to see.

The helicopter increased speed, climbing all the while, with the big engine pounding the air in the compartment. Strader looked down on the bodies at his feet. The air currents whipped the fabric of the poncho liner wildly, and a covering flap folded back revealing a face he couldn't identify. He knew that faces in death sometimes had only the weakest resemblance to the owner's living countenance—the pallor, the complete lack of muscle tone—but until now he had always been able to see through the mask and find the living face in his memory. But he couldn't place this one. Then he noticed the boots and the tucked roll of the cuffs and knew this was one of the FNGs. The eyes were partially closed and the lower pigmented orbs of the irises stared blankly at the overhead. This was a face Strader had seen only once with a name he never knew. The teeth inside the slack mouth showed dark stains, and Strader winced at the ghastly wound hiding below the chin. The short tour, he thought. Going in and coming out on the same helicopter. If people ever thought that if you were going to die, it was better to get it done early in the tour, they hadn't thought it through.

The massive torque of the rotors shook the bodies, and he recognized Tanner's face as vibration made the back of his lifeless head beat a rapid tattoo on the deck. The casualty tag tied to his shoelace flapped in the turbulence like a pennant. Looking at both bodies, he somehow couldn't reconcile the deaths with the Chief. In his experience, no Marine had ever killed another Marine on purpose. There had been accidents during contact at night, but despite blustering threats and promises, no one had ever actually followed through and committed a murder. He knew the Chief's reputation for being a hard-ass was well deserved, but he didn't think he would kill fellow Marines. He saw that the Chief was staring at him as though he was reading his thoughts. Their eyes locked and the Chief shook his head slowly.

A peripheral movement caught his eye as the gunner waved to get his attention. The helicopter was climbing under load and the noise filled the compartment, drowning the door gunner's voice, and he was forced to watch as the young Marine pantomimed twisting something and pulling it apart. When Strader's face lacked any sign of comprehension, the young Marine pointed at his own belt and then to the Chief. Whatever message the sign language was meant to communicate, it wasn't getting through. All that registered was the door gunner's frustration; the rest was pure puzzle.

Just as the gunner was about to launch another hand puppet show, the helicopter pitched forward and began to lose altitude. Strader felt his body weight vanish and began to lose his physical connection with the deck. The gunner pressed a hand to the side of his helmet and listened, then grabbed the M60, pulling it to his shoulder. Strader had been at a loss to understand the gunner's miming, but the reaction he saw now was perfectly clear, and he grabbed the grip of his own M60 at the portal.

The copilot was the first to see the four figures crossing the valley, bisecting the crook in the elbow of the northern Ong Thu, black specks moving against a beige background. As the helicopter drew closer, both pilots could see that the four were burdened with weapons and were running as fast as their loads would allow. The pilots were sure the enemy could hear the helicopter coming by now, but it was obvious they weren't stopping.

At a little over nine hundred feet, the two pilots could see the four fleeing Vietnamese clearly over the round nose of the fuselage, and the copilot kept up a running dialogue with communications in An Hoa describing the four and their weaponry.

A recent command decision made it necessary for anyone in the 5th Marines TAOR who wanted to fire on enemy sighted to ask permission first. Even when time was a crucial factor, a call to command had to be made, and while a responsible officer—or one willing to give permission—was being located, the opportunity to fire was often lost. Clearly identified enemy with weapons usually prompted those in the rear to grant permission a little quicker, but in situations where delays could be deadly, those in the field found the rule absurd and frustrating.

But Highball wasn't asking for permission to fire. Their intention was to identify those on the ground and place their movements on the map so other Marine elements could be brought into play, leaving Highball to ferry their casualties to the BAS. The copilot reported numerous RPGs along with AKs, an RPD machine gun, and what looked like a mortar. He calculated their distance from the sports team thrust point christened New York Yankees and estimated their path would eventually intersect Nam An 5.

The pilot dipped the nose and swung the helicopter in a starboard bank, showing the open door on the right side a full view of the ground. Strader held onto the bulkhead and grabbed the corner rung of the Chief's litter so it wouldn't defeat centrifugal force and slide out. The Chief dug his heels in and pushed, trying to inch away from the opening, but the slippery floor fought his efforts. Strader pulled with all his might. When the gunner caught sight of the four men running on the valley floor, he instinctively brought his weapon up, leaned his cheek close to the feed cover, and squeezed the trigger. The gun shook on its mount, and an arc of spent brass flew into the air while the weapon spewed black links onto the deck that danced like frantic spiders before finding the door and falling into space. Most of his bullet strikes were lost in the grass, but a few chunks of earth jumped into the air, providing his targets with an impetus to run faster, and he swung the barrel, letting the tracer rounds guide him along the path in the grass until he caught up to the last runner. The man pitched forward in a flurry of arms and legs and an AK-47 cartwheeled away like a discarded toy.

Immediately, the underbelly of the helicopter began taking hits, although the enemy runners hadn't even broken stride. Heavy rounds punched through the deck and disappeared through the overhead as though they were headed somewhere else and the helicopter wasn't even a serious obstacle. The strikes sounded like hammer blows coming in rapid succession. One came in under the new guy in the poncho liner, tossing him up with a jolt to land against the starboard bulkhead. The poncho liner flew free and writhed about the compartment like something alive before snagging itself on one of the jagged bullet holes.

Another burst of hits slammed the helicopter, and Strader could see frantic movement in the cockpit. The copilot was now flying an evasive action, trying desperately to lose the green tracers reaching out from the jungle with deadly accuracy. He swung the nose into the sun and increased the rpms in an effort to get distance and altitude, but a loud bang staggered the helicopter and sent the tail into a spin. The entire machine vibrated violently. While the copilot fought for control, more rounds struck the helicopter. Strader could see daylight through holes in the bulkheads on both sides.

The tail seemed determined to loop around itself again and again, and Strader knew the tail rotor was damaged or gone and that this big green machine was going down. It wasn't a question of whether the helicopter would crash or not, but how bad the crash would be, and only the skill and luck of the pilot could determine that. Above the noise of the machine shaking itself apart, Strader heard an insistent voice. "Reach! *Reach*!" the Chief screamed with all the force his lungs could muster. He also knew the helicopter was going down, and the constricting straps made him completely helpless. "*Reach*!" he screamed again.

Across the deck, the gunner lay slumped on his side with one foot hanging out of the opening. His helmet banged spasmodically against the forward bulkhead and rivulets of blood from under his body drew erratic lines on the deck following the dictates of wind and inertia.

Strader fought the vertigo that was stealing what little stability he had and grabbed the litter end, pulling it until the Chief's entire body was lying on top of Tanner. Their eyes met again, and Strader hoped that his weren't revealing the level of fear he felt. In contrast, the Chief's stare seemed to have a purpose. It was steady and intense, as if he was trying to commit Strader's face to memory, as though it was the last face he would see and he wanted to carry it with him into the next world.

The Chief's look had a calming effect on Strader, clearing his mind. There was no benefit to panic. He had to assume they would survive the landing. If he assumed wrong, it didn't matter, but if he was right, they would have to get away from the helicopter. He grabbed his M14 and pulled up one of the backpacks that had been tossed about since they left the ground. The Chief's web belt was near, and he looped it over his shoulder.

In all the dozens of helicopter lifts he had experienced in the last year, his greatest fear was that the one he was in would fall out of the sky or be shot down. One of the most profound reliefs he had felt yesterday after reaching An Hoa was that that fear would never be realized. Now here he was, living the nightmare. By all rights he should be back at the base picking up his laundry and wondering what the chow hall menu would be. Instead, he was riding a crippled machine full of the dead and dying in an out-of-control spiral to the ground.

The copilot struggled with the controls. The rudder pedals were of no use, and he tried to use the forward speed to stretch the glide. All he could do was try to keep the wheels facing down and auto rotate to the valley floor. He worked at the throttle, slowing the spin and keeping the nose up. Finally he lowered the collective at his side; without lift, the helicopter dropped like a stone. At the last second he increased the blade pitch in an attempt to cushion the landing, but the spin caused the helicopter to hit hard on the right strut, collapsing it and pitching the machine to starboard. The huge blades struck the ground with tremendous force, sending shattered chunks spinning into the air and leaving the jagged stumps to beat at the earth until the rotor hub finally stopped turning. The 34 lay like a fallen beast in a steaming cloud of its own making.

The port strut held the body up, cocking the angle of the fuselage so the deck was a slippery incline to the open doorway. Everyone in the compartment, living or dead, bounced on impact and slammed against the new guy's body on the starboard bulkhead. The odor of fuel oil and freshly turned earth filled Strader's nostrils while he tried to orient himself. The Chief's weight was pinning him in the corner, and when he tried pushing him away, the Chief's groans turned into curses in an incomprehensible language. Strader crawled free and climbed to the opening. The jungle's edge was only a few hundred feet away, and no firing was coming from it. A loosely formulated plan began to develop in Strader's mind that included getting into those trees.

The copilot's voice drifted down from the cockpit. He was giving the downed chopper's position as two points west of the Dodgers thrust point, all the while trying to get the pilot's unconscious body free of his shoulder harness. Three figures in black pajamas with AK-47s were running toward the helicopter for all they were worth. "Get away from the chopper," the copilot yelled, pulling his helmet off and dropping it. "Hostiles are on the way. You don't have much time."

The Chief was wriggling toward the opening with all the speed and agility of an earthworm. "Reach," he said. "Cut me loose."

The Chief's cartridge belt with the big stag-horn knife was still looped over Strader's forearm, and he drew the blade and slipped it under the web belt buckled across the Chief's thighs, the blade tip an inch and a slip from a castration. He pulled up hard, and the razor edge parted the ribbed layers like they were made of paper. He repeated the process with the chest belt. The Chief pushed himself up on his elbows, but his head swam and he rolled back.

"Come on, Chief. We have to go," Strader said. He retrieved the backpack from the jump seat where it had landed and looked around for his rifle.

The Chief held his hand out. "Give me my knife," he said.

Strader hesitated, looking down at the big blade in his hand.

The Chief sat up, found Strader's loose rifle, and pulled it across his lap. "Give it to me," he said.

Strader held out the knife and waited until they made a mutual exchange. While he shoved a magazine into the rifle and jacked a round into the chamber, the Chief slipped his knife between his ankles and severed his knotted bootlaces. With his legs now free he got onto his knees and crawled to the opening. When his head reached daylight, a wave of nausea washed over him and he dumped the contents of his stomach into the grass beside the helicopter, retching until the pain in his head turned into starbursts behind his eyes.

Strader got a hand under the Chief's arm and lifted him to his feet so that they stood on the ground with their heads protruding into the tilted helicopter. As the unstable Chief staggered, Strader pushed or pulled to keep him upright, lifting hard when the Chief's knees started to buckle. "Can you make it to the trees?" he asked.

The trees were a distant blur, and the more the Chief tried to focus on them, the more the overwhelming dizziness tried to turn his stomach inside out. He swallowed hard.

"Can you do it, Chief?"

The Chief wavered like a tall stalk in the wind, his red-rimmed eyes giving him the look of a drunk after a three-day bender. He wanted to answer but couldn't trust his stomach enough to open his mouth, so he just nodded.

AK rounds began striking the face of the helicopter, and the distant cracks of their reports echoed against the Ong Thu. "Get moving," the copilot screamed. "I'm right behind you."

The two Marines ducked past the shattered remnants of the main rotor, and Strader half-dragged, half-carried the Chief toward the tree line. The toes of the Chief's boots dragged in the grass like a blunt plow as Strader cajoled him with a steady stream of pleas and threats, all the while moving at an angle that kept the smashed aircraft between them and the shooters. The Chief pressed a hand to the battle dressing on his head but kept his legs churning at an awkward gait.

After what seemed to Strader to be the exertion of a marathon, they reached the trees and slipped into the shadows. As soon as Strader released his grip, the Chief sank to the ground with his head cradled in his hands. Gasping for air, Strader looked back at the empty open space they just crossed. "Where the hell are the pilots?"

⁓

Nguyen had known before the first group to cross had covered three hundred meters that there was going to be trouble. He could hear the pulsating thump of a helicopter coming up the valley. His men were already well beyond the distance where they had a chance to get back into the trees before the helicopter was within sight, and he knew they wouldn't try now because if they did, they would draw the helicopter to the main unit's position. They would keep heading away. Their only option was to present as difficult a moving target as possible, and their only hope was Co and the heavy machine gun. Nguyen ran toward the gun's position, but he couldn't run far enough quickly enough, so he stopped and cupped his hands to his mouth and yelled as loudly as he could: "*Ma'y bay truc thang.*"

Co's group already had the feet of the gun's tripod firmly anchored on a small mound with a clear view of the valley. Pham and Truong watched as Sau swung the lid on the tin ammunition box open and drew out the belt and Co positioned the rim of the first round in the jaws of the feed carrier.

Truong stood upright and looked back toward the main unit. "That was Nguyen's voice. He says there is a helicopter."

Co reached under the rear of the weapon and jerked the operating handle all the way back, then shoved it forward again with a clatter of meshing metal parts. "I hear it," he said, flipping up the vernier sight in the rear and peering down the long, ribbed barrel to the mule-ear front sight at the flash suppressor. He grabbed the two spade-handle grips and swung the barrel up, checking the elevation. "We're ready," he said.

"What can I do?" Pham said, feeling like a useless bystander.

Co pointed to the edge of the tree line. "Go there and tell me when you see the helicopter and when our people have been spotted."

Pham ran the few steps to the rim of the valley, where the entire skyline was visible. He could hear the vibrating thuds the big helicopter engine sent ahead of itself, but it took a few seconds before the green spot in the sky came into view. It was climbing fast and following the shape of the Ong Thu. "I see it," he said, not trying to hide the excitement in his voice.

Co dug his heels in and made an adjustment to the rear sight by sheer estimation.

Pham watched the spot in the sky, checked the progress of the crossing, then looked back to the sky. The helicopter kept climbing, well beyond the eastern edge of the lake. It seemed very high.

Pham had never flown in an aircraft of any kind, but he imagined it would be very difficult to see small things on the ground from that height. He had once taken a trip north of Hanoi to Tam Dao to visit the three peaks. Most everyone wanted to see the stone table on Thach Ban or the waterfall on Thien Thi, but Pham wanted to climb Phu Nghia because it was the highest of the three and because, with a name like Bearer of Good Things, it must certainly bring him good fortune. He remembered how oddly cold it was nearly 1,500 feet up and that recognizing small landmarks from that height was nearly impossible. He hoped the Americans were having that same problem now, and that they were cold too. Suddenly, the nose dropped and the helicopter went into a steep dive, and Pham knew his wishes had not been granted.

"It's attacking," Pham yelled as the aircraft swooped in a wide arc like an awkward bird and showed its underbelly to the mountain. A lethal stream of bullets rained down on the four runners, and Co pressed the trigger on the SGM with his thumbs and held it down. The big gun shook like it was possessed. Co twisted his body and forced the long barrel to follow the path of the helicopter until the glowing tracers were striking the bottom between the wheels. He could see the bullets hitting the target. The helicopter suddenly changed its angle, and Co fired into the left side. When it started to swing away again he heard the *bang* and *swoosh* of a rocket-propelled grenade being fired from somewhere near Nguyen's location. It seemed foolish to Co that Nguyen would give away his position for a long shot with a grenade, but when it hit the tail at the angle that swept up to the rear blades, he made a mental note to tease Nguyen about his incredible luck.

Pham was a little forward of Co, and his ears were ringing from the report of the big gun. He could see the rounds hitting the helicopter, and he was awed by Co's skill with such an old weapon. The unexpected sound of the RPG being fired had made him duck and had put his nerves on edge. But when the explosion followed, he could barely restrain himself from running into the valley and shaking his fists at the big machine with its mortal wound. He watched it spin and waver in the air. He could hear the engine increasing and slowing as the spin carried it out of control to the north. It got quiet in the last seconds, then twisted into the ground past the bend in the mountain and rolled onto its side.

Co stopped firing and let the barrel drop. White clouds rose into the trees from the steaming weapon, and Vo ducked down to see how many loops of the belt remained in the tin box.

"It's down," Pham said, pointing with the barrel of his AK. "Shouldn't we go after them?"

Co opened the top of the machine gun and checked the feed. He seemed unaffected by events. He closed the top and locked it down. "This is our responsibility," he said, patting the hot gun. "Nguyen knows how to command." As proof, he pointed into the valley in front of their position where Hoang Li and two others were running by, heading for the helicopter.

S trader watched from his position at the edge of the jungle and knew that no one else would be coming from the helicopter. He stretched out on the ground in a prone position with his legs splayed, propped on his elbows, and pulled the M14 butt plate into his shoulder. He wrapped the sling around his left arm and drew a sight picture from under a sagging branch laden with thick leaves. Though the distance wasn't great, the shot would be difficult. His breathing was coming in gasps, and his heart was beating like a jackhammer. Every breath and heartbeat altered his aim and magnified the deviation. If he was going to shoot, it would have to be done quickly, holding his breath while willing his heart to calm just long enough to squeeze the trigger. If he was lucky, his first shot would have some precision, but after that it would be all general direction with little chance of suppressing any fire coming back his way.

Strader watched as three Vietnamese in black crept around the nose of the helicopter, rifles raised. He could see the tall magazine pouches strapped to their bodies and the undulating brims on their canvas hats, their matching canvas hats. It seemed odd to him. There was no coordination of uniforms among the Viet Cong, at least not the village militias or regional troops. There was rarely even any consistency in their weapons. Their ubiquitous *non la* conical hats and collarless shirts and dark shorts were the national dress in rural areas. The VC main forces were better equipped but still kept the look of peasant farmers just in from the paddies. But these three were trying very hard to look like VC, and the hair on the back of his neck confirmed what he already suspected. They were NVA. And the NVA did not move in small units.

One stayed by the nose while the other two moved around the truncated rotors to the starboard opening, which was leaning sharply into the ground. The jungle boot on the door gunner's leg was still visible at the hatch. The two seemed hesitant to show themselves at the opening, and Strader watched while they worked out an angle of approach, one from the front and one from the rear. He drew a bead on the one by the nose. He was the one closest to cover. In two steps he could be behind the nose and out of sight. The other two would have to scramble for safety, giving him time to place as many shots as he could into their exposed position. At the top of the next gasp he choked off his air and focused through the rear peep sight on the NVA standing by the martini glass with olive and bubbles painted on the helicopter's nose, perching him on the sight blade at the end of his barrel. His index finger put pressure on the trigger. He was within an ounce of tripping the hammer spring when a hand grabbed his pant leg and tugged. He looked back at the Chief's bandaged face and bloodshot eyes. He could see that the crash had added a split lip and bloody nose to the earlier injury. "You're ruining my aim, Chief."

"You don't want to shoot now, Reach," the Chief said. "We should wait."

"Are you shittin' me?"

"Gunships will be coming," the Chief said, wiping a trickle of blood from his upper lip with his forearm. "I don't think the dinks know we're here. We just have to be cool."

"We'll be passing up a chance for a little payback."

"I'd rather have a lot of payback, and the gunships will bring that."

Strader pointed toward the helicopter. "Look at them, Chief. They aren't VC. There's an NVA unit here somewhere, and those bastards are part of it."

"So, on your last day in-country you want to take on the NVA? Just you and me? Call me crazy, but I think we should wait."

"I've got two days and a wake-up."

"Oh. Well that's different. After we destroy the NVA, you'll have all day tomorrow to rest up for your trip. Don't be a damned fool. We should wait for help."

Strader looked over his rifle sights again, pressing his cheek against the wooden stock. "I didn't think you'd be someone who would want to be rescued by the cavalry."

The Chief spit out a bloody wad of mucus. "If my head wasn't pounding so much I'd make sure you'd have to check your shit pile tomorrow if you wanted to see your teeth again."

Strader kept a steady aim. "One hour ago I was in the rear getting ready to catch the freedom bird. Now, thanks to you, I'd consider myself lucky to see my teeth smiling back at me from tomorrow morning's dump because that would mean I *had* a tomorrow morning."

"If you pull that trigger, we can both forget about tomorrow."

"Chief. The prisoner doesn't get a vote."

"Who's a prisoner?"

"You are. You're my prisoner. I was sent to escort you back to An Hoa. I'm responsible for you. You're the reason I'm here."

"But I didn't do anything, Reach."

Strader looked back. There was pain in the Chief's face, and it was more than physical pain. "Right, Chief. They were sending you back gift-wrapped for the fun of it."

The Chief grabbed a fistful of Strader's pant cuff. "They were wrong. They don't know what happened." Releasing Strader's cuff, he cupped the battle dressing tied to his head. "I can't remember, but I know I wouldn't kill Tanner and the new guy."

"You know, do you? You were going to shoot me yesterday."

The Chief looked away. Something familiar tickled at his brain, and his thoughts were frantically searching the black spot in his mind, looking for that spark of memory. "I was?"

Strader looked back to the valley. The two NVA at the side of the helicopter flanked the door and crept closer with cautious moves. The one by the nose stood at the ready. It was obvious that they were unaware that anyone had moved clear of the crash. The one coming from the tail could see into the opening and unleashed a small burst from his AK into the door gunner's body. The other two ducked instinctively.

Strader pulled his rifle tight and took serious aim. Anger welled, and the passion of it guided his finger to the trigger.

"What's happening?" the Chief asked, pulling himself into a position where he might see.

"They're pissing me off, that's what," Strader said, his voice full of venom.

"Don't do anything crazy, Reach. Stay cool."

"Since when are you the voice of reason, Chief? I didn't think you were the type to preach restraint."

"I'm not asking for restraint, man, just a little brains. My people knew how to beat the odds. Be smart. You shoot now you get one man, maybe two. You wait for the choppers, we maybe get every toe jamb in the valley. Look, my head is busted and I have to rely on yours for a little reason, and when I see you throwing away a chance to nail these bastards and live to go home, it worries me."

Things had turned sour so quickly that Strader hadn't had time to consider how events were conspiring to snatch a year's goal from his grasp. He cursed himself for thinking he'd seen the light at the end of the tunnel. The tension that was just beginning to ooze from his pores in the last twenty-four hours was back, and it was back with a vengeance. He had committed a fatal error; he let his situation allow him to think he had it made, and now he realized he'd been conned. It was like he hadn't learned a thing during his tour, watching the carrot-and-stick dynamic beat unlucky Marines into the ground.

A memory flashed through his mind. It was mid-July, when the heat of the day wilted the energies, and he'd spent hours of down time holed up in the dark interior of his bunker on Nong Son Mountain listening to the detailed plans Buck Henick, the short-timer of the moment, had for the minutes, hours, and days that would start when his feet hit solid ground back in the world. Buck allowed his spirits to soar higher with each passing day, until only seven were left. He even found it funny when, on a day patrol upriver, a sniper with little skill took potshots at them from high up on a three-hundred-foot ridge. He was going back to An Hoa in the morning, and his smile showed that he felt this was a fitting end to his time in the field; a last bit of excitement before leaving it all behind. After a lull, the squad broke cover and moved out again, only to be met with more wild shots. Buck's exultant laughter could be heard as he ran for the protection of a mound of rocks by a network of rice paddies, but the laughing stopped when the luckiest shot in the world nicked the rim on the back of his helmet, entered at the base of his skull, and exited through the bridge of his nose between his eyes. His life force gone in an instant, he dropped to the ground in a sitting heap, his head bent forward, letting blood clots and white clumps of brain matter drip from his nose.

From that moment on, Strader promised himself that no matter how short he got, he would never get caught up in the delusion of thinking he was home free. Even dwelling on what going back to the world would be like was a form of self-flagellation, an exercise in self-inflicted anguish. But sometimes, in moments of weakness when his mental vigilance

waned, he took solace in daydreams placing him on the moving walkway in the LA airport, seabag in hand, heading for a connecting flight
to Pittsburgh. His dress greens were sharp, his oxfords were shined,
and his service ribbons put just the right flash of color on his chest. The
walkway was always empty and he stood alone, statuesque, letting the
airport machinery sweep him along, reveling in the sensation of walking
without effort. It had seemed innocent enough, but now he could see the
pitfalls of surrendering to comforting imaginings. Here he was on the
ground in the Arizona. The carrot was gone, and all that was left was
the stick. And it was a mean stick.

Two of the NVA disappeared into the helicopter, leaving the third
to stand alone by the buckled wheel strut, the bulk of the dead machine
towering over his head. Left to his own devices, the third man let his
attention wander into the field surrounding the crash site. He stepped
forward, rifle raised. A path of crushed grass led away from the debris,
and he guided the front sight on his AK barrel along its wavering route.

"Damn," Strader said, shrinking back as though the enemy soldier
was staring into his face. He knew the line of bent stalks was pointing
to their position like footprints in snow.

"I think we're in trouble, Chief," Strader said, drawing a bead on
the curious man.

The Chief lay with his head resting on a forearm, breathing in the
dank and earthy aroma of the jungle. "No shit."

The NVA barked a few sharp words and his partners scrambled
from the helicopter, one dragging the M60 from the port mount with its
trailing belt of brass. He let it drop when he saw the interest the other
two were showing in the distant trees.

The lead man waved a hand and the other two spread out and raised
their weapons. They took their first tentative steps toward the tree line.

"Do you think you can move fast if we have to?" Strader said, gaug-
ing the rhythm of his own labored breathing so that he could choke it
off on the intake long enough to fire a quick shot.

"I don't know. Why?"

"We got unfriendly company headed our way."

The Chief raised his head and tried to see past Strader into the valley. He covered his left eye with a hand and squinted through the other.
He could see two of the three figures in the distance, wavering in his

vision as though they were dancing. "Damn," he said. "I hoped we had a choice."

"The only choice we have now is to not be here when they arrive."

As Strader watched, three more NVA rounded the shattered tail of the helicopter. They were burdened with heavy pack boards loaded with RPGs and heavy rounds for some piece of artillery. One carried the long-barreled RPK with the drum magazine.

"This day just keeps getting better and better," Strader said.

He looked around for some landmark under the canopy that he could fix on. Back where the foothills began to hint at the elevation to come, a tall tree with deeply corded bark stood out among the others. He pointed at it. "See that tree?"

The Chief tried to rally his focus on the one target in a multitude of like targets fitting the terse description. "Don't jerk me around, Reach."

Strader pointed again, making sure his hand was in the Chief's field of vision giving him a sight line to follow. "That big mother on the rise there."

The Chief could make out a massive vertical shadow and he nodded.

"Head for it as fast as you can. If you aren't spotted, I'll catch up."

"And if I am spotted?"

Strader leaned into his rifle again. "I'll take care of that," he said. "And then I'll be right behind you."

≈

As Lieutenant Diehl broke radio contact with Sergeant Blackwell, the pounding throb of a helicopter fighting to gain altitude penetrated the jungle. Although it was more than a mile away, the sound had a physical presence that sent vibrations through the air. The bulk of the platoon had climbed high enough to smell the rotting blossom of the rafflesia, and more than one had commented that there was a corpse somewhere nearby, although no one seemed able to follow the stench to the body.

The ground above the malodorous tree was scarred with the passage of many feet under load. A well-trod path cut through the undergrowth, heading north along the face of the Ong Thu, and a diminishing blood trail decorated its surface. The lieutenant let command know that a large unit of VC was moving north on the mountain, but with the R-20th Doc Lap Battalion active, large unit movements in the Arizona

were commonplace. He positioned the remainder of 1st Platoon along
the path, poised to move the instant the sergeant returned with Middleton's squad.

When he thought he had lost two men at the hands of one of his
own, Diehl's anger was tempered with a little self-recrimination for having misjudged the character of a Marine under his command. But now
that it was plain that the enemy had struck at his people and gotten
away clean, no shadow of personal failure muted his anger. His ire was
hot, and he paced the path, anxious to start tracking them down. The
radioman stayed as close as he could to Diehl without the risk of tripping him.

The lieutenant's impatience was boiling to the surface. "Get me
Four on the horn," he barked, causing Clyde to fumble awkwardly with
the handset.

Just as Sergeant Blackwell's voice squeezed through the static, the
burst of gunfire from the northern end of the valley echoed across the
face of the mountain. It was followed immediately by a long, sustained
rip from a heavy machine gun, punctuated by the explosion of a rocket-
propelled grenade.

"What's happening, Four?" the lieutenant said, cutting the sergeant
off, but no answer was necessary. Both he and the sergeant knew that it
was just the savage disposition of the Arizona reaching out to grab them
by the short hairs. They had wandered the area for most of the week
with nothing to show for it but sore feet, sore backs, and sore moods,
but now, with the op drawing toward a conclusion, the ugly furies that
seethed just below the surface of this country had decided to rear their
vicious heads. It was as though the Marine blood spilled during the
night had whetted the country's appetite. He could hear the tinny voice
coming through the handset. "Highball must be taking fire," it said.

"Get up here ASAP, Four, and I mean yesterday. One out."

The lieutenant yanked the radioman down and spun the radio dials
to the helicopter's frequency. "Pounder One to Highball," he said. The
harsh hiss of open air was the only sound when he released the handset
lever. He squeezed again. "Pounder One to Highball, come in." When
he released again he heard the stern and insistent voice of one of the
pilots dictating a grid coordinate to command, a coordinate in a northern corner of the valley. And the only way a helicopter can have a fixed

coordinate is when it's on the ground. There was no panic in the voice, but it had the serious, practiced efficiency that comes with experience in tense situations. It was an all-business report meant to pinpoint their position, but it had an underlying, unspoken message; they were in deep trouble, and they needed help, fast.

Lieutenant Diehl squeezed the handset with so much force he was surprised the plastic didn't shatter in his hand. The enemy had struck his unit with impunity, and now they had downed the helicopter carrying the casualties. Although the intensity of his desire to get the VC in his gun sights was almost overpowering, he was also a bit surprised at their brashness. The 5th Marines had encountered the R-20th Doc Lap before, but it was nearly always on Doc Lap terms. If the VC felt they had the upper hand, they would hit with everything they had and keep on hitting until their resources were spent or enough firepower was brought to bear to force them to withdraw. But this was odd. Last night they eliminated the LP but ignored the platoon, though it was blind on that flank. And now they knocked Highball out of the sky when letting it pass unmolested would have been the smart move. There seemed to be too much risk for too little gain. With its forces marshaled, the 20th could hit the base at An Hoa if it suited their purposes, but this was something else. It had another feel to it.

The two dead Marines from last night wouldn't bring any other American units into the area, but shooting down a helicopter would. The Evil Eyes from Marble Mountain would have choppers on station in no time, and 2nd Platoon, assigned to Sparrow Hawk, would be lifted from An Hoa to the site for security. Before long, the northern corner of the valley would be alive with activity. Even now, Cessna Bird Dogs would be on the way to fly lazy circles over the mayhem, ready at a moment's notice to summon a sortie of fast movers to rip the face of the mountain apart. Last night the VC chose to run, and now they seemed to want a fight. If that was the case, everyone was headed into a shit storm. But maybe it was something else. Maybe, in each instance, their hand had been forced. It could be that each tentative assault was just what it seemed: the reaction of an unlucky VC unit trying to extricate itself from a confrontation. The lieutenant hoped it was that, but he knew it didn't matter either way. The helicopter was down and the

Chief was on the ground again, wounded at best, and his guilt at having wrongly accused a good Marine ensured that he would move heaven and earth to make that right.

The lieutenant spun the dials on the radio hard, and the clatter of stops made Clyde wince. "One Actual to workhorse, over," he said into the mouthpiece, and then held the handset up to his head.

Bronsky's thin voice crackled back immediately. "Four was trying to reach you, sir," it said, interspersed with scratchy hisses.

Lieutenant Diehl wanted to spend as little time as possible getting past Bronsky's screening. "Give the handset to Four," he said with enough steel in his voice to discourage any verbal response, even one that might just be following radio etiquette.

The sergeant's voice was on in an instant.

"It sounds like Highball is down, Four," the lieutenant said.

An awkward silence followed.

"Do you copy, Four?"

"Sir, there's something you should know. Reach was on that chopper."

"Strader? That's not possible," the lieutenant said.

After another strained pause, "Gantz made it possible."

The Marines close enough to see witnessed a transformation in the lieutenant's face: the usual unflappable granite visage metamorphosed into a mask of barely restrained rage. His face darkened. His hand, holding the radio handset, shook. Taut cords of muscle rippled his jaw line. "I will wipe my ass with his fucking career," he hissed through clenched teeth.

Marines looked up, surprised at the vehemence in his voice. Lieutenant Diehl was renowned for his composure. Regardless of how dire the situation, they could always count on hearing his voice issuing orders calmly and steadily, untainted by emotion. But a single, short conversation with the platoon sergeant had drawn his temper to the surface like hot magma, and they all waited anxiously for the eruption to come.

"Saddle up," the lieutenant said and then shoved the handset up under his helmet. "Four. Disregard my last order. Head back toward Pontiac and the LZ and follow the flats to Green Bay Packers. Highball is down near there. We're on the way. And Four . . . be quick, huh?"

The radio hissed and the lieutenant tossed the handset to the operator. "Burke, your squad has point. Move fast and stay sharp. And don't lose the bastards' trail."

Lieutenant Diehl moved into the center of the column, and the remnants of 1st Platoon moved north, marching away from the wafting stink of the dead body no one could find.

Corporal Pusic sat behind his desk in the company office sipping a Coke fresh from the cooler and updating a file labeled Indigenous Base Personnel. It was a daily tally that more or less documented the Vietnamese labor that kept everyone at An Hoa in clean uniforms. It was a short list, but command insisted that it be kept current. They were confident that being on a list discouraged an enemy sympathizer from making secret maps of the base infrastructure like nothing else. The fan on the file cabinet across the room lifted the edges of the papers, and the corporal held them down with a forearm.

The landline bell rang and Pusic had the receiver to his ear in one ring. "Golf Company. Corporal Pusic speaking," he said with all the professional formality of a telephone operator. His back straightened and he subconsciously tried to sit at attention. "Yes, sir," he said. He looked at the partition that separated the front of the building from the back. "Yes, sir. He's here, sir. I'll get him." He cupped a hand over the mouthpiece with enough force to create an airtight seal. "Sergeant. Sergeant Gantz," he said, keeping his voice at a moderate level because the partition did not reach the ceiling and, more important, Gantz did not appreciate being hollered at by subordinates.

The sergeant's voice drifted over the top of the wall. "What is it, Pusic?"

The corporal tried to make his voice as contrite as possible. He wanted to sound as though any intrusion that bothered the sergeant wasn't coming from him. "It's the captain. He's calling from the com shack and he wants to speak to you."

The sergeant stepped through the door wiping his hands on a towel with his face full of questions.

Corporal Pusic shrugged. "I don't know. He sounds pissed."

The sergeant took the receiver. "Yes, sir," he said with a practiced subservience reserved for officers.

The captain's booming baritone squeezed through the wire, and Pusic could hear the overflow of sound, but not the words.

"Yes, sir. Yes, sir," the sergeant repeated. It was the usual sound of a one-sided military conversation that confirmed that shit flowed downhill. "Yes, sir. I did, sir, but . . ." The sergeant fixed Pusic with a stare that skewered him like the point of a bayonet.

That look told Pusic that he was about to experience the Corps' theory of fecal flow firsthand.

"Yes, sir. Right away, sir," the sergeant said into the receiver, then handed it back to Pusic distastefully. "The VC shot that 34 down. Get the reactionary platoon to the runway."

Pusic raised the receiver and rang the company area. "Second Platoon. Sparrow Hawk, Sparrow Hawk." He slowly lowered the receiver. "Done," he said. Immediately, hurried voices in the distance could be heard echoing the corporal's alert.

The sergeant didn't answer. He just tapped the corner of Pusic's desk with a fingernail, picking away at the surface of the comfort zone that separated the two. "That Marine we commandeered earlier for security . . . you know him?"

"He's one of the squad leaders in 1st Platoon," the corporal answered.

"Were you aware that he has only a couple days left in-country?"

Suddenly, the chair was becoming extremely uncomfortable and Corporal Pusic squirmed. "Well . . . I don't know . . ."

The sergeant slapped a hand down on a stack of manila folders next to the company Out Box. "If I look through this pile, am I going to find his damn name?"

Pusic's eyes were drawn to the pile and the protruding tab, just three from the top, with "Strader, Raymond L." glowering in black marker. "He . . . could be there."

The sergeant shook his head in exaggerated disbelief. His voice rising with each word, he continued, "I've got a captain chewing me a new asshole and a lieutenant in the field who can't wait to see my head on a stick, and I don't like it when the brass is headhunting, especially when it's my head. And you say 'could be' and 'might be.' Is that what you're telling me, Corporal?"

Pusic slumped back in his chair and turned his hands up toward the ceiling, knowing he was a supplicant praying at the wrong altar. "It was just for an hour."

"Just an hour? I'm sure his parents will be relieved to hear that. I'll bet their congressman will take that into consideration when he shows up here to crawl up every dark orifice looking for someone to take the heat for this screw-up."

The corporal's mind raced for an out, a quick fix, anything that would stop the inevitable brown flow from burying him. He was coming up empty.

"You know what I need?" the sergeant said.

Pusic suspected the question was rhetorical, but he answered anyway. "No."

"I need eyes." The first sergeant stepped into the back and returned with a flak jacket, web gear, and a helmet, which he dumped unceremoniously in the center of Pusic's desk. He grabbed an M16 from its spot next to the file cabinet and pushed it into his clerk's hands.

"I need to know what's going on, and you're gonna find out for me . . . firsthand."

The jumbled thumping of multiple helicopters coming in from the north infused the air with a subtle vibration that was growing stronger by the second.

"Get down to the airstrip and go with the 2nd, and when I radio their platoon sergeant and ask for you, you'll only have one excuse for not being there. And if that's the case, I'll write a glowing letter to your bereaved family."

≈

Strader watched the NVA multiply near the helicopter and counted at least a half dozen. The curious one was marginally closer than the others. Strader eyed the man over the barrel of his M14 and watched him signal the three new arrivals to move right. He pointed in Strader's direction then held up two fingers. He seemed to have the rank to throw orders around, and he already knew that there were two in the trees, so he could read the signs and he would track them.

Strader looked back over his shoulder, checking on the Chief's progress. He wasn't encouraged. Moving on heavy legs, the Chief was less than half the distance to the big tree, making periodic stops, grabbing at anything that could provide some support. Strader watched him go tree-to-tree, finding help for a balance he lacked. When he leaned a shoulder heavily into one small trunk, a shiver of vibration moved all the way up the tree to the leaves, which quivered audibly. When the Chief pushed away from the tree, it moved again. Strader hoped against hope that the movement wasn't visible from the valley, but a sudden burst of fire from the NVA with the long-barreled machine gun sent a swarm of bullets over his head that sent shards of bark flying from tree trunks. The recoil kicked the barrel upward, and though the first few shots were dangerously close, the remainder climbed up the trees, spending their lethal energies in the branches. Strader could see that the man was firing blindly, probing the area below the movement, using a hope of his own for aim.

Strader leaned into his rifle and timed his breaths as though guided by the sweep of a metronome. He made a silent plea that his shot go straight and true, and then regretted the thought. A prayer to guide his bullet to a kill seemed somehow antithetical to the will of a benevolent God, and he hoped that the request wouldn't be held against him. It was never a good thing in combat to antagonize the omnipotent.

He inhaled and then let half of it out and held his breath. A second burst from the machine gunner swept over his head, threatening his calm, hastening his finger to the trigger. A choice would have to be made. He would get one shot with a modicum of precision while the NVA gunner was throwing lead wildly into the foothills. He focused and squeezed the trigger. The discharge punched the butt plate into his shoulder, and his ears rang with the pealing of a high-pitched bell.

A slight puff of dust erupted from the center of the magazine pouches that wrapped the curious tracker's chest, and he pitched onto his back as though struck by lightning. Strader flicked the select fire switch to automatic and emptied half the remainder of his magazine into the area where the other five NVA had dropped, trying to keep the rounds in the grass, fighting the rifle's inclination to climb. The shots assaulted his ears in a symphony of chimes and squeals.

The sudden exchange lit a fire under the Chief, forcing him to keep putting one clumsy foot in front of the other until his hands felt the deep, wet creases of the target tree. He leaned his head against the bark and held on while the ground rocked under his feet. A wave of nausea swept over him, and he clung to the tree, gulping back his impulse to vomit, as a stream of drool from his lower lip mixed with the moisture clinging to the tree. Flashbulbs fired behind his eyelids. The rifle reports stretched from their succinct crack to an elongated echo that did nothing to restrain his involuntary need to retch. He peeked around the tree. The tableau before him was a patchwork of ominous shadows identifiable neither as friend nor as foe. He squeezed his eyes shut and opened them slowly, hoping for a fresher, clearer view.

One dark shadow moved away from the light at the tree line and ran a jagged course in his direction. The Chief blocked one eye again and picked out Strader covering ground like an Olympic sprinter, a pack swinging wildly from one hand and his rifle in the other. As he watched, Strader stopped and shouldered his rifle, using a tree for support, and emptied the rest of his magazine in the direction of the downed helicopter. The lowland beginnings of the jungle blocked any sight of the valley floor, but the shots were meant only to delay pursuers. Anything beyond that would be pure luck.

The Chief wrapped his arms around the tree, trying to absorb some of its stability. The ground beneath his feet settled, and he squeezed the trunk with all his might, willing his spirit to join with the tree's as he had once done on the edge of the mesa. He had always felt an affinity for trees; they were of a tribe he admired and respected. They were the gods of the plant world. In his mind, touching one was akin to touching all, and he wondered if they were interconnected with Mother Earth as a conduit. He hoped so. He wanted to touch the strength of the great tree in the high desert and ask its spirit for help. As he gripped the trunk, he could feel his father and grandfather as they linked hands around the great tree. A wave of comfort swept over him. His father's hand pulled on his wrist. He could almost hear his name being called. But the wrong name.

"Chief, Chief," Strader said, trying to pull the Chief's hand from its grip on the tree. "We can't stay here," he said.

The Chief opened his one functioning eye and watched Strader pull the empty magazine from his rifle and push a fresh one in with a click, all the while snapping worried glances back at the valley.

"They'll be coming," Strader said.

The Chief reluctantly relinquished his grip on the tree. "And I guess they're pissed?"

"Well, all but one."

Strader ducked under the Chief's arm and grabbed a handful of his belt in the back, taking as much of the Chief's weight as he could. "Let's *didi mau*, Chief."

The Chief clung to Strader's shoulder and the two Marines beat a clumsy retreat into the foliage that blanketed the foothills.

～

Hoang Li felt empowered when the three men from the initial crossing joined his group at the helicopter. With the new infusion of numbers they spread across the face of the crash site, and he signaled that two Americans had made the flattened swath of grass leading to the tree line. The signs showed that the two had been side-by-side and very close together, and he was sure one was injured. When the sudden burst of fire from the RPD shattered the silence, he searched the face of the jungle for the target he failed to see. There was nothing. He looked across at the others with a puzzled expression, wanting to know if the firing had purpose, and a sledgehammer slammed his chest, knocking him onto his back. The air for his next breath was gone, and he gasped, arching his back, trying without success to fill his lungs. The echo of the shot cracked across the face of the mountain, and a rapid burst of cracks followed. The tall grass that towered over his face seemed to be blocking the air and he felt he was drowning in it. His magazine vest wouldn't let his lungs expand. He was suffocating, as though he was buried alive, and panic surged through his veins.

He could hear grass stalks breaking as his closest comrade crawled through the grass in his direction. He could hear the protests of the creatures in the way. He could hear the clouds moving through the sky above him. He could hear everything in the world that made a sound, but he couldn't hear his own breathing. Just shallow, strangled gasps that he was sure would be the last sounds he would ever make.

Another rapid stream of cracks flew from the trees as a hand grabbed at his sleeve. He didn't want to be distracted from the task of finding oxygen somewhere in the universe, and he clawed at the invading hand, pushing it away. In seconds, the hands untied the magazine vest and pushed the heavy, cartridge-laden pouches away from Hoang Li's chest. But relief from the weight didn't bring air. Fingers fumbled with obstinate buttons and threw aside his shirt, exposing bare skin with a trace of blood that pooled at the sternum. A filthy hand smeared the blood away to reveal a shallow break in the skin ringed with a red halo that spread from the center like a tender wheel around its axis. The vest of magazines lay with the inside up, a jagged hole with the sharp edge of a split magazine pushing through the canvas.

Hoang Li wished he could be left alone to die with as much dignity as he could muster while smothering. His gasps were painful wheezes that did nothing to fill his lungs, and he could only wait patiently until his body no longer needed the air that it desperately wanted now.

A face moved close and he looked into eyes that seemed to be smiling. "I think fate has smiled on you, Hoang." The vest dangled before his face, the round hole in the front, the jagged one in the rear. "You'll have your wind back in a moment."

He wanted to believe. The reassurance calmed him and the panic began to ebb. Short gulps seemed to be working, and his mouth worked like that of a fish in a garden pool.

Another man crawled to his side and alternated looks at Hoang with glances at the tree line. "How bad?" he said.

The other got to his knees and held up the vest. "It saved him," he said.

The man examined the canvas on both sides and smiled. "I'm going to stay close. You have luck with you, Hoang."

Together they lifted Hoang Li to his feet, holding him up until the weakness passed. Even shallow breaths sent bolts of misery through his ribs, but the torment was a blessing, and he inhaled as deeply as his pain tolerance would allow.

When Hoang Li bent to grab his AK from the grass, the resulting pain was so intense that he wasn't sure he could stand upright again. One of the others helped him straighten. His vest was pushed into his hands, and he opened the center pouch. The enemy bullet had nearly passed through two full magazines. The heavily ribbed walls of the magazines and the fat cartridges inside absorbed the bullet's energy, leaving it flattened and spent as it tried to push through the inner side. He extracted the bullet and held it up for the others to see. It worried him that the shot had struck the center of his vest directly over his heart. It was neatly placed under fire, and he had the feeling that wasn't by chance. "Let's go," he said, and the line of NVA moved at a cautious trot toward the tree line.

18

Corporal Middleton's squad moved rapidly along the valley floor just beyond the tree line. Franklin led the point fire team and kept everyone going at a quick pace, at least as quickly as he could go while scanning the ground for anything that looked even remotely like disturbed earth. He was having difficulty weighing the need to reach the downed chopper against the reputation of the Arizona for disconnecting Marines from their lower extremities.

The sudden exchange of gunfire to the north quickened the pace. Everyone in the squad could distinguish between the signature sounds of the weapons being fired, and it definitely wasn't one-sided. U.S. and Chinese rifles were trading lead, and the urgency to be there went through the squad like a virus.

Sergeant Blackwell moved just ahead of Bronsky, and the radioman jogged a few steps to catch up. "One Actual wants you, Sergeant," he said, holding out the handset.

The sergeant took the handset without slowing his pace. "Four," he said. "That's affirmative. There are friendlies on the ground in contact." He listened for a bit. "I roger that, but we have a way to go yet." He listened again then returned the handset to Bronsky. He spoke up to the man ahead. "Pass word to Franklin to double-time."

The squad increased their speed to a tortured run. Equipment bounced and slapped, and hands flew up to stabilize loose helmets. Running in full field gear was always difficult. It was heavy, and most of it hung loosely from the waist and shoulders, working at cross-purposes to a running body. Heavy canteens, magazine holders, and grenade packs floated at the apex of the stride and slammed against hips and legs when the stride bottomed out. Unless you carried something heavy across a shoulder, like an M60 machine gun or a mortar tube, the flak jacket and pack banged against your spine like a jackhammer. The helmet would lift off and try to fly unless you clamped it down with your free hand. The contents of pockets flapped against your thighs, bruising with the force of knuckles. But if you were feeling abused by your plight, you could always take comfort in knowing that you weren't carrying one of the radios—unless, of course, you were unfortunate enough to be a radioman. Bronsky ran like an overloaded pack mule.

〜

When manning the lines, each of 2/5's four companies supplied a platoon for the reactionary force. The H-34s out of Marble Mountain used the moniker "Sparrow Hawk" when they flew these details, and the waiting platoons worked under the same name. As far as assignments went, being the Sparrow Hawk platoon was good duty. No work details. No manning the bunkers. No patrols or ambushes. The men got the sleep they needed and three square meals a day. The only responsibility was keeping field equipment ready for a quick departure. The sergeants would prowl the barracks, inspecting every area, making sure each man's gear was laid out so it could be gathered quickly.

If it was quiet in the boonies, Sparrow Hawk duty was sweet. But if anything went sour anywhere in 2/5's TAOR, the Sparrow Hawk call echoed through the platoon area and everyone had to be lined up in full battle gear along the runway before the helicopters touched down. When units were operating in the Arizona, the Sparrow Hawks generally spent their time enjoying their ease but always waiting for the other shoe to drop.

Within minutes of Pusic's alert, Lieutenant Hewitt's 2nd Platoon was forming in front of the control tower. Staff Sergeant Litinsky paced back and forth barking orders as Marines helped each other wriggle through their pack straps. A staggered line of H-34s was already across the northern perimeter wire and dropping over the runway. The sergeant divided the squads into groups that would meet the carrying capacity of a 34, and they turned their backs to the runway as the helicopters dropped to a low hover and swung their tails south before setting down. The rotor wash exploded the dust from the steaming runway plates and pelted the waiting Marines as though from a sandblaster, stinging the backs of their necks and invading their lungs. As soon as the helicopters rolled to a stop, the squads moved forward, following Sergeant Litinsky's bellowed commands, and climbed on board, filling the interiors until the last man on sat with legs dangling through the hatch above the runway.

The pilots waited, keeping the rpms high for a quick liftoff.

A lone figure crossed the rise next to the tower and ran down the embankment, rifle in one hand and helmet in the other. He waved the helmet in the air. Sergeant Litinsky pushed the new arrival onto the last helicopter and climbed in after him.

Solemn faces populated the shadows in the helicopter's belly. Marines leaned back against the bulkheads, trying not to hold anyone's gaze too long for fear of revealing anxieties, or worse, seeing them in others. Tight-lipped smiles faded as quickly as they were made; designed to comfort, they came off as masks sculpted by worry.

The burdened 34s lifted sluggishly from the runway and banked over the base, fighting for altitude in a wide circle before passing over the ammo bunker and the northern rolls of concertina wire hung with B-4 C-rat cans holding loose pebbles. Worn footpaths led away from the wire, branching out through the low brush like scars, scrubbed bare by the boots of a thousand patrols.

≈

Lieutenant Diehl set the pace of his Marines with his own speed. Those behind him had to hurry to keep up, and those ahead were driven forward by his admonitions. The lead fire team was uncomfortable moving through the Arizona at the speed they were traveling. The volatile earth of the Arizona did not reward those who threw caution to the wind, but the path they followed was well worn by the fresh imprints of feet under load, and they hoped the fleeing Vietnamese hadn't taken the time to set traps in their wake.

Though the blood trail petered out quickly, Burke's squad had no trouble keeping to the path. The point man pushed through branches and leaf stalks already bent and broken by the VC. He could see that the enemy wasn't moving single file. They'd gone side-by-side, smashing the undergrowth back and leaving a wide path, and it was obvious where they had stopped, crushing small plants down when they dropped their loads.

Further along, where signs of a second stop were found, the point called a halt. Burke pushed his way forward. "What's up?"

The point man, breathing heavily, indicated with the barrel of his rifle where the path split, one path moving downhill. "We could be walking into an ambush here," he said, searching the trees with worried eyes.

Burke turned to the Marine behind him. "Pass word to the lieutenant. Something's up. The trail has split."

While the column passed the word in hushed voices, Burke looked at the churned ground where the paths diverged. Unlike the path straight ahead, the one going down seemed to have footprints going in both directions. He pointed his rifle downhill and followed his aim, with the point man close behind. A handful of yards downgrade a hastily formed layer of leaves and branches looked oddly out of place, and Burke and the point man dragged them aside to reveal a soft mound of dirt. "Well, it's no ambush," Burke said.

Lieutenant Diehl dropped down from the main path, digging his heels in to keep from falling. Clyde was taking the lieutenant's advice to heart and stayed within arm's reach. "What's going on, Burke?" the lieutenant said.

Burke could see from the lieutenant's expression that the delay wasn't making him happy. "It looked like maybe some of the dinks peeled off to wait for us to come along, but it's just a fresh grave," Burke said, trying to make his voice not sound like an apology.

The lieutenant looked down at the raised mound of black earth. "One for the Chief," he said.

A question formed on Burke's face. "Do we dig it up?" he asked.

"Hell, no," the lieutenant said, turning back up the hillside. "We've wasted enough time already. Get the platoon moving. Now." The radioman scrambled up the incline after him.

Burke and the point man looked down at the grave. The point spewed a stream of brown spit from the wad of chew in his cheek, bitten from a Days Work plug that came in the last Red Cross parcel. It hit the mound dead center. The Marine wiped his chin with the back of his hand. "This don't feel like payback," he said.

Burke launched a droplet of clear spit—all his dry mouth could produce—in the general direction of the slurry of thick tobacco juice sinking into the grave. His contribution seemed insignificant in comparison. "No, it don't," he said. "But it will. Soon."

The two Marines dug their boots into the hill and climbed back to the platoon as fast as their legs would carry them.

～

Strader and the Chief dodged trees and staggered upgrade like two drunks in a three-legged race, Strader holding onto the Chief's belt and the Chief with an arm clamped around Strader's neck like a wrestling headlock. The Chief grunted with each step as Strader yanked up on his belt, driving his inseam into his scrotum. At least it distracted him from the pain in his head. They took whatever path was steepest, trying to get to the highest defendable ground as quickly as possible.

Below, at the edge of the tree line, the NVA fired a few short bursts, hoping a round would find a home by chance or flush one of them into view, but the two Marines were well out of sight and climbing above the line of fire. Though they weren't too concerned about being hit, the firing added an extra energy boost to their climb. Their only advantage was being able to push forward and upward as fast as their feeble gait would allow, while the enemy had to move with at least a little caution, not knowing if they were just pursuing or walking into a desperate defense. Even so, Strader couldn't imagine the Vietnamese moving any slower than he was.

Twice the Chief retched with convulsive spasms that produced a weak line of drool that swung from his chin. All the while he forced his legs to keep pushing upward, ignoring the overwhelming desire to curl over his knees and rest his forehead on the ground. Strader looked at him in amazement. He didn't know it was possible to puke and run at the same time. The streaks of blood from the Chief's head wound sucked up his perspiration and peeled away in flakes that gave him a diseased look.

"Can you keep going, Chief?" Strader asked.

The Chief's sidelong glance had reproach in it. "You'll be looking up at me when you fall," he panted.

They drove their knees into the slippery face of the mountain until their jungle pants were caked with the pungent earth of the Ong Thu. The midday sun weighed on the canopy above, superheating the air and making the jungle into an orchid hothouse. Plants hanging low with the weight of last night's rain rose up with the relief of evaporation. Wide, leathery leaves that looked like elephant ears hung on thick stalks intertwined with a lacework of other plants in bewildering variety and profusion that seemed to be conspiring to make movement from one spot on the mountain to another as difficult as possible. Strader pushed and shoved at the natural barricade, looking for weak spots to force a way through. The two Marines ducked and twisted, fighting the plants that snagged their arms and legs and equipment. They tucked in their arms and held their equipment close, hoping to reduce the target for the clinging obstructionists.

The Chief had to relinquish his stranglehold on Strader's neck and content himself with hanging onto the buckle straps on his pack. He couldn't focus his vision ahead, so he let himself be dragged along in Strader's wake through whatever holes could be found.

Strader stooped below a cluster of the obstinate branches the Marines cursed as "wait-a-minute vines" that grabbed at him like fishhooks, ripping at his utilities and stinging his ears. By themselves the vines were of little consequence, easily snapped and flung aside, but in the thickets they formed here they were formidable—natural proof of strength in numbers. "Chief. I need your knife," he said, turning as far as the vines would allow.

"It's mine," the Chief said stubbornly, thumbing the silver end cap that anchored the blade.

"Come on, Chief. Don't jerk me around," Strader said, pushing his hand backward, palm up.

Reluctantly the Chief withdrew the knife from its sheath and set the handle in the upturned hand. "I want it back."

"I'll leave it to you in my will. That way you'll be sure to get it . . . soon." Strader struggled to get his arm back through the vines. He didn't want to swing the blade like a machete—the hacking noise would be a homing beacon—so he set a vine on the hilt and let it slide up the long blade, parting it easily. He lifted the knife high and drew it down across the web of vines in his face, slicing through them like a razor through spaghetti. He dragged the blade up and down across their vulnerable green throats until they surrendered the way. Their progress improved as Strader sliced through vines the knife could defeat and sidestepped those it couldn't.

The Chief seemed to be getting his legs back and had less trouble keeping up. The suffocating vines finally disappeared beneath a fallen tree that had recently crushed the tangled surface community to the ground under its weight. The industry of a voracious termite colony was gutting the tree, and the two Marines followed the spindly-legged army marching along the dead bark. Staying close to the trunk, they trampled down the foot snags and quickly made their way to the leafless dead branches that had once graced the canopy.

They were deep inside the jungle now, where impenetrable undergrowth found little foothold in the dim light among the thirsty root systems of the larger trees. Strader swung an arm behind the Chief to help him navigate, and they moved upward through the tall trunks as through an obstacle course, climbing over and around ancient root buttresses thick with lichens.

Huge slabs of stone had slipped away from the face of the mountain at some point in the geological history of the Ong Thu and settled against one another to grow blankets of moss and fade into the natural camouflage of the jungle. Strader led the Chief into their midst and released him to slide down against the upper side of one green slab. "I need a breather, Chief," he gasped.

The Chief barely had the strength to scan Strader with the one bleary eye that wasn't obscured by the slipping battle dressing. "If you say so," he said, trying to put force into his voice but failing miserably. The Chief held his one-eyed stare until Strader flipped the long knife over in his hand and held it out, handle first.

"You sure you want a dangerous individual like me to have an edged weapon?"

Strader balanced the knife between index finger and thumb and wiggled the handle up and down. "I'll take my chances."

The Chief reached up slowly and took the knife, happy to feel the weight of it in his hand again.

Strader grabbed a canteen from his belt and took a long pull. The bitterness of the halizone battled with the flavor of plastic leached from the inner wall of the canteen to be the taste that made the water undrinkable. They both failed: thirst trumps taste. Strader wiped his mouth with a gritty forearm. "You think you can keep something down?" he said, holding out the canteen.

"I can try." The Chief took the canteen and filled his mouth.

Strader's Corcoran jump boots, stiff and hard-edged when he'd put them on yesterday, now bent with the subtle flexibility of calf skin when he squatted down. Strader watched the Chief's blood-streaked face as he drank.

"What?" the Chief said, returning the canteen.

"I don't like the look of your face."

"You're not exactly a fashion model yourself, shithead."

"Tilt your head back," Strader said, taking the canteen from the Chief's hand.

"Why?"

"Because I can't read your face covered in war paint."

The Chief searched Strader's eyes, trying to determine whether this was an insult. "My people paint their faces so there is no mistaking the read. You don't have to interpret their expressions. If you see paint, you know you're in deep shit."

"I already know I'm in deep shit, Chief. I don't need you trying to scare me, too." Strader gently pushed the stained battle dressing up so he could see more of the Chief's face. "Close your eyes," he said.

The Chief started to pull his face away from Strader's outstretched hand, but the pain of the movement made him stop.

Strader grabbed the Chief under the jaw, digging his fingers in and forcing the Chief's head back without showing any consideration for discomfort. He tilted the canteen over the Indian's upturned face.

The Chief spit and blinked his eyes under the halizone soaking. He swung his arm, knocking Strader's hand away. "You're wasting water, asshole." The cool water streamed down his neck and into the stretched-out collar of his T-shirt. He wiped a hand over his face and blinked again . . . and again, then snatched the canteen, tipped his head back, and poured more water onto his face, blinking furiously as he did. Water was running down onto his shoulders before Strader could grab the canteen away.

"Ease up, man. I might want to wash the car later," Strader said, screwing the attached cap back on the canteen. Nearly half of the water was gone.

The Chief dragged a hand over his face again, staring at Strader like he was seeing him for the first time. "I think I can see."

"Good. Let's go." Shrill bird calls and hooted answers in the upper reaches of the canopy announced intruders, or maybe just passed the time of day, but Strader hoisted the Chief onto his feet anyway and they followed the stones up the mountain.

≈

The initial pace of the lone squad's progress along the valley floor dropped off to a steady plod after a quarter mile as each squad member fell into his own rhythm, adjusting speed as necessary to keep up or to keep from being pushed from behind. When Sergeant Blackwell felt they weren't covering ground fast enough, he sent word to Franklin at the point to act as lead dog, daring the pack to stay with him or suffer the shame. The pace was pounding some of the squad, especially Bronsky, who looked as though the heavy radio was driving him into the ground with each step.

When thick reeds at the southern end of the lake sent the squad back into the trees, they moved at a cautious walk, thankful for the breather; entering the shade was like stepping off a hotplate. The cool, oxygen-rich air soothed their burning lungs.

Doc Brede could see that the heat was taking its toll on the squad and passed word to down salt pills before returning to the valley floor.

The point fire team tested the marshy ground outside the tree line until they were past the stands of bamboo on the northern bank and the ground firmed up enough to carry weight. Reluctantly, the squad filed out of the trees and back into sunlight that seemed focused directly on them by some immense celestial magnifying glass. The ground was solid and clear, and Franklin resumed the fast pace. He could see across the open valley to the northern Ong Thu that doglegged spurlike east to Nam An 3. In the crook of the mountain's angle he could see thin vapors rising above the broken body of the helicopter. He pointed to the machine, small in the distance, so Middleton could make it out.

With the helicopter now in sight, Sergeant Blackwell called a halt to contact Lieutenant Diehl. But before he could squeeze the lever on the handset, a burst of fire erupted high up on the mountain behind them. Every face turned toward the noise, though the firing was too far away to be a danger to them. The gunfire was a sustained rip that lasted only a handful of seconds and was followed by a short pause; then another burst filled the mountainside with echoes.

To the uneducated ear this was just distant gunfire, but most of the Marines in 1st Platoon were well into a yearlong tutorial in deciphering weapon noises. It didn't take long in-country to learn to recognize the voices of the different weapons. Each weapon had its own signature readily distinguishable to the initiated ear. The tones of round detonations from the AK-47 and SKS were as different from an M16's tone as the M16 was different from the M14, and the lapse of time between rounds when the weapon was on full auto easily identified the weapon spitting them out. The M16 could rip through a whole magazine so quickly that it sounded like an abbreviated snarl. The rate of fire of the M60, though using the same round as the M14, had the distinctive cadence of a full-auto machine. The .50-caliber had the methodical plodding of an automatic cannon, slower than the lighter calibers but infinitely more destructive.

From their position on the valley floor, the squad used hard-earned experience to work out a scenario for the noise up on the mountain. The first burst was definitely from Chinese weaponry, so it was clear that Lieutenant Diehl and the rest of the platoon had stepped in it. The reports were deep with a hollow ring, so the enemy was firing away from the valley. The second burst, after the pause, was the return fire from the platoon, exclusively M16 initially, but joined shortly by a sustained blast from an M60 and punctuated by the muted thump of the M79 and its sudden explosions. The sounds of Chinese weapons mixed with those of U.S. origin blended into a discordant mishmash that grew more raucous by the second.

Though the besieged platoon was short one squad, it still had two squads remaining, along with both M60s, and could bring substantial firepower to bear on the enemy. The squad in the valley stood listening to their platoon high on the Ong Thu fighting to gain fire superiority.

Middleton waited by Sergeant Blackwell's side, a question on his face. "What do we do?" he asked.

The sergeant gave the handset back to Bronsky. He knew the lieutenant would have his hands full now. From the sound of things, the VC on the mountain weren't breaking off. They were meeting the Marines shot for shot. He looked across the valley to the green slope of the northern Ong Thu and the broken helicopter on the ground. He wondered what they had all fallen into. "We follow our orders and get to the chopper," he said, looking into the trees and longing to know the situation hidden within them. "Tell Franklin to move out, on the double."

~

Nguyen led his unit into the upper reaches of the foothills, away from the valley with the downed helicopter, driving the men hard to get into the big trees where it was easier to move. The chatter of AK-47s announced his runners' arrival at the helicopter, but he didn't pause. When Nguyen felt that the elevation was sufficient and going higher would only slow their progress, he directed the column northward, out of the morass of ground cover into a sea of broad leaves with pliable stalks and pulvinus joints that allowed the leaves to track the daylight and the men to brush them aside with ease.

As he changed the direction of march, an exchange of gunfire came from the valley; a shot, then a burst followed by a sustained blast from the RPK. He knew that the first group, caught in the open, had joined up with the runners and were dealing with the situation at the helicopter. He also knew from the sounds that there were American survivors.

In a while he would be passing across the mountain face above the crash site. With luck he would collect Hoang and his people there and disappear into the Ong Thu. With luck. He felt he was beginning to rely too much on the fickle mystery of luck. So he added hope. He hoped his luck wouldn't run out.

Pham and Truong kept the heavy machine gun moving, keeping pace with the more seasoned soldiers. The exchange in the valley prodded them to keep their legs pumping, and they dug in their sandal edges under the balance of the gun. But it wasn't just the gunfire giving them the boost of power. In the weeks since they had dropped from the tailgate of the truck, they had undergone a physical transformation that neither would have previously imagined possible. Hard labor and scanty rations had chiseled their soft flesh. In the beginning, a few hours under their pack boards took them to the limits of their endurance. Their bodies ached. Their hands chafed. Dehydration made their heads throb. When they looked at the others in the unit, who carried heavier loads but seemed unaffected, they felt weak and inferior. But now, with many kilometers behind them, molded by the strain of their efforts, they had become more like the hardened men around them.

They pushed forward in between Sau in front and Co bringing up the rear of the column. The older men ignored the firing around the helicopter; they had a direction in which to move their equipment and they weren't interested in distractions. Pham looked to the veterans as barometers of imminent danger, and the men with experience showed no concern. He wondered if there would ever come a time when his nerves would be attuned to the shocks of war. Could he attain such control? He looked at Sau's back bent toward the incline of the mountain, his calf muscles knotted under the weight on his back. Maybe Sau felt the same jolt of fear. Maybe he had just learned to conceal it, to hide his reaction. Pham couldn't imagine the effort it would take to do that.

When the firing broke out far behind them on the face of the Ong Thu and the exchanges fed on one another exponentially until the noise congealed into full battle, Sau looked back over his shoulder and smiled. Pham was surprised to see the emotion on that leathery face. When Sau noticed he was being observed his smile grew. "We are not alone, my friend," he said, leaning back into his work. Pham gripped the barrel of the machine gun balanced on his shoulder and pushed harder to keep up. It may have been only a simple pleasantry, but being addressed as "friend" was like a dose of sweet oil on his aching muscles.

~

The 20th Doc Lap Reinforced VC Battalion struggled to maintain a roster of four hundred troops but seldom kept up with their losses. As a result, the battalion had to frequently impress local villagers into their ranks, much to the dismay of the villagers, regardless of their political persuasion. Being primarily farmers, the villagers were more concerned with the seasons and weather than the ebb and flow of political ideologies. They survived by the grace of their rice crops. If they had any allegiance at all, it was to fellow villagers who toiled in the paddies at their sides. Visits by troops were always problematic, no matter what uniform they wore.

The Americans they looked at with a suspicion that barely hid a tentative curiosity, especially from the young, but at least the oversized foreigners seldom used the villages as a free-market supply depot. They were usually passing through on their way to somewhere else, their columns stretching far beyond the borders of the little hamlets. It was understood that these men could erupt into a storm of destruction if the situation moved them, but as a rule, they were looked on as a sort of traveling circus on the march. The children saw them as irresistible entrepreneurial opportunities, and when their pidgin bargaining became a nuisance, the Americans told them to *didi* and called them little gooks. That seemed odd to the villagers. A gook, to them, was a foreigner in their country, and they certainly weren't gooks. In their minds, the Americans were the gooks. The children would protest, "Me no gook, you gook," but the Americans would laugh and shake their heads. There didn't seem to be any place in Vietnam for understanding. It was that kind of war.

The troops of the Army of the Republic of Vietnam looked on the villagers as lowly peasants and treated them with disdain. Their visits were always a lesson in coercion and intimidation, and anyone who did not answer their questions with complete candor could expect a fist or rifle butt or bullet, especially if the ARVNs were traveling with the Americans and wanted to demonstrate the depth of their commitment without doing anything actually dangerous. When they had an American audience, they seldom missed an opportunity to act like warriors— as long as their targets were unarmed and could deliver nothing more lethal than scornful looks. When the ARVNs left a village, they took anything they wanted with them.

The NVA sent cadres to educate the villagers, spouting their doctrine and laying down the rule of law: follow or die. Villages were required to lend support to the patriots from the North in any way that was deemed necessary, and that included sharing their crops with the freedom fighters who risked their lives to rid Vietnam of the foreign scourge and their lackey *nguy* puppets in Saigon. The NVA expected their quota of rice at harvest, no exceptions, and instructed the villagers to be grateful for the opportunity to give it. The cadres led the little populations in songs designed to arouse their patriotic fervor, such as "Liberate the South" and the alliance anthem, "The Voice of Mountains and Rivers," and took note of any voices that didn't demonstrate the proper enthusiasm. Village leaders who complained or rejected the cadre's demands were visited in the night, and the morning sun would illuminate their mutilated bodies stretched out in the center of the village square for all to see.

The R-20th Doc Lap visited the villages when they had need, and their need was always for food or men. They would slip in at night without warning, before the young and strong could disappear into the bush, and pick and choose to fill their rosters and their bellies. The villagers were adept at hiding what they didn't want to give, but the 20th's quartermasters were equally adept at finding what they wanted. Each of their visits left the villagers a little poorer and their families a little thinner.

The Americans always found it odd that there were only children and old men and women in the villages they passed through when humping the boonies. How could all these children exist when all the adults looked to be octogenarians? They assumed the actual parents were VC, off in the jungles awaiting their chance to strike, but more likely they disappeared at the approach of any troops under any flag, leaving behind only those whose age provided a modicum of protection.

This war, like the ones past and the ones to come, was just one more thing for the people to endure, like the typhoons that pounded their villages and spilled the river beyond its banks, drowning their hopes in nature's madness. But the wind and rain would stop and the river would recede, leaving the earth more fertile than before, and the farmers would go on tending their crops. The wars left the earth barren and the villagers impoverished. To survive was to prevail. The trick was to survive.

As Sau's group scrambled along the path after burying Binh, elements from the R-20th Doc Lap moved in behind them, choosing positions that provided a little cover and gave a tactical advantage over the course cut by the fleeing NVA unit.

An entire squad of the R-20th, three cells strong, squatted silently where the trampled foliage from the fleeing NVA's passage dipped down toward the valley floor. The downward curve let the track fall away from the horizontal trajectory, giving at least three of the VC a straight sight line back into the jungle where hurried feet had crushed the plant stalks into the mountain. They pulled back into the overlapping leaves until there was no trace of their existence. They would be the first to see if hurried boots followed. They would be the first to see the helmeted faces. They would be the first to fire. Three more squads waited in invisible spots just meters above them, nervously fingering the triggers of their AK-47s and SKSs, checking their ammunition with the regularity of an obsessive-compulsive, making sure, again and again, that nothing forgotten would weaken their effort and bring them shame. The still, wet air clung to their uniforms and fed nervous perspiration to sting their eyes and make dry lips taste salty. They would wait. They would wait with restrained patience until the day wore away to nothing or someone came along to fulfill their expectations.

19

The point fire team swept through the clouds of gnats swarming above the broken plant stalks, drawn to the sweet, dripping juices. Their microscopic wings stuck to wet faces and arms and were ground to flyspeck under flak jacket collars. They stuck to eyelashes and were sucked in and spit out of mouths in gritty gobs propelled by invective.

Patches of stratocumulus clouds swept over the Ong Thu, fracturing the sunlight beating on the canopy into a mottled kaleidoscope of green patches. To those on the ground the flickering points of sunlight looked like stars against the darker canopy.

Burke set Laney's fire team on point with Karns at the head and Deacon, clothed in his new trousers, bringing up the tail. The virgin waistband on Deacon's pants had crisp ridges that were finding vulnerable spots on his hips. His skivvies were buried back at the night position along with all the cardboard, used toilet paper, and discarded ham and motherfuckers.

Karns was developing a limp from the constant rubbing of soggy socks between jungle boots and skin the texture of gelatin. Walking the constant slope of the mountain twisted the boots and ground tender feet raw. The docs would give Karns hell for not changing his socks enough, but if they went through all the feet in the platoon, including their own, they wouldn't see enough difference to attract either praise or condemnation. The only two types of socks the platoon had had available for nearly a week were wet and sopping wet. Karns squeezed the butt of his M16 under one arm, the sweep of the barrel controlled by a sweaty hand on the pistol grip. The other hand dangled a machete slick with plant sap. With each step it felt like the skin under his toes was peeling away, leaving only bloody bone to scratch for a hold inside his boots.

A cloudbank with a black underbelly rolled over the mountain range, absorbing the sun and throwing the Ong Thu's canopy into shadow. It was an ominous prediction that today's rain would be early.

"Shit," Karns said, taking a swipe with the machete at an arching stalk with a broad leaf, sending it flopping. His feet hurt, and the elephant grass cuts on his forearms stung with sweat and attracted the interest of insects with big appetites. He could hear Laney swatting the same little feeders finding meals on his own arms. Looking back, he made sure Laney saw the displeasure on his face.

Laney noticed. "What?" he asked, but he brushed his hand silently over his itching arm instead of slapping, though it didn't give the same satisfaction. "Keep your damn eyes on point."

The squads of the R-20th Doc Lap held their silent positions, some sitting cross-legged, some squatting on their heels, all cradling their weapons in their arms. The front man of the cell aligned with the trail caught the first faint sign of movement, helmets in line bobbing in random cadence, emerging from the deeper darkness created by background and distance. The man's whole being involuntarily shrank, as though the slightest opening in the leaves would leave him exposed and vulnerable. His movement alerted the rest of the cell, who raised their weapons slowly, by millimeters. Tense fingers took up the trigger slack on Chinese AKs, meshing their internal parts, roughly formed and with crude tool marks, but slipping into concert as efficiently as their Russian progenitors. Sear to hammer to spring, the pieces found their places and drew to a stop, set to trip. Sweat stung wide eyes denied a blink because the flutter of an eyelid might betray their position.

The knowledge of the approaching enemy swept through the VC squads that hooked above the trail. They couldn't see the path, but they were never meant to. The cells below would spring the trap with a withering burst, then suddenly stop. Those above would wait through the inevitable lull for the return fire and let those sounds guide their aim. There would be little but leaves and soft green stems between them and their targets, and with luck their rounds would find warm homes. They raised their barrels and pointed them into the green, imagining those places where noises would beckon.

Below, the front man of the critical cell carried the burden of responsibility. He would decide when. He would choose the spot, the closest he would let the enemy come. The snare could not be tripped too soon and spoil the impact of the fire from the high ground. But these Marines could not be allowed too close because they had firepower you did not want to meet at close quarters. A poor decision now might sacrifice the waiting cell as well as the comrades hidden above.

His sights lay on the lead American swatting at wet leaves with a machete. He watched the man come, searching for that spot, that perfect spot that would satisfy everyone, the spot beyond which his nerves would take control of his finger. He settled on a broad leaf drooping to the churned dirt, its thick veins, close enough to count, fanning out to the ragged edges. A drip fell from the leaf as the AK butt pressed into his shoulder. He could let the Marine come that close, but no closer. The front post sight on his weapon wavered over the approaching figure. Not one step closer.

20

Karns dug the edges of his jungle boots into the slippery surface of the hillside, bending his ankles uncomfortably to hold his grip. He walked like a tightrope artist trying to keep a precarious balance as he poked at the foliage with the tip of the machete. The path ahead was clear except for a broad, thick leaf bending down from above and casting a jagged shadow on the ground. Beyond the leaf Karns could see the path angling down toward the valley, and he adjusted his grip on the smooth handle riveted to the wide machete blade, readying for a backhand swing that would part the leaf stalk on the bias. He swung. The well-honed blade caught the stalk on the upswing, and the leaf head shuddered then floated in a looping turn to settle on the path like an expended parachute. The force of Karn's swing threw his arm wide; before he could pull it back, the world exploded.

The arboreal hum was shattered by ear-piercing cracks that fed on their own echoes, stripping the mist out of the air and filling all the space in the jungle with noise, so much noise that there wasn't room for anything else. The noise of AK-47s spitting out the contents of their magazines occupied the entire sound spectrum. But even as the first firing pin struck the first round in the first AK, Marines were already diving for the security of Mother Earth.

Life for the Marines in the Arizona was always tense and spring loaded. You stayed wired tight so your reaction time would be instantaneous and you could leave the Arizona with the life that carried you in. The platoon went to ground like dominoes, but the first down, and with the least effort, was Karns. The opening round struck his chest just inside the loose zipper of his flak jacket. The second shot went in under his left collarbone and shattered the shoulder blade behind, flinging him around and dropping him in a heap. His helmet bounced back and got in Laney's way as he was trying to become one with the earth. Laney frantically scooped it aside and pushed his chest into the trail. The only thing between his bare chest and the dirt was his dog tags, and he cursed the Marine Corps for making them so thick.

Bits and pieces of plants filled the air like a green dust storm, and bullets sounded like demented mosquitoes as they ripped through the jungle to spend their energies against the trees or lose their momentum far beyond the last fire team in the platoon. Deacon found himself buried in the foliage on the high side of the trail, wanting to move but afraid that the slightest twitch would shake the leaves above him and draw fire. He could see the new guy on the low side of the trail darting wild looks and jerking physically with every blast as though being struck with an electric cattle prod.

Everyone knew that the VC fire was coming head-on, making the air above the path a very dangerous place, but the remembered gravel-voiced screams of DIs from Parris Island to Pendleton pounding in the importance of fire superiority. You didn't assume control of the battle-field, you took it—and you took it by force. Whatever advantage the enemy grabbed, you grabbed it back, and made him pay a high price for his audacity.

Burke raised himself on his elbows and fired a full magazine over the sprawled Marines ahead of him. He wasn't sure of a target, only a direction, but apparently his newly bestowed authority brought with it a responsibility to act. To his surprise, he found that he was the kind of squad leader who led by example. He ejected the empty magazine and slapped in a fresh one as the firing ahead stopped. The jungle went silent. The air seemed to vibrate with the quiet. Ahead Burke could see Karns on his back in the middle of the path, arms spread, coughing a geyser of blood. He looked back at the empty ground behind him. "Corpsman up," he screamed. He could hear the lieutenant's voice barking orders, and then the entire platoon opened fire.

Lieutenant Diehl was less than a month away from rotating to a new assignment in the rear. He'd spent enough time in the bush to feel he deserved to coast awhile in an area that offered a little more security than a flak jacket and good aim gave him. He wouldn't miss being in the field, but he wouldn't change anything either—especially now. The VC firing stopped as though killed by a command, and the silence rang in his ears and teased the dark corners of his experience. He saw the pattern develop as though it were a tangible entity he could reach out and touch; and he knew he had to touch it on the high ground, and fast. One of the gun teams was strung out just behind him, and he called out to the gunner. "Direct fire uphill! Now!" he said with enough force to leave no question about the urgency.

The gunner unfolded his lanky frame, rolled onto his knees, sat back on his heels, and raised the M60. Fifty rounds hung over the C-rat can wired to the side of the M60, keeping the angle of feed honest so the gun could be fired single-handed without it jamming. He clamped the butt stock under his arm and pulled the trigger. Black links dragged the brass cartridges over the can as the muzzle blast jolted the foliage into frantic spasms. He swung the barrel up and forward, covering the ground above the line of Marines ahead of him. He held the trigger down, making his feed man jump to get another hundred rounds from the bandoleer around his neck to the belt vanishing into the chattering receiver.

The third man in the M60 team had the gun's extra barrel in a soft bag slung over his shoulder. He glanced nervously at the gunner. It was his job to remind him to fire short bursts and save the barrel. A cyclic rate of 550 rounds per minute and a determined trigger finger could fry a barrel in short order, and it was never fun to change one under fire; your concentration always seemed to be needed elsewhere. He raised his M16 and ripped a full magazine into the high side of the mountain.

From behind, the M79 fired, sending the fat explosive rounds up onto the mountainside as fast as fingers could break the breech and reload the chamber. The muzzle *ponk* and pause ended in a sudden blast hidden in the trees. As the second 40-mm round detonated high up the slope, the mountainside erupted in a storm of firing, sending the Marines pitching back down onto their faces.

As was often the case when the firing began, the only targets moving were the corpsmen. When Burke used the eerie silence to call for help, Doc Garver was already crawling forward, a demo bag full of battle dressings hanging from his neck and his compartmented medical bag dragging along the ground, the strap wrapped around his right hand. He climbed over prone Marines in the path. Those with room squeezed aside while firing to give him room to pass. He was just starting to get to his feet when the mountain burst open again, raining lead down on their position and sending him headfirst to the ground. He landed next to a Marine who was lying on his back and trying to get two LAAW rocket launcher straps from his neck. The tubular launchers always snagged on vines and branches, and when you went to ground they always managed to get in the way. The Marine seemed especially agitated. "Doc," he said.

Doc Garver spit out a bit of the muddy path. "I'm busy, Bishop," he said, getting ready to start crawling again.

"Take a look at this," Bishop said, pulling his left pant leg up to the knee. A dark hole in the inside of the calf led to a gaping red mouth on the outside where a round had split the muscle and flesh on exiting.

The doc wiped his mud-caked hand on the side of his pants and felt the Marine's shin from knee to ankle. "Tibia's good," he said.

The Marine assumed that was a good sign and finally got the tangled LAAWs free, setting them at his side.

Garver unsnapped a compartment on one of his bags that held small bits of shiny metal. He scooped out two safety pins and thumbed the tines open. "You ready?" He said.

"Ready for what?"

Garver hooked the pink edge of the gaping wound with the pin's point and, squeezing the flesh together, skewered the opposite side and locked the pin closed.

"Shit, Doc," Bishop whispered through clenched teeth.

Garver pushed the second pin through the puckered skin like hooking a worm. He pulled a battle dressing from the bag and tore the sterile plastic wrapping open. The pad had a pinkish hue, and the four gauze leads, meant to encircle anything from a leg to a torso, seemed excessively long. The doc folded the bandage around Bishop's calf. Instead of cutting them, he crossed the filmy tails and wrapped them tightly, again and again, until their length was used up. He could hear Burke calling up ahead. The distant and frantic voice cut through spaces in the noise. "I gotta go. Tie these in a knot over the outside of your leg." He handed the loose ends over so they wouldn't unravel.

"Hey, Doc. Do you think they'll send me home?" Bishop said, sounding like a youngster on a department store Santa's lap asking for a pony but uncertain whether the tired guy in red could deliver the goods.

Doc Garver turned away and started crawling again. "Tie it tight," he said over his shoulder.

Firing from both sides shredded the lush green vegetation of the Ong Thu. Wildly aimed projectiles punched through everything in their way, and patches of the mountain shuddered under the impact of M79 rounds. The muzzle blasts of dozens of weapons reverberated against the canopy ceiling like thunderous echoes in a drill hall. Instinct dictated that the only position that provided even the illusion of safety was flat on the ground. And if you could burrow, you burrowed.

The incoming rounds kept Doc Garver low. He slithered on his belly like a snake, trying to pull himself forward without raising anything up that could be shot off. Bits and chunks of plants landed on his back, and the gunfire from the Marines he passed set his ears ringing into temporary deafness. Pieces of the path jumped into the air ahead of him as the strikes of a line of bullets skipped across. He stopped, staring at the unsettled ground. He didn't subscribe to the theory of lightning never striking twice in the same place, and the chewed ground he would have to cross made him feel irrationally vulnerable. When his body scraped over the churned earth, he squeezed his eyes shut and held his breath, steeling his body for the impact of another stream of rounds and hoping he would take the pain of being hit with a stoicism that would do him credit; but he passed by with nothing more than frazzled nerves. Ahead, he could see Burke waving an arm, as if hand signals would get him there faster. He dug in his elbows and toes and inched forward as fast as he could go.

In front of Burke, a pair of legs jutted from the bush. Jungle boots with the toes scuffed to tan pointed awkwardly at the canopy high above. The corpsman looked into the little alcove made by the crush of the falling body and saw a green towel draped over a face, but instead of being supported by facial features, the towel sank into a red crater. He started to reach for the limp wrist, but Burke tossed a spent cartridge brass to get his attention and pointed forward to where Karns lay in the path, his back arched over his pack.

"He's dead, Doc," Burke yelled, his face inches from the ground. "See what you can do for Karns."

The corpsman reluctantly pulled away from the body. It was his job to determine if someone was dead or not, entrenched in the description of his MOS, and he didn't like having it usurped by anyone but Brede. On the other hand, some deaths didn't require a studied opinion. Gruesomely fatal damage was as obvious to the layman as anyone else, and he was sure Burke was right. He moved on until he reached Karns' head.

Fragile red air bubbles rose above faint breaths and fed streaks of blood that made tracks down into Karns' ears. His arms were spread wide and his feet were together as though he was awaiting crucifixion. His flak jacket hung open, and Garver could see the dark hole in the left side of his chest percolating gouts of bright blood.

Garver moved his face close to the Marine's ear. "Karns," he said. "Karns." But whatever life force the Marine had left wasn't being wasted on hearing. Doc Garver pulled out an empty plastic wrapper from a battle dressing and cut it in two with his KA-BAR, found his widest roll of adhesive bandage, and taped the wrapper over the chest hole. Bright red oxygenated blood smeared against the plastic. His shaky fingers fumbled for a pulse at the Marine's neck, but he couldn't tell if the beat he felt belonged to Karns or was just his own charged system pounding in his fingers.

The platoon's position went no further than the mud caked into the worn tread of Karns' boots, and the doc shot apprehensive glances at the shadows in the virgin green jungle ahead of him while freeing the buckles on Karns' pack straps. Once they were loose, he rolled Karns to the left, wounded side down, and pulled up the back of his flak jacket. Another red hole fit neatly between a pair of ribs, and he used the other half of the battle-dressing wrapper to seal the leak. Blood made a sticky pool where Karns' face caressed the path.

Burke and Deacon fired full magazines into the mountainside, and Garver flinched from the assault on his already overcharged nervous system, but the noise had no effect on Karns. The doc squirmed around until he could see the Marine's face, eyes half closed, unseeing, thin streams of blood dripping from both nose and mouth. Stinging sweat burned the corpsman's eyes, and he wiped it away with the back of a bloodstained hand, leaving dark streaks across his forehead. His hand shook. An involuntary mantra ran through his mind: stay cool, stay cool, stay cool.

Behind Garver the voices of squad and fire team leaders were cutting through the gunfire, directing their people to concentrate all their efforts on the upper slope. The telltale flash of a LAAW launcher sent a rocket into the trees that shook the ground with its blast. The doc thought he heard the muffled explosion of a hand grenade and wondered to himself what crazy bastard threw a grenade in this dense foliage when the odds of it getting caught up in the branches and falling back on you instead of hitting the enemy were even money.

Karns' breaths were shallow and short, and his color was more gray than tan. Even the bulldog tattoo on his arm seemed dull and color-less to Garver, and he dug into the three-tiered pouch that hung from his web belt next to his .45 automatic. The two top tiers held bottles of serum albumen; the bottom contained a Kodak Instamatic camera wrapped in plastic. He withdrew a bottle and stopped to look at Karns again. With Brede off with Sergeant Blackwell and Middleton's squad, he only had the two bottles of serum for the rest of the platoon, and he couldn't guess what injuries he would face before this little gift from the Arizona was over. What he did know was that Karns did not look good. It was quite possible that Karns would not survive such wounds even if he were hit while lying on a treatment table at the aid station in An Hoa.

Doc Garver hated the awful decisions of triage in the field, the tyranny of priorities. Who was too far gone to receive live-saving aid? Who, being so damaged, was a waste of vital medical supplies? Though Karns was a long shot, he had to try.

He could see Burke screaming at his squad to slow their rate of fire before their ammunition was exhausted. An M16 lay barrel-down in the brush where it had dropped from Karns' unconscious hand. The doc kicked the sole of Burke's boot and pointed at the rifle. Burke tossed it over impatiently, as though angry that his concentration was broken, but he looked back to see if the corpsman intended to exact a little revenge of his own or just needed a twenty-round security blanket. The doc pulled the magazine free and ejected the round from the chamber, then tossed them to Burke. The new squad leader nodded his thanks and turned away. It was better not to dwell on a fallen Marine or what it took to keep him alive lest you begin to see it as prophecy. Turn away and leave the wounds to the corpsman. What you don't see won't fill your mind's eye and become an unconscious guide to your every movement.

Doc Garver fished Karns' bayonet from the scabbard on his belt and snapped it under the barrel of the M16, driving it into the rich earth. The butt stock wavered over Karns' head, and the doc hung the bottle of serum albumen from the trigger guard. He unraveled the plastic tubing and, with shaking fingers, searched the inside of Karns' left arm for a target vein. The skin was as pale as the underbelly of a fish. Intravenous injection had never been Garver's strong suit. Even during his year at the naval hospital at the Great Lakes Naval Base he often had to enlist the help of a more experienced hand to find a successful way into a patient's bloodstream, and this with veins that weren't in the process of collapse. His mind raced to remember the lectures on the "cut down" when it was necessary to open the flesh above the target artery. He hoped he wouldn't have to dig with a scalpel in this place. After three probes came up empty, he plunged the barrel of the beveled needle in and sighed in relief as blood infiltrated the tubing. He reached up and let the liquid flow free.

The intensity of the fire coming from the high ground seemed to be diminishing. Rounds were still slapping through the branches, but from fewer sources. The lieutenant's voice cut through the machine-gunner's heavy trigger finger, and the M60 shifted to bursts that had ends. Burke sent Laney and Deacon forward past where the doc leaned over Karns.

The acrid smell of burned cordite hung in the air and mixed with the odor of shredded plants and the pungent wafts of churned earth. The gush of enemy fire slowed to a trickle, and the Marines knew that the VC were holding true to form. They would hit from invisible positions then fade into the jungle, leaving nothing behind but spent brass—and more often than not, not even the brass.

Lieutenant Diehl already had fire teams leapfrogging up the mountain. The incoming rounds petered out until the only sound was the alternating fire of M16s covering the fire teams on the move. There was no doubt that they were advancing on abandoned positions. With luck they would find dead or wounded with their weapons, but generally that happened only when the Marines designed the surprises. But the VC were running the game plan here, and everyone knew that their plans always included an exit strategy.

Burke stepped around Doc Garver and moved Laney and Deacon into positions that could cover the point while Bishop hobbled up using his M16 as a crutch. The tails of the battle dressing on his leg hung from his cuff like drab pennants. He gave a questioning nod at Karns' limp body and got a hopeless shrug from the corpsman, then turned his face away to the tortured slope of the Ong Thu where his fellow Marines were in pursuit of ghosts.

≈

The formation of H-34s flew an awkward path over the valley beyond the Thu Bon, their tails slaloming in the turbulence. Corporal Pusic was crushed up against the grunts crowded into the last bird. His shoulders were crammed against those of the men on either side, and his knees were pulled up against his chest, with Sergeant Litinsky's pack pushing against his shins. Vibrations from the big engine passed from the deck up through the occupants, who passed them along to one another in an impossibly rapid Morse code, an ominous message being shared by osmosis. The helicopter's interior was infused with the odor of oil and fuel, and even the air currents from the rotors couldn't rid the heavy atmosphere of the musty warehouse stink of web and canvas gear. And overlaying that Pusic could detect the sweet aroma of gun oil on freshly cleaned weapons.

Some faces looked in his direction with suspicion, but concerns of their own quickly drew them away. The Marine leaning into Corporal Pusic's left shoulder looked him over from his Kiwi-blackened boots to the bright camo cover on his helmet. The man's own boots were scuffed and worn and had holes at the ankles. His utilities were faded, and his tattered helmet cover showed burnished steel through holes around the rim. Both men were part of the Corps, but from different worlds within it, and that difference made Pusic uncomfortable. The Marine held his thumb up and smiled around a wad of brown chew. "Get some," he said, as though he thought the clean corporal was satisfying his curiosity, going on some wild outing of his own choosing. Pusic tried to smile, but his heart wasn't in it.

The first helicopter lowered its tail and bounced to a stop fifty yards from the crash site, and Marines gushed from the side like blood from a burst artery. They jumped from the starboard opening so quickly that they risked landing on those who had exited ahead, as though they were anxious to get out into the rain. They spread out and ran hunched over toward the downed helicopter—not because they had an overwhelming desire to join the squad closing on the crash but because the sight of the big, awkward 34s jockeying for position on the valley floor would draw fire like magnets if any hostiles were nearby, and the smart move was to get as far away as possible. You ducked down in case the machine took a hit large enough to change the rotational plane of the big rotors enough for a jolted blade to cleave you in half, and you kept moving away until you couldn't feel the swirling turbulence on your back. The pilots knew they were the object of every enemy gunner's eye, too, and the instant the crew chief announced that the last grunt had cleared the deck, the engine would roar and the machine would lift and bank away, dipping its nose, swinging its tail, and heading for high air.

≈

Approaching the crash site from the mountainside, Sergeant Blackwell sent a flank of two men into the tree line to warn of ugly surprises while Middleton spread his fire teams out and headed for the helicopter. They waded through the knee-high grass, rifles set on full auto, anxious to pour fire on any moving object that would show itself. The closer they got, the higher their rifle barrels were raised. By the time they were close enough to see the shiny bullet craters in the 34's paint and the spider webs spreading around the cluster of holes in the windscreen they had their M16s pulled tightly into their shoulders and looked at everything over their gun sights. They could smell the battered helicopter, and the rain gave the dull green fuselage a freshly washed sheen.

The firing on the mountainside had stopped as abruptly as it had started and the sergeant wondered what the platoon was doing, but he would have to wait to satisfy his curiosity. At the moment his full attention was dedicated to the broken H-34 in his sights.

The fresh Marines pouring onto the valley floor gave Middleton's squad a warm feeling. It was like coming in from night ambushes or day patrols in the deadly Phu Locs and seeing the concertina wire and bunkers on the perimeter of An Hoa. You didn't feel so alone and exposed anymore. You felt the benefit of safety in numbers. If misery loved company, it especially loved heavily armed company joining the fight, and with the Sparrow Hawk platoon spreading out behind them, the lone squad felt they had the upper hand for the first time, or at least sufficient numbers to prevent them from being overwhelmed. Whatever they found at the crash site, they wouldn't have to face it alone. Their tentative steps changed to deliberate strides filled with a confident aggression that said peers were watching.

The distant thumping of the transport 34s heading back across the valley drummed an eerie echo from the wreck that sounded like ghostly pleas, like a dying goose calling to its fading gaggle. Sergeant Blackwell signaled Middleton to skirt the tail, then waited at the nose until he could see the squad leader and a fire team at the tail. With a wave of his hand, they moved on the starboard opening in unison, rifles raised, taking short steps that wouldn't jar their aim. They reached the dark port together. The abandoned M60 and its sprawling belt lay just beyond the door gunner's boots.

Middleton could see nothing past the gunner's body and shrugged at the sergeant's questioning look. Sergeant Blackwell aimed his M16 into the cargo compartment and nodded almost imperceptibly. Middleton nodded back and ducked into the dark interior. Light from the port opening chased the darker shadows into the corners, but the pitch of the deck was steep and Middleton's boots slipped back toward the opening. He pushed a hand down to keep from falling. It came back red and sticky. Two bodies lay in an awkward stack against the lower bulkhead, a tangle of unrecognizable arms and legs.

"Reach?" Middleton said tentatively, throwing out the name with no real expectation of an answer. Then he noticed the fresh boots and bloused cuffs on the FNG. "It's just Tanner and the new guy," he said, regretting the "just" as soon as it crossed his lips. He climbed forward, trying not to slide down into the gunner's helmeted head, and pulled himself up far enough to see into the blood-spattered cockpit. He lowered himself until his weight was off his arms. Of all the things the squad leader thought he wanted in this world, nothing compared to being away from this dead machine and the men who flew it beyond their lives. He squatted on the stained deck and slipped back into the daylight.

"No Reach, no Chief," he said, searching the areas of flattened grass with a worried gaze, half expecting to see more bodies. "Do you think the VC took them?" He could see on the sergeant's face a passing flinch of pain as that possibility was considered.

Sergeant Blackwell studied the ground outside the chopper, searching for a clue, anything that would ignite a spark of hope that capture wasn't the case. He prodded the grass with the toe of his boot. "Someone blew lunch," he said. "Does that look like turkey chunks to you?"

Middleton looked down at the mash and globs of mucus without comment, thinking that if it was turkey, the meal looked much the same as it did before being eaten.

"And why did they leave the M60 on the ground?" the sergeant continued. "It looks like they started to take it." He pushed at the linked rounds with the same inquisitive toe. "And they didn't even try for the other one."

Two squad members dragged Tanner's body into the open air and went back for the new guy whose name they couldn't remember. The sergeant stooped and grabbed something from the shadows where the bulkhead met the deck: a web belt sliced neatly through both layers. He held it up, looking across the grassy expanse where staggered paths of trampled grass led zigzag courses to the tree line. "It looks like the bastards went across on line," he said. "Why would they do that?"

Middleton looked at the abandoned 60, the riceless puke, and the belt. "I think Reach skyed up and took the Chief with him," he said. He looked to the edge of the tree line where shadowy shapes could have been anything. "And I think they had to *didi* because Charley was after them.

$\approx$

The Sparrow Hawk platoon filed past the wreck, their legs soaked to the knees by the wet grass. Lieutenant Hewitt peeled away with a radioman and one fire team, leaving Sergeant Litinsky to take the rest into the tree line to secure the dark green areas from where danger was likely to come. Corporal Pusic followed the officer's CP to the chopper. He was out of his element here, and he knew it. In just the last hour he had gone from eight long months in-country to being the FNG in the field. It was the kind of culture shock he had been sure he could avoid, and the short-timer's calendar in his desk drawer agreed with him more each day. That desk seemed far away now. His mind raced to find a way back there so he would have a chance to mark that calendar again. He could see Staff Sergeant Blackwell from 1st Platoon standing beside the chopper wreckage with Bronsky while other Marines labored moving heavy loads from inside.

When Sergeant Blackwell saw Lieutenant Hewitt heading in his direction he called out, "Sir, I have people in the tree line," pointing vaguely to the general area where he imagined they might be.

The lieutenant spoke over his shoulder to his radioman without breaking stride. "Tell Litinsky we have friendlies in the trees."

When the small group got close enough, Pusic could see the fruits of the Marines' labor lying in the grass: five bodies, too still, too quiet. The dead had an awkward composure of their own. Their angles lacked life, and they conformed to any uncomfortable position they were assigned without complaint. Death had freed their limbs to assume attitudes restricted only by the limitations of human joint dynamics. The position of their heads didn't seem quite right. Viability gone, they were just grotesque husks of stolen potential.

Pusic's daily efforts had all been designed to avoid the realities of combat. Now, ten lifeless boot bottoms were showing him the blind grooves in their treads. That was the trouble with Vietnam. No matter what your job and how safe your situation, the horror of battle was always close.

≈

The distant murmur of a Cessna Bird Dog droned down from where it drifted just below the cloud ceiling. The engine had an almost soothing sound. It spoke to the Marines with a familiar voice that reminded them of home and clear summer days with civilian pilots in their Pipers and Cessnas, looking down on Home Town USA from a bird's perspective. The six-cylinder engine that filled the cockpit with noise was a calming voice from the other side of the world to those on the ground. But there were other, more significant reasons for taking comfort in the little aircraft's ethereal song. The Bird Dog pilots were forward air controllers, and though the FACs had no real armament beyond the marking rockets under their wings and the pilot's personal firearms, their innocuous sputtering carried with it a lethal promise, like the tip of a dorsal fin at the ocean surface held the promise of flesh-ripping teeth below. With a map, a radio, and some calculations scribbled on the windscreen with a grease pencil, the FAC could rain death down on any spot he chose. The Fowler flaps could drop the little machine into a rollercoaster dive, swooping close to the ground and teasing the enemy into a lethal mistake.

The Bird Dogs were like the weak kid in school who thumbed his nose at the bullies because he had strong brothers who would pound the snot out of anyone with the lack of foresight to think he was an easy target. The FAC's big brothers were F-105s and F-4s that could split the sky at five hundred knots and make the ground shudder. With the Bird

Dog's simple direction to "hit my smoke" a jet-powered arsenal would rip and burn the jungle until the trees themselves wept in regret.

Sergeant Blackwell looked up at the little aircraft hanging suspended on invisible air currents. "The LT must be pretty pissed to put eyes in the sky," he said. "Get ready for some fast movers." Those around him looked up as though seeing the strutted wings ducking the clouds could put a face on Lieutenant Diehl's anger.

When the sergeant's eyes dropped back to earth, they settled on Pusic lurking behind the Sparrow Hawk radioman. He couldn't have stood out more had he been wearing dress blues. The sergeant's brow wrinkled in confusion at seeing a familiar face outside its normal habitat, like seeing your priest in his street clothes. It took a minute for the juxtaposition to work itself out in his mind. "You lost?" he asked, watching Pusic try to wilt behind Lieutenant Hewitt's people.

Pusic focused his attention on Corporal Middleton, who was kneeling by the bodies reading from dog tags while Doc Brede filled out the casualty cards. "Woods, Daniel A., Warrant Officer, Protestant," Middleton said in a hushed voice, trying not to look at the damage AK rounds had done to the young copilot's body. Brede filled in the appropriate spaces on the tag and wrote KIA in big letters. Pusic watched the two Marines at their task. This was something he could understand: paperwork. Everything in the Corps boiled down to a clerical notation somewhere, from a lost gas mask to a lost life. Middleton moved on. "Kobert, Eric R., Lance Corporal, Catholic."

Corporal Pusic forced himself to search the still bodies with his eyes. Two wore pilot's flak gear; one wore new utilities; one was too young, with a pockmarked face; and the last had the wrong color hair. He moved to get a better angle on the helicopter's interior. "Anybody else in there?" he asked, trying to ignore the sergeant's stare.

Sergeant Blackwell looked past Lieutenant Hewitt's people, expecting to see faces further up the Corps' food chain, the kind of rank with the weight to drag a company clerk along when they went into the field. Maybe the captain, or worse, someone from the battalion's larger brass circle that Corporal Pusic orbited. Nothing was obvious. It appeared that the spic-and-span corporal was here alone.

"I asked if you were lost," the sergeant said in a voice meant not to be ignored.

Middleton looked up to see who the sergeant was talking to with such an edge.

Lieutenant Hewitt barked a sit rep to An Hoa over the radio and beckoned Sergeant Blackwell with an impatient wave of his hand.

Sergeant Blackwell pointed a finger at the clerk's face without comment, as if to punctuate a pause in a conversation that was far from over, then turned toward the Sparrow Hawk CP.

Pusic craned his neck to see into the damp shadows of the helicopter, half hoping, half expecting to see Strader's sun-browned face crawling out, prisoner in tow, to save his clerical ass and the lifestyle to which he was accustomed.

Middleton hurried through the information on the new set of dog tags in his hand. "Crowell, Fredrick P., Warrant Officer, Protestant," he said. There was no need to bother with the other two bodies, familiar corpses he had helped carry from the mountain, tags with all the information needed by posterity already flapping from their bootlaces. He stepped away from the bodies, leaving Doc Brede to finish his work.

Pusic surveyed the wide expanse of wet grass that ended at the lush green tree line and the Marines from the Sparrow Hawk platoon moving along it. Being this far outside An Hoa's perimeter gave him an odd, exposed feeling, like he was standing on the parapet of some tall building gazing at the emptiness below, with nothing but empty air between him and a wet stain on the pavement. He could hear the voice of Sergeant Blackwell in animated conversation with Lieutenant Hewitt. Other members of the squad from 1st Platoon worked close to the wrecked helicopter, and though he knew he had plenty of company standing on this green building's precipice, he still felt alone, as though everyone around him was blind to the portent of the view and he was the only one with acrophobia.

"What the hell are you doing here?" Middleton said, standing by the feet of the dead Marines as though moving away would be a kind of betrayal.

Pusic examined the tired-looking Marine with his M16 slung barrel-down over a shoulder. "They sent me to find the . . . the prisoner," he said, then let his eyes sweep over the bodies.

Middleton looked the clerk over as though he was giving an inspection and didn't like what he saw. "You won't find him there, pogue."

The Cessna Bird Dog finished a lazy circle that carried it from the valley to the higher slopes of the Ong Thu. It banked to port, then dipped its nose. A sudden *whoosh* sent a rocket of white smoke into the trees that rose into the air like a ghost trying to escape the confines of the jungle.

Sergeant Blackwell finished with Lieutenant Hewitt and started back, tethered to Bronsky's radio by the coil of cord. He signed off and tossed the black handset back to Bronsky. Despite all the rain and wet grass, the handset was still dry inside its coating of clear C-rat plastic. "The platoon is on the way down with two dead and three wounded," the sergeant said, stopping by the open side of the helicopter between the wreck and the line of bodies on the ground. "Lieutenant Diehl says they should come out onto the valley somewhere just south of the lake in about an hour."

Middleton looked to the mountain where a diffuse column of white smoke was struggling through the weave of branches. "Who's dead?" he said, watching as the lazily rising smoke and the humming Bird Dog worked in soothing concert before their intended collaboration rained a pyrotechnic shitstorm onto the slope.

The sergeant seemed not to hear the question. He only had eyes for the company clerk standing in the wet grass, his starched uniform soaking up the light rain. "Are you people out of your fucking minds back there?" he said to Pusic. "The stress of beer limits at the EM Club or not enough pogey bait at the geedunk making you soft in the head? Sending a Marine into the Arizona with only a couple of days left in-country; that was a shit-for-brains move."

Pusic felt the sergeant's words like punches. He had to deflect the anger to another target, but he had to do it without burning any bridges, especially bridges that he needed to carry him across the rest of his tour. He had to point an accusing finger, but it had to be nonspecific, the target anonymous. The only thing that could help him was the natural enmity between the ranks. "I didn't send anyone anywhere. I'm not running this company. I take orders like everyone else. If you're looking for someone who gives orders," he added, "you're going to have to look a lot further up the totem pole than me."

Blackwell and Middleton exchanged glances. "Is he making a joke?" Middleton asked in disbelief.

"I don't know." The sergeant looked the clerk over from helmet to boots and back again, as if the trip might provide a better understanding of the man's motives. "That wouldn't be a crack aimed at the Chief, would it?"

Pusic's face registered his confusion, and he looked around cautiously in case 1st Platoon's wild man was somewhere near. Maybe totem pole was a poor choice of images that might be misconstrued as an insult, and he didn't want to say anything that would set the Chief off.

"Why the hell would I do that?" Pusic said.

"You said you were looking for him," Middleton said.

"Like hell, I did."

"You said you were here looking for the prisoner."

"Yeah, the prisoner escort and, of course, the prisoner, too."

The sergeant stepped up close to the clerk, uncomfortably close. "The Chief *is* the prisoner. And you people sent Reach . . . Strader . . . out here with two damned days left on his tour."

The clerk felt his throat constrict like the Chief already had a crushing grip on it. It was amazing how quickly the status quo could dissolve into garbage in the Crotch. One day things were going along smoothly, and the next the villagers were screaming for your blood. He didn't see how he could possibly catch any blame for the Chief being a prisoner. Beyond that, any personal responsibility he might bear for Strader's presence was speculation for these Marines. "I don't know anything about crimes the Chief committed," he said, though horrifying transgressions he might envision only in nightmares were, to his thinking, well within the Chief's capabilities.

The sergeant seemed to be suddenly uncomfortable with the direction of the conversation. "That communication with the com shack was in error. There was no prisoner. And since no prisoner, there was no need for an escort."

Pusic was confused at the sergeant's discomfort, but he just shrugged. The backbone of discretion is silence, and since anything he might say would only fuel the fire or provide information he didn't want to share, he kept his mouth shut.

The sound of a distant blast furnace forced its way into the valley from the north, and two machines dropped through the clouds and materialized in a roaring streak above the bridge at Phu Loc. F-4 Phantoms in mottled camouflage banked to starboard, and the dripping thatch roofs of Phu Phong 3 passed in a blink below their wingtips. The F-4 pilots confirmed the Bird Dog's position then zeroed in on the mountainside. The trailing Phantom banked to port, showing its light underbelly to the trees, and pointed one wing at the ground, ripping a wide arc that would carry it around to its starting point in a circle filled with crushing G-force. The lead Phantom concentrated on the distant smoke. Two air-to-surface missiles flashed from under its wings, and it was already into its own arching circle when the missiles punched through the smoke and great chunks of the Ong Thu leapt up in protest.

Pusic moved to where he could see over the tail of the downed chopper and watch the aerial ballet. Phantoms flying close air support were always an awesome spectacle. The fighters' turbojet engines made the ground quake, and it took a special effort not to suck your head down into your shoulders when they split the air overhead at mach speeds. The other members of the squad looked up for a second, then went about the business of collecting gear from the helicopter. They had witnessed the Phantoms' aerobatics before and didn't need to watch them to appreciate their presence. A sense of ease ran through ground troops when two such formidable weapons were on station. They also knew that any VC in proximity were already burning up their sandals trying to get clear. The only question was whether they could run fast enough and far enough to avoid the Phantoms' reach.

Right now, the task at hand overrode all else. Belts of M60 ammunition from the crew compartment, crew weapons, and maps and personal gear from the cockpit were added to a growing pile in the grass. The ground Marines' only nagging concern was that the F-4s might not know exactly where the U.S. troops were. Often, the distance between friendly and enemy was negligible, and not one of the weapons of death in the Phantoms' arsenal could discriminate between them.

The second Phantom closed on the spot where the air-to-surface missiles struck, then lifted and banked to port. A 500-pound general purpose bomb with a fuse extender fell away from the undercarriage. The long nose guided the bomb's trajectory like the point of a knight's lance, ensuring that detonation would be aboveground. The blast was enormous. Trees shook and shed their leaves, and a shock wave spread out from the blast's center like ripples in an arboreal pond. All the

Marines in the valley felt the impact of the distant explosion through the soles of their boots. The first Phantom streaked back in and another GP struck the mountain a little higher up than the first. Again the trees shuddered and leaves fell and the ground telegraphed a spasm of its pain to the valley floor.

Until that moment Pusic hadn't been able to think of a worse place to be than in the miserable, wet valley next to the still congregation of bodies and their dead machine, but the mountain sounded like Hell itself had split open, and for a second he was grateful to be where he was.

The Phantoms spun in turn on their deadly G-force merry-go-round delivering high explosives to the face of the Ong Thu. They would continue until their arsenal was exhausted or the FAC in the Cessna called them off like a handler calling off a pair of attack dogs.

One of Lieutenant Hewitt's CP caught Sergeant Blackwell's attention. "The lieutenant wants you," he said, indicating the spot where the officer was trying to block the jets' roar, covering one ear with a hand and pushing the radio handset up tight against the other, barking into the mouthpiece like a DI on a drill field to make himself heard above a cluster bomb ripping a hole in the high slope.

Lt. Mark Hewitt stood a little shy of five feet eight inches with muscular shoulders and thick forearms. Like Lieutenant Diehl he had been a collegiate wrestler. Back in those days he worked the weight room until his opponents would groan when they found themselves matched with the "little guy." He was fair skinned, and his arms below the faded green sleeves of his T-shirt bore patches of red with white edges of peeling skin where the Southeast Asian sun was trying to congeal his freckles into one solid mass. He made up for his lack of height with a no-nonsense attitude and a single-minded focus on his position as platoon commander. He was a decisive leader who never showed a second of hesitation or doubt and would not tolerate either in his men.

After Hewitt was finished screaming into the handset he turned to Sergeant Blackwell. "My people say they found a spot just inside the tree line with a bunch of freshly spent 7.62 brass," he said, pointing to the tree line where Blackwell could make out Marines stepping into the open.

The sergeant nodded. "We've got two men missing from this crash. One is wounded, and the other carries a 14."

The lieutenant's face revealed sympathy. "That could explain it; maybe they're on the run." He looked away and didn't hint that it could be anything else. "My sergeant found lots of tracks leading toward high ground, but I'm not sending my people after them. We're ordered to set up security here until this bird is stripped and lifted out, and I'm guessing that won't be until sometime in the morning."

"I don't think I can wait, and I know my two missing people can't."

The Bird Dog flitted just above the valley floor, the pilot watching the Phantoms' exercises through the transparent window in the wing above his head. He directed the Phantoms to move their strikes higher and five hundred yards north. He assumed the direction would be to high ground, but this was just speculation, and he knew he was shooting blind. The jungle canopy cloaked both the terrain and movement on the mountain, and he knew he could direct sorties all day with no guarantee that the expended ordnance would hit anything but trees.

Sergeant Blackwell moved to the opening in the helicopter and shoved an arm into the shadows, drawing out a pack. "Second Squad, mount up," he said. When he got close enough to where Middleton stood he tossed the pack into Pusic's arms.

"What's this for?" Pusic said.

"I noticed that you didn't have your pack with you. I guess you were planning on a short trip."

Pusic dangled the pack by its strap like it was something distasteful. He wondered which of the men on the ground had owned it, then decided he didn't want to know.

"You said you wanted Strader and the Chief," the sergeant said. "Well, let's go get them."

The sergeant was right. Pusic *was* planning on a short trip, and it was already longer than he thought prudent for his health. "I'm here with the Sparrow Hawk platoon," he protested. "I should stay with them." He was on the ledge of that green building again, and now the ledge was crumbling under his feet. What little stability there was in his situation—and there was precious little—was dissolving, threatening to leave him hanging in thin air.

"Bronsky," the sergeant said, "get me Golf CP in An Hoa. Let's find out what role the pogue played in this fuck-up. He sure as hell didn't volunteer for this trip."

Pusic wanted to intervene. If there was something he could say that would stop the radioman from reaching An Hoa without admitting his part in Strader's situation he would say it, but the words weren't there.

The corpsman from the Sparrow Hawk platoon was helping Doc Brede with his pack. They knew each other well enough to use first names. All the corpsmen were members of a small, exclusive fraternity in the battalion. There were only two for each platoon. When they found time in the chow hall they sometimes shared some unique, personal slant on field treatment that had been successful for them, but mostly they just exchanged knowing glances filled with futility. Being the first responders in combat put them in an untenable situation, and they knew it. They were there because the Navy physicians' medical degrees were far too valuable to risk in ground combat. The corpsmen's job was to keep the wounded alive long enough to reach the golden hands of the overworked surgeons, and to stay alive while doing it. They did this whenever possible, but sometimes, they knew, it wasn't possible to do either.

Bronsky passed the radio handset to the sergeant while the last of the Phantoms' munitions struck the Ong Thu. The explosions echoed across the valley, leaving Blackwell bellowing into the handset while the jets swept a blistering arch and rose up through the cloud ceiling to disappear like winged specters, leaving only the roar of their engines as an ethereal proof of their existence.

"Pusic, right?" the sergeant said, holding out the handset. "Sergeant Gantz wants to speak with you."

Pusic stepped up and took the handset, tentatively holding it to an ear. He didn't want to hear anything Sergeant Gantz had to say, but he couldn't refuse. Sergeant Blackwell moved away, not to give the clerk privacy but because he already knew the outcome of the conversation.

Franklin came around the tail of the helicopter and stopped where the bodies compressed the wet grass. "Are we going after Reach and the Chief?" he said, tugging at the straps on his pack.

Middleton cocked his head toward Sergeant Blackwell and shrugged. "Don't ask me. I'm only the squad leader."

Franklin smiled, knowing how much Middleton hated to have his authority usurped.

Sergeant Blackwell held out his M16 by the sight mount as though it was the handle on a piece of luggage. "Let's pretend the Crotch is a democracy. Who votes for going after our people?" A short pause followed while he waited for the voices of the constituents. "How about it, Middleton. Do we go?"

Middleton nodded.

"What about you, Franklin. Put your two cents in."

"The Chief always makes me nervous, but if you're goin' after Reach, I'm cool with that."

The sergeant smiled and let the M16 swing down at his side. "Now don't you feel good about having participated in the democratic process?"

Franklin shifted his weight from foot to foot, as though he was either embarrassed or anxious to stop being a stationary target. "We was goin' no matter what we said, right?"

"That's right, Franklin. In case you assholes didn't notice, this green machine is *not* a democracy. If the Marines wanted you to have a vote, they would have issued you one."

Pusic gave the handset back to Bronsky and stood there waiting for a bolt of lightning to reach down from the gloom and strike him dead; the way things were going, it wasn't an unlikely possibility.

Sergeant Blackwell watched him standing there like an orphan with the borrowed pack dangling at his side and put on his best Cheshire Cat smile. "Gantz tells me you're a good man and that he can't remember a time when you didn't complete an assignment. He says he's sure you won't come back without completing this one. I don't know if that means that he has confidence in you or that if you don't find Strader and the Chief, he doesn't want you back at all. Either way, you belong to me."

Pusic stepped over, dragging the pack limply through the grass. "Gantz is just a sergeant," he said pompously. "He can't make decisions that impact the whole company, not without the captain's okay." He knew as soon as he said it that his self-important tone wouldn't sit well here.

"Really?" Sergeant Blackwell said, his grin showing real pleasure. Besides wanting to pop Pusic's delusions of grandeur, being a staff sergeant himself, he didn't like to hear someone in his rank structure being described as ineffectual. "Tell me the last time you heard of a captain taking a corporal's side against a first sergeant." He didn't wait for an answer. "That's right. Never happened, never will. So don't give me a ration of shit." He softened his smile and put his hand on Pusic's shoulder as though he were Father Flanagan welcoming a wayward child to Boy's Town. "As of now you are our own personal rear echelon mother fucker." The smile disappeared. "So, get your REMF ass in gear, strap that pack on your back, and fall in behind the radio. What are you complaining about, anyway? You'll finally get to see how the 0311s live, because as of now you are one."

Pusic didn't move, couldn't move. Gantz had thrown him to the wolves and now he was being abducted by the pack.

"That's an order, Corporal. You disobey it and I'll show you how much power a sergeant can have in the field."

Pusic resignedly pushed an arm through one of he pack straps, then balanced his M16 between his knees and struggled with the other. Bronsky lifted the pack and helpfully guided the strap onto the clerk's shoulder with a slap. "Don't mess with the sergeant, man," he said. "He's in a piss poor mood. This morning he took my .45 and stuck it in the Chief's face and threatened to blow his brains out. And he wasn't kidding."

"So he's not that fond of the Chief either?"

"It ain't that. He just thought the Chief killed Tanner and the new guy last night. Now he thinks maybe the VC did it."

Pusic gave the radioman a puzzled look. He'd always known that he left sanity behind when he landed in Vietnam, but he'd always been able to keep the madhouse at arm's length. Now, here he was, getting his own personal glimpse at the inner workings of Bedlam. "Killed two guys?" he said, shrugging the pack into a more comfortable position.

"Well, Diehl and Blackwell say no, but I'm not so sure."

Sergeant Blackwell looked back along the fuselage to see if his people were ready. "Franklin. Your fire team is on point. Follow that wide path through the grass to the tree line, and don't bunch up." This last was said with enough volume so everyone could hear.

Second Squad of Golf Company's 1st Platoon began moving away from the downed chopper in prescribed intervals until their elongated line stretched halfway to the jungle.

Doc Brede handed the casualty tags to the Sparrow Hawk corpsman with an apologetic look. "These are for the chopper crew. Make sure they get on the right . . ." He couldn't think of a description that wasn't so final and cold. "You know . . . where they belong. I gotta go."

"Yeah, don't worry. Catch you later."

It was funny how simple terms that slipped easily from the tongue took on an ominous overtone in Vietnam. Back in the world you might say "see you later" or "I'll be right back" with a negligent assurance that didn't elicit another thought. The element of doubt was absent. But in-country, nothing in the future held even a hint of a guarantee. "See you later" was just a wish. The target of the remark wasn't even important. Only the idea of being around to make good on it was.

The impermanence of life in the field was also fertile ground for superstitions to take root. Everyone seemed to have something in his possession that lent an artificial comfort to his travails—a symbol of religious faith, a memento from home, some talisman that accompanied a stroke of luck that could rub off on the present, anything that might exert a supernatural influence. For Doc Brede it was a book. Not a specific book, but whatever book he was reading. There was a point, beyond the first pages, where your mind was absorbed by the story. You slipped into another reality and lived there until the end. It would be unthinkable to leave that reality unfinished. Even the vagaries of fate must see that. So Doc Brede would never finish a book before going into the field. The story would have to be finished later. And the only way for it to be finished was for him to come back and finish it. Dying was something you did when there was nothing left to do. And he always had to finish a book. Even now, stuffed into his seabag in the company storage tent in An Hoa, the remaining chapters of H. G. Well's *The Time Machine* sat waiting for his return. He also planned ahead. In his field pack, crammed in next to his jungle shirt and extra tee, he carried a paperback Steinbeck novel with the bookmark creeping its way into the volume. If it wasn't finished before the next trip, it would be left behind to wait, a mystical assurance that he would return. That he must return.

Every step Strader and the Chief took disturbed something winged or clawed that escaped their presence with a rustle of feathers or a scratch on stone. What little noise the Marines made went ahead of them like a warning, and any creature with speed in its makeup scampered aside.

The huge stones they were moving through had cool, damp surfaces carpeted with green moss that was soft to the touch. The two Marines struggled up through the angular slabs until the Chief tugged at Strader's arm. He was too winded to speak, but looked up with a haggard face and pointed to a niche in the stone with enough clearance for them to pass through. Beyond the opening, a pocket of natural space provided protection on all sides. The Chief slid down into the scuppers, his head in his hands.

Strader climbed up to where the weight of vines dragged a sapling over to touch the stone rim and peeked through the tangle of branches. A panoramic view of the mountain below lay before him, giving a clear field of fire all the way to the fallen tree at the foot of the slope. He was satisfied. He slid down to the Chief's side. "They'll play hell getting us out of here."

The Chief looked around at the stone enclosure that had waited for decades, possibly centuries, for two needy Marines to come along and find it useful. "We'll play hell getting ourselves out of here."

Strader squatted down, standing the M14 between his knees, and rested his forehead against the barrel. "What the hell am I doing here?"

"You signed on the dotted line, Reach. The shores of Tripoli and all that."

"I mean, I was home free. I was packing my bags and making peace with the guys in the rear with the gear." He held up two fingers in a miniscule measurement. "I was this close to a mixed drink with ice served by a stewardess on an air-conditioned jetliner, looking forward to Vietnam being nothing more than a last-page story in a newspaper." He shook his head in disbelief.

"Oh, you mean what are *you* doing here?" the Chief said, watching Strader trying to come to terms with his predicament. "And maybe you think I'm to blame for that."

Strader took a long, hard look at the Chief as though seeing him clearly for the first time. "Aren't you, Chief?"

The Chief looked away, embarrassed at his inability to give a straight answer. "I don't know. I don't remember. I don't . . . think so. But I do know one thing." He fixed Strader with a hard stare. "We'll get along a lot better if you stop calling me Chief. I don't call you Governor or Mayor."

Strader searched the Chief's blood-smeared face, trying to gauge his mood. "What would you like me to call you?"

"I think I told you before, my last name is Gonshayee." The name came out with guttural stops and sharp hisses of air.

"Gong . . . sha . . . ee? It couldn't be something like Jones or Smith? What do your friends call you?" Strader couldn't remember the Chief being close to anyone in the platoon, but he had to assume that somewhere in the Chief's past he had to have had some kind of human interactions that could be loosely construed as friendships that might generate a nickname.

"My people call me Kle-ga-na-ai." Again the name came out chopped into blunt syllables with the tongue.

Strader looked at the Chief like he was begging for a little cooperation. "Come on, man. Give me something I can work with."

The Chief squeezed his eyes shut and cocked his head, listening to a faint sound in his head trying to get his attention, a whistling spirit piercing the black shroud that consumed his memory. He opened his eyes to mere slits and pointed a finger at Strader. "I did tell you my name before, didn't I?"

"Yeah, I think you did. Right after the lieutenant asked if you wanted to shoot me."

"I remember that," the Chief said happily. He looked back at Strader. "You know I wasn't going to shoot you, right?"

Strader checked his web belt. The magazine pouches had four snapped inside, but one was empty. There was one full in the weapon. The stacked pouches for his fragmentation grenades held nothing. He pulled the backpack close and tossed the flap open. Inside were two C-rat meals—one turkey, one ham—a pair of socks, a Kodak Instamatic camera, half a box of 5.56 ammunition for the M16, three packs of grape Kool-Aid, and a bundled jungle shirt with lance corporal chevrons on the collar. The roll of the shirt protected a leather-handled KA-BAR without a sheath. He knew it was Tanner's pack.

"Did you hear me, Reach? I wasn't going to shoot you."

Strader tore open one of the Kool-Aid packs and dumped some of it into the remains of their water. He shook the canteen. "Yeah, I guess I knew that."

The Chief nodded with an expression of relief.

Strader sniffed the water then screwed the plastic cap back on. "But you know why Diehl singled you out for the job, don't you?"

"Why?"

"Because of the doubt. No one could be certain. You're fighting two wars here, man. Nobody knows which you hate more, whites or the VC. Your back is always up. To your way of thinking, you're surrounded by enemies, and you don't seem to mind which one you fight."

The Chief drew in a lungful of air, pushing his chest out. "I'm Chiricahua Apache. We are warriors. And we've been at war with whites for generations. Hell, we've been at war with everyone. Do you know what the word 'apache' means? It means 'enemy.' We were given that name by the Zuni, who learned our true nature the hard way . . . and we adopted it as our own. Before that we were the Ndee, but 'enemy' was a more accurate description of who we were. Imagine that. We were named by people who feared and hated us, and we liked the name. That should tell you something."

Strader was dumbfounded. He couldn't remember the Chief stringing this many words together since he joined the platoon. "This ain't the Old West, Chief, or, ah . . . Kleg-a-neg . . . ah, shit, man."

The distant mountain erupted with a pitched firefight that sounded like a coming storm. The two Marines traded knowing looks. After days of wandering about the mountain and valley, their people had finally stumbled onto something big, and the something was biting them. Strader turned to crawl up the rocks.

"Reach," the Chief said, grabbing at Strader's arm.

Strader stopped.

"Kle-ga-na-ai," the Chief whispered, as though the distant firefight demanded a sudden quiet here.

"Yeah, Kleg-a . . . something, right. I know."

The Chief pulled Strader near, as though he needed to say something confidential, something even the trees shouldn't hear. "Kle-ga-na-ai," he said. "It means 'moon.' My people call me Moon."

≈

Hoang Li knew that Nguyen would lead the main unit across the face of the mountain; if he could hold his little group to their present course, he would intercept Nguyen's path somewhere in the heights. The problem was the Americans somewhere ahead.

The three-man cell worked their way up through the trees, spread out but within sight of each other, carrying some of the load dispensed by the survivors of the team caught in the open. All three were alert, their weapons at the ready, expecting at any second to trip over the fleeing Americans. The track cut before them was easily followed, though this in itself was a reason for caution because it was never wise to allow yourself to be led in the South. But once past the downed tree, the close cover thinned and they had to watch the ground for fresh disturbances in the soil. Hoang Li knew that if the enemy was tired enough or injured enough, or just angry enough to stop running, he and his men would walk into their rifles. Hoang pushed a hand up under his magazine pouches and touched the sore spot in the middle of his chest. He didn't think he could count on being lucky again.

The battle that ran its course back along the mountain did not concern Hoang much. It was a distant, grumbling storm, so Nguyen's detachment was surely not involved. He guessed that the Americans were butting heads with some of the R-20th Doc Lap, and the thought made him smile. It was good to have company. He looked back to the line of bearers downslope, the snags and natural foot snares sapping what little energy they had to drag their heavy loads back into the heights, and signaled a halt. Everyone stopped and squatted in place. The only sounds were the muted clatter of raindrops and chittering birds flitting through high branches searching for a dry perch. Hoang's cell partners watched him with interest, their faces coated with a glossy sheen of rain and sweat and expressions of admiration. They seemed to have a newfound regard for him. The gods had smiled on Hoang, and when he faced certain death, had aligned conditions in just the right way to spare his life. He was charmed, and a recipient of divine dispensation bore watching. While they squatted, the ominous thuds of multiplying rotors filtered up from the valley. Every pulse confirmed that they would be wise to stay close to Hoang Li.

$$\approx$$

A movement below caught Strader's eye, and he watched as the three NVA felt a path along the dead tree and began to thread their way upward. The three moved apart, painting the hillside with the silent sweep of their weapons. Strader sank until his eyes were level with the stone, slid his M14 slowly to his side, and swallowed hard.

Pressed into the moss-covered stone with his three magazines of ammunition, watching the enemy move closer, each burdened by a load of lethal weapons that proved they had no lack of resources, he could see the awful decision to be made, and there was no optimistic slant that could change his estimation of the result. It would be the last decision of his life, and he would be making it for both of them.

Strader looked down at the Chief leaning against the stone. He wondered what the Indian might decide. The Chief looked up to meet his gaze, his face mottled with patches of red and purple, one eye now as dark as a blood marble. Without speaking, the Apache drew his long knife from its sheath and moved to the narrow opening in the stones. The fissure was small. Only one could pass through at a time. Those who did would find the blade waiting. Strader nodded. Their situation was dire and they both knew it. It didn't need analysis. They were a consensus of two without saying a word, mutually screwed by circumstances.

Turning back to the rock rim slowly so that his movement wouldn't attract an enemy eye, Strader saw that all their pursuers had sunk to the ground. He watched them and wondered. Had they made a decision of their own? As he looked on, the center of the three stood, his AK with its long, curved magazine held tightly, the butt working its way to his shoulder. There was something familiar about this soldier. Strader concentrated on the man's face, the shape of his hat, the bearing of his shoulders. He could hit him easily now where he stood, but that seemed somehow redundant. He had looked at this man over his sights before.

He had put that face down. The tracker from the valley should still be in the valley, but instead he was standing below the tumble of stone, alive, alert, and promising trouble.

An odd relief swept through Strader like a sudden chill. The decision he dreaded making slipped away. A decision deferred was a decision lost. There was no choice now. This man could and would track them through the stones. This enemy who had come back from death to stand at the edge of their seclusion would read the mountain and invade their sanctuary. The assumption of choice had been an illusion.

Strader eased his rifle upward, inching it forward by fractions through the clinging branches until its vented muzzle pointed in the direction of the standing Vietnamese. Pellets of rain smacked the bent tree's leaves and thumped the moss coating the rock. The drops slapped the brim of his soft cover, sending splashes into a spray, and struck the back of his shirt, soaking through the already saturated material to his skin. He aimed at the standing man. Just because a decision had been forced didn't make it any easier.

≈

The path the Americans had made passed right under Hoang Li's squat, and he could see the line vanish into the trees, heading toward an ancient rock slide. If he were the one running injured, with finite energies, that was where he would go. If they were looking for a place to rest or hide, or even fight, they would find nowhere better. Far behind him, the shuttle of helicopters sent vibrations up the mountain. The two Americans above him would soon be joined by others of their kind. Time was short. Hoang peered up the mountain and considered the possibilities. At the sound of movement on his left, along the face of the Ong Thu above the Gordian knot of ground cover, he rose to his feet and slowly pulled the butt plate of his AK toward his shoulder. It was unlikely that the Americans had come this far this soon, but their mobility always made the unlikely possible.

Before the AK barrel reached a level aim, the forward members of Nguyen's bearers scrambled into sight, pushing forward under the weight of their burdens as fast as their legs could carry them. Hoang lowered his weapon. His two companions were drawn to their feet as though a magnet was pulling them from above. They waved their arms frantically. The sight of the main unit drew the others waiting below with a resurgence of energy. They kicked and clawed their way up the mountain, fulfilling a natural need to rejoin their main element like errant beads of spilled mercury are drawn to the mother pool, a human quicksilver.

The recoilless rifle rocked by on unsteady shoulders, still bound with leafy branches that gave it the appearance of an uprooted tree. The carriers nodded at Hoang Li but saved their breath for their load.

Nguyen came from behind the decorated gun and stepped out of the column. The heavy pack board laden with recoilless and mortar rounds made him stagger on the wet ground. Before he could speak, Hoang Li lowered his head and pointed behind him. "We lost one in the valley," he said, not looking at his commander as though the news would not be well received or might be misinterpreted as a personal condemnation.

Nguyen's breathing was deep and sounded painful. "And the others?" he gasped.

Hoang Li met Nguyen's gaze. "All here," he said with surprising satisfaction.

Nguyen nodded. Another man lost, but acceptance was his only option. "Good," he said.

Hoang seemed puzzled. Was it congratulations for leading the survivors back to the fold, or was it just an appreciation for the succinctness of the report?

Nguyen started to turn back to the drudges passing by him. Hoang Li grabbed his arm. "Two of the enemy got away from the helicopter. I'm sure one is wounded." He could see from the look on Nguyen's face that this was an unwelcome problem. "We followed them this far."

Nguyen scanned the upper mountain, feeling the weight of feral eyes. He felt suddenly exposed. "You think they are close?"

Hoang let his attention wander to the closest of the mossy boulders and nodded. "They could be," he said.

The deep roar of jet engines suddenly filled the valley, startling the birds from their dry roosts. Worried faces in the passing column sought out Nguyen's reassurance and guidance; the American jets could be lethal. Would they seek cover or run? Only Nguyen could decide. He waved them on with an impatient swing of his arm that wordlessly demanded a jump in pace. He would not fail to move again.

The mechanical lion's roar from the clouds was followed by an explosion that seemed to crack the heart of the mountain, broadcasting a stutter that found the column's feet and drove them forward with a new passion.

"Join your comrades, Hoang," Nguyen said, leaning in close to be heard. "These fugitives are not our concern."

"They killed one of our comrades," Hoang Li said incredulously.

A new and larger explosion made the earth jump and the trees shake.

"We are not here to avenge our fallen, Hoang, at least not today." Nguyen pointed at the passing bearers. "Our revenge is in these weapons. We will spend what lives are necessary to get them to their destination, and then we will have our day."

S trader watched the enemy multiply in front of his sights. Instead of coming on, though, as he expected, the tracker turned away and met the new group of soldiers trotting by like an overloaded mule train carrying a variety of large weapons that made the first group appear unarmed. He drew his rifle back. The armament this new group was carrying would overmatch a full platoon of Marines in the field. Shooting now would be like bailing the ocean with a teaspoon.

F-4 Phantoms hit the distant mountain, and the rocks shivered below their moss coating as though they were alive. Strader could imagine the insults to the mountain's structure reanimating the rockslide and sweeping him and the Chief down to be ground into pulp in the confusion, carried away and buried so thoroughly that only opportunistic insects would witness their end. But the Phantom strikes were also a godsend, manna from a gray and leaking heaven that would redirect the NVA's efforts to self-preservation. The bombs hitting the face of the mountain were loud reminders that they were also hunted; and, for prey, unnecessary distractions could be fatal. A fresh explosion with more heft shook the trees, and the little sapling suffocated by attacking vines seemed to be fighting back.

Strader felt the Chief sidle up next to him. "Can you see them?" the Chief whispered. Strader nodded, and the Chief could see the concern in his eyes. "How many are there?"

Strader gave a short, involuntary laugh, forced out by the overwhelming hopelessness of their situation. "If Ho Chi Minh himself isn't there, it's because there isn't any room for him." He peeked back over the rock rim.

The Chief pulled himself up, digging his fingers into the moss until he was upright and the mountainside opened up in front of him. The column of NVA were filing by below the slide, a procession of mute stevedores shouldering their loads through the trees with determined faces as though they were on a tight schedule and their destination was just out of sight. The Chief adjusted his sagging bandage. "Do you think they'll come for us?"

Strader scooted down to a position where he could rake the opening to their little den with fire and turn the narrow passage into a slaughter-house. "I don't know. I'm hoping they have more important problems." He leveled the barrel of his rifle on the opening. "We'll find out soon."

The Chief looked down on the passing parade of weaponry, the NVA equivalent of the legions of tanks and missile launchers that rumbled through Moscow's Red Square on holidays in an arrogant demonstration of firepower. The drooping brims of the men's hats shed water, and their bare arms had a slick sheen that matched that of their clinging black tunics and pants. The footing became less certain with each passing bearer, and they struggled to stay upright, pushing their bundles forward.

The Chief blinked, trying to clear away the gossamer spots that obscured his vision. A chatter of metal on metal drew his attention back to the trees below, where a man trotted by with ammunition tins straining his arms. He was followed by one with a large tripod balanced across the hump of his pack. Then came two bent under the weight of a heavy machine gun of large caliber, working in tandem like a brace of yoked oxen, the black receiver and finned barrel spanning the distance between them. He watched them pass, the last of the column. Even with his barely functioning vision he could see that the final two seemed fresh-faced and younger than the others. He stared at the last man and then reached up to touch the empty space over his heart, clinching the center of his wet T-shirt within the curl of his fist.

Dancing on the sweeping arc of a rawhide pendulum around the neck of the second man was a kachina-like figure in polished beads, its lapis and turquoise body waving its arms at the perfectly fitted circle of melon shell moon. His grandmother's tribute to little Kle-ga-na-ai summoned his namesake across the face of the deerskin pouch rimmed with knotted dogbane.

At his birth, Gonshayee's grandmother had unraveled two of her finest heishi necklaces and stitched the miraculous little cylinders into a tribal pictograph of a young warrior in communion with his spiritual guide in a dark heaven. A drawstring squeezed the pouch's neck tight over a little curl of meat the consistency of dried beef, the same little curl that once connected Gonshayee to his mother's life source and was sliced away as he entered the world. Later, the little bit of umbilical was joined by talismans and charms of Gonshayee's choosing: a bear cub carved from a shard of horn; a black bracelet of woven horsehair; a smooth, round stone with dark spots marking the surface like the face of the full moon; and others, like the shaman's coin—all reminders of milestones in his tribal life that he cherished as lucky pieces. But the fragile birth cord was the guarantor of his self. As long as he counted it among his effects, his path would be true and just and honorable. His value as a man and a warrior was wrapped in the little coil, the guardian of his character and protector of his spirit. It was his first and most important possession and an essential part of him.

The line of NVA moved out of sight. The Chief craned his neck beyond the rock rim in hope of catching another glimpse, but they were gone.

Strader sidestepped through the narrow opening, keeping the muzzle of his rifle low so it wouldn't stick out and give advance warning that he was there. He leaned far enough forward so one eye could make out the natural path down through the stones. It was empty. He pulled back into the safety of the enclosure.

The Chief had slipped down to the foot of the inclined stone and was sitting there, bleary-eyed, his head wavering like the capital of a flagpole in a strong wind. "Gone?" he said as Strader backed in.

Strader crouched down, resting the rifle across his thighs, the barrel pointed toward the opening. "Maybe," he said. "I guess with all the other attention, we've become a low priority."

The Chief leaned back, resting his head against the soft moss. "An army of NVA against the two of us; they better run," he said.

Strader smiled at the bravado. "We'll wait awhile in case they have a rear guard, then head back to the valley."

The Chief raised his head, then let it sink back to the stone. "My head is spinning so much it feels like the whole damn mountain is moving. I don't think I can walk. You'll probably have to carry me down."

Strader looked at the Chief as though he'd just heard the final proof that the Indian had brain damage. "Like hell I will. You crawled up here, you can crawl back."

"No can do, white man. I go piggyback or not at all."

"I'm not gonna lug your ass down this mountain like a donkey carrying you on some canyon tour. We'll go down the way we came up."

The Chief shook his head, then regretted the movement. "I'm too sick to put one foot in front of the other. This is a good spot. Leave me here. You'll move faster without me anyway. You can be back here with the platoon in no time. It won't be the first time they carried me off this anthill today."

"I can't leave you here."

"Sure you can. Just head back the way we came until you run into a bunch of guys dressed like we are."

"Don't give me a ration of shit, Chi—I mean Moon. I'm responsible. I can't leave you here."

"Responsible for what? Me? You mean I'm your prisoner, don't you?"

"I mean that Gantz will bust my ass back to boot if I don't come back with you."

The regularly spaced explosions ended and the roar of jet engines faded to a distant rumble. The Phantoms were already blistering the air beyond the bridge at Phu Loc on their way back to Da Nang, leaving behind bald and smoking patches of mountain as the only evidence of their presence.

"I didn't say to leave me here permanently. I expect you to come back. I'm counting on you coming back. Hell, you're not really leaving me. I'm sending you . . . for help."

Strader searched the Chief's face with a skeptical eye. It was one thing if the Chief was truly unable to walk, but if he was making some noble sacrifice so a fellow Marine's short-timer calendar would end well, it wasn't going to fly. The swelling from the head wound had spread across the Chief's face, giving his blood-red eye a pudgy wink. "You're sending me? Who the fuck do I look like to you, Lassie?"

The Chief squinted. "For all I know, you do. I can't really see you that well."

Strader reached out to lift the Chief by the arm but had his grip torn free.

"You're not listening to me, Corporal. I'm not asking you for permission to stay. I'm telling you that I'm staying." The Chief pulled the long knife from its sheath and let the blade rest against his wet pant leg.

"Like you said, I really don't care who I fight. I don't know how much energy I have left, but if I have to use every last bit of it fighting you, I will."

Strader stepped back a pace, feigned disappointment on his face. "So, I guess this means we're enemies again . . . Moon."

The Chief let the knife slide from his leg to rest under his hand on the mossy stone. A long, exasperated breath gushed out. "No, it doesn't. It means that one friend shouldn't have to threaten another to get some help."

"This is the Corps . . . Moon. No one gets left behind."

"You're not abandoning me. It's going to take more than one man's sweat to get me off this mountain alive. I'm just asking you to go and get me some sweaty Marines. Is that too much to ask?"

Strader watched the Chief's head waver as though its weight was becoming too much for his neck to support. If he lost consciousness on the way down the mountain, it would be nearly impossible to carry him. Maybe he could be dragged, but even that would be a chore with someone the Chief's size, and his head wound would likely sustain further damage. It could be the Chief had a valid point.

The Chief's clear eye detected the hint of doubt lurking behind Strader's stubborn expression. "I'll be safe here," he insisted. "Just make sure nothing happens to you. You're the only one who knows where I am."

The legions of insects stunned to silence by the explosions returned to their rhythmic chant, an almost subterranean hum like electric circuits pulsing just below the surface of the jungle. Strader crawled past the Chief and peeked over the rock rim. The enemy was nowhere to be seen. "I think Charley skyed up. They probably expect mean green company. If we just sit tight and wait, the platoon will be along eventually."

The Chief looked at Strader like someone tired of explaining the complexities of long division to a moron. "I don't have time to wait. I've got a clock ticking in my head, and it's running down." He reached out and grabbed a handful of Strader's shirt. "I need to be somewhere else, and soon, or I won't be anywhere."

Strader wrapped a hand around the Chief's thick wrist and pulled the clutching fingers free. "Okay," he said. He pulled the canteen from its pouch and took a long pull on the Kool-Aid-fortified liquid. He wiped his mouth and handed the canteen to the Chief. The Chief's hand missed the canteen on its first try. Strader took note.

The Chief took a drink, letting the two oddly discordant tastes of halizone and sweet grape fight for dominance as they slipped into his roiling stomach. "I'll keep the canteen here with me," he said, struggling to thread the cap onto the neck.

"You move one inch from this spot and I'll personally put you in a world of hurt."

The Chief set the canteen on the ground between his feet. "I'm there already, shithead."

A weak smile spread across Strader's face. "I have a name, too, and it isn't shithead."

A similar smile, though lopsided, crossed the Chief's swollen features. "Yeah, I know. It's Raymond. How many mail calls have we been through together? Maybe you should ask yourself how I could know your name but you didn't know mine."

"Probably because everyone who called the mail stumbled over your name like it was a trip wire. I think it came out different every time." Strader stuck out his hand and let it hang there. The Chief looked at it as though it had a bad odor. "Come on, make it official," Strader said. The Chief pushed his right hand into the one waiting and gave it a limp squeeze.

Strader squeezed back. "Moon, I'm Ray."

The Chief looked up at Strader with the biggest scowl he could force his facial muscles to produce. "Ray, I'm Moon. Now go get me some damned help."

Strader let the Chief's hand drop. "I'll do what I can, but you listen up. If you hear shooting after I go, assume that you have to find your own way home."

"I'm filled with confidence."

"I shit you not, Marine. I would have bet that I'd be catching three squares in the chow hall and packing my bags today. Instead, I'm here. So nothing is a sure thing."

"I'm betting on you."

A nagging tug in the back of Strader's mind didn't stop him from sliding through the narrow opening and following the natural path down through the stones.

At the bottom of the slide, the path made by the NVA turned the soil into a black furrow that might have been cut by a plow. Strader crouched by the last boulder, letting the creature voices establish a pattern in his ear. The jungle seemed empty. The enemy column had kept moving, he was sure of that, but maybe a rear guard was near. Too often they were there when there was nothing to be seen. He scanned the trees high and low. He stretched beyond the rock and pointed his rifle down the path after the enemy column. Nothing. He could wait a bit, hoping for anyone near to make a mistake and expose himself, but there was no time for that.

Strader ran, bent at the waist, letting caution hold little sway over the speed of his steps. He passed through the trees like an open-field runner without blockers. He soared above the ground cover like a hurdler, landing heavily with the magazine pouches slapping his hips, expecting gunshots at any moment. He tightened his jaw muscles against the imminent impact of AK rounds striking his body. Nothing. His legs churned, and the slope and gravity increased the length of his stride until he was at the edge of control.

The trees seemed to converge on his path, and he twisted and contorted his body to keep his shoulders from making a disastrous contact. Then the fallen tree was there, crushing the ground plants, and Strader slowed so he could high-step the branches pushing out from the trunk like outriggers. His breath came in hoarse gasps. At the upended roots he stopped and looked back. The community of tall trees conspired to block any distant view, and the rockslide was a blur of green and earth tones, hidden but for slivers of clear air between the standing trunks. From where he stood the hidden tumble of stone seemed a lost place, a place were an abandoned man could be hidden forever.

Guilt lay on his chest like a tangible weight. The Corps never left men behind. They would marshal hundreds to retrieve a single body, and they would face any resistance to make that retrieval. Marines would willingly risk their lives to recover a fellow Marine already dead. It was a promise, a pact that bound one Marine to another. Whether you had breath or not, you would be reunited with the whole, and each man found comfort in that credo.

Strader wondered what the platoon would say when they found that he had left the Chief alone on the mountain. He could already see the disappointment on the lieutenant's face. Just this morning he had been home free, and now he was facing humiliation and shame that would live in the minds of men he respected and thought of as brothers. He looked down beyond the fallen tree to the path cut through woven twigs and whiplike tendrils, then back to the indistinct smear of mountain above the trees. He couldn't go on. If the Chief needed to be carried, he would carry him. If he was going to be branded a failure with the Corps, it would be for attempting the impossible, not for denying a fundamental tenet of the Marines. If the impossible needed to be done, he would do it or die trying with a clear conscience.

Middleton's squad filed out of the valley and, after a momentary pause to examine the spent cartridges at the tree line and trade congenial insults with the Sparrow Hawk platoon, threaded their way into the foothills, the point fire team in hushed discussion over which of the many tracks would be the best to follow. The enemy had obviously entered the trees on line, then slowly congealed into a single column with their own scouts picking the line of advance heading for high ground. Middleton stayed on the heels of his lead team, pushing Franklin to keep a steady pace.

Pusic scrambled along behind Bronsky's bobbing radio, his pristine boots slipping on the wet path blended to muck by those who had passed before. He kept looking back at the line of Marines stringing out to the rear and the light from the open valley fading away behind them. He shuddered. Each step drew him further from the light.

Franklin slipped back to third position where his voice could carry to Middleton with whispers. "Does the LT know we're doin' this?"

"Does it matter?"

"It should. You're in charge. If Diehl gets pissed about being left out of this decision, he's gonna chew some squad leader ass, and that ass is ridin' about three feet above your boots."

Middleton looked back over his shoulder. The squad was struggling with the slick ground, never getting a full stride without slipping, cursing under their breath at each stumble and slide—and looking vulnerable. It was best to move in the Arizona in large numbers, and a squad was not a large enough number. "You see that trigger-happy brother with the stripes in front of the radio? He's the one in charge here. If this thing turns into a cluster fuck, he'll be the one with the chewed ass."

Franklin looked back with a big grin. "I hope you're right," he said.

"Are you really worried that I might be wrong?"

"No. I'm worried that we won't survive this cluster fuck."

After a short pause to examine a new scattering of 7.62 brass where the path cut through a stand of thick trees, the squad dug in their heels and pushed upward. It seemed evident that their people were on the run, fighting a rearguard action.

Pusic examined the squad with a critical eye as they moved onto steeper terrain: their stained and frayed pants rolled at the drawstring cuffs above mud-caked boots; their flak jackets sun-faded nearly to beige sucking up the rain, turning their shoulders dark; their tattered helmet covers littered with marker graffiti. He wondered how good these Marines were at their jobs. None seemed to be worried about moving deeper and deeper into a forest that was closing in on all sides with a claustrophobic intensity. He tried to estimate their ages, but their bedraggled clothing and dirty faces made it difficult. He himself would be twenty-one in January with nearly nine months in-country and guessed that with the exception of Sergeant Blackwell, he was the oldest in the line—the oldest and the least experienced. Most of the others would be denied a beer on a barstool back in the world, but here their faces were ageless. They were the age of all Marines at war, and their casual attitude indicated that they were conditioned to live in the moment. He hoped that would change if something happened, but until then he would assume that their nonchalance was a necessary economy of emotion, because eternal vigilance had a price.

The trees grew taller as they went deeper into the jungle, raising the ceiling to a green canopy that seemed to be spitting down on them. Pusic felt even more out of his element in this insular world. An Hoa was all brown or tan or tinged red from the dust thrown up by the wheels of the passing parade of giant green machines. No plant life survived to grace the compound with color. But in this place, the trees and other plants convened in a primeval tangle, coloring everything with the dripping green of their dominance.

Pusic had seen the country outside the wire from the back of the occasional six-by shuttling between An Hoa and Phu Loc. There were huts and paddies and footpaths, the ground always showing the hand of people. But the muddy boot prints ahead of him were the only sign that humans had ever been here. In this place, man was not a consideration; he was an intruder. As twists and turns took the column further up the mountain, Pusic noticed some squad members peering back. At first he thought they were just being cautious, but the furtive glances seemed aimed at him.

The path entered a tangled thicket with a hole cut in it. Franklin's fire team came to a stop, and the entire column hung stationary on the mountainside. Some squatted. Others just stood, thankful for the rest from climbing. Franklin didn't like the idea of being caught in that sheath of vines under fire, and he balked at entering. He looked back until he caught Middleton's eye. "Go around or through?" he asked with no more volume in his voice than was needed. Middleton scanned the expanse of impenetrable brush that spread out like a wall before them. If he'd read the sergeant's mood correctly, going around was not an option. He pointed a finger at the hacked branches and stabbed the air for emphasis. Franklin shrugged and ducked into the opening.

~

Burke's inherited squad led the platoon out of the tree line just south of the lake, skirting the marshy ground beyond the reed and bamboo stands. Behind them came the others, struggling with the wounded and two dead loads wrapped in poncho liners. Bishop hobbled along between two Marines, his arms draped over their shoulders, one leg avoiding the ground and still trailing the loose leads of the stained battle dressing. Some of the insects that flitted and danced over the still surface of the lake interrupted their routine, drawn to the sweat and blood.

An OH-6 Loach came out of the east and banked its skids to the mountain, buzzing a curved path over the lake like a turbo-charged bee, the helicopter's speed exaggerated by its lack of altitude. It swung a tight arc over the platoon, then turned back toward the valley.

The lieutenant called a halt. The casualties were moved to a single spot, a combination staging area and morgue, and Doc Garver moved among them, uncovering and covering the dead and checking dressings on the wounded. There were two dead now. Despite his best efforts, Karns had not survived the trip. His failing body drank up all Doc's serum and morphine, but it wasn't enough.

A fire team stayed just inside the tree line for security while the rest of the platoon found comfortable spots and lay back on their packs, their helmets tossed to the ground, letting the drizzle cool their sweat-soaked heads.

Haber moved to a clear spot and dropped to his knees. Playing the part of the surviving FNG, he leaned into his M16, using it as a stay to keep him from pitching forward onto his face. Nearby, a black private named Eubanks watched with casual interest. "Hey, man. Drop the pack and take a load off while you can," he said. "We'll be movin' again soon." Some Marines resented the FNGs because their inexperience presented a danger to everyone. Others took pity and offered advice that was not only beneficial but demonstrated the wide expanse between themselves and a needy novice.

Haber peeled the pack straps from his shoulders and let the bundle drop to the ground. He leaned his rifle against it and sat back with his arms wrapped around his knees, pulling them close, folding himself into as small a package as he could. His baptism of fire over the last twenty-four hours had pounded him like a heavyweight boxer. He had finally seen the elephant, and he couldn't get the sight of it out of his brain.

Burke moved through his squad, warning them not to get too comfortable. When he reached Haber, he looked at the new guy's boots. "Lose the blousing springs," he said, pointing at Haber's ankles with the barrel of his rifle. "They ain't worth shit in the field."

A wide grin spread over Eubanks' face. "That ain't true, man. They worth something good. Real good."

Burke gave him a look that said, we may be close in rank, but I'm the one in charge. "Don't fuck with the new guy, 'Banks."

"I ain't shittin' this young man, Burke. I'll show you what I mean." He pointed a finger at the new guy. "What's your name, man?"

Haber looked at the Marine, wondering if he was being had. "Haber," he said.

"Okay, Haber. You miss puttin' the long and hard to your lady?"

"Huh?" Haber struggled to find his bearings in a surreal world that was not only horrific but incomprehensible as well.

Eubanks put on his most serious look. "Sex, man. Fuckin'. Do you miss the feelin' you get when you fuckin'?"

Haber dipped his head, letting the question sink in, then looked at the Marine out of the corner of his eye. His mind was presently consumed by many concerns, but the lack of sex wasn't one of them. He had to pull the thought of it up into his consciousness to provide the requisite response. "Yeah, I guess so. Why?"

Eubanks pointed at Haber's legs where the pants cuffs curled in tightly above his boots. "Unhook those bad boys."

Haber looked at him in confusion.

"Come on. Pop those motherfuckers off."

After a brief hesitation, Haber looked up at Burke. The squad leader just shrugged and nodded.

The blousing springs clamped the cuffs in a tight pucker against his wet skin, and Haber struggled with the hooks until both coils lay in the grass like dead snakes. Neat dents ringed each leg above the soggy tops of his socks. "Okay, they're off."

Eubanks leaned forward with a knowing smile. "Scratch 'em," he said.

"What?"

"Scratch your damn legs, man."

Haber slowly pushed his fingers up under his pant cuffs and dragged them tentatively over the indentations. Eubanks watched, nodding. A light of recognition flared in Haber's eyes and he met Eubanks' look with an unexpressed question.

"That's right. Go ahead, scratch," Eubanks said.

Dirty nails sought out the ridged creases and dug in. Haber dragged his fingers over the marks, increasing the intensity with each pass. His eyes closed in ecstasy and his fingers flew with manic delight. He bit his lip.

Eubanks laughed. "See what I mean? If that don't feel good as fuckin', it's so close it don't matter."

Haber continued his clawing, moving his fingers about in search of fresh nerve endings. It felt good, too good. After last night and today he hadn't thought anything would ever feel good again, but here he was, in the throes of self-induced rapture, a gratification he could not have imagined an hour ago, and he clung to it like a life raft.

A high-pitched buzz bounced off the face of the tree line, and the Loach streaked out of the valley again, banking high over the platoon as though performing at an air show. Lieutenant Diehl had his radioman in tow, barking into the handset. He waved at Doc Garver and pointed to the empty air over the valley. Garver nodded his understanding. The plangent thump of a larger engine drifted in over the grass, and the profile of a medevac H-34 appeared high over Nam An 5. It dipped to port and headed in their direction. Damaged Marines were leaving the field, and their transportation was on the way. The doc pulled a handful of men away from their rest to lift the dead and wounded in preparation for their departure. Garver pulled Bishop to his feet and draped one of the wounded man's arms over his shoulder, helping him hop on his good leg.

"I'll write and let you know what it's like back in the world, Doc."

The corpsman looked at the Marine with knowing sympathy. "You won't be going home, Bishop. All you have is a through-and-through. You'll be back here in a couple of weeks."

"Come on, Doc. Gimme a break."

The doc gave that some thought. "Actually, that would work. If we break your leg, they would definitely send you home."

Bishop seemed to be considering the option.

Karns and Price hung heavily in poncho liners in front of them, waiting in their green shrouds for their ride. Doc Garver nodded in their direction. "There's going home," he said, "and then there's going home."

The H-34 flared just beyond the platoon and settled to the ground with a bounce. Turbulence from the rotors whipped at the Marines rushing to its side. The two bodies were slipped in first, then the ambulatory and the hobbled Bishop climbed in with help. Bishop turned back and shouted. "Keep your ass down, Doc."

"I'll be here when you get back," Garver started to say, but the sound was lost as the rpms roared for takeoff. Everyone ducked and ran, and the big machine lifted into the air, nose pointed east, away from the Ong Thu.

Lieutenant Diehl had the platoon up and moving while the sound of the helicopter still hung in the air. The security team from the tree line scrambled to join up. In the distance they could see the Loach doing slow fishtail turns close to the ground east of the downed helicopter, like something in the grass was drawing its attention. A handful of Marines could be seen headed for that spot. Lieutenant Diehl pointed at the crash site, and the lead fire team pushed off in that direction.

Haber, his pants rolled loosely above his boots, fell in with his squad and watched the tail of the medevac helicopter shrink away, tracking the fading heartbeat of its engine with an overwhelming sense of being left behind.

≈

Strader pushed back up the mountain, legs tightening with the effort, covering ground that he had just leapt over on the way down. On reaching the bottom of the rockslide he leaned against the nearest rock, catching his breath. The natural rhythm of the jungle seemed undisturbed, everything in quiet concert. He wanted to call out, warning the Chief that he was returning, but thought better of making a discordant noise. He would wait until he was closer.

Moving up between the boulders, he pushed an index finger forward in the rifle's trigger ring, slipping the safety off, leaving the finger to hover. A few feet from the narrow opening he tried a restrained hail that came out as little more than a hiss. "Chief," he whispered, then caught himself. "Moon. *Moon.*" The silence made him nervous. He waited, listening. Primate chatter was answered by a screech somewhere in the mountain heights above. He inched forward. "*Moon,*" he said, irritated at being forced into a spot that made him feel both guilty and exposed.

The ground he could see through the narrow passage seemed much as it was when he left. "Answer me, Moon," he said vehemently. He raised the rifle, pulling the butt tight against his shoulder. In one step he was inside, sweeping the interior with the weapon. The space was empty. "Son of a bitch," he said, the heat of the words filling the little alcove. He let the rifle sag under its own weight. At the base of the ramped stone, the pack sat soaking up the rain, the canteen perched atop the flap. He stared at this, all the evidence left of the Marine charged to his custody. Thoughts clashed in his mind, trying to sort their way to a rationale for the Indian not being there, but nothing made sense. The backpack was neatly positioned, not tossed aside in a struggle. The canteen was balanced with precision. "Damn you, Chief," he said, mixing concern with anger, both aimed at himself.

On closer examination he saw that the canteen was there to hold down the top flap torn from a C-rat box. He slid it free. The drizzle had darkened the beige cardboard, except where the canteen covered it. Printing on the face marked the meal as ham slices; on the back, written with pencil in block capitals, was a single line, the graphite already starting to surrender to the rain: "went to get my honor back."

Strader stared at the note, trying to decipher its meaning. There was no sense to it; the scribbling of a damaged brain. The only thing that seemed certain was that the Chief didn't vanish on impulse. It was an intentional move, a plan. Maybe a crazy plan, but a plan nonetheless. And all he'd needed to execute the lunatic particulars was to suck in the gullible. Strader flushed at the realization that he had been so easily duped. He took a long pull on the canteen then hung it on his web belt, swung the pack onto his back, and shoved the note into one of his cargo pockets. He didn't know what the note meant, but he planned to ask the Chief as soon as he caught up with him.

Back at the bottom of the slide, Strader stopped to examine the chewed ground. Overlaying the imprints of shoe-shaped tire treads and designs cobbled in Hanoi, the pattern of tapered squares surrounding a clover leaf center stood out: U.S. jungle boots. The Chief was headed north after the Vietnamese. Strader followed the trail with his eyes. It twisted and turned for twenty yards, then vanished into a curtain of green. He stared at the spot where the trail disappeared. Everything beyond that was the unknown. He'd thought he was finished with walking blindly into a questionable future.

Sounds from the valley floor filtered up through the trees, and he longed to go in that direction and find the protection of his platoon. At least he knew they would come after him. They would pass this spot, but he wouldn't be here. He took the Chief's cardboard note from his pocket, folded it into a tent, and placed in on the nearest stone in plain sight, an enigmatic signpost pointing the way.

How hard could it be to catch a man who could barely walk? How long could it take? All he had to do was overtake the stumbling Chief, get him to listen to reason, and drag him back. How hard could it be?

T he dark trail lay before the Chief like a tracing on a road map, the rich, dark soil kneaded into a malleable consistency by many hurried feet. The enemy had no time for subterfuge. Their numbers were too many and their need to travel too desperate to waste time concealing signs of their passing. Their only safety was in distance, and they knew it. The circuitous trail they left behind swam in the Indian's vision as though through steam rising above a desert highway. With every step, a painful pulse pierced his wounded temple, making him screw that swollen eye closed under the battle dressing.

The clatter of rain in the treetops diminished, and the drips made their long fall without reinforcement. The Chief looked up, making the jungle ceiling spin. He guessed the rain was stopping. Small favors, he thought. He clutched the handle of the knife on his belt and concentrated on moving forward. Short steps, like those that might drive any daily constitutional, grew into long, loping strides. The jolt of each footfall resounded in his head. The collision of bones was jarring his damaged brain into flashes of blinding light and he went to his toes and bent his knees, absorbing his weight with muscle and sinew. He would have to think beyond the pain and the body's need to acknowledge the cost of exertion. He would have to think beyond the pain, beyond the body's need to acknowledge the cost of exertion. It was a trait encouraged by his people and practiced at White Mountain, a pride celebrated by the young and strong. The historical Apache on horseback was a terror; afoot he was still a formidable threat. He could cover great distances at a steady run, crossing all manner of terrain, in pursuit of game or horses, and Kle-ga-na-ai slipped into the learned reverie that monopolized the mind, letting it find the mental rhythm that pushed the pain of physical effort down until it lost all influence.

The spirit of his mind flew free, and the black runnel of the beaten path solidified under his feet. The claustrophobic closeness of the jungle vanished. The glare of desert sunlight forced the green shadows back, opening an arid vista before him, and his feet flew along the jagged edge of an arroyo whose steep sides dropped into the dormant path of an ancient rill. The tails of his plaid flannel shirt flew out behind him like pennants in a high wind, and his feet, forsaking the traditional deerskin moccasins, smacked the hard earth with the rubber soles the Keds Shoe Company made with basketball in mind. He followed a *brecha* made by wild hooves, threading through sage and weaving himself into the chaparral that he knew as home. His legs were strong and quick. His breaths drew deep with the regularity of a new pump, filling his chest and driving him like a locomotive. A distant mesa shimmered in the hot air, and he felt he could reach its slope in the passing of a minute. He could run forever.

A coil of rope hugged his waist and slapped at his right thigh because he knew wild mustangs were close, and luck and speed could snag one. But it didn't matter if he was successful, or if he even saw one. He was the horse today. Air rushed over his face, and wet strands of his long, black hair slapped the back of his neck like a mane. He was free and wild and would never feel more alive.

Flatlands spread out before him, the wild path marking a wavering line to follow, luring him onto the heat of eolian sands. His strength allowed no fear. His drive pushed him out onto the range, and he ran until he thought his white man's shoes would melt. He saw a mound of dirty white and brown ahead and slowed to a stop by its side. The carcass of a dead horse lay still, the mottled hide hanging over the bony prominences like a collapsed tent. A line of large, square teeth sat atop the bare jaw like grotesque dice in a grimace of death that drew a cloud over Kle-ga-na-ai's mood. The mechanisms of nature placed a reminder of the destination for all; the universal conclusion.

The cloud grew, darkening the sky and moving in close to smother the light until the weight of it stuck to his face and stung his eyes. A putrid smell rose to fill the Chief's nostrils, and his half-blind stare found the source beside the jungle path. A four-legged creature lay in the undergrowth, its decomposition defying identification beyond an ungulate of short stature, the victim of some disease or predator, or the unlucky recipient of wild artillery fire from An Hoa meant to harass and interdict. Or perhaps it was placed as an intentional obstacle to be stepped around, a repugnant cause for a designed detour.

The suppurating flesh moved in waves as maggots crawled through the turgid body cavity, filling its dimensions with their appetites, giving the hide an impression of animation that no longer existed. Winged thrips formed a cloud above the carrion beetles that were ripping apart the flesh with their mechanical jaws. The Chief's head swam, and he had to fight to keep himself from pitching headlong into the offal. He was suddenly weary, like he had made a long journey only to arrive at a place he would rather not be, and the skin on half of his face felt hot and stretched and tight. He moved along the path to the nearest large tree and leaned against the trunk, pressing his swollen cheek to the slippery surface. The strength of the tree, the fibrous muscle below the bark, invaded his consciousness like encouragement from a wise elder. The spinning in his head subsided. Against the steady base, his failing equilibrium found the stability to continue. He thanked the tree and pushed off.

≈

Less than thirty minutes after reaching the edge of the jungle, the point fire team of Lieutenant Diehl's column entered the Sparrow Hawk platoon's perimeter at the downed helicopter. They ducked the smashed tail section and filed past the line of bodies under wet ponchos, small puddles in the folds reflecting fragments of gray sky like shattered mirrors. An enemy's black-clad body lay to the side, tossed unceremoniously into an awkward lump. When Haber saw the bodies, his hands and knees began to shake, driven by some involuntary trigger that had taken root in his mind and was already exercising its influence, a demonstration of power showing Haber that, like the reflexive kick resulting from a doctor's hammer blow below the knee, there were some things he would never control.

A pair of new boots protruding from one of the ponchos had blousing springs holding the pant cuffs in a neat tuck. He wished he could show DeLong the ecstasy of relief they offered, the rush of pleasure, but he pushed it from his mind. Just being this close to DeLong made his insides twist as though the Marine's body were a dead planet with a gravitational pull that was sucking him in. He wanted nothing more than to get away. But he was afraid that if he lived to be a hundred years old, he might never get far enough away from this day.

All eyes of 1st Platoon were drawn to the still ponchos, and Lieutenant Diehl ordered the men away from the helicopter, toward the tree
line where they could take a meal break using the advantage of the Sparrow Hawks' vigilance.

While his men tromped away through the wet grass, Lieutenant
Diehl left the line to meet Lieutenant Hewitt coming in his direction.
"How's it goin', Tom?" the Sparrow Hawk commander said with a
somber edge to his voice. The lieutenants always addressed one another
with casual familiarity. They spent most of their time with the enlisted
members of their respective platoons, and whatever conversations they
had there outside the realm of military business were conducted with an
underlying tone of deference to rank. There was no verbal exchange on
an equal footing. There were boundaries in the military class structure
that the ranks knew were crossed only at great peril. Familiarity was
one of those boundaries.

"Just another hard day in the Arizona, Mark, but we're kickin' ass
and takin' names," Lieutenant Diehl answered, giving the expected
response, though he felt more like the kicked than the kicker.

"Do I have a squad around here somewhere?" Diehl asked, looking
about for a familiar face.

"Here and gone, Tom. Your Four was hot to get after your missing
people." Hewitt pointed to the tree line in the approximate spot where
they left the valley. "He wanted my help, but I'm locked into security
here until this machine is lifted out, and even then we're still the reaction
unit; they may call me back to the base to sit and wait for some other
shit to hit the fan."

Lieutenant Diehl studied the distant trees, imagining what shit was
out there waiting for him to step in it.

"I suggested that he wait for you, but he was strainin' at the bit,"
Hewitt said. "I figured he had your orders. Was I wrong?"

Diehl turned to look at the dead helicopter with the row of draped
bodies. He shook his head. "No. He's doing what needs to be done."

A corpsman stood by the bodies making notations on a pad of casualty cards.

"What was the pilot's name?" Lieutenant Diehl said.

"You know the Highball crew?"

"No. I just spoke with him yesterday when he dropped our resupply."

Lieutenant Hewitt flipped the pages of a notebook. "Fredrick Crowell. Second seat was Dan Woods. I didn't know them either." He looked at Diehl staring at the ponchos. "You want to take a look?"

Lieutenant Diehl turned away and looked at his watch. He wiped droplets of water from the big crystal with a swipe of a finger and looked to the tree line. "No. I've got other problems right now." He started into the grass then turned back. "You keep yourself handy, Mark. I have a feeling that the Arizona isn't finished with us yet, and I may need you before this miserable day is over." Trailed by his radioman, Diehl headed for the tree line where his platoon squatted around improvised cook stoves.

"That's what I get paid for, Tom," Lieutenant Hewitt said to the receding officer's back. "You watch your ass," he added, though they were out of earshot.

Lieutenant Diehl spoke softly without looking back to see if anyone was near. He assumed that his earlier order to the radioman was being obeyed. "Clyde. Get me Blackwell."

Looking ahead, he could easily pick out his Marines from the Sparrow Hawks. The Arizona had left its mark on them. Each day in the field wore away the veneer of civilization. It showed in their clothes, their skin, and their demeanor. By comparison, the Sparrow Hawks looked fresh and their faces were clean, lacking the sags and shadows of long days and sleepless nights. The rush of battle left behind a residue of fatigue that made his platoon's steps look heavy and each movement labored. They needed sleep and chow hall food and the relative safety of An Hoa's perimeter, but he knew that wasn't in their immediate future. They still had a long way to go.

Burke looked up from his squat over a boiling tin of chocolate, a shard of cheese-coated cracker between his teeth and a question in his eyes. Lieutenant Diehl held up a hand, fingers spread: one minute per finger. Burke nodded and looked back to his brew, no indication of disappointment. Earn sixty, expect thirty, and get five; life in the Crotch.

Clyde held the radio handset close to his face, his voice bouncing off the waterproof wrapping. The response vibrated under the plastic like a trapped insect. "Yeah," he said. "One Actual wants Four." He held the receiver out and waited for the officer to take it from his hand.

From the time a young staff sergeant berated him mercilessly on pick-up day beginning Officers Candidate School at Quantico, Lieutenant Diehl had carried a grudging respect for the noncoms who would happily chew out candidates they might meet as officers later in their careers, hard-edged men who would bite down on an assignment even if it might eventually bite them back. He came to see many of them as men of abilities, especially at distasteful tasks. He placed Sergeant Blackwell in that group.

A distant, hesitant voice pushed through the static-filled airwaves. "Four here."

"But you're not here, Four," the lieutenant said. He tried to make it sound like the confirmation of a simple fact without putting so sharp a point on his voice that it would wound.

The sergeant chose to block any rebuke by remaining formal. "That's affirmative," he said without explanation.

"What's your position, Four?" The rubber-coated levers on each handset spit static at one another, and Diehl imagined he could hear the folds in the sergeant's map unbending. Finally, the voice swept in to smother the interference. "Two clicks north of Studebaker."

The lieutenant ran his finger past the automobile thrust point on his map near the crash site to climb along the face of the Ong Thu. It was a good distance, and the inhospitable terrain made it seem further. He chose a grid coordinate beyond the sergeant's position and improved on it by upgrading the Studebaker to a Corvette. When he suggested that the squad hold there until the platoon could link up, the radios seemed to strangle on the lack of communication. "That's a negative, One. Hostiles a threat, time is critical."

"Copy that, Four." Prolonged static carried an air of relief from the other end. "I'll find you," he added.

A relieved voice came back immediately. "Roger that," it said, then lapsed into silence.

"One out." The lieutenant handed the receiver back to the waiting private. He scanned the remains of 1st Platoon hugging the face of the tree line and working the magic of C rations into their mouths. One of the gun teams was just off to his left. "Ask Lieutenant Hewitt for the belt ammo from the chopper, and be quick." Faces looked up to witness the inevitable announcement. "First Platoon," the lieutenant shouted. "Saddle up."

≈

Sergeant Blackwell nodded at the inert handset. He had an appreciation for the lieutenant. Platoon sergeants always had considerably more time in service than their platoon commanders. In fact, their job was to lend their experience to new lieutenants who were putting the theory of their recent officer training into practice. Sometimes sergeants complained to each other that they had drawn a bad lot as their young officers stumbled through the trials of combat, but Sergeant Blackwell had no such misgivings. Lieutenant Diehl was hard but fair, and most of all he was competent. Combat was an unforgiving OJT, but the lieutenant learned quickly and kept his mistakes to a minimum.

The squad was stopped, waiting for the radio message to slap them back into line and casting glances at Sergeant Blackwell, searching his posture for any sign that he was catching that slap. But instead the sergeant held the handset by its mouthpiece and shook it forward, up the mountain, pointing the way with punctuated arcs like a priest wielding his aspergillum of holy water blessing his little congregation. He returned the handset to Bronsky's care and the squad resumed their climb.

≈

The Cessna Bird Dog banked in from the valley and climbed the face of the Ong Thu, searching the sea of green concealing the ground, hoping for some breach in the trees large enough to give him a peek at the opposing players in this deadly game. Thousands of rounds from An Hoa's artillery had punched holes in the canopy, leaving openings where a discerning eye might find something hidden, but what he really needed was a spot where an airburst of white phosphorus had shriveled the leaves with molten heat or a plummeting drum of fuel oil had burned away everything within its splash. He needed a window.

Staying above the contour of the mountain that seemed probable for foot traffic, the pilot stuck to a northern tack, following the slope toward the dogleg where the mountain bent to the east. Ahead, a long gash split the green like a gaping wound, revealing the dark flesh of the jungle floor. The Cessna's airspeed slowed. The dip of a wing put the little aircraft into a slow circle above the scar where, looking over his left shoulder, the pilot could see bare earth and the dark line of a fresh path that bisected the cut. It looked wider than an animal trail or a villager's footpath to a desirable stand of wood. He let the aircraft do another lazy turn. With his map on his knee, the pilot made some quick calculations on the surface of the windscreen with a grease pencil, figuring airspeed and marking distance in kilometers from the thrust points circled in black marker. He estimated foot speed and time elapsed, stabbing a spot on the map with the pencil; an educated guess, but a guess worth making. He turned back to the valley and radioed the fire direction center in An Hoa.

≈

Metal tendrils rose in clusters above the sandbagged roof of the communications hut, sensitive aerials reaching out to touch all the rifle companies working from An Hoa in the surrounding TAOR, some tall enough to reach the darkest corners of Antenna Valley or all the way back to Division in Da Nang. Compared with the other structures on the base, the command, operations, and communication center was a fortress. The walls and ceiling were staggered layers of sandbags on beams and corrugated steel, designed, in theory, to take a direct hit from a mortar round or RPG, though no one inside wanted to see that theory tested.

The interior of the huge bunker was divided into areas of responsibility, each working under the requisite glare of a bare lightbulb. S-3 operations took the lion's share of the space running the entire battalion. S-2 intelligence filled a corner, poring over their maps, analyzing information that filtered in from Division, Recon, and 2/5's rifle platoons as well as friendly whispers from the ARVN. Information flowed in from the ever-present Popular Forces, too, who posed as guardians of the surrounding hamlets in their skin-tight uniforms with U.S. helmets sitting on their heads like huge colanders. Their M-1 Garand rifles from World War II drew even more attention to their modest stature. Their suspect local information might be ignored, investigated, or occasionally tickled with HE from the artillery battery.

S-2, monitoring the incoming call to Fire Direction Control, scrambled for their maps. "Fire mission" rang through the compound, and gun breeches clanged as the battery fired a single shot, jolting the ground within An Hoa's compound, rattling the plywood hooches, and shaking the C-rat cans laced to the razor wire on the perimeter.

The Bird Dog's radio hissed, "Shot over," and the Cessna sprinted for the valley, away from the incoming round. The pilot watched and made an adjustment. "Add five hundred and fire for effect."

The first projectile split the air over the valley far ahead of the sound of the muzzle blast, pushing through the cloud cover with the pulsating *whoosh* of the atmosphere's resistance. The Sparrow Hawk platoon looked to the gray ceiling as the round passed invisibly, evaluating the sound to ensure that it was in fact passing, until the distant thunderclap from An Hoa caught up. Back at their work, each kept an ear tuned to the ever-present possibility of a "short round."

More shots passed over 1st Platoon like distant steam locomotives high above the canopy, and in a mere second flew beyond Sergeant Blackwell and Middleton's squad.

Strader's practiced ear could tell the round was passing over but was on a downward trajectory. He hoped the Chief wasn't too far ahead.

From where he stood, the Chief could see a large swath of the jungle floor illuminated by a massive break in the trees, the gray sky pushing in to reveal bare ground where the wash of relentless monsoons had scoured away anything green with aspirations of a foothold. He doubted the reliability of his hearing, but the sound of the incoming round was palpable and he went to ground as quickly as his head would allow, hugging the base of the nearest tree. The shot struck the ground just beyond the northern boundary of the opening. The explosion was sharp and deep, and the concussion filled the space below the canopy like a shotgun blast in a rain barrel. His ears rang and he worked his jaw up and down as though he were flying high in an unpressurized aircraft and needed relief from the pain. The ground spasm traveled through the tree's root system into his arms. When he looked up, spinning chunks of the jungle were raining back to earth.

≈

Self-preservation schooled the ears of the NVA, and the column knew from its earliest whispers that an artillery round was coming in their direction. With the exception of Pham and Truong, each man's interest turned to the air above the trees. Nguyen called a halt. They all stood perfectly still, fighting their gasps and pounding hearts to hear the growing friction as the projectile pushed through what sounded like heavy air in their proximity. Some eyes searched the canopy; others scanned the terrain for a spot that might offer some protection. Nguyen barked an order, and everyone dropped their loads and dived for cover. He stood alone on the path, watching his people disappear leaving behind precious weaponry to fend for itself in the mud. When he was sure all were down and concealed, he stooped and ran uphill, dropping to the ground between two trees, letting the heavy pack board drive him downward until the rising earth conspired with the pack to punch the air from his lungs.

The round hit the mountain far back on the trail with a tremendous crack. As soon as it hit, Nguyen knew that it was too far away to be any danger to them. He pushed himself up onto his knees and looked around. Heads were popping up all about him. Pham's sweaty face was so near that Nguyen could see trickles of perspiration making tracks past eyes wide with concern. Their gazes met and Pham blinked, maybe to clear the burning sting of salt from his eyes, or perhaps to gain some control over eyes that were betraying his panic.

The rest of the unit made tentative moves to stand before Nguyen spoke. He knew the single shot from the muzzles on the American base would not be an orphan, and he pushed himself erect. Expectant faces turned to him like sunflowers to light, not because they didn't know what needed to be done but because they needed it to be said. Nguyen looked back at them with frustration. "*Cu-dong*," he yelled, triggering instant movement. His people fell on their abandoned loads, jerking the weight onto their backs with renewed energy.

As Pham passed, Nguyen grabbed his arm, redirecting him away from the heavy machine gun at the end of the column. Many in the unit were carrying double loads, and Nguyen pressed a heavy pack board strapped with rounds for the recoilless rifle into Pham's arms. Pham looked back to the heavy gun. An objection was forming on his lips when Nguyen cut him short. He pointed in the direction he wanted Pham to move. "*Cu-dong*," he said through clenched teeth, pushing him forward.

T he Chief struggled to his feet, holding the tree, using its stability to find some of his own. The smell from the detonation wafted across the gash in the jungle, a burnt chemical odor mixed with vapors of plants obliterated in the blast, the only thing left of their existence. Though the Chief was not unfamiliar with the smell, he always found the recipe of sudden destruction mixed with earth's green life offensive to his senses. But it occurred to him that this particular blast could be of benefit. If his quarry sought cover from this shot and the promise of more, he could make up lost time. All he had to do was run onto ground of interest to a fire mission. Though the logic was questionable, he crossed the gap and skirted the smoking crater left by his TNT benefactor.

━

The sound of the explosion spent itself fighting through the curtain of foliage, reaching Strader as a deep growl without sharp edges. He didn't think the shot was random and figured there were eyes on the heavily armed enemy column somewhere up ahead, eyes determined to turn the NVA into bloody pulp, and the crazy Chief was leading him straight into the slaughter. The commandeered pack beat against his unprotected spine, reminding him of how naked he felt without his flak jacket. In his entire thirteen months in-country, with the exception of a couple of night ambushes, he had never been on the move outside a perimeter without his flak gear. Now he had no helmet, no vest, nothing between vital organs and nasty projectiles but the green weave of his jungle utilities. He pictured the jacket, pack, and helmet lying on the borrowed rack in the corner of 3rd Platoon's hut, enjoying the view of the runway.

The reasonable portion of his brain screamed at him to turn around and go in the other direction. The Marine portion pushed him forward. He trailed his M14 in one hand, saving the other to slap away plants that might slow him down with a snag or a trip. He stayed to the center of the well-worn path, trying to make sure his feet didn't strike ground that didn't already have a footprint on it. The Chief's jungle boot pattern was plainly visible, and Strader tried to match his stride step for step, hoping to run right onto his heels soon and . . . what? He needed time to think. What would he do? How would he do it? All he was sure of was that he would need help, and any help that was coming was still far behind following the shallow imprints of his stateside Corcorans on the soggy floor of a jungle where they were never designed to be.

~

Franklin sent word back through the point squad that the faint paths they were following merged with a larger, well-used trail that pointed north along the face of the mountain. He could see the overlapping footprints, each imposing its signature over the ones that preceded it. The mélange was as busy as a Jackson Pollock, and the point man hesitated to speculate on the number that had passed, simply leaving his estimate at "a shit load" without elaborating. He moved onto the new path, superimposing his boot prints over the existing ones, making a connection between himself and the enemy somewhere ahead, a connection that sent a chill up his legs that raised goose bumps. The trail was fresh and obviously made by a superior force. It seemed they were chasing a tiger with a fly swatter. When he looked back, Franklin could see Sergeant Blackwell pumping his arm up and down to increase the squad's speed. He knew the sergeant was more interested in what the tiger was chasing than what they would do when they caught up to the tiger.

Silence reigned after the initial artillery round struck the mountain far ahead, broken only by the distant boom from An Hoa. The target was obviously so far off that no one felt they were near the coming impact area, and they pushed forward without concern—until Franklin called a halt. He stood a few yards from where the trail passed a large, moss-clad stone and waited, scanning the surroundings. Something was out of place. Aside from the intrusion of the muddy path through the tangle of nature, something odd and geometric, an anomaly in straight lines, was perched on top of the stone, standing out as something designed, manmade, and therefore wrong. Bringing his M16 up, he swept the trees as though the muzzle had the power to detect an enemy in hiding.

His alert had safeties clicking through the squad. Pusic, still behind Bronsky's radio, looked down at his own weapon in his hands. He had often imagined a personal need for the M16 when the lines at An Hoa were probed in the middle of the night and flares and tracer rounds lit the darkness, but his imaginings were never so perverse as to set him on a jungle-covered mountain in the Arizona looking to a flawed plastic rifle for his salvation. The faces near enough for him to see didn't seem to register an inordinate amount of concern, so he left his selector on safety, waiting for the reactions of the squad to confirm that a nightmare was actually in progress and he truly was in Hell.

The VC often marked mined trails with subtle changes to the environment meant to warn those initiated to the signs that the route was lethal. The jungle was a place of nuance, easily read by those living there, so the signals were designed to mimic the natural texture but with a twist that moved them just beyond the likelihood of normal occurrence. A few stones stacked in an impromptu pyramid, twigs positioned on the ground pointing out the deadly way, a branch snapped down at an intersection of trails dissuaded those native to the cause from taking the wrong path. But the cautions were always from nature, blending into the surroundings, easily noticed only by those in the know. This was different.

Franklin crept forward, the rest of his fire team covering the flanks, until he was close enough to see the folded cardboard tent sitting on the boulder like a dinner place card waiting for an invited guest. He crept forward and reached out to the little folded piece, touching it gingerly as though it might bite. Unfolding the crease, he looked at the cryptic message written in pencil in block letters. He turned it on its side, then back again, as though a different angle might give it a sense that wasn't apparent at first glance.

The second man back tore his nervous eyes away from the trees long enough to eye the point. "Franklin, what is it?"

Franklin passed him the note, never taking his eyes from the jumble of stone that held the promise of defensible ground, and was therefore the most likely spot from which to launch an ambush.

The second man looked at the note with the same befuddled expression.

"Pass that back to Blackwell," Franklin said, peering over the big stone to the chewed footprints winding up the mountain through the jumble.

The note made its way back through the squad, stopping in Middleton's hands.

"Why are we stopped?" Sergeant Blackwell said, stepping forward.

"Point found this." Middleton held up the folded meal flap, supple from being handled wet.

Blackwell took the darkening piece of cardboard. Getting a sign from his people lost in the bush was more than he could have hoped for, but this fell short of anything he might have dreamed. "Went after his honor?" he said, his voice rising in question.

All Middleton could do was shrug and be thankful that he was not the one responsible for deciphering the odd message.

Sergeant Blackwell held the note and stared past it into the trees, trying to see nothing, freeing his brain to work out not the meaning of the scribble but the implications of the note's very existence. A wry smile worked its way onto his face. Captives would not be in a position to leave notes behind. His people were free. But any note left to be found should at least make sense. The fact that he held it in his hand, though it erased a major concern, raised more questions than it answered. If they were being chased, why didn't the pursuers find the note? If they weren't running, where were they? What the hell did the note mean? He looked back at the questioning faces behind him. "Hey, pogue. You're a paper pusher. This mean anything to you?"

Pusic moved past Bronsky and his radio, trying not to step off the path onto unknown ground, and took the wet cardboard from the sergeant's hand. He turned it from the turkey side to the pencil printing inside the fold. He looked to the sergeant's face, then back to the note. He was skeptical about being included in the workings of the squad and hesitant to proffer an opinion, but it didn't matter. It couldn't have meant less to him if it had been written in hieroglyphics. He could feel Bronsky squeezing close, peering over his shoulder, so he held the surface so the radioman could see.

"I'll tell you one thing. Reach wouldn't leave no dumb-ass note like that for us to find," Bronsky said, punctuating the statement with a twist of his mouth that said something was being left unsaid.

Pusic and the radioman exchanged knowing glances. "The Chief," they said in unison, a duet without a pleasing harmony, Pusic's part more a question than an assertion.

The sergeant took the note back and looked at it with a new appreciation. It still had no meaning to him, but he could see the hand of the Chief in it.

Middleton whistled from where he squatted in the bush. "Franklin wants somebody in charge to come up. You want to flip for it?"

Brushing past the kneeling squad, Blackwell looked down on the squad leader. "You don't have the stones or the stripes to even ask that," he said, weaving his way toward the point fire team with Bronsky following, the radioman's loyalties wavering but finally settling comfortably with the precept of rank and its attendant privileges.

Middleton looked back at the office clerk, who was bent at the waist, trying to look unobtrusive without actually getting down in the mud. "How do you like it so far, pogue?"

Sergeant Blackwell worked his way to the front where Franklin leaned against the big rock, making sure the impenetrable bulk of it was between him and the slew of rocks above.

"Where did this come from?" the sergeant said holding out the note.

Franklin tapped the top of the stone. "It was sitting right here, like it was waiting for us to come along."

"No other sign of Reach or the Chief?"

Franklin wiped his face with a forearm etched with healing scratches that showed pink on his brown skin. "Somebody squeezed up through those rocks," he said pointing to the path around the lichen-covered boulder. "And that there looks like a U.S.-issue boot print to me."

Sergeant Blackwell looked up the mountain. "You think our people are up there?" he said, speaking as much to himself as to anyone else. Franklin shrugged. The sergeant had never seriously asked his opinion before, and when the rank seemed pissed, you walked on eggshells.

Blackwell looked down at the note in his hand. "Some think the Chief wrote this."

"I know he did," Franklin said. "He was telling me about his honor yesterday."

"What about his honor? What the hell does this mean?" The sergeant shook the note, making it flop.

Franklin felt put on the spot. "I don't know what that note means, but he said he carries his honor in that bag he wears around his neck."

The sergeant folded the note and stuffed it into the breast pocket on his flak jacket. "I think I'm gonna regret not shooting that jackass."

Bronsky stayed back a bit, leaning forward, hands on thighs, positioning the weight of the radio over his bent knees. The congregation at the big rock was growing too large and might attract a strike of righteous lightning, and he didn't want to be in its path.

The sergeant looked up at the scrambled stones and the path through them. "Franklin, take your team up there and have a look, but be quick."

The three Marines dug in their toes and climbed through the rockslide, pushing their rifles at any chink in the stone that promised a hiding place. They were back in minutes, dropping down with heavy plods, moving with none of the vigilance they demonstrated on the way up.

Sergeant Blackwell watched them come, surprised at how disappointed he was that they were alone. "Nothing, huh?" he said.

Franklin looked back at the massive slide as though refreshing a memory, or making one. "There's a natural blind up there built like a stone bunker. I think our guys spent some time in it."

The rush of projectiles far above the trees ignited the birds into shrill protests that clashed with the rumble of echoes from An Hoa. The sounds seemed to add an increased urgency to the passing of every second.

"You just *think* they were there?" the sergeant asked.

Franklin held out the top half of a paper envelope with "presweetened" printed across it. "Unless the gooks are drinking Kool-Aid now, I'd say they were there for sure."

The passing rounds struck the mountain in brutal succession. "Let's get going, Franklin," the sergeant said, crumpling the packet top and tossing it aside.

Franklin looked back at the men crouched on the trail. "Which way?" he said.

The sergeant hooked his thumb north toward the noise. "Move it out, Marine."

One of the other fire team members pointed at the muddy path and Franklin knelt down for a closer look. "Sergeant," he said, looking over his shoulder with a satisfied expression. "My man here says he thinks our people were the last ones over this ground."

Blackwell moved close so he could see. Bronsky couldn't resist following. Curious faces hung over the muddy imprints, their attention directed by Franklin's finger pointing at one boot print overlaying another. "That looks like a stateside boot impression to me," Franklin said. "Who the hell is wearing statesides out here?"

Blackwell could see the mark of a jungle boot half concealed under the crosshatched pattern of another foot. "My two strays are chasing the VC. What the hell is going on? Has everyone in this damned country gone crazy but me?"

Franklin stood, sending his fire team ahead. "Maybe," he said to the sergeant. "And we ain't too sure about you anymore."

Sergeant Blackwell waved an arm to get the entire squad moving behind Franklin's lead. Once a drill instructor at Parris Island, he often felt the need to lapse into a DI's descriptive colloquialisms for recruits, "puke" and "turd" being among his favorites. But the young Marines past the trials of boot camp resented the characterizations as both insulting and inaccurate, so he made an honest effort to not invalidate his platoon with his words. "Son of a bitch," he said, confident that no toes were tromped on unjustifiably.

~

Halfway along the trampled path transecting the elongated gap in the trees, the parade of artillery rounds made their lethal hiss overhead and Strader began to run. The gap was bare. The only cover, the tree line ahead, seemed miles away. Having a clear view of the sky made him feel irrationally exposed, and he stretched his stride, trying to believe he could win an impossible race, the tortoise pitted against a hare with a muzzle velocity.

The rounds began striking the mountain one after another, unevenly spaced, and he fought to stay upright on the shimmering ground. All stability seemed to have vanished from the solid platform that was the earth. The big projectiles of explosive steel pounded the mountain beyond where he could see, but he still felt their force compress the air in his ears and constrict his chest. Standing near the big guns when they fired was an experience that commanded awe. The power was impressive: the thud of the recoil, the jolt that stole all confidence in solid ground, the air shifting as though trying to get away. But being on the receiving end was a plunge into an inferno from Dante's hellish imagination— an imagination complete with flames and heat and ear-rupturing noise

and jagged shrapnel and disgorged earth. There was a fundamental dis-
connect between the experiences of the sending and the receiving, a psy-
chological schism like seeing a listless tiger in a zoo and seeing a hungry
one eyeing you on a jungle trail. Unable to maintain his balance, Strader
dropped to his knees. When the first salvo ended he was up and running
again through a lull that left only a threatening roar rebounding from
the clouds.

≈

Nguyen drove Pham forward with a hand against his back, pushing him
past those with heavier loads, not listening to the objections the younger
man tossed back over his shoulder. Everyone knew that the American
artillery would likely reach out with more. If the location of the first shot
had been sanctioned, the ground behind them would be the target and
they had to put as much distance between themselves and that unlucky
real estate as they could. Even as they grunted and dug in their feet, the
munitions searching them out could be heard growing ever louder in the
air like angry hornets. Nguyen barked orders, driving them on. If any
had the notion of ducking for cover again, he disabused them of that,
the hiss of the oncoming rounds adding emphasis to his demands.

The leading shot hit the mountain high on their left, deep in the
trees. The ground jumped and the force of expanding air hit them like
an atomic blast. Those who were knocked from their feet struggled up
again as the second and third rounds struck high and behind. A fourth
shot hit closer, back along the path. The explosions engulfed them like a
living entity, sucking the air from their lungs and choking their throats.
Shrapnel ripped the trees. The concussions spread in spherical shock-
waves that shook the branches where their influences collided. Nguyen
knew that the target coordinates had been changed from the initial spotter round, and that they were now in the kill zone. They could not stay
here. The big guns would fire again, unloading death onto this place,
and if they were here, they would die. He yelled with all the force he
could muster without sounding panicked. He had to keep them together,
solid to their purpose, and he had to keep them moving.

They lurched forward through clouds of fragrant green confetti, the
urgency to be gone and the threat of immediate death putting renewed
strength in their efforts. Pham, staggering, looked back, but Nguyen

waved him on with an impatient hand, not wanting the handicap of caring about this fledgling bird who could bury him with his needs.

Once again they heard the rending of air above the trees foreshadowing a new onslaught of artillery rounds that were homing in on their very heartbeats. The new salvo slammed into the mountain, the explosions forcing the atmosphere away in concussive blasts that left burnt voids that sucked in the surrounding air, creating a storm of currents that pushed and pulled at the Vietnamese while the ground jolted under their feet. Their voices screamed in defiance, matching their futile sounds against the explosions as earth rained down on them in chunks, and they scrambled and crawled to get away, knowing they were in a race they could not win.

26

The Bird Dog pilot revved away from the mountain, turning his head only to watch the rounds find their spots. They punctured the canopy, exploding below the green surface and making the trees perform an unnatural dance. The blasts spread across the treetops in undulating waves. The shells struck unpredictably, the result of miniscule disparities in load and barrel condition in the weapons that sent them. Even the density of the air currents played a role in determining the specifics of their trajectories. Fire control radioed the new warning that rounds were on the way, and the pilot banked off to clear skies, keeping the implications of the big guns' disparities in mind.

Sergeant Blackwell barked over his shoulder to Bronsky, bent under his radio. "Get the LT. Quick."

Bronsky grabbed the handset from where it swung on his breast pocket and squeezed the plunger. "Golf Four to Golf One Actual," he gasped. An unresponsive hiss returned. "Four to One Actual," he repeated, economizing on words to save air better used to curse Clyde for being slow on the uptake. "Pick up, shithead," he said, after first releasing the plunger to be sure that he wasn't sending.

Lieutenant Diehl's voice cut through the static, terse and demanding. "One Actual."

Blackwell snatched the handset from Bronsky without ceremony. "Call off the guns, sir. Our runaways are in the zone."

"Roger that," Diehl said into the mouthpiece, then turned to Clyde standing next to him, the coil of handset wire stretched between them. "Clyde, get me fire control," he said, letting the coil retract the handset by tensile memory. Clyde looked back with a blank expression that the lieutenant easily read. "Turn around," he said. The radioman turned, and Diehl spun the frequency knobs on the radio with deep clacks. "Go," he said. In seconds Clyde had a reply. He held out the handset again. "Sir." The lieutenant snatched it away. "This is Golf One Actual.

Cease fire. Friendly troops at that coordinate. Stop that fire mission, now."

≈

The Chief lay prostrate, hands clamped over his ears, trying to block the impacts of the rounds from pounding the bruised tissue in his skull. The ground under him jerked with each detonation, transferring the spasms through his body. He willed himself to shrink. The target area was close, so close that streaks of shrapnel ripped the leaves overhead. They fell to the earth all around him, curled into ugly fists by the heat. In the lull between salvos he pushed himself up onto his knees, still holding a hand over his damaged ear, which was replaying each throb like a reverberating drumbeat. Before he could stand, fresh thunder cracks erupted ahead, and he curled into a fetal position and waited to meet the Great Spirit.

≈

Two rounds hit just behind where Nguyen estimated the column ended. Ears stinging, he stepped aside and waved his people past, refusing to acknowledge the fear in their eyes. The jungle lapsed into silence again, another lull as the enemy reloaded. He swung his arm frantically, desperate to take advantage. The high-pitched pealing in his head seemed to pass, and he heard a faint, guttural groan behind him, an animal sound, alien yet familiar, something recognized by primordial receptors deep in his brain that triggered alarms. Nguyen grabbed the last of the passing bearers, who was struggling under the bulk of the recoilless rifle. "Where is Co?" he asked, looking back where the trail twisted into the trees, his mind ticking off the ominous time gap between those ahead and those behind. The man shrugged and pushed on, concerned only with the assault on the physical space he occupied, wanting to move that space as far away as possible. The silence seemed filled with threat. Nguyen watched the empty path, tuning his ears to the ominous stillness in the sky.

The last of the column left Nguyen where he stood, never looking back. Co and Sau and the heavy machine gun were somewhere back along the trail, bathed in the smell of burned air and shredded earth, waiting for the American gunners to blanket more of the mountain with steel. Nguyen wanted to call out. He even wanted to run back and find them, to admonish them for holding up the column, but the column had to be his focus. Sacrifices had to be made, and risks had to be avoided; no more regrets at not moving. His thoughts now were not for the men lost but for the men left.

Pham stepped out of line, letting the trailing unit push past until the recoilless rifle crew went by. He knew the big machine gun was at the tail of the column, but now there was nothing but empty jungle behind him.

Nguyen shouldered his load and followed after his unit, each step he took away from those behind lying on his mind like an accusation. Pushing through some overhanging branches, he was surprised to see Pham just ahead, the extra pack board thrust on him earlier hanging from one hand by the shoulder straps. The comfort he felt at being joined in the empty jungle, where the trees now felt too tall, the shadows too dark, and the silence deafening, was overmatched by anger at having his orders disobeyed.

Pham looked past Nguyen as though he wasn't there, searching as far as sight could reach. "Co?" He gulped. "Truong?"

"Keep moving," Nguyen said, not looking back to emphasize that there was nothing back there that should concern him.

"But Truong," Pham said. He let the extra pack board roll into the foliage beside the path. With a hop, he adjusted the position of the pack digging into his shoulders and started back over ground that smelled of cremated humus, ozone, and scorched trees.

Nguyen slipped the AK sling from his shoulder and tucked the butt into one arm. "Pham," he said, louder than he intended. Pham continued to move away as though Nguyen's words were not reaching the world he occupied. Nguyen raised the weapon. The sight ring on the barrel wavered over the pack roll partially concealing Pham's head. He drew a bead. "My word is law here, *con trai*," he said, testing the label "boy" for impact, but finding none. Nguyen held his aim on the spot until Pham moved out of sight, then let the weight of the weapon pull it down. Pham wasn't a boy. He was a soldier. He could go and drag the boy back, but not the soldier. He turned and headed after the column. He expected the mountain to explode again at any second, but the lull stretched on. He tried to will his worn legs to trot, but the weight on his back held him to a barely controlled stagger. Maybe Pham would survive. He himself might survive. Maybe they would all survive.

≈

Truong pushed himself into a sitting position, letting his head hang forward as though the gyroscope whirling in his skull couldn't find a way to balance it on his neck. He tried to marshal his thoughts but found it impossible. His body felt bruised inside. He wanted to put his hands over his ears to block the screams but knew it was useless because they were coming from inside.

When he raised his head and was able to focus he saw nothing but empty path before him. He looked behind and saw the barrel of the heavy machine gun spanning the path like a tipped hurdle and a sandaled foot protruding from the bushes nearby, as though a runner had missed his leap. A rhythmic whisper and a weak drone that might have been the jungle finding its breath for a feeble protest caught his attention. He tried to stand, but searing pain gripped his left thigh and he crumpled back to earth, grabbing his leg. Blood squeezed between his fingers. He realized he could taste it, too, and spit a red glob onto the path. He explored the inside of his mouth with his tongue and felt a sharp foreign edge invading the familiar interior landscape. Reaching up, he discovered a shard of splintered tree piercing his cheek, feeding blood into his mouth that oozed out as pink bubbles on his lips. He struggled to his feet again, squeezing his thigh, desperate not to make a sound that would seem unwelcome in this mute wilderness.

He reached the solitary foot extended into the path and let his eyes follow the leg up to where the other twisted at an odd angle, tucked behind in a runner's pose, then further up to Sau's staring eyes, unblinking, specks of debris lying on the whites and irises to no effect. A chunk of Sau's neck was gone, and the ground underneath him was soaked, the black soil taking back blood for blood. Truong had to tear his eyes away from Sau's face. There were hardships to be endured and forgotten, and then there were shocks and horrors to be absorbed and carried away like a malignancy to grow in the memory. The difference was in the seeing.

"Co," he called, weakly, leaving Sau and stepping over the tilted barrel. Making his way through the remains of a tree ripped apart by a ballistic force nature had never equipped it to resist, he found Co lying in a bundle just off the path. Scratch marks on the ground showed where Co's feet had searched for footholds as he pushed himself into the cover he sought with the instincts of a wounded animal. His pinched respirations were the jungle whispers Truong had heard. Co's breaths came short and forced, as though they were losing a competition with his heart for which would end first, and the back of his black tunic was soaked by a spreading stain.

Truong knelt at his back. "Co?" he said with a question in his voice, unwilling to accept that a man who exuded such invincibility was down. If men like Co and Sau could be broken, what chance did he have? Truong gently lifted one shoulder until Co rolled onto his back, leaning against his pack in a semi-sitting position. The front of his tunic was as wet as the back and sagged with the weight of a thickened mass pushing under the hem in bluish-purple convolutions. When he realized that he was seeing Co's spilled intestines Truong was transfixed by the image. He reached out and touched Co's shoulder lightly. "Co," he said, his voice equally light, afraid that any stimulus might add to the pain.

Co met Truong's look with tired eyes that registered recognition. When he tried to speak, he coughed a spray of blood droplets and then smiled, his teeth stained red as though he had been chewing betel nut.

"I'm here, Co," Truong said, hoping his attempt at giving comfort would conceal the panic he felt.

Co looked down at himself and smiled ruefully, as though this was some cosmic joke. He gave Truong a weary look that begged him to make everything right again, or at least to verify that it was all a dream to be brushed away when they both awakened.

Truong ducked his head under the strap on his canvas satchel and fumbled with the ties, his hands shaking, then dumped the contents onto the blood-soaked ground. The white cloth that protected his beloved books was safely sealed inside a cocoon of plastic, and he tore at the folds with manic intensity. "I'm here, Co," he said again, not knowing what else to say, the solitary sound of it catching in his throat. He looked past the fallen machine gun to the empty path beyond and felt lost and abandoned. Holding a tail of the cloth, he dumped the precious books unceremoniously into an eclectic pile of East and West.

Co noticed Truong's interest in the empty path. "You think they will return for us?" he whispered. "No. Nguyen has a responsibility to the assignment, to the weapons."

Truong pushed an end of the cloth under Co's back and draped the rest over the twisted blue bulges escaping the confines of torn muscle and flesh. The pristine white expanse grew spreading red bouquets while he concentrated on tying the ends with just the right tension for support. "Well, maybe he'll come back for the gun."

Co nodded. "He will do only what he thinks he must."

Truong studied the older man's face, the skin stretched tight by the sun, tired eyes slipping into resignation, an expression of acceptance ushering in serenity. "Then we must go to him," he said, slipping his pack from his shoulders. He worked at the buckles on Co's pack, and the man drooped when its grip was released.

Truong slipped an arm behind Co's shoulders and started to lift, all the while wondering why the mountain wasn't being ripped apart by the American artillery. "We should go now, while we can."

Co stiffened and gasped for air as though the sudden pain had stolen his breath. "Stop, stop," he said, grabbing at Truong's arm. Truong let him settle against the pack again. Co struggled to breathe, and his skin had a clammy pallor that made Truong afraid. He looked at the empty path. "Maybe I can go and get help," he swallowed hard, "and come back for you."

Co relaxed against the pack under his shoulders as if it were a favorite old chair molded to his contours where he could happily spend the rest of his days. He waved a hand, the wrist weak and loose. "You go . . . and don't come back."

Truong lifted his pack and balanced it on top of Co's, making a pillow. "I cannot . . ." He let his words fade. A battle waged in Truong's mind, a conflict between self-preservation and loyalty. The allegiance nurtured in the last weeks made thoughts of self-interest as distasteful as treachery. Before his pangs of patriotic fervor sent him south, he wouldn't have given a man like Co a second thought, and now he was fighting his own instincts, putting his own life in peril for a dying peasant in some nameless patch of wilderness. And he knew it was the only thing he could do.

The dilemma held him frozen in place, unable to go, unable to stay, unable to help. It occurred to him that the pragmatic thing to do would be to shoot Co, gather up everything he could carry, and go after the unit with all the speed he could muster. But pragmatism was the purview of a commander, and he was not in command of anything—not even, he was surprised to discover, the shaking of his own hands. He was a slave to an affinity he would not have thought possible before. All he could do now was wait. Wait for Co to die. Wait for the artillery to begin again. Wait for the Americans to come. Wait for some external force to take the decision from his hands. He hung his head, pitying himself, a victim of circumstance, and wondered what name he would be assigned to enter the next world, and who would be there to assign it.

His books were strewn beyond where his knees pushed wet dents in the jungle carpet, and the sight of them exposed to the elements made him mourn their loss as though they were already being deconstructed by nature, reduced to nutrients for plants and little sharp-jawed beetles. He grabbed the plastic wrap and reached for the discarded volumes. Saving them was something he *could* do.

The love tale of Kieu, with its worn leather binding, brought his mother's face to mind, and he held it to his nose hoping for her scent. Knowing it was her favorite and often caressed by her hands made it special. He laid it gently on the plastic as though its existence was fragile. The well-thumbed westerns had collected more stains on their thirsty pulp pages, and their dust covers looked more worn than before. He held one up, examining the cover art. A hot, dry mesa. Wide open spaces. A wild red man riding bareback on a spotted horse, free—and so far away from this place. He always imagined that one day he would visit the dry, hot land and the men in feathers and skins who lived there. His shoulders sagged a little more. Of all the things he felt he was about to lose, his lost dreams stung worst of all.

Co drifted in and out of consciousness, mumbling incoherently, moving his feet as though he was walking, and then lying still again. He groaned and tried to push himself up. Truong picked up the next novel and looked fleetingly at Co, afraid to see his own future in the man's face. But Co wasn't looking his way. He was staring at the bush beside Truong, and the blood vessels in his face and neck seemed about to burst under the strain. Truong looked up and his own blood stopped pumping.

A huge, bronzed man who looked like he belonged on the cover of Truong's Zane Gray western had risen from the plants a meter away. A leather sheath with brass rivets at his waist held a large knife. Truong watched as the long blade slipped free of its confinement. He couldn't take his eyes from the honed edge and the dark hand pulling it out. The blood of the man's Indian ancestors was expressed in the broad face and short black hair bound tightly in a bloodstained dressing. The red streaks on his face and the dark red eye peering from under the bandage accentuated the fierceness of the image. Truong looked down at the ragged books in his hands and then back at the man, who surely was a figment of his own mind. But the clear eye, the one not swollen and clouded with pain, was looking only at the leather bag around Truong's neck, and in an instant Truong knew who he was. An involuntary flood of relief swept through him like a sudden chill. The conflict he felt over the Indian's death was resolved, only to be replaced with the very real danger of his living presence.

Co reached for his AK, pulling it to him by the butt. He raised it with feeble hands and clawed for the trigger. The figment suddenly moved, snatching the weapon away by the barrel and tossing it across the path to land with a crash out of sight. The misshapen face turned so the good eye could assess this enemy's condition, then turned away, satisfied. Co dropped back against the packs, spent.

The hallucination, if such he was, was real enough to plant a boot in the middle of Truong's chest and knock him backward, away from his AK lying in the mud. Before he could kick his feet in defense, the western nightmare was upon him like a hungry predator. A bent knee pinned him to the ground. Truong still clutched the pulp novels, and he held them up like charms that could ward off evil spirits, though the authority of Brand and Grey seemed far less than what was needed at the moment. The red-streaked face loomed over him, a ceremonial mask of war. Something cold touched the side of his neck, and he froze. The flat side of the big knife blade pressing against his skin made him shiver. How could something be so cold in this heat, he thought? And how strange that the last thing he would feel while bathed in sweat would be cold, a cool release from the heat of life. He forced himself to look into the last face he would ever see. The man was looking not at him, though, but at the books in Truong's hands.

For Truong, the world seemed to stop. The air stopped moving. The trees stopped growing. The planets stopped spinning. The only movement in the universe was his heart, and that was beating like a drum.

The specter's good eye wandered from the books to Truong's face, as though the sound of his beating heart had attracted its attention. Truong tried to put everything he was into his aspect, everything he thought, everything he felt, everything he dreamed, sending it spiritually into the eye, which seemed to have all the compassion of a shark's.

The wild man's free hand snatched one of the books away and studied the cover, holding the knife in place all the while, making sure any movement on Truong's part would be short-lived. He leaned in closer, as though his next decision would be decided by smell. Truong's body had turned to stone. He couldn't even blink. He wondered how much pain there would be when the knife plunged into his throat. How long he would suffer. But the blade lifted from his neck until it stretched the little bag's rawhide cord taut, then cut it free. The man stood, dangling the bag from the knife blade, admiring it like a trophy, a buckskin scalp.

≈

Pham pushed one foot ahead of the other, leaning forward against the weight of his pack but not moving too quickly, afraid of what he might find. The ground he was revisiting had changed from just minutes ago, and he concentrated on the path that wormed its way through a landscape scarred and broken. He was going back so he could do something, but he didn't know what that something might be. He moved forward with tentative steps, clutching his AK as though the feel of it held solutions. The world around him now smelled acrid and burnt, making his nose question the wisdom of taking a breath. Ahead, he could make out something long and dark crossing the path: the straight lines of the big machine-gun barrel. Beyond that, a figure in green blended with the brush, a figure with broad shoulders, a wide back, and a round head wrapped in tan cloth. Pham blinked hard, trying to make the unbelievable real.

The man in green seemed to be focusing his attention on something in his hand. His big arm rose up and the thing of interest swung free by its rawhide cord: the beaded bag, the prize from Co that Truong had worn about his neck.

The AK suddenly felt heavy in his hands; the wooden parts slippery to his touch. If Truong had worn the bag the enemy now held, then where was Truong? He heard an unrecognizable voice screaming in rage and brought the rifle up to bear on the enemy. The voice was that of a wild animal, and it was coming from him. He pulled the trigger and the weapon jerked, spitting spent cartridges and invading the dark silence with a string of sharp cracks that joined his own guttural roar in a mad duet.

Pieces of muddy path jumped into the air—his trigger pull rushing ahead of his aim—and Pham extended his arms, hunched his shoulders, and forced the barrel up and over into the trees, firing until the magazine and his lungs were both empty. His finger still crushed the trigger in an emotional cramp he couldn't release, though all the weapon could do now was send wispy clouds of steam into the humid air.

The man in green was gone. A high-pitched peal filled his ears, making him want to stretch his jaw muscles to clear the deafness, and he pointed the impotent barrel at every shadow where his fear imagined the enemy could be. His hand shook. He'd never fired a weapon at anyone before. He'd never tried to kill anyone before. He'd never wanted to kill anyone before. The AK-47, once heavy, seemed both weightless and harmless now. He snapped the empty magazine free and fumbled a fresh one from the pouches on his chest. Its curve and fit seemed incomprehensible to his shaking fingers, and he struggled to match the end to the opening on the gun, finally feeling the comforting snap as it locked into place. As the bolt drove a fresh cartridge into the chamber, he felt restored, ready again but not prepared. He looked around at the vast emptiness alive with threats.

Pham reached the place where the machine gun barrel blocked the path without knowing he was moving. Sau's crumpled body off to the side captured Pham's attention, and he tightened his grip on his AK. He straddled the barrel, feeling the hardness of the steel with his knees, not wanting to take his eyes from the shadows. The spot where the enemy had stood was just ahead, ominous in its emptiness, and he kept his rifle trained on the place, expecting a sudden reappearance. His eyes flitted about the trees, but the rifle held to the spot, an involuntary compass unable to point anywhere else.

He was close now. Close enough for anyone to hear his pounding heart. Close enough to see the slightest movement that would unleash the firepower in his hands. From where he stood he could see Co leaning against the packs, the bloody bulge protruding from his stomach, his skin pale, eyes rolled back. A movement nearby drew his head back with a snap. A blood-encrusted hand rose up from the undergrowth, a tattered book in its grasp, and Pham's brain battled at synaptic speed to control his trigger finger. Time lost for recognition struggled against a nervous desire to empty his magazine into the bush, but he knew that book—the garish colors, the wild man on horseback, the belching locomotive. "Truong," he said, hope overriding caution. Wet black hair appeared, followed by eyes opened wide, then the rest of the face. "Pham?" it said, still holding out the book as though it had mystical powers that might be offered in trade for a life.

Pham kept his weapon leveled, his hands not yet willing to believe the evidence of his eyes. "Truong? You're alive."

Truong looked down at himself as though he wasn't sure Pham's statement was true. He touched his throat with his free hand. "Pham. I saw a spirit. It was here. It stood where you stand now."

"I saw it, too, Truong, but that was no spirit. It was a man."

"It was a spirit." Truong tapped the cover of the book with a stained finger. "A spirit from here. Co told me he was dead, but he came," he touched his chest where the beaded bag had hung, "for me, for this."

Pham searched the shadows for any spirit shape in hiding. "I truly hope it was not a spirit. We cannot kill a spirit."

Truong reached for his AK but felt only the empty spot in the dirt where it had been.

The Chief squatted with his spine pressed into the trunk of a wide tree and the stolen AK lying across his legs, a welcome addition to his sorely limited armament. The spoils of war lay at his feet, a book with an artist's rendition of a Native American warrior on the cover. And more important than both, the pouch he held up by its severed cord, amazed that it was back in his possession. Though he'd never wavered in his resolve to get it back, he'd understood that the likelihood of success was small. The social conventions of his people required him to attempt its recovery—or die trying—but it was only stubborn determination that pushed him on through a quest that he felt could only end badly. The success of his efforts was due to an amalgamation of both Apache and Marine ethos that he had come to discover complemented each other perfectly. A tension deep inside of him released as the weight in his hand made him whole again.

He reknotted the rawhide cord and hung the bag around his neck where it belonged, tucking it inside his shirt. The thought that other hands—enemy hands—had touched the pouch made it appear somehow tainted to him, its sanctity invaded, and he felt responsible. Its loss was the result of a lapse in his vigilance that would not be repeated. He swore never to let it go again.

He looked down at the book and was disconcerted to find the title incomprehensible. The words found no resonance in his sagging mind, and he wondered if the blow to his head had knocked English from his brain. He recognized the Sioux warrior, but the letters of his alphabet were jumbled beyond meaning. He thumbed the pages. French, he thought in relief, recognizing only the famous author's name. The young Vietnamese was a reader of white man's tales of the Old West. His smile felt tight on his face.

A few feet away, a pale spider with long white legs scrambled over gossamer cords of its own creation. He watched the spider spin its translucent fiber, creating a strength and design that would ensure its survival. With the enemy no further away than he could throw a stone, the Chief

watched the spider at its labors, the concerns of the world removed. He
envied the little creature, not for its ignorance of human folly but for its
apparent trust that it was innately equipped with everything it needed
to do what must be done. He wondered if the spider chose the design of
its web or was blindly following some genetic blueprint, released from
the messy burden of free will. Was it a machine or was it in control of its
life? He knew he could not answer that question. But it was something
he could certainly answer about himself.

The bark of the tree caressed his vertebrae from his belt to his shoulder blades and had a friend's calming effect on his mind. He grasped the
pistol grip on the AK in his lap and lifted, testing its heft. It was much
heavier than his M16 and even more fearsome looking than the spider,
and the long curve of the magazine promised a firepower that might
meet his needs. He looked at the spider as it pounced on a moth that
foolishly strayed into its trap, then back at the AK in his hands.

≈

For the second time in a handful of minutes Strader flung himself to the
ground at the sound of firing up ahead. The first was a sustained burst
from a single weapon. The second was an exchange, a clash of opposing
yet oddly similar weapons. And they were close. The number of weapons firing grew from one to two to three, and finally became an eruption
that defied counting. There was no doubt in his mind that he was not
the target, just as there was no doubt that he knew who was. The way
his luck was going there couldn't be any other answer. The Chief was
the wellspring of his woes, and from the sound of it, the Indian was in
serious trouble. He began crawling slowly forward, abandoned that for
a stooped run, and then switched to a headlong dash between the trees.

≈

Franklin led the squad at a pace as quick as the mountain would allow.
He wished there were flanks out, but that would only slow them down,
with the flanks having to beat their way through virgin ground. The
squad would have to rely on an instant reaction to anything that might
happen.

The shadows of the jungle fell away into a clearing open to the sky,
the light illuminating a scramble of muddy footprints crossing to the tree

line on the other side. He stopped at the edge of the exposed ground, not wanting to rush into the opening where he would be a tempting target. It seemed a long way across. The big guns had been called off, so he wasn't worried about sudden death from friendly fire, but he was still deep in the Arizona, and if the guns weren't threatening him, they weren't threatening the VC either.

The ominous quiet allowed the soft sputtering of the Cessna Bird Dog to be heard. Franklin caught a glimpse of the little aircraft cutting the edge of the gap down on the valley end before it banked away and vanished behind the cover of the canopy. Franklin mopped the sweat from his face with an end of the green towel hanging around his neck. It stank of a thousand such wipes, the decay of the jungle, and the pungent smell of the explosions the terrycloth seemed hungry to absorb. A member of the fire team strung out behind Franklin relayed word from back in the column. "Sergeant says get your ass in gear." Franklin looked ahead at the open ground, took a deep breath, and started across at a quick pace. The squad followed.

Pusic stood silently behind Bronsky, thankful for the rest. The rain and jungle moisture had taken the starch out of his utilities, and he looked like a wilted plant. He could feel sweat trickling down over his ribs. Wiping at his face with a shirt sleeve he smelled the stiff chemical labors of the mama-sans in the camp laundry and wondered why he was out here while they were safely back there, probably counting the paces between the perimeter, the com shack, and the chow hall so their relatives could map out a target for their midnight mortars.

Finally the rear of the squad began to move, like a stretched and now retracting spring. Bronsky looked back with a remark forming on his lips when sudden gunfire broke the silence. Pusic ducked before looking to the rest of the squad for a cue to what his reaction should be. They seemed cautious and alert but not too concerned. Apparently the firing was far enough ahead to warrant only modest interest. It was an abstract threat that promised peril, but only in the future.

The squad pushed on across the opening. Before the tail reached the tree line the second course of firing erupted and grew to consume the air and all of their imaginations about what was ahead.

≈

When Nguyen heard Pham's weapon firing he was already headed back with Hoang Li and a few other bearers. He sent the remainder of the unit on, carrying all they could manage and leaving packs behind for Nguyen and his detachment to retrieve later.

As they came within sight of the big machine gun spanning the path, firing began again, tracer rounds burning the air both up and down the mountain. Pham's AK was kicking in his hands, the barrel swinging wildly as though he didn't know where his target was and had chosen to paint the whole mountain with his lethal brush. Truong was across the path, frantically thrashing the weeds. He finally found a weapon and joined Pham's efforts to shred the mountain.

Nguyen directed his men's fire upslope, their rounds blindly searching for the origin of the tracers angling down. They were so close together that the firing battered their ears, and when the RPK with its seventy-five-round-drum magazine opened up, they moved apart. One of the men shouldered an RPG and scanned the mountain for a spot to send the rocket. The firing from above began searching them out in turn, and they dove for cover. Nguyen leapt over the old Chinese machine gun blocking the path and ran in a crouched stoop to where Pham was frantically changing the magazine in his AK with fumbling fingers.

Pham looked at Nguyen in shock. His sudden appearance in the path was no less surprising than that of the knife-wielding Indian. But Nguyen couldn't appreciate the bewilderment on Pham's face. He was transfixed by the gruesome sight of Co leaning against his pack, bloody intestines lying in his lap like a bundled infant. Nguyen pointed his AK uphill and emptied the magazine into the shadows that held the killers of his friend. Truong limped to Nguyen's side, and along with Pham they poured fire up the mountain until the *swoosh* of the RPG made them duck.

The explosion, hidden in the trees, was followed by the crack of a returning shot. The empty grenade launcher fell from the shooter's hands and he crumpled to the path a lifeless sack. Hoang Li directed the RPK gunner standing nearby to fire into an area his ears told him needed destruction, but as soon as the weapon began to chatter, a single shot dropped the gunner where he stood, the long-barreled gun hitting the ground with a thud. Hoang Li threw himself down. Again his ears identified the shot. It had a familiar voice. He was sure he'd felt that shooter before.

he first shot pierced a latticework of branches and leaves, catching the rush of movement that launched the RPG. The explosion lit the trees to Strader's left, and he waited a breath before pulling the trigger, threading the needle to his target. He could see fragments of movement below him where the path cut through the trees, and he struggled to find another clear shot. A movement to the side caught his eye, and he swung his rifle around, catching the Chief in an awkward lope from tree to tree, coming from the direction of the grenade strike. A long rip of firing from below sent tracers careening off anything hard enough to deflect a round's hot path, and Strader took aim again and fired, knowing that his round planted pieces of leaves into the shooter whose muzzle blast had betrayed his position. The gun went silent. Each time Strader fired he felt the rounds go true to their targets. It was just a feeling, like getting a solid hit on the sweet spot of a baseball bat: the skill, the training, the need. He didn't see the enemy fall, but he felt them fall.

The Chief was moving as though his torso was too heavy for his legs. He grabbed at trees and crashed through bushes that a steadier gait would be able to sidestep. Strader watched him come. He wanted to call out but didn't want to paint a target on himself. As the Indian stumbled, a new fusillade climbed the mountain, blindly biting at everything in its path. Strader smiled. He was pleased to see that the Chief could piss off the VC as much as he pissed off his fellow Marines. He felt somehow less singled out.

Bracing against a tree, Strader pressed in the selector on his M14 and snapped it to automatic. There was no definite target below, so he raked an imaginary line where he thought the path would be, walking the fire north until the magazine was empty. When he stopped shooting everything went quiet.

The Chief came on, cutting an unsteady path between trees, stopping at each one, grabbing hold like a drunken partier at a class reunion. When Strader fired, the Indian looked up with faint interest; his energies were occupied elsewhere, with little left for showing surprise.

Strader waited for some response from below, but none came. He could hear voices down in the trees, and though they sounded angry, his grasp of Vietnamese—limited to negotiating purchases and shooing away children—couldn't begin to make sense of it. There was a chance that he could reach out and touch those voices, but with less than sixty rounds left, he decided not to gamble away precious resources he was bound to need later. He snapped a fresh magazine into place and glanced over to the Chief. All he could see was the top of the Marine's head. He had slumped into a squat against one of the trees, unable to come any further.

Strader made his way through the trees until he reached the one bracing the Chief. From a distance it seemed the Chief was convulsing, but when he got close enough he could see the bounce of shoulders and hear the sound of muffled laughter. His suspicions were confirmed: the Chief was crazy. As he knelt, a twisted and swollen smile greeted him.

"I never thought I'd see *you* again," the Chief said.

"You should have had more confidence in the white man." Strader had imagined he would rip into the Chief when he caught up to him, but the swollen, purple face changed his plans.

"Don't take it to heart, jack-wad. I didn't expect to see anyone again."

"You were supposed to wait for me in the rocks."

"And you were supposed to bring help. I guess we're both full of shit."

Strader peeked around the tree to see if anyone was coming up toward them. There was no movement. "What the hell are we doin' here?"

The Chief pulled up the front of his T-shirt to reveal the beaded pouch nestled against his skin.

"You got me out here for a damned leather bag?"

"I came for the spirit pouch. You're not supposed to be here at all."

"I've been telling you that all day. I should be in the rear starching my civvies." Strader could see a cluster of shrapnel wounds speckling the Chief's ribs. "Jesus, Chi . . . Moon. How much punishment are you gonna take?"

The Chief looked at the lacerations leaking blood down to stain his waistband. He gently touched the pouch, pressing it into his chest. "They're all honorable wounds." He touched the battle dressing on his head gingerly. "I ain't ashamed of any of them."

"Okay, Moon. I believe you." Strader looked downhill again. There seemed to be movement on the path. "I suppose you got some payback? Really pissed them off, huh?"

The Chief was surprised to find he still had the empty AK-47. He tossed it aside. "My head is killing me and I can't see well enough to hit anything." He pulled his shirt down and patted the lump the pouch made. "I found the one who had my spirit bag, though . . . and I let him go."

Strader raised his eyebrows at that. "You're becoming a real humanitarian, Moon."

"Screw you, Raymond. He just didn't seem to be an enemy, or not much of one."

Strader leaned in close, as though imparting a secret. "I hate to suggest this to a warrior and lunatic of your standing, but he *is* the enemy, and I think we should *didi* . . . and I mean now."

The Chief struggled to get his feet set under him. "If you're waiting for an argument from me, you'll be here waiting long after I'm gone."

Strader slipped under the Chief's arm and they started back through the trees, harnessed together in green brotherhood. They crawled across the face of the mountain until the *zing* and *thwack* of rounds blindly searching for a home drove them behind the trunk of an uprooted tree, its exposed root system clawing the air with gnarled tendrils. Strader had hoped to make more distance, but this would have to do. Even Olympic sprinters couldn't outrun a bullet.

The Chief seemed pleased with the spot and the rest. "Are they coming?" he asked in between gasps.

Strader raised an eye above the trunk and scanned the trees. "I don't see anything, and I don't think they see us either. Those shots are wild, just anger." He sank down beside the Chief and looked into his good eye. "You didn't make any friends there, did you?"

The Chief blinked stiffly and waited for his breath to come. "I guess the Corps didn't train me to play well with others."

Strader stretched his neck for another view over the tree as hot rounds spent their energies blindly. He slipped back. "I don't see anything, but we can't stay here and just hope they go away."

"Why not? They went away last time."

"Yeah. I went away, too. And yet here I am."

The Chief put as much intensity into his stare as one eye could provide. "I told you to go. Your problem is, you don't listen."

"And you don't stay put."

A twinge of guilt made the Chief uncomfortable. "I had something to do," he said.

"I had something to do, too. Like shine my boots and pack my bags and get the hell out of this damn country."

"Don't blame me. I didn't stop you."

~

Hoang Li found Nguyen kneeling by Co's side testing the weak pulse in his friend's neck. He pointed to the bodies of the machine-gunner and the RPG man lying on the path. "I know who did this," Hoang said, feeling for the hole in his magazine pouch.

Nguyen looked up, thinking he might see an accusatory finger pointed his way, but he could see that Hoang Li's anger was focused elsewhere.

The spark of recognition ebbed and flowed in Co's eyes until he got control of his consciousness. "Get . . . away," he said when he saw who was kneeling by him.

Nguyen wasn't sure if his friend was in too much pain to be touched or was just disappointed to be an excuse for jeopardizing their mission. As gently as he could Nguyen rested a hand on Co's shoulder. "We'll be going soon."

Hoang Li pointed his rifle uphill with one hand. "And they'll follow. They must have been in our shadow since the valley."

Truong listened to Hoang Li's anger. He wanted to say that the enemy was following only him to retrieve his property, but they might think him *dinky dau*; or if not crazy, they could blame him. Either way, the acceptance he had gained within the unit would be lost. He needed to clear his thoughts but couldn't. Until now his experience in the South had been nothing more than an agony of labor: long days, heavy loads, and little sleep or food. The tormenting insects and heat and rain had made him miserable, but what he felt now was a misery of another caliber. Physical pain and mental confusion clashed in a battle to pilot his mind.

Co, resting a limp hand on the bulge lashed to his abdomen, marshaled enough energy to force some words. "You cannot stay. I cannot go."

"You will be carried," Nguyen said without looking at his friend.

"No power on earth can get me from this mountain."

Nguyen looked into his eyes and knew it was the truth. Whatever they did for Co would just bring him more pain and still have only one result.

Co grabbed Nguyen's arm and pulled himself up a few inches from his pack. His face showed the strain. The tracks of swollen veins mapped his face. "You must not leave me like this," he pleaded. His grip faded and he eased back again.

Nguyen stood slowly, letting each joint ratchet him upward, feeling each vertebra click into position with a finality and stiffness he hoped would bolster his resolve. The truth of Co's words was inescapable. He discovered he was gripping his weapon as though it might fall to his numb feet with a lesser hold, and he wished it would.

Truong inched over close and knelt down. Co didn't notice. His eyes were closed over a peaceful expression, as though he were just waiting. Truong touched his shoulder. Co smiled when he saw Truong's face. "So, you have survived, *linh*."

Being called a soldier would have warmed his heart before, but now Truong just touched the place on his own neck that could still feel the cold flat of the knife. "The Indian took back the rawhide bag." He felt he should apologize for losing the gift acquired at such great risk, but there was no anger on Co's face.

"You may have been right about those people." His eyelids sank under their own weight. "It would have been good to know them."

Truong noticed the thick sight on Nguyen's weapon rise up to point at Co. Before he could protest it fired, once into Co's chest, then twice more, quickly, to hasten the end. Co's body contorted with a newfound strength, then sagged to limpness. Truong was stunned. Even though it was an act he too had considered, the sight of it burned through him like a fever. Some turned away. Others stood frozen, looking to the broken body on the ground. Whether they saw the brutal act as merciful or harsh didn't matter to Nguyen. It was an unavoidable outcome tailored for his shoulders alone, and he would have to wear it.

Hoang Li moved up the mountain like a bloodhound following a scent. His two disciples were close on his heels, confident that the aura of protection surrounding Hoang would be large enough to engulf them both. Hoang's heavenly protector would be their shield, and the jungle floor would be their guide. They followed, and others fell in behind.

Nguyen watched them fade into the shadows, his objection dying on his lips. He should order them back and chastise them for their insubordination, but his taste for command was sour in his mouth, especially since he was guilty of violating his own rules. He stood silently and let them go, his offending weapon dead weight in his hands. They had a purpose even he could justify. It was his own purpose that was now giving him trouble.

The RPK man in the path lay curled around the bullet hole that killed him, his weapon lying within reach. Nguyen let his own AK slide to the ground and picked up the long machine gun. He could see Sau's lifeless leg protruding from the bush. A second body lay prostrate by the empty rocket launcher, its face a mask of calm put there by a single shot. Things were going wrong, and the decay was gaining momentum. Any control he had ever had was crumbling away, and he hated feeling helpless. If it was his fate to fail, he could at least strike out at his tormentors. "*En bas*, Hoang Li," he yelled, his French out of character and the force of it loud enough to ensure that Hoang's cell would hug the ground. Then he raised the long-barreled weapon and pulled the trigger, sending a stream of tracers into the mountain where he hoped they would kill his pain.

With the empty, steaming machine gun hanging lifeless at his side, Nguyen realized why the artillery had stopped. The bodies at his feet told him. Someone in the enemy camp had discovered that their own people were in the target zone. Someone close by had called off the guns. He retrieved his AK and looked toward the shadowy trees where Hoang Li had disappeared. He knew he should have stopped him. Each error he made seemed to feed on the last, compounding its effect, growing like a cancer that would kill his mission. Around him lay the lifeless products of his missteps. He knew he had to regain control, and he saw a way. Hoang Li's anger would keep the Americans busy, and he could use that. Maybe letting Hoang's cell go would be something other than a mistake. Maybe it was a sacrifice, a necessary sacrifice. He could stop the cancer. But he would have to excise some of the good with the bad. To kill the malignancy he would have to abandon valued comrades to their fates. He still had enough strong backs to carry the dead or the heavy machine gun and its equipment, but not both. It was another decision of rank that really left no choice.

The bodies were dragged a few meters downgrade and arranged in a ragged line as respectfully as possible, touching arm to arm as though this would be a comfort, if not for the dead then for the living who were leaving them behind. Equipment was collected, and the big Chinese gun was lifted onto shoulders. Overloaded bodies staggered under the weight of double loads. Nguyen pushed the heavy tripod into Truong's hands without regard for the man's limp or the track of blood coming from his cheek. Another pack board and the canisters of ammunition for the machine gun were left wanting a pack mule.

The jungle behind seemed empty and used. "Where is Pham?" Nguyen said, nearly pushing Truong aside.

Truong stumbled with pain and looked away, willing his torn leg to hold the load. Nguyen grabbed his arm. "Answer me," he said. "Where is Pham?"

An apology was on his lips. Truong wanted to say the fault was his, and that Co's gift had Hoang and the others searching the trees for an enemy who already had what he came for, but all he could do was point the way uphill with his chin to where Pham was pursuing Hoang Li and the others.

Nguyen's anger rose in him like a sudden fever. This was truly an obstinate cancer. It deftly parried every move he made. It knew how to eviscerate his strengths and tease his weaknesses. His anger was so thick that he couldn't trust his voice, so, looking over to assure himself that the others were moving the big gun back up the path, he surrendered to the mountain's lure, dug in his feet, and climbed into the trees.

~

Pham felt weightless. His pack lay back on the path and all he carried was his weapon and the magazines in his vest. Though the slope was steep, climbing without the crushing load seemed effortless, and he wondered why he wasn't lifting off the ground and floating up through the trees. Ahead, the jungle was empty and quiet, brooding over its wounds. Dark chunks of bark had been ripped from tree trunks, revealing the slippery white core beneath; sap dripped from the black-eyed holes where the bullets struck. His legs pumped hard and he climbed from tree to tree with no direction in mind other than up. He didn't know where he was going, but he knew he had to go. The ones below without voices were demanding it, and their dull, lifeless eyes were watching.

Sweat stung his eyes and he dragged a forearm across them without benefit. He stopped to listen but heard only the beating of his own heart. The damaged jungle seemed deserted and uninviting, and every beat of his heart made him feel more isolated, every shadow more threatening. He wanted to call out to the others but knew he wouldn't. A month ago he might have, like a lost child in a frightening place, but not now. He had changed. His world had changed.

A chirp in the trees, a faint squeak from a startled bird or rodent, came from somewhere ahead. When Pham ignored the sound it turned into a hiss, insistent and pointed. He somehow missed that he was the target of the sounds until one of Hoang Li's men rose from the undergrowth with a louder *pssst* and tossed a small stone. The sudden appearance of a familiar face eased some of the anxiety that was filling his brain. It was as comforting a sight as he could have hoped for.

He followed the man uphill, moving silently from tree to tree until they came to Hoang Li kneeling in the bush, his rifle raised. With a swipe of his arm Hoang signaled them down. The cell leader pointed to gaps in the trees ahead that showed a downed trunk with gnarled roots at one end. Above, Pham could see another of Hoang's men creeping upward. Pham sank down and swung his weapon toward the dead tree without knowing why. The jungle was quiet and empty. The only life he saw or heard was the men around him, and he wondered if Hoang Li was being overcautious, assigning importance to a natural blind simply because it was there, but the look on Hoang's face told him he would not be voicing that question. He would defer to experience and then rely on that experience as though his life depended on it, because it did.

When the man above signaled he was in position, Hoang pulled his AK into his shoulder, pressing his face down to peer over the barrel.

Shuffling sideways, Pham put a standing tree between him and the distant trunk nestled into the ground. He raised his own weapon and aimed into the shadows. If there was something there, he was ready. As he watched, a sliver of movement showed above the dead tree, a Lazarus in green rising up from the jungle floor, and before he noticed Hoang Li's signal to wait he pulled his trigger.

S trader was on his knees, looking into the Chief's face. "I don't think we should wait. I need to be somewhere else, and I'd like to *didi mau* in that direction, if you don't mind." The Chief reached out and Strader took his arm, rising up, pulling until his backpack rose above the cover of the tree. Pieces of bark jumped up from the dead trunk, and the air screamed with rounds passing overhead. He dropped down again, hugging the tree.

"I guess they didn't go away," the Chief said.

Strader searched the bruised and distorted face before him, looking for something that would explain their situation, justify the dilemma they were in—some expression of remorse, a contrite grin, fear, any-thing. He was disappointed. "No shit," he said.

The single weapon turned into many, their shots crowding the space above the tree and slamming into the trunk. The rounds struck the decaying wood like hammer blows, sending jolts through Strader's body as the tree spit fibrous bits of itself into the air.

"I'm . . ." Strader looked into the Chief's responsive eye, "we're screwed." Strader pushed the M14 up over the trunk and fired blindly, sweeping the trees at random, letting the weapon's recoil decide the aim. The incoming fire balked, a momentary stammer, before regaining its voice, renewing its intensity. Strader pulled his rifle back and held it close. He couldn't help the expression of hopeless resignation crossing his face. The Chief looked back expressionlessly.

Strader turned and crawled toward the upturned base of the tree where he might fire unnoticed through the tangle of roots. The precious cartridges he had left would have to count. Hot rounds burned streaks in the air above, and the odor of wood pulp from bullet strikes filled his nostrils. Clumps of dried earth clinging to the root knuckles filled in some spaces, and Strader found an opening large enough to take the muzzle of his M14.

The Chief watched him go. He knew their resources were almost gone, and then the enemy would come and he would have to fulfill his warrior destiny with a white man at his side. Drawing the big knife from its sheath, he looked at the heavy blade. If they came close enough, their blood would mark the steel . . . again. Bursts of night shadows popped in his mind. Dark figures full of groans and thuds: alien sweat, whiffs of tobacco and oil and fear, pungent flesh crouched nearby, full of menace. His knife moved in the night and found a breathing resistance; a body shuddered. Pain stabbed his head. He looked at the knife again as though it were an oracle revealing a hidden truth. He turned it side to side, letting the revelation sink in. "I didn't do it," he said, surprised to hear his own voice and the relief it carried.

Strader leaned into his weapon, waiting for something in his narrow field of fire to make a fatal mistake. He felt the Chief move close but didn't move his eyes from the gun sights.

"Reach, it's not my fault," the Chief said, keeping his head close to the tree trunk.

Strader seemed unaffected by the news.

"Did you hear me? It's not my fault."

Again no visible response.

The Chief reached out to touch Strader, then thought better of it.

Strader's muffled voice worked around the rifle stock. "What's not your fault?"

"You being here. It's not my fault. That screw-up belongs to someone else. I just remembered what happened last night, and Tanner and the new guy ain't on me. I didn't do it, so it's not my fault you're here."

Strader looked over his shoulder just long enough to see if the Chief's head injury was driving his words. He seemed lucid enough. "What a relief," Strader said, leaning back into his rifle. "For a minute I thought I was in trouble."

"It's a relief to me. This is all a mistake, and I didn't make it."

Strader seemed absorbed with the concentration required to aim. "Moon, I hate to burst your little happiness bubble, but I'm just a poor city boy, and I don't think I could have got this far up shit creek without an Indian guide." He looked over his shoulder to see if his words had hit their target.

The Chief's old ethnic sensitivity flashed across his swollen face. His spark of memory had brought a relief that was all too short. He wanted to argue his case further, but he could see Strader take in a deep breath, let half of it out, and tighten his grip on his weapon.

≈

Nguyen dug his sandals into the rich soil and pushed his legs to the limit of what energy they had left, letting the sounds of the exchange drive him forward. Ahead, Hoang Li's cell was firing bursts across the face of the mountain. He couldn't see the target, but they were all firing in the same direction. He leaned against a tree, checking his weapon and letting his breathing settle. Hoang Li was barking orders through the noise. It all seemed one-sided to Nguyen. If he could get close to Hoang, he would order him to withdraw. He would pull them all back into the mission, demand that they focus on the assignment. His AK seemed alive in his hands again. They would not dare refuse him.

Nguyen charged to the next tree, then the next, keeping a wary eye on the empty distance drawing all the fire. The nearest of Hoang Li's men, replacing an empty magazine, saw Nguyen coming up behind them. He leaned out of his concealment and waved an arm for Nguyen to get down. A discordant crack spoke back from the distance, and Nguyen watched the man fold his body around the point of a bullet's impact. The man pitched backward, contracting his limbs into a knot, twisting around an unbearable pain. Nguyen crawled to his side. He watched the man unfurl. He watched him release his grip. He watched the surprise fade from his face.

30

The squad of Marines climbed away from the path, following the lure of the clash on the mountain above them. Sergeant Blackwell opened the point fire team up, moving them on line. He didn't have to warn them to stay sharp. The gunfire was pounding home the need for caution.

Pusic stayed behind the metal square on Bronsky's staggering back. He looked around at the faces bent to their tasks, seeing only the effort of the climb in their expressions. The sounds that were jolting Pusic's nerves seemed less urgent to the others—not unimportant, just a noisy destination that needed their attention.

Corporal Middleton watched the clerk search for some model of behavior. "I'll bet you feel a long way from home, huh, pogue?" the young squad leader said, his voice low and airy, his smile out of place given the situation.

Pusic didn't trust his own voice, so he tried a smile that came off weak and tentative. He felt there was something inherently wrong with moving toward the sounds of battle. It was counterintuitive, going against everything his brain was telling him was the wiser course. Bad things were happening ahead. To consciously move in that direction was a form of insanity, an insanity that could be created only with training designed to ignore the sane path, to allow yourself to be carried along on the current of like behavior, putting one foot in front of the other because everyone around you was doing the same. He dug his boots into the mountain and let the green mentality sweep him upward.

Looking at the young men around him, he wondered if it was courage or conditioning that kept them moving. If you did nerve-wracking things often enough, did you develop a tolerance for danger that could be seen as bravery, or were these the faces of truly fearless men? Was courage an innate quality beyond the common, or was it the lack of some genetic survival trait removed by training? It would be comforting to think he was in the company of brave men and not just a bunch of robots whose senses were dulled by repeated exposure to the abuses of war. The faces looking back at him showed no reservations about their assessment of his qualities. He was an interloper. And worse, he was a liability.

~~

Farther back down the mountain, behind the web of trees that filtered the sounds of the battle, the platoon pushed on, with Lieutenant Diehl driving Burke's squad to eat up the ground. The distant shooting grew in volume, each shot reproducing itself, bouncing between the tree trunks and mountain and canopy like light reflected in a house of mirrors. His wayward people were up ahead, behind that veil of green shadows.

The lieutenant looked over his shoulder. "Get Four on the horn," he said without breaking pace. In seconds he had the handset pressed to his ear. "Is your workhorse in contact?" he asked. He was relieved by the answer but didn't bother to conceal the anxious tone in his voice. "How close?" he said. "Roger that, Four. Keep me advised. Out." Nothing else needed to be said. Sergeant Blackwell was as capable a Marine as he had ever met, and the lieutenant would have to rely on that capability. He handed the receiver back to the radioman. To ease his anxiety the lieutenant passed word forward for Burke to get his people motivated.

When the word arrived, Burke felt the weight of "his people" like an extra load in his pack. The responsibility and delegated authority presented fresh concerns. It was up to him now to field the orders from above and pass them along. He was the squad leader, and it was too new to be anything but an ill fit.

The path rose and dipped, skirted trees, and cut through vegetation, marking the mountain as abused by many feet. And the mountain fought back. It made every step a struggle and told every offending boot that, as in all of Vietnam, it could not come here without effort. Every step, every breath, every day would be a struggle. They might mark its earth, but it would mark their hearts.

Burke pushed up ahead until he caught the point fire team. The column moved without sound, each man wrapped in his own mind, sweating his load, listening to the noise in the distance, trying to imagine the best possible outcome. The clusters of shots pushed against their progress as though they were at repellant poles of a magnet.

"Quit draggin' ass, Deacon," Burke said, irritated at his new accountability. "If you can't hack it, get the hell out of the way." Not being able to "hack it" was a common rebuke, especially to those who lacked the tenure to establish their worth. The acceptance of the platoon was a daily process that ebbed and flowed based on successes and failures that could dog a new man, marking him permanently as a substandard shitbird or elevating him into the ranks of the brotherhood. Every hour in the field was a test. You humped your load. You ate your pain. But most of all you hacked it.

Deacon cursed and increased his pace, stretching his strides until the fabric of his new jungle pants thrummed in protest. The smell of death and decay was becoming stronger with every step.

The others in the fire team watched Deacon pull away and swore under their breath. They felt no obligation to demonstrate anything but would have to keep pace with this insecure rookie trying to prove his mettle. He was far too eager for their taste, especially in the Arizona. "Slow the hell down, Deek," one said, not wanting to break into a run.

"What's wrong, can't you hack it?" he hissed back over his shoulder, sniffing the air at the insistent odor of death. A spot on the path slick with ooze from an animal carcass caught his step, and he slipped and fell sideways, plunging his hand into the bloated body and releasing a burst of stink that clung to his fingers in a putrid gel alive with squirming maggots. The choking fumes rising from the carcass drove Deacon up with a guttural groan. He looked in horror at the slimy gore coating his hand. An unintelligible sound escaped his throat, a prelude to something more substantial. Before anyone could tell him to shut up, Deacon staggered backward, stepping off the path and sliding on the slick surface onto virgin ground.

In unison and without thought, the rest of the platoon threw themselves to the ground just as a detonation swept over them in a tidal wave of pure concussion. The blast hung in the air, masking all other sounds, turning the distant gunfire into something disconnected and irrelevant. The alien odor of burnt earth, burnt air, and burnt flesh supplanted the jungle smells. Everyone lay still, as though paralyzed by the concussion. They clung to the ground, waiting for this new assault to show its shape, as an end unto itself or the beginning of something worse.

Lieutenant Diehl raised his voice. "Burke." He waited. The air seemed sucked free of life. It occurred to him that he might be calling for someone who no longer existed. "Burke, answer me, damn it."

A voice came back hugging the ground like a low morning mist. "Yeah."

"What happened?" The lieutenant felt a small relief that someone could answer.

"Ah, I'm not sure," Burke replied.

"Well, now would be a good time to find out, squad leader."

"Roger that," came back with a hesitancy that would be the subject of the lieutenant's next council with his noncoms.

Burke got to his knees slowly, as though movement was a violation of rules the explosion had just established. Moving in the Arizona was the offense. No transgression, no punishment. He could hear Lieutenant Diehl organizing the platoon, readying them for anything that might come next—a question on everyone's mind that would be answered in the next few minutes. Was the lethal device passive, lying in wait, abandoned? Or was it the opening salvo of a snare that lacked only the stumbling participation of a victim? He got to his feet and moved forward without straightening, keeping that proximate connection to the ground that might be needed in an instant.

Two of the point fire team lay on the path ahead, propped up on their elbows and pointing their weapons at a gray fog rising through the branches, a sinister cloud marking a destination. "You hurt?" Burke asked.

"No," they answered in unison, and with a hint of surprise.

"Where's Deacon?"

They pointed at the mist.

Burke stepped over them, making sure each pace stayed on the path. "Get my back," he said as he passed. They rose and followed.

The call for "corpsman up" ran back through the ranks, and they made room for Garver to pass. When he reached the lieutenant, Diehl touched his arm. "I'm right behind you, Doc," he said, and they moved forward with Clyde struggling to keep the radio the requisite distance from the lieutenant's needs.

When Doc Garver reached the point fire team, he could smell the change in the air—the fried chemical smell of cordite mixed with the rich aroma of disgorged earth and something else, the fragrance of burnt meat and a foul stench of decay. He closed his nose with a pinch of a thumb and forefinger. Ahead, a chunk of the path was missing next to where Burke stood pointing into the bush. "Over here, Doc," he said without looking at the spot his finger was indicating.

Deacon lay on his back just off the path. He was reaching out for something that only he could see, and pieces of his left hand and forearm were missing. His eyes were wide and beyond seeing, and his lips were moving with a silent, airless question. Garver knelt by his side. The young Marine's new jungle pants were a shredded drape hanging from his belt over red meat and pink flesh folded back to reveal bits of pelvis. The explosion had been powerful, probably made from a dud round from heavy mortars or part of a 155. Whatever Deacon was missing was gone for good; there would be little left to see, and nothing to save.

The smell of ruptured bowel combined with the stench of decaying meat coming from nearby nearly made the corpsman gag. He ripped open the snap on one of his bags and unwrapped a canvas instrument case. There were severed arteries and veins to clamp, massive tissue damage to cover, and fluids to run, if it would do any good, although he knew it wouldn't. He pulled morphine syrettes from the case and squeezed their contents into Deacon's shoulder. The Marine didn't feel the needles penetrate his flesh. His pain was beyond that. The shock of what had just happened to him was all-consuming, blinding him to all but whatever he was seeing just beyond his reach. Doc Garver took hold of the Marine's damaged right hand and held on. There was nothing else he could do.

≈

Rounds continued striking the downed tree, but with less volume. There seemed to be a rotation of firing coming from one angle and then another, some closer, some farther away. Strader knew the enemy was moving in, one covering the advance of the next, firing only enough to fulfill their purpose until they were in position. He raised his weapon over the dead trunk and fired blindly, sweeping the barrel back and forth.

As Strader replaced the empty magazine, slamming the bolt on a fresh round, he wondered what day it was. In the morass of days in which he was mired, which was this? His mind couldn't find it. He wasn't surprised. A Sunday was a Friday as much as it was a Tuesday. He knew that few in his platoon could even name the month, let alone the day of the week. At home he might know by the smell in the air, the color of the leaves or the clarity of the sky, but not in this place. Time blurred here. His need for specifics now bothered him.

Rounds struck the dirt-encrusted roots, exploding clumps of dirt into an earthy spray that settled on the two Marines in a brown mist. As Strader turned away, he noticed that bullet strikes were kicking up dirt behind the tree trunk close to their outstretched feet. Someone was flanking the tree on the high side. The cycle of intermittent firing was positioning someone for a clear shot. They would be easy targets. He crawled across the Chief's legs unceremoniously, staying close to the trunk, clutching his rifle and moving like a three-legged dog. Shots flew over his head from another angle, ending harmlessly somewhere in the jungle behind him.

"There's one moving in above, Moon," he said, tucking the butt plate into his shoulder and slipping his left forearm through the strap. He would try to find this target, but he would have to expose himself above the tree to do it. When the turn came for the man above to fire, he would be waiting. Shots slapped the ground, and the Chief curled his legs up out of the line of fire. Strader popped up, braced the rifle against the tree, and pulled the trigger. The M14 bucked and he held the muzzle climb down by force. The expanding gasses from the AK above shook some leafy branches, and Strader hit the spot and moved rounds through the trees behind them. The AK went silent. Chunks of the tree trunk leapt up as his head drew attention from the distance. He crawled back to the Chief.

"You do any good?" the Chief asked, still holding his legs out of harm's way.

"Some, I think, but not enough," Strader said, looking down at his rifle's bolt, locked back over the empty last magazine. When he looked up it was to meet the glare of the Chief's good eye.

"Maybe its time for you to go, Raymond."

"Go where? My flight doesn't leave until the day after tomorrow. I've got one whole day and a wake-up."

"Get the hell out of here, man," the Chief said, feeling the guilt rise in him again.

"The trouble with you, Moon, is you don't like to be called 'Chief' but you think you are one. You give orders like you're in charge and you got a say in things, but you don't."

"And who has the say now, you?"

A new flurry of shots streaked the air and beat at the tree. Strader hooked a thumb. "No. They do." He laid the empty rifle across his legs and tried not to imagine his future. "And the worst we can do is spit."

The Chief held up his knife and turned the darkened blade side to side, letting the light touch the edge and shadow the blood groove. "Speak for yourself, white man."

Strader shrugged out of his pack and dumped the contents on the ground. He quickly unwrapped the jungle shirt and held up the hidden KA-BAR, testing the edge with his thumb. It would have to do. He looked from the blade of the Marine-issue fighting knife to the Chief's weapon and knew the result of the comparison was evident.

The Chief followed his gaze and managed half a grin. "I guess size really does matter," he said.

≈

Nguyen crawled to a tree and squirmed up behind its protective trunk. An AK fired just ahead, then another from above. He waited for a response from the jungle, but none came. Another tree a short distance away promised cover, but Nguyen knew that Hoang Li was right; this enemy was a marksman. He could choose his targets from the slightest movement, and reaching the next tree would require a move. It wasn't far, but a single step could be too far with this shooter. An AK fired close, and up above a dark figure dashed forward under its cover.

Nguyen watched the crouching shadow move. "Stop, Hoang Li. Stop now."

The figure knelt and looked back, his angry expression twisting into surprise at the sound of Nguyen's unexpected voice. "They are just ahead, *Dai uy*. They are within reach."

Nguyen looked into the deceptively empty jungle filled with ugly potential. He raised his weapon and pointed it in Hoang Li's direction. "And you are within mine," he said with an edge to his voice that could not be misinterpreted. As leader you didn't request obedience, you demanded it. And if they didn't respect your commands, they must fear your reactions and the deadly consequences.

≈

High on the mountain, the cadre split the R-20th Doc Lap unit in two and spread their descent above the firing. The sounds of the exchange were not far below them. The artillery could begin again at any moment, and the safest place to be was near the point of contact. The enemy would not shell their own troops, and it had been agreed that the VC unit would get in close and stay there until their comrades could pull free. They would drop down and fulfill their commitment before vanishing back into the jungle.

31

The firing gradually slackened to an eerie silence, and Strader cocked an ear and looked up as though he could see the quiet.

"Do you think they're leaving?" the Chief said. There was no hint of concern in his voice, and no hint of hope. It was just a simple question searching for an honest opinion.

"Not a chance in hell, Moon."

The Chief wiped his lips with the back of his hand. "My mouth is dry, Raymond. You got any pogey bait? I'd kill for a stick of gum."

Strader leaned forward and stirred the debris of Tanner's belongings with the point of the KA-BAR. Tight little rolls of toilet paper mixed with packs of instant coffee and narrow boxes of cigarettes tumbled about with tinfoil envelopes of heat tabs packaged like condoms. He stuck the blade into the ground and released the handle. "I don't think so, Moon." He squeezed his cargo pockets against his thighs; nothing there. The side pockets of his jungle shirt produced only the coveted sign-out sheet with its lone signature—the single testimony that he was qualified to go home, the young doctor's okay for him to survive. He pushed it back out of sight. "All we have is a few swallows of grape water." Reaching for the canteen, he absently patted the angled breast pockets on the front of his jungle shirt. "Damn," he said, feeling the shape hidden inside the right pocket.

"The Chief looked up. "Gum?"

"Better." Strader struggled with the buttons until the flap was free. He dug deep inside and drew out a closed fist. When he'd climbed on board the helicopter in An Hoa, the young powder-burned door gunner had reminded him, as he did every grunt passenger, to clear his weapon. It was the price of admission, the cost of flying his friendly skies. And now it was a gift. He unfolded his hand and the bright brass of a single 7.62-mm round stood out on his filthy palm like a jewel.

The Chief looked down at the little jacketed gift and grinned, nodding at the menace beyond the dead tree. "Oh, they're in trouble now."

"This is our last punch. Use it now or save it for later?"

The Chief pointed at the pristine cartridge with the tip of his knife. "You're probably crazy enough to think you can end the war with that one shot."

Strader thumbed the round into the open chamber of his M14 and sent the bolt home with a metallic *clack*. "I can end it for someone."

The Chief took the canteen and filled his mouth with the flavored water, swishing the liquid over his teeth before taking a gulp. He spit purple onto the ground between his legs. The attached cap fought him as he tried matching the threads, but he managed. He gave Strader a satisfied look.

"You don't seem too concerned," Strader said, turning toward the tree and getting to his knees so he could position the rifle for a final shot. "Ain't Indians ever afraid?"

"You keep calling me an Indian. My people were never anywhere near India, shithead. We always knew where we were. It's your people who couldn't find their asses with both hands."

"That's no answer."

The Chief wiped his mouth with a hand that betrayed a slight tremor. "When my grandfather's spirit passed, I told my father I was afraid and asked what it was like to die. He told me I was too young to worry about such things and that he didn't know much about dying anyway, but he imagined it was like going over Niagara Falls in a barrel. The rush of life ending pulled you over the edge. You couldn't resist it. You couldn't refuse it. You just went with a force greater than your own and were swept away."

Rounds slammed the tree trunk, sending chunks flying, chipping away at what Strader imagined were the remaining moments before they both faced the pull of that watery precipice. "And what did you take from that little bit of Apache wisdom?" he said, resting the sight end of the rifle on the upper curve of the tree.

"I was just a kid, so I figured he meant if you're so afraid to die, don't get in the damned barrel."

Strader gave the Chief a knowing grin. "But you got in anyway."

"That's right *quien más sabe*," the Chief said, holding his arms wide, revealing himself as an unrepentant example. "And the barrel is mean and green."

≈

Hoang Li froze where he was. The murderous look in Nguyen's eyes reminded him of the leader's capabilities. "I owe that one," Hoang said, absently touching the center of his chest.

Nguyen's weapon didn't waver. "You owe the *dau tranh*, and you owe me. Beyond that, all you owe is your life."

Hoang Li felt the anger rise in his throat. He wanted his day. "But this one will follow us. He came all the way from the valley, and we will not be free of him unless we act now. We can stop him here."

This seemed to strike a note with Nguyen, but then a voice came from behind them.

Truong stood shakily, his leg wrapped in a battle dressing and blood pushing through the hole in his cheek with his words. "He won't follow," he said. "He has what he came for."

Nguyen growled at seeing another of his people gone astray. "Do my orders mean nothing?"

Truong limped forward. "Co gave me a leather pouch he took from the enemy last night because he knew it was something I would want. That enemy came and took it back. I think that is all the American wanted."

Nguyen held up his AK with one hand on the pistol grip, pointing it like an awkward handgun at the barely visible tree trunk in the distance. "I'm not asking for opinions. We are finished—" He felt the bite of the distant bark before he heard it, the pain traversing his chest from one armpit to the other, passing through his body like a flaming comet, burning his life away, engulfing his very existence in fire. Every muscle in his body tensed, encasing his torso in a spasm of agony, a contraction sealing inside the destruction that was tearing him apart. His legs buckled, and only Pham's quick hands stopped him from hitting the ground as dead weight.

His people were all firing their weapons now, but they seemed far away. Pham's shimmering face hovered above him, and though his lips were moving, no sound reached Nguyen's ears. He felt so tired. Maybe he would rest for just a minute. His peripheral vision contracted into black edges. Just a little rest so he could catch his breath.

S trader slumped back behind the cover of the tree trunk. The firing from the jungle was coming at a madly increased level, smacking the dead tree, tossing chunks of soil, and ripping the air over their heads. The sudden torrent seemed to have a wild emotion behind it. Strader looked at the expended shell casings spread about as though a particular one should stand out as unique. The Chief pointed at one with the tip of his knife. When Strader picked it up, the brass felt warm in his palm and he held it tightly, letting the warmth make a memory impression on his skin before he slipped it back into the pocket it came from.

Bullet strikes were pounding everywhere, and the look Strader gave the Chief left no doubt that he had no solution. There was no next move. They were back in the air above the valley in the dying helicopter looking at each other through eyes short on future.

The Chief forced a smile and raised his twisted voice above the noise. "Sounds like you got someone's attention. You better go before they get here."

The KA-BAR stood in the ground where Strader had pushed it and he jerked it free. "Well, when the bastards come I can always blame everything on you."

The Chief's grin looked genuine. "I would expect nothing less of a white man."

"I guess you'll spit in Chuck's eye?"

"I'll spit in all your eyes."

The details of Strader's surroundings filled his mind. The smells, the sounds, the feel of this place in this land where he was always too tired because the days were too long and the nights even longer, the weather was too hot and too wet and too humid, the ground was too muddy or too dusty, and the flora was too thick and too sharp and too green. And all of it was too far from home and ending in a life too short. "In the valley you said we should pick our battles, choose what we could win. Well, this is a no-win. I say we run for it."

"You run. I'm staying."

"Are you telling me you can't run or you won't? Because I'm not buying that 'can't' bullshit again."

"I'm saying that I'd rather get lunched out fighting than running."

"Is that more code of the Apache warrior? Well, I say fuck that." Strader stabbed at the air with the KA-BAR. "When I say 'go' we crawl to that tree with the split trunk and then start running."

"You run your way, I'll run mine."

"What the hell does that mean?"

A trickle of blood from the Chief's nose spilled across his upper lip, and he smeared it with a wipe of his hand. "I wouldn't get far. At least I can keep them busy. You'll have a chance to get clear."

Strader's face showed his exasperation "Cut the shit, Geronimo. We're getting out of here together if I have to drag you by the short hairs."

Instead of being insulted, the Chief smiled. "You got it right."

Strader struggled to make sense of the Chief's words but failed.

"Geronimo," the Chief said with an air of pride. "He was Apache. One of ours. You got the right tribe."

Strader's anger intensified like steam pressure looking for a release valve. He pointed the KA-BAR at the Chief with a menace that said if he couldn't bring the Chief back he would at least bring back his head. "I'll call you Geronimo or Indian Joe or fucking Tonto if it gets you moving."

The Chief's smile hardened. He set the long blade of his knife across his thigh. "Don't make me forget that we're friends."

Strader grabbed the Chief's wrist and pointed to the target tree with his own knife. "Head for that damned tree, and I mean now." Movement caught his eye, between the splayed legs of that distant tree, something green and familiar. He thought he was hallucinating, but other flecks of movement in the background drew his attention, and then Franklin's face rose from the tree's crotch, aiming his weapon. Strader grabbed a fistful of the Chief's T-shirt and pulled him over. "Get down."

The jungle behind them exploded in gunfire. Franklin's single M16 snarled through a full magazine and was joined by others in his fire team, ripping at the air, drowning the enemy fire. Within seconds a full squad was pouring everything they had into the shadows beyond the downed tree, making Strader and the Chief hug the ground and hope that the excitement of the moment wouldn't spoil the Marines' aim.

Though still tense, Strader couldn't seem to get the smile off his face. He'd thought he was climbing the gallows stairs to his own execution, but once again fate took a hand, and the relief of that was showing involuntarily across his face. He was surprised he wasn't laughing out loud.

All the fire was one-sided now, and he could see the squad's fire teams moving forward, leapfrogging, covering each other's movements. Franklin's fire team reached the downed tree first and, leaning against the trunk, fired into the trees on the other side. Middleton's voice was audible above the noise, pushing his teams, while Sergeant Blackwell bellowed orders from behind. When the second fire team reached the tree, they climbed over and kept going.

Franklin looked down at Strader. "What the hell are you smiling about, shithead? The sergeant is gonna kick your young ass."

"I don't have a problem with that," Strader said, still feeling the silly grin tightening his cheeks.

Middleton came to the trunk, running in a stoop, waving the third fire team around the exposed root end. "Get your team moving, Franklin," he said, filling the space Franklin vacated as his team crawled over the tree and followed the others. "So, what's new Ray?"

The release valve Strader needed had arrived, and he felt a welcome draining of tension like a deflating balloon. He just kept smiling.

"You think this is funny, you crazy bastard?"

"I'm just glad to see you," Strader said, finding his voice.

Middleton looked around at the shattered bits of tree and spent brass on the ground. "I'll bet," he said, slapping Strader's shoulder. He looked over at the Chief leaning against the tree like he was relaxing at a picnic. "Chief, you've looked better."

The Chief focused his good eye on the squad leader. "I can't say the same about you."

A voice came from behind, and Sergeant Blackwell strolled up to the tree as though he were crossing a drill field. Bronsky, Pusic, and the doc were close on his heels. "Middleton, break up this circle jerk and get after your people."

Middleton matched Strader's smile tooth for tooth then disappeared over the tree.

Sergeant Blackwell didn't bother to duck down. It was always his policy not to show the enemy he could be intimidated. He looked down on the two worn Marines and winced at the Indian's appearance. "Doc, take a look at the Chief."

"Moon," Strader corrected. No one paid attention.

Doc Brede knelt and looked first into the Chief's good eye and then at the swollen slit that was the other. He noticed bloodstains that he thought were from the Chief's dripping nose spotting his T-shirt front but pulled the shirt up anyway. Numerous punctures from shrapnel peppered the Chief's torso, and the doc moved the beaded bag aside for a better look. The Chief grabbed it away. Doc Brede tore open the top of a demo bag full of battle dressings and chose one labeled Abdominal Bandage. "I see you found your leather bag," he said, pressing the big sterile square to the Chief's chest.

The Chief managed a smile. "It's always in the last place you look."

The doc just shook his head.

Bronsky knelt down also, taking the load of the radio off his shoulders. "How do you feel, Chief?" he said, trying to show real concern but missing the mark.

"I feel like throwing up, but then I usually do when I see your ugly face."

"You see?" Bronsky complained. "He always busts my balls." Bronsky struggled to his feet and moved a few feet away, leaning back and letting the tree take the weight of his heavy pack board.

While the corpsman tied the bandage leads around his body, the Chief looked up at the sergeant. "I didn't do it," he said with as much indignant conviction as he could muster.

Sergeant Blackwell waited before answering, listening to Middleton's squad firing in the trees, everything going out, nothing incoming. "I know," he said. "Why do you think I'm here?"

The Chief hooked a thumb in Strader's direction. "I figured you came for young Raymond here."

The sergeant didn't bother looking. "Who, Reach? Hell, he ain't here. He's back at An Hoa packing his seabag, trying on his civvies, decidin' which seat he wants on the freedom bird. He'd have to be a damned fool to be here." He finally turned his attention to Strader. "Are you a fool, Marine?"

The relief of the squad's arrival had drained much of Strader's residual energy, leaving him with hardly any to form a stink eye, especially with the smile an uncontrollable fixture, but he managed.

Pusic tucked himself in behind the trunk, unsure of what he was supposed to do, where he should go. He decided this was as good a spot as any.

The firing was dying out in the trees, and from the sound it was getting farther away.

Blackwell noticed too. "I better rein those boneheads in before they cross the DMZ. Come on, Bronsky, get the lead out. Pogue, you stay here." He gave Strader a long, hard look, nodding all the while. "And shit-can the grin," he said, knowing the toothy smile would follow him over the tree and into the noisy distance.

Pusic didn't know whether to feel fortunate or abandoned. If there was strength in numbers, he wanted to be with the largest number, but he was in no position to make demands. He could see Strader and the Chief looking him over as though he were some rare jungle creature, and in fact he did feel like a rare thing here, deep into his tour but as inexperienced as an FNG, outside his cloistered position insulated by forms and files that were the clerical by-product of this war. This ground was the jagged point of the war's industry where the product was made, and he was not comfortable seeing the process, much less being a part of it.

Strader spoke over Brede's back. "Did I forget to sign something, Pusic?" The Chief turned his attention back to the doc's labors as though Pusic was so insignificant that he was beneath notice.

"Very funny," Pusic said. "Gantz sent me to find you."

"He sent *you* . . . to find me. Why?"

Pusic looked away, wondering if he should chance a peek over the bullet-riddled trunk, feeling there might be less danger on the other side of the tree. "I was just the first one he saw." Expediency was a safe harbor from culpability.

"I know how that feels," Strader said, addressing anyone and anything within earshot.

In the trees beyond them, hidden Marine voices barked orders and directed movements, little sputters of firing snapping away at unseen targets. As usual, the Vietnamese pulled back and left the jungle so empty that it held only frustration for anyone hoping to find evidence that they were ever there. Pusic chanced an eye above the trunk, but there was nothing ahead but hollow voices and shadows. He shrank back behind the protection of the dead tree.

The doc knotted the ties over the massive dressing and pulled the T-shirt back down, making the Chief look even more barrel-chested. "I can't give you any morphine, Chief," he said. "Not with a head wound." He repacked his bag and slung it on his shoulder.

The Chief repositioned his spirit bag over the battle dressing under the shirt and patted the pronounced lump. "No sweat, Doc. I have all I need."

A sudden burst of shots in the distance was followed by Middleton's voice trying to get some control of his people. The weapons were again of mixed origin, and another voice, strained and high-pitched, called for a corpsman. "Gotta go," the doc said and was over the tree in an instant, sprinting toward the noise.

Pusic watched the corpsman go with rising horror. He was used to working in manpower figures, and he knew a 25 percent reduction in personnel when he saw it, especially when it was personnel needed to keep him alive. Everything in Pusic's being told him to follow. The sergeant had said to stay, but his confidence in Blackwell's concern for his personal safety wasn't very high. Gantz was only interested in finding Strader, and here Strader was, safe and sound; mission accomplished. "Doc, get back here," he said, trying to be heard and not heard at the same time. He looked at Strader and the Chief sitting there in relative comfort smiling at his panic.

The exchange in the distance grew more intense and came from higher on the mountain, and hurried voices filled the spaces between shots, trying to marshal efforts and concentrate the needed response.

"Don't sweat it, pogue." Strader's unwavering smile was unnerving Pusic.

"What do you mean, don't sweat it? We're stuck here in the middle of nowhere with just two weapons between us."

Strader's smile took on a sinister bent. "Think again." He held up the M14 as an offering to the god of impotence. "Empty," he said. As proof he pulled the magazine free and slapped it back in with a hollow clack. "I've fired my last shot in Vietnam."

Pusic had a recurring nightmare in which he found himself in the field alone, the last survivor of an unknown unit, surrounded by invisible enemies. He would awaken with a start, drenched in sweat, struggling to recognize something familiar that would put him back into his partitioned corner of the company office. The whirl of the fan pushing the dark air around usually provided the rescue. Now he was living the nightmare with no chance of a cool reprieve. He hazarded another look over the trunk, hoping to see Marine faces returning, but instead saw only shadows full of ugly noise.

On the mountainside above the dead tree, not fifty yards away, three black-clad figures moved like shadows themselves, bent over their weapons. Pusic ducked down out of sight. The invisible phantoms of his dreams were there in the flesh, peopling his waking nightmare.

"Strader," Pusic said with undisguised urgency in his whisper. "Look."

The expression on Pusic's face told Strader his attention was genuinely needed. Above him three figures moved tree to tree with military precision. He grabbed Pusic's collar and pulled him close. "They're moving in behind the squad," he said through clenched teeth.

Pusic looked back dumbfounded, as though he'd expected something more from Strader but wasn't sure what.

Strader's face was inches away from his, and the smile was finally gone. "Stop them."

Pusic heard the vehemence in Strader's voice. It was another dream gone bad, an unlikely request in an impossible situation.

"Do it now, Marine."

Pusic slipped his M16 onto the trunk and peered over the sights. The trio was still moving, well within reach, even closer now. His breaths were in a race with his heartbeats, and his hands felt wet where he held the weapon. He felt ill.

Strader moved in close. "Get control. Breath easy." He looked over Pusic's shoulder, trying for a similar sight picture. "Listen to me. Breathe. Okay, now breathe again. Slowly. Select fire on single. Hit the one nearest cover first, then the others.

Pusic tried to swallow but his mouth was too dry.

"Breathe in. Now let some out . . . and do it."

Two of the unsuspecting wraiths were in the open with one just passing behind a tall tree with a trunk wide enough to conceal him completely. Pusic positioned the front ramp sight at the edge of the tree, and when the Vietnamese stepped out, he squeezed the trigger exactly the way every range DI instructed. The man dropped as though he was following the dictates of target protocol. The others ducked, unsure of where the shot came from, and with Strader growling "lead man" in his ear, he fired again. They were still in plain sight, and the lead man pitched onto his side. The third bolted for the cover of the trees behind him only to be knocked over by the next round. He was up in an instant, moving to higher ground. Pusic could hear Strader screaming "fire" like a man possessed. The next round found its target, putting the black uniform down again.

It seemed over, but Strader slapped the back of Pusic's helmet. "Again," he said. "Hit them all again, and keep firing until I tell you to stop."

There didn't seem to be any movement, but Pusic fired into the last man again, then the first, and then the second, again and again. Their bodies jerked but went back to a stillness that filled him with both relief and dread. He kept squeezing the trigger even after the magazine was empty, moving the sights from body to body, not seeing but feeling the imaginary hits until Strader pulled him around. "What?" Pusic said, with more force than he intended. He didn't know why, but he was suddenly angry at the world and everyone and everything in it.

"Stop," Strader said, his voice trailing off. "Just stop."

Pusic slid down behind the tree, cradling the M16 in his lap. When Strader lifted it away, he didn't protest or even show that he noticed. He didn't move when one of the magazine pouches on his belt was snapped open and the empty magazine in the rifle was replaced. When Strader pulled the charging arm back and let it loose, the metallic *clack* drew his attention and he held out his hands with beckoning fingers.

Strader set the safety and returned the rifle. "You okay, Killer?" Strader asked, anointing the clerk with the kind of spontaneous nickname that followed such baptisms.

Pusic stared as though making no sense of Strader's words. "Slow, easy breathing, right?"

"That's right. When the shooting is over, it's always good to be breathing."

≈

Pham and Truong struggled with Nguyen's weight between them. They crashed and stumbled down the mountain, ignoring the moans from their leader, trying to get beyond the explosion of firing that ripped into the trees behind them. Hoang Li and his remaining devotee dragged their other cell member's body by the straps of his magazine vest, bouncing him along the ground, barreling through clusters of plants with no concern for the remains of their comrade. Their only goal was to remove the evidence of his death from the battlefield and deny the Americans a single number for their tally. His partner kept glancing over at him with a reproachful expression. Hoang Li's mystical umbrella was apparently flawed, or maybe his god didn't extend coverage to others. Either way, the evidence hanging between them proved the man would have to find his own way to survival, and he felt betrayed.

There *was* remorse in Hoang Li's heart. Not for the lifeless weight plowing the soft earth between them but for allowing himself to be lured into contact with a larger unit. The single shooter had drawn him in with the bait of revenge, and now he would be lucky to escape with his life.

A new element joined the firing on the mountain behind them. The echoes of the exchange reverberated through the trees, and Hoang Li saw a chance to escape. They might live. He might live.

Nguyen awakened at the sound of the firing and groaned a demand for Pham and Truong to put him down. His insides felt like they were filled with broken glass and every jostle was death by a thousand cuts. Once he was down, Pham wiped away the frothy blood from Nguyen's mouth and Nguyen grabbed his wrist. "Do you hear? They have not forgotten the importance of the cause. The *dau tranh* is everything."

Hoang Li and his comrade stumbled down and drew up beside them. "Why are you stopping?"

"Listen," Nguyen said in a voice that sounded wet and strangled. "That is the R-20th. They have taken a hand. They are buying time for us with their lives. Do not waste that gift."

Hoang Li pointed downhill with his rifle and began pulling the dead body again.

"Hoang Li," Nguyen gurgled. "It is on you now. You must finish."

Pham and Truong lifted Nguyen again and, despite his wet protests, started down. His coveted binoculars, wrapped and tucked in their shabby case, swung freely from the lanyard around his neck, and he tried reaching them without luck. All the strength he had left was devoted to pain. But the binoculars were important. They were the only sign of his station among the troops. They verified his status and worth. He felt there was something to be regained by just holding them again, feeling their weight, and he needed the comfort of this identity once more. The rocking, jarring movements that cut like razors faded to an ache, and the black edges of his vision grew lighter until they burned white as an arc light. He knew his eyes were closed but felt like he was staring into a bright sun, a warm, soothing sun that smothered his pain and his worries and promised the rest he needed.

When they reached the path, Hoang Li and his partner moved past the piles of cargo waiting for their return and carried their comrade to the group of bodies hidden below. They stripped away his useful equipment and set him down at the end of the morbid queue. There was no time for mourning. The firing above was growing more intense. They clawed their way back to the path as Pham and Truong arrived and leaned Nguyen against a discarded pack, searching for some sign of life.

Pham pressed an ear to Nguyen's chest, and Truong wet his fingers and held them in front of Nguyen's mouth to feel for expelled air. Neither wanted to admit what both already knew.

Hoang Li pulled the young men back and went roughly through his commander's pockets. He took his ammunition and his map case. He took an old, scratched compass and a French cigarette lighter. He found a whistle wrapped in a handkerchief and faded photos of loved ones stained around the edges. He kept the whistle and gave the photos to Pham.

The two young soldiers felt they were witnessing a desecration rather than a pragmatic necessity of war. Hoang Li tried to lift the lanyard holding the binoculars case over Nguyen's head, but the dead owner's hand still gripped the case tightly. He pried the fingers free and slipped the lanyard over his own head. The mantle was passed, the succession was confirmed, though Pham and Truong thought it looked more like a coup.

Hoang Li pointed down the mountain to the spot waiting for Nguyen, and the two young soldiers lifted their *dai uy*'s slack body and carried him to join the macabre collection. They made room next to Co and set the two friends with shoulders touching.

"Who is at fault here?" Truong said, a worried expression on his face.

Pham looked up the mountain to where busy hands were collecting the waiting gear. "There is enough blame for all," he said.

Having assumed command, Hoang Li shoved equipment into his cell members' arms, snapping orders with a new authority. He stepped off the path and looked down on the two heads protruding above the foliage. "Come up now," he yelled above the gunfire. "We have a long way to go."

Pham's and Truong's faces showed their disenchantment with their new commander. At their feet lay the evidence that the *dau tran* demanded only sacrifice. The cause had no rewards, took no responsibility; it only issued demands.

S trader and Pusic kept their eyes on the high side of the mountain, expecting more NVA to appear, but the firing seemed more distant. It looked like Pusic's three were just a flanking movement not yet missed, the main unit being somewhere further out and higher up. In seconds the jungle ahead of them began to move, almost imperceptibly at first, and then bobbing Marine helmets made sporadic dashes through the empty spaces between the trees, firing uphill as they moved. Strader watched them come, knowing that the enemy would be following from the high ground.

"Pusic," he said, pointing to the dark areas above, deceptively empty. "Suppressing fire uphill. Full auto."

"I don't see anything," Pusic said.

"Just do it." Strader knelt and touched the Chief's shoulder. "We may be in trouble again."

"I thought the squad chased all our troubles away."

"Well, it looks like the troubles are chasing them back."

Pusic tucked the butt stock into his shoulder and flicked the select fire switch to full automatic. But he didn't pull the trigger. Instead he glanced back at Strader with a look that said he didn't need or even want to fire, that maybe it was outside his job description and that he wouldn't mind if Strader took the weapon.

Strader could see the uncertainty in Pusic's eyes. "I told you, I've fired my last shot. Now hit that damned mountain with everything you have and get our people back here."

For an outcast, "our people" sounded good to Pusic; it felt inclusive.

Strader shrugged. "What's the problem? You already have a dog in this race, Marine, so get the job done and let's get the hell out of here."

Pusic leaned back into the M16. The dark and empty spaces above seemed dangerous simply by virtue of their existence in this hellish place, and though he could see nothing in those spaces, for some reason Strader's words carried all the weight he needed. He squeezed, sending the rifle into a spasm, the buffer assembly kicking back, countering the recoil, easily sending the rounds anywhere Pusic pointed the barrel.

The squad was returning in rotating fire teams. When three riflemen were moving, the rest were firing, keeping the enemy's heads away from their rifle sights; it was fire team assaults in reverse. Sharp voices barked the timing of leaps: who went when and where and how far. Sergeant Blackwell's and Corporal Middleton's directions stood out over the replies of team leaders, and the trees themselves seemed to be expelling bodies in spurts.

The first fire team scrambled over the downed tree in seconds and joined Pusic in firing up the mountain. The arrival of the second team brought Sergeant Blackwell and Bronsky with the radio. The sergeant had the handset pressed to one ear. "Copy that location," he said over the noise. He flipped the handset back to the radioman and waved the first fire team away from the dead tree and back toward the valley.

Middleton and the last fire team were loping toward the trunk, and an injured Marine's arms were stretched over Franklin's and the doc's shoulders as he limped and half-dragged a hastily bandaged leg. Those already at the tree fired above and behind them. Middleton jumped the tree while the others circled the root end.

"The lieutenant wants us across that bare spot back there." The sergeant indicated a direction with his thumb. "Get your people moving."

Pusic kept firing as the second fire team pulled back. The sergeant noticed him and raised his eyebrows at the Chief and Strader.

"I know," the Chief said. "You can't take him anywhere."

Strader was still having trouble looking at the sergeant without breaking into a grin. He pointed wordlessly over the trunk to the three bodies on the slope.

"The pogue?"

"That's killer pogue to you, Sergeant, and he saved your ass."

The sergeant stared at Strader in disbelief then shook his head. "Doc," he said, "keep moving, and don't stop for anything until you're across that bald area."

The remaining fire team kept sniping at any spots in the trees that seemed to be spewing green tracers, with Pusic keeping an honest pace.

The sergeant squatted behind the trunk, using the excuse of conversing at eye level for ducking rounds that were beginning to send wood chips flying. "What are you two shitbirds waiting for, an engraved invitation?"

"He doesn't think he can go," Strader said, nodding at the Chief.

"I didn't ask what he thinks. I'm telling him what he's going to do. Now get your malingering asses up and get moving."

Strader grabbed one of the Chief's arms and struggled to lift him. "Pusic. Give me a hand with Moon."

"Who?" Pusic said, pulling himself away from the tree.

"Just get on his other side and lift. You want to get the hell out of here, don't you?"

"More than anything."

They each took an arm and lifted while the Chief groaned in protest. They looped his arms over their shoulders and moved away from the trees. The sergeant and the last fire team fired into the trees with an intensity meant to discourage any heroics from the other side, and the explosion of fire put a burst of energy into Strader and Pusic.

"A little help, Moon," Strader said, struggling under the Chief's weight.

The big knife dangling in the Chief's right hand slapped menacingly against Pusic's arm.

"Hey, watch the damned knife, Chief," he said, feeling like a horse being goaded with a riding crop.

"As long as I've got it, it's you who needs to watch it. And the name is Moon."

Bronsky and the sergeant trotted by, ducking away from the second fire team's zone of fire shielding their retreat. "Get the lead out, Strader," the sergeant barked. "You're not a civilian yet. I'll let you know when you're off the clock."

The squad moved tree to tree, turning to fire and then moving on, making sure the enemy behind them would have to gamble their lives to move close.

Strader watched the Marines around him interact, meshing in a common purpose like the teeth of matching gears, and felt oddly at ease. He remembered standing beside the runway in An Hoa last night, looking out into the darkness and wondering about his long-awaited homecoming with all its familiar faces and places, and feared that this place, this awful place with these men, this bruised and bleeding society of Marines, might be the only place he would ever feel at home again.

≈

Hoang Li, bent under the enormous load he carried, harangued the others for their lack of speed, though he knew they were beyond what any reasonable commander would consider their carrying capacity. They had gathered up all the documents of identification from the dead, including photos, letters, and insignia. It was assumed that the bodies would be found and searched, but there would be nothing there to satisfy the taste for military information, or even for souvenirs. They would be counted, but that was all.

The firing on the mountain behind them continued unabated, but the sound receded. No one was following them, that was evident, but the combatant sides lost in the trees were not disengaging. They seemed locked together in some mutual need to bring things to a conclusion, a driving taste for blood that comes with the realization that a weakness has been discovered.

The main unit of bearers far ahead twisted and turned along the muddy path, rising and falling with the contours of the topography, until the trail split, one spur leading down toward the valley and the other climbing an awkward angle in the crook of the mountain's bend. They waited there for Nguyen's return. It would be his decision whether to move downward and head for Minh Tan 1 and the crossing, or climb north and look for a notch in the crest that would let them through to the other side. The high route would lose a day, so none of the tired men waiting was willing choose a direction. The risk was too great.

When the small band of survivors arrived, all eyes remained on the empty path behind them. When finally their eyes settled on the new arrivals, not one would meet their gaze . . . and they knew. Nguyen would be making no decisions.

"Portion the loads," Hoang Li shouted, and the overburdened shed their equipment with groans. The others seemed confused at the authority in his tone. As the equipment was quickly portioned out in equitable amounts, worried eyes searched Hoang Li's face. Hoang Li moved down the line, checking that nothing would be left behind, trying to appear resolute while everyone knew that all the qualified heirs to Nguyen's command lay back in the jungle, aligned side by side in a makeshift queue to the hereafter, leaving a pretender in charge. Though every face showed concern, no one objected.

Hoang Li eyed the path in both directions; one dipping down toward the valley, the other twisting up through the trees. He looked for some sign that would point the way, some mark or feel or spark of intuition that would act as a signpost, but nothing stood out. Though it was obvious the paths were not equal, the high path looked especially brutal.

"The enemy is below. We go up and over," he said, not knowing if it was the right decision but knowing that the only thing worse than a wrong decision was no decision at all. At least it would be unexpected, and in this place the unexpected often made all the difference.

34

T he squad moved through the trees as fast as the slowest of the wounded could move, the fire teams rotating as rear guard, firing and moving and firing again, all the while pushing the others to move faster. Bullets snapped around them with only distant sounds to serve as targets. One wounded man sagged, blood loss draining his consciousness, and Doc and Franklin reached down and scooped his legs up, taking his full weight without losing stride.

They ran a jagged course through trees and over ground freshly chewed by the work of An Hoa's big guns, the acrid odor lingering as silent testimony to their power. Strader and Pusic moved the Chief to the forefront, keeping up with Franklin and the doc, Sergeant Blackwell and Bronsky just behind them. The Chief tried to contribute, but his legs seemed to be wading through deep water; every move was an effort that required more than the last. As his feet slowed, his helpers added lift, driven by a need that had him covering ground without actually touching it. He wanted to stop. He wanted to complain that his head was bursting. He wanted to squeeze their necks until they let him lie down. But he knew that in the Corps, nothing had anything to do with what he wanted. He would keep going. He would hang on to these two Marines with all his might. If they eased their grip, he knew he would fall, but he wasn't worried. They would not drop him and they would not stop. No matter what, as long as there was breath in their bodies, they would not stop; and as long as there was breath in his body, he would be with them.

Behind, they could hear the fire teams calling out to one another. Ammunition was low, and those with more kept to the rear. Someone screamed and cursed, and Blackwell stepped in for the doc, who was running back toward a voice spewing anger through clenched teeth in a manner the corpsman knew well.

Sergeant Blackwell barked orders between gasps.

The Chief lifted his chin from his chest, and flavored water erupted from his mouth.

Pusic looked over at Strader. "It's purple," he said incredulously.

They plunged into the opening with Strader and Pusic half-dragging, half-carrying the Chief. It seemed a much wider span than when they'd crossed it earlier. Until they reached the other side there would be no place for refuge. They were easy targets for anyone unseen and waiting. Where unimpeded daylight once seemed inviting it now felt threatening, and everyone who entered the clearing looked to the other side, with its concealing shadows, and longed to be there.

Though the squad's lead struggled under the weight of their loads, no one came forward from the other side to help. Sergeant Blackwell searched the distant trees for the rest of the unit but saw just another tract of empty, anonymous jungle. More of the squad poured into the gap, and in seconds the space was littered with running Marines bouncing under their equipment, slipping and sliding across the exposed ground. A few stayed at the trees' edge, firing back into the shadows, using what was left in their magazines to cover those in the open.

Strader and Pusic carried the Chief into the shadows on the other side, arriving first with the sergeant and Franklin close behind. They weren't on the well-worn path, but their only concern was to get into the trees where the platoon was hiding and find a place to stop. The barrel of an M16 protruded from a clump of vegetation clinging to the edge of sunlight, and Sergeant Blackwell looked down to see Burke's face looking back.

"Keep going and don't stop," Burke said, waving an impatient hand to keep them moving.

A smile spread across the sergeant's face as he saw the plan Diehl had formulated. A simple snare that needed the retreating Marines as bait, to be seen moving deeper into the jungle. The open ground was a killing zone, and if the pursuers saw the pursued stopping they would not expose themselves. They had to have the draw of blood lust toward a weaker prey to override their caution. The chance for an overwhelming victory might pull the VC into the open if they knew their targets lacked the will or munitions to resist. And Diehl's Marines would be waiting. It would be the retribution Diehl had never expected to experience in his time left in-country. But first they had to sell the flight.

As more of the squad reached the relative safety of the far side they were warned not to stop. No one was to turn and face the enemy. They kept moving, letting the light from the gap push them deeper into the shadows. The enemy, watching from behind, would see that their quarry lacked the resources to turn the open ground to advantage.

"When do we stop?" Pusic panted as they moved further from the security of numbers.

Close behind, Sergeant Blackwell pushed against Strader's and Pusic's need to rest. "When those bastards are convinced we never will."

"And how will we know that?"

"You'll know. Just keep your ass moving."

The rearguard fire team was the last to cross, making no pretense of covering their own retreat as shattered pieces of sunlit dirt leapt into the air around their feet. One of the team grabbed half the weight of the wounded man the Doc was carrying, improving their speed, their chances, and getting the undying gratitude of the corpsman. The trees on the other side were their only hope of protection. Their only defense was speed, so they ran. They crashed through the bushes at the edge of the forest, nearly stumbling over the Marines hidden there, and considered themselves lucky to have crossed the open space without getting hit. It was an odd phenomenon. Sometimes Marines caught on open ground came through a hellfire of bullets and tracers completely unscathed, and were amazed that they did. The last men across the clearing were experiencing that amazement now.

The squad continued to move away from the scar on the mountain, maintaining a pace that proved they were running for their lives, but each felt a pull drawing them back to where they needed to be. The nucleus of their comfort was behind them, and each Marine felt the growing distance. Shooting only furtive glances back, they kept running.

≈

The platoon lay silent and unmoving just beyond the edge of the open ground. Lieutenant Diehl had given explicit orders that no one fire until he did, promising that anyone who jumped the gun would be burning shitters until the ARVN rotated; and the intense look on his face made it clear that ignoring his order would bring dire consequences.

Private First Class Haber lay within arm's reach of Lance Corporal Eubanks. He could see figures in black moving in the trees on the other side of the clearing. They were firing their weapons after the fleeing

Marines and beginning to show themselves in the opening. He caught himself looking for DeLong, wondering what he thought of all this, until a flash of memory slapped him back to his senses. Another wave of guilt washed over him. DeLong was gone, and he was still here. As bad as this place was, he was alive. After his first full day in the field the only friend he had in-country was dead. His first day in the field, and the ghostly enemy most combat troops never even saw were standing right in front of him. His first day in the field, and the only thing he could think of that could be worse was a second day in the field. He looked to Eubanks with fear and disbelief on his face.

"You stay cool, young blood," Eubanks said in a stern whisper. "You don't shoot unless I do."

Haber nodded. He was operating in a state of mental exhaustion, going through the motions, being pulled along by the momentum of others. His hands shook. "I'm nervous," he said, "and I'm . . ." He let the confession die on his lips.

Eubanks smiled. "Don't pay no attention to froggy talk you hear. We're all nervous, and we're all afraid 'a dyin'."

Haber suddenly understood that being killed was only a part of it. "Maybe I'm more afraid that the guy I was yesterday is already dead."

Eubanks' smile faded. "Oh, yeah. He's dead and gone. That's for sure."

At least six of the VC were in the open now, and Haber aimed his rifle at the closest one. Not a paper target, a person. The objective was not a qualifying score on the range but a death. The man was stopped and seemed to be sniffing the air, an inkling or flash of intuition warning him. Maybe the openness of the area was enough to hint that a mistake was being made. But before he could resolve the conflict between need and doubt he was dead.

⁓

The instant the platoon unleashed their weapons on the enemy, Middleton's squad stopped running. Those carrying wounded abandoned them and ran back toward the gap as fast as tired legs could carry them. They needed to be there. Their platoon was punishing the squad's tormentors, and they had to be there to witness it and help with the punishing. And it was a rare thing indeed to witness: a unit of VC tripping an ambush in the Arizona. Lieutenant Diehl had rolled his dice many times during his tour, but now he was making his point the hard way, and he would push the advantage for all it was worth.

With his helper running back to the gap, Doc Brede slid the wounded Marine off his shoulders and lowered him to the ground. The man's T-shirt under his flak jacket was soaked with blood that ran down to stain his web belt and trousers. Doc Garver arrived as Brede examined the holes in the Marine's torso.

"You okay?" Garver said, real concern on his face.

Brede kept searching the Marine for wounds. "So far," he said. "But the day isn't over yet."

"I thought you were invincible."

"No, I'm pretty sure I'm vincible."

Strader and Pusic started easing the Chief to the ground, but the Indian stopped them, waving the blade of his big knife toward a large tree with buttressed roots and sleek green bark. They shifted him over and settled him between the buttresses, the sloping roots hugging the Indian's sides like the arms of an easy chair. He leaned back with an air of comfort.

Pusic straightened, the pain in his back ratcheting him up, and watched the other Marines heading back to the gap.

Strader couldn't help but notice the indecision on the clerk's face. "What's wrong?"

"What should I do?" he asked, nodding in the direction of the cacophony.

Strader glanced toward the gunfire. "Nothing. You stay put. I'm empty, so you're the only security we have. If the gooks send out another flank, we'll need you."

Pusic looked back toward the roar of firing and felt the weight of real responsibility. Not for the accuracy of pay records or accumulated leave, but for the safety of fellow Marines. They were entrusting their lives to him, and if anything were to happen here, it would be on him to respond. He gripped his M16 tighter. What else could he do? The corpsmen were working over the wounded Marine without looking up, assured that their backs were covered. He knew immediately that he would do whatever it took. Marines were putting their trust in him, and for one reason—because he, the pogue, was one of them. At this time, in this place, he was not the pariah behind the desk. They didn't see him as the conspirator aligned with the upper ranks, but simply as another grunt, an essential cog in the combat machinery, a brother Marine.

The firing from the gap stopped as abruptly as it began, the jungle so silent now that a whisper sounded like a shout. The voices of the Marines in the trees were a violation, breaking a quiet so fragile that even mere talk might set off another frenzy of violence.

The trap was sprung, and the orders filtering back through the trees were for a reconnaissance of its success, a success calculated in bodies and weapons.

The Chief dragged his spirit bag from under his shirt and pulled it open, pouring the contents into his lap. He moved his precious possessions about with the tip of a shaky finger, taking inventory from memory. The count made him chuckle. Everything was there but the coin.

On the night before he left for Parris Island, his father borrowed Benito's new truck and drove him into the hills where the *gutaat* lived in an old clapboard shack with a drooping porch. The news beyond the reservation was full of the troubles on the other side of the world, and his father wanted some spiritual protection for his son. A small pack of dogs barked on their arrival until the holy man whistled and shooed them away. They sat in the cool darkness inside the house, the glow of a kerosene lantern moving the shadows about in air currents, and listened as the old man recited chants and song-stories in a language they knew only in ceremony, his eyes closed, his white head bobbing in cadence with the words that communed with the spirits. On the palm of one hand the shaman had a tattoo of the sun, on the other, the moon. He stretched out the moon hand and placed it on young Gonshayee's head, bestowing an incomprehensible prayer that somehow made the future Marine feel better, safer.

The ceremony ended abruptly, and the old man offered them coffee from a blackened pot atop his woodstove. They drank and talked about the tribe and the world outside, listening to the dogs' claws clicking across the wooden floor as they moved in and out of the light. When the younger Gonshayee said he was sure to be going to Vietnam, the holy man raised a finger. "I have something that's been waiting here for you many years." He disappeared into the shadows and rattled things about in the darkness, finally returning to his chair. "When I was younger, long before you were born, I was paid for work off the reservation by a

white man who thought it would be funny to slip me something worth-
less in the payment. I didn't object because it was a thing unique to me,
and I knew you would be coming." He opened his hand to reveal a
bronze coin sitting on the moon tattoo. "Take it," he said.

The coin was tarnished gray and had a hole in the center. Kle-ga-
na-ai remembered holding it up to the lamplight. Two draped female
figures sat on either side of the center hole, surrounded by the words
REPUBLIQUE FRANÇAISE, with 1 CENT at the bottom.

"A penny?"

"A French centime," the holy man said. He flipped his hand. "Turn
it over."

The obverse side said INDOCHINE FRANÇAISE and 1923 around
four Chinese symbols. "It's meant for me?"

"Yes. Its home is Indo-China, once the name of the place you are
going. Take it with you." The moon on the old man's palm flickered. "It
will complete a circle."

He held it up so the light shining through the hole made a spot on
his eye. "I'll bring it back."

The shaman leaned back in his chair and one of the dogs laid his
snout in the old man's lap. "The coin has a path of its own, young warrior, and you have yours."

The Chief searched again and squeezed the bag just to be sure. It
was really gone. But he wasn't angry. All the cherished things of his own
choosing were still there, he thought, slipping them back into the pouch,
and it seemed somehow fitting that the coin should return to its home.
He picked up the knife and rested the blade—the symbol of his warrior
status—across his thigh and tried to squeeze his thoughts through the
pain. "Warrior" seemed an elusive title now, a tribal assumption, a male
birthright providing only an identity on the reservation. Maybe his only
valid purpose for being here was to return a penny to Vietnam. If so, it
seemed a lot of trouble.

The corpsmen worked on the wounded, and Pusic and Strader stood
guard while the distant jungle roared under the triggers of the platoon,
his platoon. He closed his eyes and leaned his head back against the tree.
The validation of a warrior must be an earned acceptance into a warrior
clan, and surrounded by his Marines in a jungle far from home, Kle-ga-
na-ai felt fulfilled.

Strader squatted down to the Chief's eye level. The eyes that looked back lacked focus. "You okay, Moon?"

The Chief fumbled in one of his cargo pockets and came out with the western novel. "Give this to the doc," he said.

Strader took the book and examined the dust cover with its French printing and Wild West illustration. "Which one?"

"The bookworm." The Chief's words slurred through sagging lips, and a stream of drool swung down to his T-shirt. The stag handle on the knife slipped from his hand, the blade clattering against the tree.

Strader picked up the knife and set it back in the Chief's hand, but the fingers wouldn't grip the handle. "Moon, are you okay?"

The Chief looked like he had something to say, but his sagging mouth wouldn't cooperate. The light in his good eye was fading. He shuddered, and a spasm swept over him like a hot ocean wave, making him feel as though he was wading through thick, boiling water. Bright lights pulsated across his vision like exploding sunspots, and a bright horizon opened up, the rise ahead illuminated in a warm refulgence he longed for, the kind of light that baked a dryer soil. He wanted a moon that traveled across a sky with different stars and a sun that roasted the humidity out of the air. He could feel the Arizona heat of home surging behind his eyes, passing under his scalp like a sun-baked wind.

Silhouetted in the brightness beyond the rise, figures stood waiting, mountain spirits, drawing him to them. One had a familiar posture, stooped and angular, a muscularity twisted with age but with recognizable family traits he shared. His grandfather raised a hand and waved a greeting. Kle-ga-na-ai smiled and waved back.

Strader stared into the Chief's face, but the twisted smile wasn't for him, and the gaze went through him like he was invisible.

The Chief felt the strength of the tree against his back reaching out and merging with his own. It called to him like a siren, summoning his spirit, inviting him to merge in a timeless collaboration that had spoken to him since he was a boy . . . and he surrendered. He entered the core of the tree, traversing its sinew from its roots buried deep to the tallest reach of its endless branches. He shared its sap, enriching his blood and adopting him into another new and timeless brotherhood.

Strader watched as the Chief's life transmigrated into the tree. "Doc, I need help here," he said softly.

≈

The NVA weapons bearers, fighting the mountain's slope, heard the change. Some dynamic in the conflict behind them had shifted. The eruption of sound made that fact clear, and the suddenness of it spoke volumes. A catastrophic turn in the balance of power had occurred somewhere back in the shadows under the endless canopy, and they were all glad that Tet was pulling them away like a physical destination.

They would not cross the Vu Gia tonight as planned, but there was a chance they would all be alive to cross tomorrow night if they were lucky—if they kept moving and were lucky. Everyone looked at Hoang Li growling at the line, driving them much like Nguyen did. They wondered if he was any luckier than Nguyen.

Whatever had happened back on the mountain was over. No smattering of fire. No sporadic returns. It ended as though someone executed a maneuver and then called a ceasefire, seeing that all aims were accomplished and nothing more was needed.

Pham and Truong kept looking back. They would do all they could to fulfill the mandate that drove Nguyen south, and they would do it carrying all the debts owed to Nguyen, to the R-20th Doc Lap, and to all the others whose spirits were left behind.

Lieutenant Diehl moved his platoon away from the gap at a determined pace, the radio handset pressed to his ear and Bronsky trotting alongside to keep up. With his map open, the lieutenant relayed grid coordinates to fire control, estimating distances to his target. The VC were running for safe ground, and he wanted to make sure that run was through a storm of high-explosive rounds. The Bird Dog softly sputtering above the trees stayed to adjust fire.

Bronsky collected the handset and clipped it to his pocket when Diehl ended communications. His pistol was buttoned down in its holster, where it had been since morning and all through the ambush.

The lieutenant had fired the first shot, setting off the rest of the platoon in an explosion of firing so well coordinated that it came as though from the pull of a single finger. All the Vietnamese in the opening of the gap were felled in the first blast, then the shadows in the trees behind them, then every branch and leaf within reach of the platoon's barrels. In thirty seconds it was over. The sound died like the fading peal of a bell, quickly replaced with Marine voices directing movement, checking squads, and just verifying that they were alive, proving it to themselves by communicating with those around them.

Sergeant Blackwell took a squad across the gap, counting five dead in the open and four more within twenty yards of the tree line, but the rest of the VC had withdrawn true to form. He counted, collected the weapons, and searched the bodies. He took satisfaction in forcing the VC to run now, to somewhere safe where they could lick their wounds, but he wouldn't be chasing them. He was just one of the boots-on-the-ground grunts who dragged the enemy into the light so technology could prove that a war of attrition was a viable policy. And he was tired, just as tired as the men around him, so letting the big guns take over was okay with him.

Burke's squad followed the lieutenant away from the gap and set up a perimeter when they reached the corpsmen and the wounded. The docs had the Chief stretched out flat on his back, partially covered with a poncho liner. They had already done what little they could and were repacking their medical bags while Strader and Pusic stood near. "You okay, Ray?" Middleton said, seeing that the silly smile was finally gone from his friend's face. Strader just nodded. Doc Brede stood and slung his bags over his shoulder. Strader held out the book. "He wanted you to have this," he said.

The doc took the book and turned it over in his hands. "The Chief reads French?" he asked, unwilling to use the past tense so soon.

Strader shook his head. "I'm guessing the previous owner did."

The lieutenant arrived as Doc Garver pulled the poncho liner over the Chief's face.

"A cerebral hemorrhage or a clot, or maybe just the shrapnel in his torso, sir." The corpsman shrugged. "I don't know how the hell he got this far."

Diehl nodded but focused his attention on Strader. "Corporal, I gave you an order to leave the field. Have you willfully disobeyed that order?"

Strader took a second to respond. "No, sir," he said.

"And yet here you are, in the field."

"I'm catching orders from all sides, sir. I don't know which ones to disobey first."

The lieutenant almost smiled. "Are you hurt?"

"Not a scratch, sir," Strader said, then held out the beaded pouch with the little figure below its lunar companion. "This should go to the Chief's . . . to Moon's family. It was important to him. I think they would want it."

Lieutenant Diehl took the bag, dangling it from its cord. "I don't see a problem with that. Do you Corporal Pusic?"

The clerk, once more trying to be inconspicuous, was startled to hear his name. Then he realized he was being questioned on a duty connected to a job he knew he was good at, and wanted desperately to return to, a question that seemed to indicate he *would* be returning to it. "Yes, sir," he said, with renewed enthusiasm. "I'll make sure all the Chief's personal effects are sent to his home of record."

"And what can I do for you, Corporal . . . I mean Mr. Strader?" the lieutenant said.

"I'd like to go home, sir."

"I sent you home yesterday. You don't stay sent. What do you think Corporal Pusic? Can you give this young Marine a huss?"

The clerk felt more relaxed with the familiar bent of the conversation and let his rifle hang casually at his side. "I think I can expedite his transition out of country, sir."

The lieutenant fixed the clerk with a hard glare. "Maybe Sergeant Gantz can help."

Pusic swallowed hard. "I'm sure Sergeant Gantz will bust a gut to get Corporal Strader out of Vietnam, sir."

"Make sure of it," Lieutenant Diehl said with no trace of humor in his voice.

Sergeant Blackwell and the rest of the platoon came through the trees laden with AK-47s of every configuration slung on their shoulders and strapped across their packs, and Strader thought how amused the Chief would be to see the Marines returning like a band of raiding Apaches with their booty.

The energy drained from his body along with the last of the adrenaline as he watched the tired squads find defensible places in a perimeter with the lieutenant's CP at the center. They had given the R-20th Doc Lap some pain and absorbed some of their own, and now they would leave. They would win the battles but cede the ground. There was no real estate they could claim that wasn't surrounded by bunkers and barbed wire, and even that ground was often in contention.

The air above the trees hissed in resistance to heavy projectiles, and a distant thunder from An Hoa signaled the coming storm. Strader watched the Marines around him, and a profound sadness overtook him as he suddenly recognized a flaw inherent in his species, a quirk in the shared biology that allowed his people to be here now, as in the past, and in all the futures to come.

The ground shook.

EPILOGUE

The tour bus from Albuquerque collected bugs on its face all the way down Route 25, following the Rio Grande to Las Cruces, then across Route 10 into Arizona. It left the interstate near Apache Pass for a quick rest stop before visiting a nearby national monument, one of the last stops before Tucson. The big diesel engine pushed the coach onto the gravel drive in front of a cluster of buildings. The sign at the roadside said EATS AND GIFTS, with GAS and SERVICE painted over but showing through white paint worn translucent by weather. The diesel shuddered and stopped, and the door across from the driver opened with a sudden hiss like the release of a vacuum-packed seal. Air-conditioned coolness rushed out into the Arizona heat. The uniformed driver, who looked like a cross between an airline pilot and a mailman, held a radio handset to his mouth and pushed the button with his thumb. A megaphone speaker above the windshield scratched to life.

"Folks, we'll be at this rest stop for an hour or so. You'll have time to do a little shopping and catch some lunch. The restaurant has lavatories for your convenience, and Bernice makes the finest enchiladas in the Southwest. Tell her Arnie sent you," he said, hooking his free thumb at his own chest. "I'll blow the horn when we're ready to leave. The next stop is the Chiricahua National Monument."

Passengers began climbing out of their seats and stretching stiff joints in the aisle. The tourists on this trip, as on most trips the driver carried, were retirees enjoying their pensions and leisure time by traveling the country, searching for the Wild West of Hollywood imaginations without the burden of driving themselves. The women sported pastel culottes, flowery blouses, sun hats, and sunglasses too big for their faces. Too-red lipstick and rouge complimented their sunburns. The men's Bermuda shorts clashed with their sport shirts, and their white socks kept sweat from invading new tennis shoes bought specifically to ease their feet through every historical site on the schedule.

The Pavlovian response to the mention of food vied for dominance with their need for bathrooms as they squeezed to the front of the bus where Arnie stood out in the heat, helping each down safely to the parking lot. "Don't forget to tip your waitress," the driver said.

In the back, a dark-skinned passenger in black trousers, black dress shoes, and a white short-sleeved shirt draped a beige windbreaker over one arm and joined the end of the queue. Patches of gray accented his black hair at the temples. He stooped to look out the side windows to see his fellow travelers, released from their confinement, making a beeline for the restaurant.

The last out, he stood beside the bus until the driver closed the door and trailed the others into the comfort of the restaurant's controlled environment. He thought to follow, but dry heat wasn't an issue for him, and the allure of the gift shop with its adobe façade pulled him in that direction instead.

A blue-and-gray station wagon was parked in front with a license plate emblazoned with PENNSYLVANIA across the top in raised letters. A long way from home, the man thought, remembering the colorful divisions in his new road atlas. A round sticker in the corner of the rear window had the globe and anchor of the United States Marine Corps.

An extended roof on rustic-looking posts shaded the gift shop's front, keeping the afternoon sun from a long wooden bench and a row of upturned milk crates parked below a wide window. A newspaper dispenser with chipped yellow paint showed photo headlines of yesterday's celebration for the one-hundredth birthday of the Statue of Liberty and the accompanying article detailing President Ronald Reagan's meeting with French president François Mitterrand.

The opening of the shop door triggered a small bell attached to a coil of spring steel that shook even after the door was at rest, effectively announcing all arrivals. Inside, a ceiling fan pushed around the odors of new carpet and paint. A row of glass showcases ran down the left side of the room and across the back, breaking to give access to a doorway leading to a back room where the whirl of a smaller fan could be heard.

A couple with two young boys moved past him in a flurry of activity, the parents working to contain the enthusiasm of their kids' need to flee boredom and see what was next. The door chimed frantically as they left.

The shop featured a moderate selection of commercially made items: porcelain and terra cotta kachina figurines, dream catchers, framed illustrations with the look of ancient petroglyphs, and bows and arrows with colorful fletching for the children. Shelves held Papago and Apache baskets made of tightly coiled grasses and Pueblo polychrome pots. Authentic native clothing decorated with porcupine quills hung on the walls behind the showcases. The visitor let the ambiance of the room wash over him. It was like a museum where everything was for sale. He felt he could spend hours taking it all in.

A young woman appeared from behind a hanging rack of Navajo blankets. She smiled and waved a hand with a tinkle of bracelets. "Hello," she said. "Let me know if you have any questions." The black hair hanging over her shoulders and down her back reflected the fluorescent lights like sun on a crow's wing. Her Apache features and bronze skin told the visitor that she was from one of the nearby tribes, and she drew his interest as much as any of the artifacts on display.

He waved back. "Thank you," he said, working hard to get the inflection just right.

He moved slowly along the showcases in her direction, looking at each of the glass shelves inside holding examples of native craftsmanship: turquoise jewelry, polished squash blossom necklaces, and Apache concho belts with bright silver discs. There were Hopi mudheads, bone hairpins, and an Osage quirt made from antler etched with pictographs. A ring of keys lay on top of the nearest showcase, an assortment for house and car attached to a beaded chain that held an empty rifle cartridge. An odd keepsake, he thought. It had a familiar significance to him. It was a military round designed for war: a 7.62-mm NATO. A row of four beaded leather bags on the shelf beneath the keys caught his attention, and he leaned in until his nose nearly touched the top of the case.

Noticing his attention, the young saleswoman came around behind the display case and stood directly across from him. "Can I show you something?"

He touched a finger to the glass over the bags.

She reached inside and lifted one decorated with turtles and lizards encircling a scorpion. He pointed to the right and she moved to the next. He pointed again. At the third he nodded and she removed the bag from the case. Beads depicted a blazing sun sprouting rays of dyed quills with a stylized horse galloping below. On the other side, a gray wolf bayed at a silver moon. A smile spread across his face.

"It's an Apache spirit bag," she said. "It holds charms and amulets and anything else important to a warrior's life." She looked at his face as she handed him the bag and noticed a starburst scar sprouting lines like a spider's legs on one cheek.

"Apache?" the man asked carefully.

She nodded. "Yes, this was made right here at White Mountain."

He set the little bag on the case and fished for the wallet in the pocket of his windbreaker.

The girl checked the paper string tag attached to the rawhide cord. "This one is twenty-four dollars, plus tax."

The man examined two green bills from his wallet. Their design, color, and colonial portraits were still foreign to him. Unsure, he handed the money to the girl. While she went to the cash register, he held the bag by its cord, letting it spin and transport him to another time and another place.

She returned with his change and placed his purchase in a paper bag printed with a feather motif. "I hope you'll visit us again," the girl said.

He smiled across the counter at the young American Indian woman, making the lines of his facial scar bend oddly. "Thank you," he said with a well-practiced enunciation.

He turned from the counter and the girl called. "Don't forget your keys."

The door chimed again and the harried father entered along with a flash of reflected sunlight from the parking lot. "Did I leave my keys here?" he asked.

The salesgirl picked up the keys and jingled them like tiny wind chimes. "These them?"

The father came forward. "Yeah, thanks. I wouldn't get far without those."

The customer shifted his purchase and scooped the keys from the girl's hand with a deft movement before she could protest and met the father along the showcases. He held the keys out, dangling them by the spent cartridge.

The father took hold of the keys while the helpful man still pinched the cartridge between his fingers. "Thank you," the father said, staring into the man's dark eyes and taking note of his scarred face. There was something he recognized in the eyes looking back, something shared. Not a familiar face, but a familiar type from his past.

The man released his hold and the cartridge swung free. Then he extended his hand. Hesitantly, the father took it and held on. "You welcome," the man said, working the words out with some effort, feeling his delivery was not quite right but not certain why.

The father nodded, and the two men released their grips.

The door opened and the boys' mother leaned in. "Come on, Ray. The boys are making me crazy in this heat."

The man nodded slowly and followed her out the door.

"Enjoy your spirit bag," the girl said, breaking the spell of the encounter.

"Yes," he said, holding up the paper bag. "Yes." He was on solid ground with "yes."

The door jingled again and he was back in the Arizona heat, his prize clutched to his chest.

The bus stood alone in the lot; the station wagon was gone. Semis rumbled by on the roadway. A few cars were now parked in front of the restaurant, and a small boy sat on one of the upturned milk crates below the gift shop's display window worrying a beetle with the toe of his tennis shoe. He looked up as the man came out of the gift shop. The boy's black hair touched the collar of his T-shirt, and the cuffs on his faded denims were turned up. A small leather bag hung from a rawhide cord around his neck. The man reached into his paper sack and produced his own spirit bag. The boy held his up for comparison and gave it a shake, making the contents rattle. He seemed proud. The man turned his upside down, showing that his was empty.

After examining the stranger's face closely, the boy dipped into his bag and chose an item by feel, a dark, flat onyx stone with a white starburst in the center radiating lines like spider legs. He smeared it with spit so moisture would enliven the imperfection. The boy held it up and the man took the stone, involuntarily touching his cheek. He cupped the stone in his hand. It seemed an appropriate award for wounds received, an honorable gift, warrior to warrior. Smiling, the boy held his bag up for some reciprocation, but the man just shrugged at his lack of fair exchange. Suddenly remembering, he dug into his pants pocket and felt through the gift shop change. He chose one piece, holding it up for the boy to see; a bronze coin with a hole in the center. One French centime from 1923 once given in payment for a debt he still felt he could never repay. The spoils of one spirit bag returned to another. The boy took the coin and turned it over in his hand. A toothy grin said the trade was acceptable and it disappeared into his bag. The man felt an odd sense of harmony in the universe, the closing of a circle, a needed symmetry. Reaching out, he touched the top of the boy's head, ruffling his hair.

The sun was hot in the parking lot, and Truong thought it might be interesting to see what an enchilada tasted like.

About the Author

J. M. Graham was born in Pittsburgh, Pennsylvania, and educated at the University of Pittsburgh and the Ivy School of Professional Art. He enlisted in the Navy in 1965 and served as a combat corpsman with the 2nd Battalion, 5th Marines, in 1967. He was wounded in Operation Essex and evacuated to the Philadelphia Naval Hospital. CBS News reporters covering Essex sent film to New York, and his story was featured on Walter Cronkite's Evening News. He currently lives and writes in western Pennsylvania.

The **Naval Institute Press** is the book-publishing arm of the U.S. Naval Institute, a private, nonprofit, membership society for sea service professionals and others who share an interest in naval and maritime affairs. Established in 1873 at the U.S. Naval Academy in Annapolis, Maryland, where its offices remain today, the Naval Institute has members worldwide.

Members of the Naval Institute support the education programs of the society and receive the influential monthly magazine *Proceedings* or the colorful bimonthly magazine *Naval History* and discounts on fine nautical prints and on ship and aircraft photos. They also have access to the transcripts of the Institute's Oral History Program and get discounted admission to any of the Institute-sponsored seminars offered around the country.

The Naval Institute's book-publishing program, begun in 1898 with basic guides to naval practices, has broadened its scope to include books of more general interest. Now the Naval Institute Press publishes about seventy titles each year, ranging from how-to books on boating and navigation to battle histories, biographies, ship and aircraft guides, and novels. Institute members receive significant discounts on the Press' more than eight hundred books in print.

Full-time students are eligible for special half-price membership rates. Life memberships are also available.

For a free catalog describing Naval Institute Press books currently available, and for further information about joining the U.S. Naval Institute, please write to:

Member Services
U.S. Naval Institute
291 Wood Road
Annapolis, MD 21402-5034
Telephone: (800) 233-8764
Fax: (410) 571-1703
Web address: www.usni.org